PRAISE FOR ZION'S FICTION

"This splendid new anthology will open a window on contemporary Israeli fantasy and science fiction—a stream of powerful work that we need to know more about."

—**Robert Silverberg**, author and editor of SF, multiple winner of Hugo and Nebula Awards, member of Science Fiction and Fantasy Hall of Fame, and a Science Fiction Writers of America SF Grand Master

"*Zion's Fiction* will supply a distinctive bright line to the spectrum of futuristic fiction, which stands in sore need of broadening, in the cause of promoting cross-cultural understanding as well as showcasing exciting new talent."

—**Brian Stableford**, author of over 70 novels and renowned SF historian

"*Zion's Fiction* explores the unlimited dreams of a people who have learned to stand on shifting ground. To face a future filled with danger and hope, forging into territory that can only be surveyed with the lamp of imagination on our brows."

—**David Brin**, multiple Hugo and Nebula Award recipient and author of *EARTH* and *Existence*

"When my collection *Wandering Stars: An Anthology of Jewish Fantasy and Science Fiction* was published in 1974, it became a classic. And now . . . we have the first ever anthology in the entire universe of Israeli fantasy and science fiction: *Zion's Fiction*. . . . Go forth and read . . . and may you find *Zion's Fiction* unexpected, delightful, and delirious!"

—**Jack Dann**, award-winning author and editor of over 75 books including *The Memory Cathedral* and *The Silent*

"The basic joy in science fiction and fantasy is the chance to look inside minds different from your own. Here's your chance. Some bright minds in the nation of Israel have been exercising their imaginations, sharing their different dreams and nightmares, and the results are ours to enjoy."

—**Larry Niven**, a multiple Hugo and Nebula Award-winning author of *The Ringworld Series*

Zion's Fiction

Zion's Fiction

A Treasury of Israeli
Speculative Literature

EDITED BY

Sheldon Teitelbaum *and* Emanuel Lottem

FOREWORD BY Robert Silverberg
AFTERWORD BY Aharon Hauptman
ILLUSTRATIONS BY Avi Katz

Mandel Vilar Press

"Foreword" by Robert Silverberg, © 2018 Robert Silverberg; "Introduction" © 2018 Sheldon Teitelbaum and Emanuel Lottem; "The Smell of Orange Groves" by Lavie Tidhar, © 2011 Lavie Tidhar; "The Slows" by Gail Hareven, translated by Yaacov Jeffrey Green, © 1999 Gail Hareven; "Burn Alexandria" by Keren Landsman, translated by Emanuel Lottem, © 2015 Keren Landsman; "The Perfect Girl" by Guy Hasson, © 2004 Guy Hasson; "Hunter of Stars" by Nava Semel, translated by Emanuel Lottem, © 2009 Nava Semel's estate; "The Believers" by Nir Yaniv, © 2007 Nir Yaniv; "Possibilities" by Eyal Teler, © 2003 Eyal Teler; "In the Mirror" by Rotem Baruchin, translated by David Chanoch, © 2007 Rotem Baruchin; "The Stern-Gerlach Mice" by Mordechai Sasson, translated by Emanuel Lottem, © 1984 Mordechai Sasson's estate; "A Good Place for the Night" by Savyon Liebrecht, from *A Good Place for the Night*, translated by Sondra Silverston, © 2006 by Savyon Liebrecht, reprinted with the permission of Persea Books, Inc. (New York), www.perseabooks.com, all rights reserved; "Death in Jerusalem" by Elana Gomel, © 2017 Elana Gomel; "White Curtain" by Pesakh (Pavel) Amnuel, translated by Anatoly Belilovsky, © 2007 Pesakh (Pavel) Amnuel; "A Man's Dream" by Yael Furman, translated by Nadav Almog, © 2006 Yael Furman; "My Crappy Autumn" by Nitay Peretz, translated by Emanuel Lottem, © 2005 Nitay Peretz; "Two Minutes Too Early" by Gur Shomron, © 2003 Gur Shomron; "They Had to Move" by Shimon Adaf, translated by Emanuel Lottem, © 2008 Shimon Adaf; "Afterword" by Aharon Hauptman, © 2018 Aharon Hauptman

This book is typeset in Alegreya. The paper used in this book meets the minimum requirements of ANSI/NISO Z39-48-1992 (R1997). ∞

Publisher's Cataloging-In-Publication Data
Names: Teitelbaum, Sheldon, editor. | Lottem, Emanuel, editor. | Katz, Avi, illustrator. | Silverberg, Robert, writer of supplementary textual content. | Hauptman, Aharon, writer of supplementary textual content.
Title: Zion's fiction: a treasury of Israeli speculative literature / edited by Sheldon Teitelbaum and Emanuel Lottem; foreword by Robert Silverberg; afterword by Aharon Hauptman; illustrations by Avi Katz.
Description: Simsbury, Connecticut: Mandel Vilar Press, [2018] | "The stories come from Hebrew, Russian, and English-language sources."—Provided by publisher. | Includes bibliographical references.
Identifiers: ISBN 9781942134527 | ISBN 9781942134534 (ebook)
Subjects: LCSH: Israeli fiction (English) | Fantasy fiction, Israeli. | Speculative fiction. | Science fiction. | Short stories, Israeli.
Classification: LCC PR9510.8.Z56 2018 (print) | LCC PR9510.8 (ebook) | DDC 823/.010895694—dc23

Printed in the United States of America.
18 19 20 21 22 23 24 25 / 9 8 7 6 5 4 3 2 1
Mandel Vilar Press
19 Oxford Court, Simsbury, Connecticut 06070
www.mvpress.org

To my wife, Lilith, and kids, Adam, Shiran, and Liam, for keeping my sense of wonder afloat; to my mom, Roz, whose fortitude is something to behold; to my late father, Harry, and to uncles, Jack and Ben (ZT"L), who would have had a hoot with this, and to Grand Master Bob, who bent space and opened portals.
—Sheli Teitelbaum

To Larry Niven, who showed me how science fiction ought to be written; to my friends at the Israeli Society for Science Fiction and Fantasy, those who feature in this anthology and everyone else as well; and to my wife, Liana, my sons, Amos and Eran, and their children.
—Emanuel Lottem

IN MEMORIAM

Keren Embar
Amos Geffen
Mordechai Sasson
Nava Semel
Aharon Sheer
תנצב״ה

CONTENTS

Foreword

Robert Silverberg

What we have here is something like a message from another world: a sampling of the powerful imaginative work that emanates from a small, struggling nation on the shores of Asia, a nation created in the twentieth century on a foundation that dates back into biblical antiquity, a nation of thinkers and fabulators that exists in constant uncertainty and has used that uncertainty as the fuel for deep and often very moving speculative thought. That is to say, an anthology of Israeli science fiction and fantasy.

The Jews have often been called the People of the Book, and the Book meant by that phrase is the Hebrew Bible—known to the non-Jewish world as the Old Testament but to Jews everywhere as, simply, the Bible. To believers of all faiths, the Bible is a sacred scripture, the record of God's dealings with mankind from the moment of creation ("In the beginning," the very first sentence tells us, "God created the heaven and the earth.") through the travails of a wandering desert tribe, the Hebrews, who had renounced pagan idolatry and polytheism in favor of belief in a single deity of austere and remote nature, the migration of that tribe out of Mesopotamia into Egypt, the escape from the tyrannical rule of Egypt's Pharaoh into the land of Canaan, more generally known later as Palestine, and the foundation in Palestine of the Hebrew Kingdom of Israel, where the Jewish people, as the Hebrews came to be known, attempted with varying degrees of success to live according to the moral and ethical codes of their religion. The later books of the Hebrew Bible provide a chronicle of the division of the Jewish land into two kingdoms, Israel and Judah, the struggles of the two kingdoms against external enemies—the Moabites, the Philistines, the Syrians, the Assyrians, the Babylonians, and others—and, finally, the loss of Jewish independence as God's punishment for a relapse into idolatry and other iniquities.

The Hebrew Bible isn't just an historical chronicle plus a set of law codes, of course. It also contains an anthology of poetry—the Psalms of David—and a collection of proverbs, and what is essentially a short novel, the Book of Job. Nor is the Book of Job the only story that the Bible tells. It is, in fact, full of stories throughout, stories that have held the attention of mankind for three thousand years. It begins with the story of creation, goes on to tell of the life of our first ancestors in the Garden of Eden ("And the rib, which the Lord God had taken from the man, made He a woman, and brought her unto the man."), continues to the temptation of Eve and the expulsion from the Garden, and on and on: the murder of Abel by Cain, the coming of a great flood from which only Noah and his family escape, the episode of the instructions of God to the patriarch Abraham to sacrifice his only son Isaac and everything that proceeded from that (and Isaac was not exactly his only son, and a long story descends from that, too) and on and on, a richness of narrative that can stand comparison with any other body of literature ever created. (The adventures of Joseph in Egypt; the career of the shepherd boy David, who became king of Israel; the Exodus from Egypt; the little affair of Samson and Delilah; the visit of the Queen of Sheba to Solomon—oh, yes, on and on. One doesn't have to be a believer of any sort to succumb to the storytelling power of the Hebrew Bible.)

A potent fantastic element runs through many of the biblical tales as we have them now. (*All* of them are fantasy, if you are a nonbeliever and evaluate the whole collection from the premise that God is an imaginary being.) The Deluge of Noah, which has its antecedents in Sumerian and Babylonian legend, is a splendid apocalyptic fantasy. Moses miraculously parts the Red Sea so that the children of Israel can depart from Egypt on dry land. God manifests Himself as a pillar of fire to guide them by night in their journey through the wilderness. Samson is an early version of the superman, and like the twentieth-century comic-book incarnation has a special area of vulnerability. The visions of the prophet Ezekiel involve humanoid creatures with four faces and four wings, who carry him on something much like a voyage through space to bring him before the Lord on His throne. (The postcanonical Book of Enoch, which probably dates from the third or fourth century before Christ and has survived only in an Ethiopian translation, offers a great deal of astronomical lore and describes yet another prophet's space voyage.) And there is ever so much more, a vast wealth of wondrous imaginative incident that remains alive and vivid in our minds even after nearly three thousand years.

Eventually the kingdoms of Israel and Judah disappeared. Their people were sent into exile by the Babylonians and brought back to Palestine by the next set of conquerors, the Persians, and upon the defeat of the Persians by Alexander of Macedon were swallowed up into his new empire, and then into the one founded by the Romans. Under the Romans, Jews emigrated to every part of the Mediterranean world, but some always remained in Palestine, which now was beginning to be called the Holy Land, the Jews sharing it with non-Jewish tribes that eventually coalesced into a population of Muslim Arabs.

Through those years of exile, diaspora, and shared occupation of Palestine, the hope of a return to the ancient days of the Kingdom of Israel surfaced again and again in Jewish thought and writing, reaching its most explicit form in Theodor Herzl's utopian novel *Altneuland* (*Old New Land*), published in 1902. Herzl had first proposed a self-governing Jewish republic outside of Europe in his 1896 book *Der Judenstadt* (*The Jewish State*). He thought Palestine was the preferable location, for historic reasons, but at that point would have found Argentina just as acceptable. But *Altneuland* explicitly locates the Jewish state in Palestine. Jerusalem would be the capital; Haifa, the center of industrial activity. (Tel Aviv did not yet exist at that time. That was the name, meaning "Mound of Spring," that the first Hebrew translator of Herzl's novel gave to the book, and which also was given to the new Jewish settlement on the coast of Palestine that was founded in 1909.) Herzl's republic was an egalitarian one that verged on socialism, with agricultural cooperatives and public ownership of land and natural resources but also private ownership of industry, and its citizens would converse mainly in German or Yiddish, though some attempt would be made to revive the ancient Hebrew tongue.

Thus a thread of speculative thinking, often mingled with a degree of mysticism, runs through the whole history of the Jewish people, from the visions and wonders of the Bible to Herzl's prophetic work of utopian fantasy. It should be no surprise to find that elements of speculative fantasy and even science fiction appear in Jewish literature over the many centuries that separate the Book of Genesis from

Altneuland. An episode in the Talmud has Moses traveling in time, making a brief visit to the future. The ninth-century Jewish merchant Eldad HaDani imagined an independent Jewish state in East Africa, perhaps Ethiopia. The medieval Jewish legend of the Golem foreshadowed the Frankenstein story and provided one of the first examples of the robot in literature. Medieval lore also gives us dybbuks, wandering ghosts who take possession of living bodies, a theme often used in modern science fiction. For good and proper reasons I hesitate to use any such broad generalizing term as "the Jewish mind," but there does seem to be some affinity between Jews and speculative thinking, an affinity that has produced not only some great works of philosophy but also many works of fantasy and science fiction.

Science fiction in its specialized modern form, though it had its origins in the nineteenth-century works of Jules Verne and H. G. Wells, was largely a product of American creativity—and a significant number of Jews were involved in its development. Jacob Clark Henneberger, the publisher who in 1923 founded *Weird Tales*, the first all-fantasy magazine, was Jewish. So was Hugo Gernsback, who brought *Amazing Stories*, the pioneering science-fiction magazine, into being three years later. Such notable magazine and book editors as H. L. Gold, Donald A. Wollheim, David Lasser, Samuel Mines, and Mort Weisinger were Jews. The roster of Jewish-American science-fiction writers includes such illustrious names as Isaac Asimov, Alfred Bester, Avram Davidson (who completed a stint as an army medic during the 1948 Israeli War of Independence), Harlan Ellison, Norman Spinrad, Joanna Russ, Stanley G. Weinbaum, Cyril Kornbluth, Philip Klass, Robert Sheckley, and Barry N. Malzberg. Even the German-speaking novelist Franz Werfel, born in Prague, turned to science fiction for his last work, the magnificent imaginative fantasy *Star of the Unborn*, when he was living in exile in the United States in 1946. (It takes place a hundred thousand years in the future, but Werfel places a small congregation of Jews in that otherwise utterly transformed distant epoch, presided over by a leader called Saul, whose title is "the Jew of the Era.")

But modern Israel, too, a country of which it could be said (without stretching things too far) that it owes its origin in part to a work of speculative fiction and which is compelled by external forces to live in a state of perpetual existential crisis, has been a center of the sort of intellectual inquiry that leads to the writing of fantasy and science fiction. *The Jewish War II*, by Reuven Rupin, sends its protagonist back to Roman times to provide the rebellious Jews of Palestine with sophisticated weapons with which to establish an independent Jewish state. *Secrets of the Second World* by Yosef Soyka puts the Ten Lost Tribes of Israel, living in subterranean tunnels, in contact with alien species who watch over mankind. Yaakov Avisar's *People from a Different Planet* shows Israeli spacefarers encountering Hebrew-speaking aliens, with whom they defeat a third species, a warlike one that threatens galactic peace. Other novels portray an Israel jeopardized by neo-Nazi plots or by the seizure of control by Orthodox Jews, strife between Israel and its Arab population, a postapocalyptic Israel that consists of little more than Tel Aviv, and many another possible futures.

Contemporary Israeli writers of speculative fiction have been active as well in the short-story form, which since the time of H. G. Wells has had a central position in science fiction. Such magazines as *Fantasia 2000*, which was published between 1978 and 1984, provided a venue for original Israeli science fiction as well as stories translated from English and other languages, and there also have been more than a few one-author collections of short science-fiction stories.

But nearly all of this work was written in Hebrew, and Hebrew is not a language widely spoken beyond the borders of Israel; and so this plethora of rich and stimulating Israeli science fiction might just as well have been published on some other planet, for all the impact it has had on science-fiction readers in the rest of the world. Hence this anthology, the first English-language collection of recent Israeli speculative literature. Some of the stories, like those by Lavie Tidhar, Nir Yaniv, and Eyal Teler, were written in English and even published originally in American science-fiction magazines, but the bulk of those included here, those by Gail Hareven, Gur Shomron, Nitay Peretz, Nava Semel, and others, have been translated from the Hebrew and thus brought back to Western readers from beyond the linguistic barrier, and there is one, by Pesakh (Pavel) Amnuel, that is a translation from the Russian.

Messages from another world, indeed. Bulletins about a version of the future different from the one that most of us perceive, sent to us from a far-off place that happens to share this small planet with us.

Zion's Fiction

Introduction

Sheldon Teitelbaum and Emanuel Lottem

The State of Israel may be regarded as the quintessential science fiction (SF) nation—the only country on the planet inspired by not one, but *two* seminal works of wonder: the Hebrew Bible and Zionist ideologue Theodor Herzl's early-twentieth-century utopian novel *Altneuland* (*Old New Land*).

Only seventy years old, the Jewish state cranks out futuristic inventions with boundless aplomb: wondrous science-fictional products such as bio-embeddable Pill-Cams, wearable electronic diving gills, hummingbird spy drones, vat-grown chicken breasts, microcopter radiation detectors, texting fruit trees, billion-dollar computer and smartphone apps like Waze and Viber, and last but not least, those supermarket marvels, the cherry tomato and the seedless watermelon.

What Israel has yet to generate—and in this it stands virtually alone among the world's developed nations—is an authoritative volume, in any language, of Israeli speculative fiction.[1] *Zion's Fiction: A Treasury of Israeli Speculative Literature* is intended to remedy this oversight. The book will pry open the lid on a tiny, neglected, and seldom-viewed wellspring of Israeli literature, one we hope to be forgiven for referring to as "Zi-fi."

Zi-fi: We define this term as the speculative literature written by citizens and permanent residents of Israel—Jewish, Arab, or otherwise, whether living in Israel proper or abroad, writing in Hebrew, Arabic, English, Russian, or any other language spoken in the Holy Land.

In the main, however, this volume spotlights a small but growing pool of Israeli writers who have pursued deliberate vocations as purveyors of homegrown Hebrew-, English-, and Russian-language science fiction and fantasy (SF/F), and other brands of speculative fiction, aimed at both the local and international markets.

We showcase here a wide selection of stories whose authors range across the entire gamut of the modern Israeli SF/F scene: men and women, young and not-so-young, Israel-born and immigrants, professional writers as well as amateurs; some continuing to live in Israel and some expatriates. More than a few have already published stories overseas; for others this is their first foray into the international arena. Many are part and parcel of Israel's SF/F fandom (more about which, see below); others are mainstream writers who at some point in their careers decided to use SF/F tropes as the best vehicles for their message and their whimsy. All of them, however, share one thing in common: by adopting the tropes of speculative fiction, they have all bucked, if not kicked in the teeth, a deeply rooted, widely held, and long-standing cultural aversion, shared by a preponderance of Israeli readers, writers, critics, and scholars, to most manifestations of indigenously produced as well as imported speculative fiction—science fiction, fantasy, and horror.[2] It is the underlying contradiction between the aforementioned science-fictional roots and this primal aversion that, we believe, renders the very publication of this book a wondrous event.

Author Hagar Yanai lamented in a 2002 essay in the daily *Haaretz* that "Faeries do not dance under our swaying palm trees, there are no fire-breathing dragons in the cave of Machpela [the Cave of the Patriarchs], and Harry Potter doesn't live in Kfar Sava." Local fantasy is so weak, she declared, that an original series like the Harry Potter books "couldn't be published in the state of the Jews."[3]

Hence a paradox: In a nation whose very existence was inspired by an SF/F vision, SF/F was until recently completely beyond the pale, and even now most cultural luminaries shun it. This despite the fact, pointed out by scholar Danielle Gurevitch, that "in early Jewish tradition, fantasy literature . . . [involving] marvelous acts, magic, and miracles aimed at hastening the Redemption, as well as a rich diversity of unbelievable stories of journeys to the Holy Land . . . was a driving force in the nation's history and thinking."[4]

Scholar Adam Rovner reminds us that whatever value they place on imagination, and however much they may have stigmatized some forms of fantasy, *all* nations and countries become the incarnations of fabulous stories told by their inhabitants or their invaders. This was certainly true of England, for instance, which took its cue from Arthurian legends, and it is also true of the early incarnations of the biblical Jewish homeland, which derived inspiration from the Book of Joshua. "Zionist historiography and literary history," says Rovner, "have long demonstrated the intimate bond between what is now alliterated as nation and narrative."[5]

On the other hand, in present-day Israel, as during the nation's prestatehood years, "willingness to open the door to weird strangers and unusual occurrences that benefit nothing but the spirit of whimsy is minimal," says author Gail Hareven.[6]

How come? Where did this allergic response to imaginative fiction come from?

Several explanations have been offered. One is the simple importation of the aversion to SF/F from abroad. After all, we must admit that for many a year,

Western culture had regarded SF/F with mild condescension, to say the very least. Until quite recently it was not culturally accepted as High Literature: fit for teenage boys (not girls!), lacking in veritable literary qualities, ignoring the exigencies of ordinary life, or worst of all, escapist—choose or add your favorite condemnation—for which alleged faults it has not historically passed universal muster. It was (and often continues to be) ghettoized, relegated to special-interest shelves in bookstores and libraries. This attitude was carried forward to and prevailed in prestatehood Israel, thoroughly unmodified. Furthermore, since cultural influences tended to spread rather slowly to and through the Jewish state, it has persisted well after the attitudes towards SF/F in the United States and the United Kingdom, for instance, became more congenial.

Yet another explanation hinges on the unusual contempt normative Judaism held even for its own nondidactic and lighter-hearted forms of literature. The Hebrew word for "imagination," *dimion*, did not appear in this sense in the Hebrew language until the twelfth century, in Maimonides's *Guide to the Perplexed*, despite the fact that seminal biblical and postbiblical Jewish texts often resorted quite freely to narrative embellishment. Frequently they crossed over into outright fantasy, either to fill in gaps in the original Torah narrative or to resolve textual contradictions.

Such imaginative works included Midrashim (exegetic tales); Meshalim (parables and fables); Aggadot (rabbinical legends); and medieval apocalyptic literature, including hagiography, Ma'asei Merkavah (mystical theories of creation), or apocryphal and pseudepigraphical Heikhalot texts describing heavenly journeys, such as the *maqama*—rhymed prose narrative—by Abraham Ibn Ezra (twelfth century), *Hai ben Mekitz*, about a journey to the six planets of the medieval solar system and their imaginary inhabitants. The sages nevertheless dismissed this massive corpus as "mere stories and profane matter."

It is possible, of course, that outright faith even in the most outlandish events trumped whimsy, obviating any acknowledgment of the fantastic. Magic and sorcery, despite the miraculous deeds of Moses, Elijah, and other biblical figures, were and continue to be considered off-limits by most observant Jews. "Thou shalt not suffer a witch to live," commands the Bible (Exodus 22:18).

While admitting the existence of grains of truth in both these explanations, we would prefer to emphasize the inherent tension between having a dream and actually living it. Forging a semblance of Herzl's *Altneuland* vision in a long-ravaged ancestral homeland very nearly forced the nascent Jewish republic, by dint of human cost alone, to deplete its imaginative reserves. "If you will it," the latter-day prophet (depicted on the cover of his book in his role as space-bound SF/F writer *cum* ideologue) famously declared of his proposed Jewish state, "it is no fairy-tale."[7]

The publicistic intent implicit in Herzl's choice of classical late-nineteenth-century science-fictional romance as a vehicle for proposing the Zionist enterprise to the masses, however, probably added an inconvenient literary fillip to the nation-building effort—one that, although inherently fanciful, regarded unfettered imagination as anathema. The very idea that Israel might have been inspired by a science fiction novel would have rankled. Consequently, *Altneuland* was deliberately misconstrued by Zionist ideologues as sui generis.

Creating a nuts-and-bolts nation, whether or not inspired by a literary fantasy, called on resources of faith of a much more practical nature. This task proved totally consuming, utterly grueling, costly in blood as well as resources, and fraught with calamity. Implementing the Zionist project left little capacity and even less taste for imaginatively unfettered ventures, whatever their pedigree. An avowedly pragmatic lot, the Zionists remained painfully wary of pie-in-the-sky schemes and stars-in-your-eyes stories.

The Zionist enterprise, moreover, was from the outset an all-out effort: each individual was expected to make his or her contribution to the fulfillment of the joint dream to the utmost of their abilities, regardless of personal cost, desire, ideal, or proclivity. It was a dream of a new nation, a rightful member of the world community, living in peace and harmony with its neighbors; of a new, just, vibrant society, where everyone has equal rights and duties and works for the common good; of a newly revived language, Hebrew, used for any and all purposes, lofty or mundane, to replace the various languages spoken by Jews in the Diaspora; and of a new person, the *sabra*: an independent, strong-willed, prickly, hard-working, idealistic individual, the diametric opposite of the downtrodden Diaspora Jew. Epitomized in the character of Uri, the hero in Moshe Shamir's 1947 novel (later a play, then a movie) *He Walked through the Fields*, and depicted in numerous other stories, poems, novels, plays, and films, this idealized new breed of Jew became perhaps the greatest hope and ultimate achievement of Zionism.[8]

There was no room in this scheme for freeloaders, including people who wished to write about imaginary worlds or predicaments. They had no moral right to pursue their idiosyncratic leanings; what they should write about must relate directly to the building of the new nation. Criticizing its faults in their stories was allowed, even encouraged; extolling it was still more welcome. Divert from these options, and no one would publish or indeed read your work.

Furthermore, the leadership of the highly politicized Yishuv, the Jewish community in prestate Mandatory Palestine, had become, since the turn of the twentieth century, increasingly socialist in orientation. By the late 1920s the political domination of the labor movement was nearly complete. The significance of this in the present context lies in the fact that both socialism and Zionism put a great emphasis on the role of intellectuals in the shaping of a new society—with a new culture and a new kind of people—and the combination of these two ideologies tended to make this emphasis even stronger.

Well before the Jewish state came into being, therefore, Israeli writers were expected to render the outlandish fantasy of a Jewish homeland in starkly mimetic, or naturalistic, literary terms. This is an activity commonly referred to by fantasy and science-fiction writers (that is, when they don't avoid it as a tiresome cliché) as worldbuilding.[9] Yet this necessity, paradoxically, required stripping a then-fifty-year-old body of Hebrew literature of its artificial biblicism, its romantic strivings, its unduly nostalgic, unrealistic, idealized concerns and tropes. These characteristics, some argued, had rendered nineteenth-century Hebrew literature dangerously escapist. To counter this tendency, ideology demanded that writers, poets, and other artists depict the Zionist mission—as unlikely and fraught an undertaking as the Exodus from Egypt—with all the grit and realism they could muster.

Ideological control was rather exacting, even though few would say it aloud. The Yishuv had always been a democratic polity, and theoretically any artist, poet, author, or thinker enjoyed complete freedom of expression. Yet social pressures were overwhelming: it was the intellectuals' sacred duty to inspire and be inspired by the common venture, enrich and if so inclined criticize it, and above all imbue the younger generation with the values, attitudes, and aspirations of their elders. Deviation from this role was frowned upon, sometimes fiercely, and on a more practical level, those not inclined to hew to such strictures could hardly find the means (for instance, a publishing house) of reaching out to the general public. Institutional publishers with telling names like Am Oved ("A Working People") or Sifriyat Po'alim ("Laborers' Library") had very clear agendas. But even private-sector, bourgeois publishers regarded themselves as part and parcel of the Zionist enterprise.

Thus developed a cohort of gatekeepers that effectively controlled the Yishuv's cultural output: publishers, literary magazines' and journals' editors, literary critics, professors of literature, and so on. This small but highly influential group had a final say over what the public could read, and steeped as they were in ideology, Zionist-socialist or just Zionist, their say was practically final.

Needless to say, aversion to speculative literature was but one of the gatekeepers' endearing qualities; in fact, it was quite a marginal facet of their overall control, since they had very few cases to contend with in that sphere. Much more than that, they were the keepers of ideological and moral purity.[10] Consider the case of Dr. Yaacov Winshel (1891–1980), a well-known physician who also dabbled in writing. In 1946 he authored a novella, *The Last Jew*, which offered up one of the first postwar alternative history scenarios postulating a Nazi victory in World War II—a forerunner of what would become a distinguished SF subgenre. Winshel was able to find only a minor publisher for this work, which was simply ignored by the Yishuv's literati. Ironically, the reason for this cold shoulder had little to do with the novella's literary quality, nor even its genre affiliation. Alas, Winshel was a prominent member of the Revisionist movement, a disciple of its leader, Ze'ev Jabotinsky. The Revisionists were Labor Zionists' mortal enemies (sometimes literally so); therefore, Winshel's writings remained firmly outré.

Although susceptible to a secular messianism that promised redemption through national renewal, the Labor Zionists in those days turned their backs on the mystical, supernatural aspects of the Hebrew Bible. They had no use for miracle-ridden Hassidic lore. Yet they also despised outright the supposedly more rational Judaism professed by the Mithnagdim, the fervently religious but excessively dogmatic opponents of Hassidism. They believed that religiosity in all its guises had helped instill and perpetuate Jewish rootlessness, passivity, frailty, hyper-intellectuality, dependence, and helplessness, brought to its horrific culmination in the Holocaust. Instead, the founders focused on geographical, historical, and archaeological accounts of a continuous Jewish presence in the Holy Land that could, they believed, ultimately be validated by empirical means.

Not surprisingly, speculative literature—what the rest of the world commonly referred to as fantasy, science fiction, and horror—did not have any kind of place in the world of Hebrew-language belles lettres, or even in what counted as popular literature. Certainly, some Israelis read commercial fiction in translation or in the original language of publication, and this may have included some SF/F. But indigenously produced genre fiction, mainly in the form of the particularly low-rent, originally Yiddish, offshoot of pulp fiction called *shundt*, "trash," held no possible relevance to the ongoing effort of building up the nation and consolidating its gains—or to the attempt to accrete a vibrant Hebrew corpus of literature. Consequently, it found neither reputable publishers nor widespread readership.

According to Hebrew University sociologist Nachman Ben-Yehuda, an expert on social deviancy, Israel's cultural commissars designated science fiction as a particularly egregious example of cultural inauthenticity.[11] Apparently unaware that Herzl had modeled his utopian novel *Altneuland* on Theodor Hertzka's utopian work *Freiland*, while seeking to emulate the success of American protosocialist Edward Bellamy's 1888 bestseller *Looking Backward: 2000–1887*—a genre classic of no uncertain stature—they regarded SF/F as a childish distraction.

Ironically, some of these very same people had championed the wholesale importation of Russian, particularly Soviet, literary forms and tropes that had informed their evolution as revolutionaries. The more left-wing ideologues among the Yishuv's literary gatekeepers saw a parallel between Labor Zionism's nation-building enterprise and the supposed success of the efforts to create a Workers' Paradise in the USSR.

These proclivities extended as well to the types of books selected for translation into Hebrew. To be sure, publishers were expected to import, translate, and publish works from the accepted Western literary canon. Otherwise, they published books that ostentatiously reflected the supposedly uplifting, revolutionary spirit of the times in the Soviet Union (yet another form of wild fantasy, in retrospect) or the perceived decadence of its adversaries. In a publisher's note added as a postscript to the Hebrew translation of Allen Drury's *Advise and Consent*, for instance, the publishers (the aforementioned Sifriyat Po'alim) felt duty-bound to explain to their readers—this as late as 1960—that "the author purported reassuringly to show us the triumph of the spiritual-moral strength of the spokesmen for that great nation [the United States], but truthfully, he gave us reason for much anxiety. It turns out that even the honest and decent ones among them are consumed by hatred [of the Soviet Union]," and so on.

Meanwhile, light entertainment and easy diversions were left largely to the aforementioned *shundt*, to the cinema, to the communal campfire, to sing-alongs, and, much later, to television. Indeed, TV serves as perhaps the best example of Israeli cultural gatekeepers in rearguard action. Until as late as 1966, it was simply banned in Israel, because Prime Minister David Ben-Gurion feared that it would "distract children's minds, so that instead of studying and expanding their knowledge, they would be captivated by vulgar entertainment."[12] And even after TV had been introduced (well after the Old Man had left office), for twenty more years the country had just two channels, both under government control. The transition to the current situation, with numerous public as well as commercial channels, cable, satellite, and, ultimately, streaming venues, was motivated by the same forces—to be discussed below—that have made Israeli literature much more variegated.

Once the State of Israel came into being in 1948, writers of the younger generation—the so-called Dor haMedina, or Statehood Generation—should have been able, one might have thought, to reverse the trend. After all, the Zionist dream was fulfilled: there was a Jewish state in place, so perhaps the time had come for its intellectuals, specifically writers and poets, to let loose their imaginations. The ground was ready, one might have concluded, for a poststate literary scene more enamored of fancy. Alas, the kind of fabulation these men and women engaged in proved quite unlike any genre of speculative literature the world has ever seen.

For with each passing year, the normalcy Israel so desperately yearned for proved ever beyond its grasp. The country emerged from its formative War of Independence without recognized borders. Palestinian and other Arab opponents vowed to rectify what they termed the Nakba, or catastrophic defeat, with future rounds of warfare—as many as it would take to rid the region of its nonnative Jews. Similarly, the Israelis awaited Round Two (and then Round Three, and Four, and . . .), which they hoped would end with more tenable borders replacing the unsustainable cease-fire lines of 1949.

The more uncertain the country's prospects, the more its storytellers strove to enshrine the boring, mundane, quotidian realities that eluded them—thus the wholesale appropriation of a peculiar literary genre governed by Eastern European conventions of social, political, and psychological realism. The fact that in Israel such conditions could rarely be found outside of isolated pockets dissuaded few.

Early Israeli literature therefore, author and scholar Elana Gomel and others have observed, restricted itself to desultory ruminations over the narrower aspects of kibbutz life; to bourgeois melodramas set in Tel Aviv; to depictions of the dire predicaments of nearly destitute Sephardic and Mizrahi immigrants dispatched to peripheral regions; to often self-serving reminiscences of the prestate underground; to the then still shame-inducing Holocaust, encapsulated by the biblical expression "as lambs to the slaughter" (this attitude would change, drastically, only during the Eichmann trial in 1961); to the exigencies of army life; and, infrequently, to various romanticized aspects of daily life.[13]

"Our generation's Israeli literature," argued author and critic Ioram Melcer, "adheres to the framework of Israeli reality, and barely exceeds it. Israeli time, Israeli man, Israeli sociology, Israeli problematics, the ideological partition in Israel—or in other words, the Israeli existence and essence—are the main referential framework of the greater part of Hebrew Literature written in Israel." The template set, realism itself, as Gomel comments, was slated to become a particularly Israeli form of fantasy, one that would become more inventively inward-looking and self-reflective (often to the point of ignominious narcissism) with each passing decade.[14]

All this should not be misconstrued, we must stress, as a reflection on the quality of the literary output achieved by these writers, poets, and playwrights or their predecessors. Authors such as Moshe Shamir, Yizhar Smilansky, Hanoch Bartov, Nathan Shaham, and Aharon Meged, and poets such as Avraham Shlonsky and Nathan Alterman, alongside others, many others, have produced literary masterpieces while working within the constraints mentioned above. Still, there is no denying they were constrained in ways their successors are not.

In *Structural Fabulation*, scholar Robert Scholes defined his subject matter as the "fictional exploration of human situations made perceptible by the implications of recent science."[15] Israeli fiction, by contrast, imagined a Jewish commonwealth made perceptible by degrees of normalcy that cannot properly exist or endure under the conditions extant in the Middle East. Israeli literature celebrated the banal, often ignoring or downplaying those local and regional circumstances that threatened most strivings toward routine, everyday existence with implosion or worse. With apologies to Scholes, we might call this perhaps unique subgenre "Fabulistic Realism."

The story so far can be recast in terms of a particular and problematic concept central to speculative fiction since its very inception: Utopia. "Israel," argued sociologist Baruch Kimmerling, "was [however briefly—Eds.] considered the only successful materialization of utopia in the world." As such, notes Gomel, Israel "represents a horizon of expectations, a vision of perfection against which the muddle of actual history inevitably appears as a mere transitional and fleeting stage.... Israel exists in the same generic continuum of other post-apocalyptic and post-utopian texts." Denizens of the Jewish homeland have been seeking physical, psychic, or digital respite from the unrelenting hostility endured over the course of the last one hundred years (the catchphrase often used by Israelis in this context is "a villa in the jungle"). Israelis, writes cultural observer Diana Pinto, now think of themselves as "living in [their] own cyberspace at the very heart of a globalized world, [their] postmodern future being built on scientific innovation."[16]

Social scientists Dan Horowitz and Moshe Lissak believe that these trends and inclinations augur big trouble for little Israel's utopia.[17] The country, they argue, is overburdened and overwhelmed by competing voices, centers of power, and belief systems. It is also caught in a wind tunnel, wherein echoes of perennial arguments imply more internal Sturm und Drang than the stabilizing effects of existing institutional, cultural, and political checks and balances can damp out.

A continuum that, as per all utopias, can never achieve its stated goals poses special existential difficulties. The whole point of reinhabiting the ancient Jewish homeland was to avoid the Territorialist approach that would have rendered East Africa, Argentina, or upper New York State refuges for stateless Jews.[18] The Land of Israel, in whole or in part, was not incidental to this process of repatriation. It was essential.

* * *

Israeli readers have distinguished themselves as among the most voracious anywhere. But for them, experimentalism, egotism, and whimsy, which they had disdained before the establishment of the state in 1948, remained a nonstarter afterwards. The self-appointed literary gatekeepers remained in place and continued to rule the roost as before. There was still no tolerance for cultural (never mind personal) deviancy. There could certainly be no room for apocalyptic musings, especially since these were not the stuff of fantasy but of hard-core reality, and therefore intolerably discomfiting. As SF/F author Larry Niven once said, "I don't know how to frighten Israelis." Under such circumstances, notes Hareven, Franz Kafka himself never would have forged the literary career he chose had he fulfilled his dream and settled in the Land of Israel.[19]

As for importation, there were a few notable exceptions; some scientific romances by H. G. Wells, Jules Verne, Edgar Allan Poe, Arthur Conan Doyle, H. Rider Haggard, and Edgar Rice Burroughs did slip past the watchtowers (most of them directly to the bookshelves dedicated to young readers), as did some works by mainstream authors, such as Orwell's 1984 or Huxley's Brave New World, as well as short stories by André Maurois, on the strength of those writers' reputations. But commercial literature, popular fiction, and dime-novel subgenres remained, for ardent Zionists, unfit for serious people bent on building a nation.

How, then, do we get from all this to a solid compendium of Israeli speculative fiction? Like so many things big, shiny, and, to skeptical Israeli eyes, somewhat preposterous, SF/F initially came from America. It arrived first in the guise of 1950s B-movies and then in a quirky trickle of Hebrew translations that often bankrupted their overly optimistic purveyors. A trio of short-lived magazines published during the late 1950s and early 1960s met the same end.

At the time, even translated modern SF novels were few and far between, appearing almost exclusively in the Hebrew version of *shundt* called *roman za'ir* (tiny novel)—in other words, pulp literature. Original works were unheard of, and fantasy existed only on children's bookshelves. Asimov? Clarke? Heinlein? Not a chance. Science fiction was so rare that no one even knew quite what to call it. Israeli fans would spend a generation arguing the respective merits of *mada bidioni* (fictional science) and *mada dimioni* (imaginary science). The former ultimately gained the wider currency (although some continue to argue against it).

In the early sixties, one of the editors (E. L.) fell upon a Hebrew translation (in pulp format) by the late Amos Geffen of Robert Heinlein's *The Puppet Masters*. Fascinated, he started looking for more of its ilk, but to little avail. It was only when he went to London in 1970 for his graduate studies that he discovered the wealth of modern SF/F. The realization that all one needed to do in order to get the kind of books one liked was to go 'round the corner to the nearest W. H. Smith's proved a life-changing revelation.

The only putatively Israeli SF to emerge during that period came from the pen of Mordecai Roshwald. This Polish-born writer and academic, who lived in Mandatory Palestine/Israel from 1933 to 1955, published his apocalyptic opuses, the hair-raising nuclear war-themed *Level 7* (1959) and the satirical *A Small Armageddon* (1962), in the United States and England, respectively. These generally well received novels, written abroad and not directly reflective of his Israeli experiences, have yet to be translated into Hebrew.

Two Israelis who ultimately defied these strictures by experimenting with science fiction—poet and filmmaker David Avidan and prose writer Yizhak Oren—consequently found themselves marginalized and were only posthumously granted critical reconsideration.

The sea change would come, however, during the mid-1970s. Between mid-1967 and late 1973, Israel fought three major wars, not to mention numerous border clashes with terrorists and cross-border Israeli retaliatory raids. The Six-Day War in June 1967 filled most Israelis with arrogant pride, not to say hubris, and fueled no dearth of messianic illusions. To many, the Zionist dream was realized in full during those six short days—not coincidentally, some would say, the same amount of time it took God to create the universe. Conceivably, the time had come to stride forward. Having become "a regional superpower," Israel could now afford to normalize its society, economy, and culture.

This too proved an outright and dangerous fantasy, as demonstrated by the gruesome War of Attrition of 1968–70, followed by the near-disastrous Yom Kippur War of October 1973. Israel's superpower illusions lay shattered. More importantly, the traditional hegemony had clearly failed its faithful adherents, not to mention the country as a whole. Even the military, the consensual symbol of social cohesion, national unity, pride, and sense of mission, had failed to deliver on all its promises. Authority was now up for grabs.

The immediate consequences were political. In 1977 the Labor Party, which had long held the helm of the Yishuv and then the State of Israel, lost the general elections. But fracture lines spread much farther than the political arena. The national economy changed, evincing occasionally dizzying levels of growth and an increase in conspicuous consumerism. The electoral demise of the Labor Party led to a shift from socialist to liberal economics and, though lifting the economic prospects of many, to a growing inequality in income distribution. A once cohesive Israeli society broke down into competing tribes (as, for instance, left-wing idealists, right-wing nationalists, Orthodox settlers, Ultra-Orthodox Jews, freebooting liberals, and Israeli Arabs of various religious and political persuasions. Most of them, needless to add, are further split among themselves). Education, too, became more fragmented and commoditized. Culture, ever both the reflection and the harbinger of social change, followed suit.

Traditional hegemony in culture, as in politics, rapidly lost ground. Diktats from above about what was proper in literature, the stage, music, and the visual arts were losing their authority. Weeds began to proliferate in the cracks. Political satire, for example, hitherto moderate and well behaved, now became vicious. The stage was thus set for a more widespread appearance of SF/F in Israel, first of all in translation (a corps of native writers was yet to emerge). But from the mid-1970s on, mainstream Israeli publishers infused bookstores with some several hundred fairly expensive translations of commonly accepted genre standards.

At the same time, mainstream Israeli literature was changing apace. Until then, under constant ideological and geopolitical duress such as Israel's, those Israeli writers who found themselves stifled by traditional notions of Hebrewness, and sought respite in globalization and multiculturalism, remained stifled. But now, as literary scholar Rachel S. Harris observes, despite their manifold cultural origins and varying geographic orientations, the cohort of writers that emerged from the 1970s on and began publishing at the start of the following decade sought to "redefine Zionism and to create a new, more inclusive Israeliness" under the aegis of so-called Post-Zionism.[20]

Later on, having gained access to the Internet, some of these newcomers showed themselves eager to transact with the rest of the planet on their individual terms.[21] Along the way they also appear to have successfully wedged open Hebrew literature, once the sole domain of European Jews, almost exclusively male. It now extends entry to women with feminist and nonfeminist, secular or religious worldviews and to non-Ashkenazi writers functioning in Hebrew, English, and other languages.

In the process, they have also opened forums and markets and afforded legitimacy to religious Jews often averse to secular literature; to Hebrew-speak-ing-and-writing Arabs; to Russian-speaking Jews and non-Jews, and to people with a variety of sexual orientations. Soon they will give voice—if voice is still to be given rather than wrested—to the ingathering masses of French immi-grants and to other skittish European-Jewish communities considering egress from an increasingly anti-Semitic Europe. More recently, we have seen the first glimmerings of writing by authors of Ethiopian descent.

Most important, from the perspective of this book, not a few among these writers have taken up commercial genres and subgenres, including detective stories, erotica, police procedurals and techno-thrillers, science fiction, fantasy, and even horror, with an aplomb that would have been unthinkable a mere generation ago. Some of them, in fact, have become extraordinarily adept at genre skipping, segueing from the detective format to science fiction to magical realism with a fluidity once inexpressible in Israel.

This has unnerved many among the older-generation Israeli literati. Writers, readers, publishers, critics, scholars all seemed increasingly prone to motion sickness. Ultimately, however, Israeli literature spared itself the fate of terminal navel-gazing and self-delusion under the lingering influence of earlier generations of literary critics. This impulse, though, endures to the present day and accounts for the existence and grudging acceptability of some limited forms of indigenous speculative fiction—the kind that, like Orwell's *1984* or Burgess's *A Clockwork Orange*, addressed recognizable social and political concerns head-on. As Israel's late president Shimon Peres intoned to an international writers' conference in Jerusalem in 2008, Israeli writers were latter-day prophets whose job was to admonish the nation. "We like to be rebuked," observes Hareven, "and we especially like to envision ourselves as people of conscience who want to be rebuked."[22]

Rebuked, but not duped.

With the floodgates breached and the watchtowers shaking on their foundations, the gatekeepers were rapidly losing their power (faint vestiges of which, due to flailing attempts to maintain some modicum of relevancy, still reverberate within the Israeli cultural landscape). The road to SF/F lay open.

First, starting in 1975–76, came two series of translated SF hosted by mainstream publishers: Massada's was edited by journalist, translator, and later publisher Amos Geffen; Am Oved's, by journalist and translator Dorit Landes with—for a short time—poet-businessman-lawyer-scholar Ori Bernstein. The White Series (so called for its earlier covers), now edited by Landes alone, became and remains a mainstay of Israeli SF/F.

Other major publishers soon joined in, notably Keter, whose series was originally edited by philosophy professor Adi Zemach, and Zmora-Bitan, which was the first to include modern fantasy as well (most notably Tolkien's). A few more publishers, while not launching dedicated SF/F series, still saw fit to include some genre titles in their lists of translated fiction.

A handful of magazines accompanied this boom, the most notable and enduring of which, *Fantasia 2000*, ran to forty-four issues, from 1978 to the end of 1984. Organized fandom, usually considered integral to the development of a viable SF/F scene, would not come into existence until the mid-1990s. Individual readership, however, was another matter.

Under the stewardship of editors Aharon and Zippi Hauptman and Eli Tene (and with modest assistance from both editors of *Zion's Fiction*), *Fantasia 2000* replicated many of the didactic hothouse functions of its American counterparts such as *Astounding* and *The Magazine of Fantasy and Science Fiction*. It did so while surpassing those pulp digests in production values and approximating those of the large-circulation magazine *Omni*.

A glossy monthly with a subscription base of two thousand, plus peak newsstand sales of about three thousand, *Fantasia* launched a vigorous letters column, book and film reviews, a popular science department, author interviews and profiles, and, most significantly, the first glimmerings of homegrown SF/F. In a country of only 3.6 million at the time, it approached the typical per capita subscription base of its American, certainly its British, counterparts—no mean feat for a niche publication, otherwise ranked the second most expensive on Israeli newsstands at the time.

Fantasia 2000 took on, consciously and conscientiously, the task of cultivating local talent. The results were mixed. Not a few prospective writers sought to emulate American and British magazine SF/F, producing anodyne stories with clunky plots and nondescript characters. Very little about these offerings could be construed as particularly Israeli, or even Jewish, except by dint of authorship. But there were some standouts. In 1980, short story writer David Melamed published *Tsavo'a beCorundy* (A hyena in Corundy), an accomplished collection featuring several stories first published in *Fantasia 2000*. But the book received little critical recognition, leading Melamed ultimately to flee the genre. Hillel Damron, a filmmaker for the Histadrut, the national trade union, published the novel-length version of his memorable short story *Milhemet haMinim* (The war of the sexes) in 1982. Shortly after, Damron immigrated to the United States, where he self-published several mainstream novels in English.

Other notable *Fantasia 2000* alumni included geneticist Ram Mo'av, Ruth Blumert, Yivsam Azgad, Ortsion Bartana, and Mordechai Sasson. Sasson's story, "The Stern-Gerlach Mice" (1984), featured in this anthology, is a typical example of the original stories published in *Fantasia*. Editor Aharon Hauptman pursued a career as a futurist and is currently a senior researcher in the Unit for Technology and Society Foresight at Tel Aviv University. Gabi Peleg, *Fantasia 2000's* last editor, went on to computer programming. Illustrator Avi Katz, who had joined *Fantasia* early on, later contributed covers to *HaMemad haAsiri* of the Israeli Society for Science Fiction and Fantasy (ISSF&F, on which see below) and to the *Jerusalem Report*, and still later provided art for this anthology.

Despite the emergence of a nascent fan scene, and the staging of the country's first SF/F convention in 1981, the bloom fell off the boom in 1982. That was when the June War with Lebanon helped sink an already strapped international convention in Jerusalem. Subsequently, the Israeli economy plunged into hyperinflation. (For example, the newsstand price of issue no. 33 of *Fantasia 2000* (July 1982) was 37 shekels; issue no. 44 (August 1984) cost 750 shekels. In terms of purchasing power, these sums were roughly equivalent). In 1984, *Fantasia* ceased publication, having lost a major part of its readership.

The next attempt at a commercial SF/F magazine, *Halomot beAspamia* (Pipedreams in Spain, the place where castles are built, according to both Hebrew and English idiom), would begin publishing original Hebrew fiction in 2002 under the aegis of Nir Yaniv and Vered Tochterman. That effort, too, folded in 2008, to be revived in early 2016 as a web-based publication. An English-language fanzine, *CyberCozen*, published in English since 1988 by a fan club based in the town of Rehovoth, can be found online.[23] Israel's first SF-oriented website was created by Yaniv for the Israeli Society for Science Fiction and Fantasy in 1996.

The boom and bust cycle of Israeli SF/F faithfully reflected the vicissitudes of the Israeli economy (itself often subject to the vagaries of intermittent military crises). This view was taken by sociologist Nachman Ben-Yehuda, who attributed downswings to lingering ideological rejection by the wider culture of pluralism and its suspicion of individuated social subcultures. The cultural gatekeepers had lost much of their power, but they still held some of the keys to publication, controlling as they did the editorial boards of major publishing houses and various influential, if little read, literary magazines.

This went on until the mid-1990s, when the Internet hastened the ultimate fragmentation of the Israeli cultural matrix. As scholar Oren Soffer observes, its advent, and especially the penetration by cable and satellite television, resulted in a proliferation of global or, more specifically, American influences. These factors have been blamed by observers for a decrease in social cohesion and the reinforcement of (sub)group identity and individualism. These, Soffer says, "appear to be part of the social and cultural processes linked to the decline of national solidarity and, alternately, to the reinforcement of individual trends and consumer culture."[24] Decentralization is still going on, helped by the diminished ability of the nation-state to supervise and control media messages.

Not surprisingly, Israel's remaining cultural gatekeepers now found themselves with their backs against the wall. Although still intent on setting and patrolling the border between canonical and pop literature, they simply no longer had a single point of entry over which to stand guard. The walls themselves had become permeable, leading to a gradual yet unavoidable fragmentation of national identity. "Realism," says Elana Gomel, is now "the Israeli fantasy."[25]

The social margins, as cultural commentator Stuart Hall argues, had paradoxically become highly charged and increasingly powerful places, especially insofar as the arts and social life are concerned.[26] Not surprisingly, science fiction fandom, which combines the two, suddenly began to flourish in Israel.

A more robust fan scene started emerging during the mid-1990s. In 1996, Hauptman, editor and translator Amos Geffen, and others joined the prolific translator (and *Zion's Fiction* coeditor) Emanuel Lottem in founding the ISSF&F. Within the next few years several narrower special-interest groups took to the fore as well, including Starbase 972 (catering to the Israeli *Star Trek* fan contingent) and the Sunnydale Embassy (*Buffy the Vampire Slayer* fandom). Both are now moribund. The Israeli Tolkien Community, the Israeli Society for Role-Playing Games, and AMAI, the Israeli Manga and Anime Society, all currently active (the last despite the oddly expressed displeasure of the Israel Defense Forces, which for a time refused to recruit its members), have shown greater staying power.

The ISSF&F, among its other achievements, has regularly staged several annual conventions, notably ICon, Olamot (Worlds), Me'orot (Lights), and Bidion (Fiction), some as collaborative events with one or more of the groups mentioned above. Its major thrust at international recognition within world fandom was to have been ArmageddonCon, intended to usher in the new millennium at Har Megiddo, known worldwide as Armageddon (on the correct date, namely midnight on December 31, 2000); alas, it had to be canceled because of the outbreak of the second armed Palestinian uprising, or Intifada.

Like other such organizations, the ISSF&F inaugurated a semiprozine, *HaMemad haAsiri* (The tenth dimension), which took over where *Fantasia 2000* had left off in publishing original fiction by Israeli writers. It also features short original fiction on its website. In 1999 the ISSF&F inaugurated the annual Geffen Prize—named for its cofounder, revered translator and editor Amos Geffen (1937–98)—for the best original and translated SF/F material published in Hebrew during the previous year. Another award, the Einat Prize for hitherto unpublished short work in Hebrew, was launched in 2005 by the ISSF&F with the support of a private family-based foundation. Genre aficionado Ron Yaniv publishes the Geffen nominees and winners annually as e-books in a private venture. The Geffen Prize volumes began publication in 2002. In 2009 the ISSF&F replaced *HaMemad haAsiri* with the annual softcover volume *Hayo Yihyeh* (Once upon a future) to showcase new and unpublished short stories written for the most part in Hebrew. The scarcity of venues for short fiction in Israel in general affords these collections added import.

One area in which the ISSF&F utterly failed was its attempts (in which coeditor E. L. was involved) to persuade educators and Ministry of Education officials to include SF/F in school curricula. Some stories, they argued, possessed sufficient literary value to be included in literature classes' reading lists. Others could be usefully included in science classes to bring some life into a regimen of eye-glazing textbooks. All these efforts were in vain: the remnants of the Old Guard had not yet perished, nor did they surrender. The gatekeepers still controlled what schoolchildren could read in classes.

On a more positive note, the organization of Israeli fandom proved crucial for budding writers who hitherto felt there was neither readership for their work nor colleagues with whom they could interact. Meeting like-minded individuals at conventions, and reading stories—and later on, novels—by aspiring writers just like themselves, there was no stopping them now. Some of their stories are included in this volume, and more, hopefully, will be showcased in subsequent ones.

More strikingly, several important mainstream writers, including three Prime Minister's Prize recipients, decided to trade in their chips for a new stake in SF/F tropes and trappings. The late Nava Semel, for instance, published three SF novels (one of them under a pen name), an opera libretto, and a play; Gail Hareven, a masterful collection of short stories; and Shimon Adaf, a mammoth SF/F novel of great wonder and complexity, one that the unusually peripatetic and internationally acclaimed British-based SF/F writer Lavie Tidhar has described as the first Israeli genre masterpiece. Upon first anteing up, however, they discovered that one of the tables in the room had already been taken by such public luminaries as Shlomo Errel, a former naval commander-in-chief, and Amnon Rubinstein and Yossi Sarid, both past ministers of education.[27] None of the latter would admit to having actually written science fiction. But their literarily established counterparts showed no such reticence. Their work, brazenly genre, proved exemplary.

The Internet provided an extremely useful tool in the service of genre proliferation. No longer did writers have to submit their creations for editorial consideration; they could publish themselves, either on their own blogs or on any one of several dedicated websites. The most outstanding one, Rami Shalheveth's *Bli Panica!* (Don't panic!), was inaugurated in 2001 and is still going strong.

As Haifa University's Keren Omry reported in a paper published by the Science Fiction Research Association in 2013, the field has proved sufficiently fertile to attract and sustain academic attention.[28] Each of Israel's public universities currently offers survey courses on speculative literature, both of the foreign variety and increasingly of the homegrown kind. The Department of English and American Studies at Tel Aviv University, for example, hosts a series of annual SF symposia. Students, meanwhile, have been awarded graduate degrees in this field from Israeli institutions, including at least one doctorate so far.

In 2009, moreover, Graff Publishing released *Im Shtei haRaglayim Amok baAnanim* (published in English as *With Both Feet on the Clouds: Fantasy in Israeli Literature* by Boston's Academic Studies Press as part of its Israel: Society, Culture, and History series). Disregarding Ortsion Bartana's more esoteric tome *HaFantasia beSiporet Dor haMedina* (Fantasy in literature of the statehood generation, 1986), as well as Rachel Elboim-Dror's 1993 *HaMachar Shel haEtmol* (Yesterday's tomorrow), *Im Shtei haRaglayim Amok baAnanim* was described by its editors as "the first serious, wide-ranging and theoretically sophisticated exploration of fantasy in Israeli literature and culture."[29] It did not, however, address Israeli science fiction in a thorough manner, leaving room, we hope, for a companion volume.

"As the field grows richer," writes Omry, "so too [do] the pleasure and insights the locally produced genre fiction provides, leaning less and less as of yore on Anglo-American themes, traditions, and locations and becoming more quintessentially and more complexly itself: Hebrew-language Israeli SF."[30]

What, then, do Israeli writers write about when they write speculative fiction? With some notable exceptions, many of them write about the end of all things. Or, to be more exact, all things Israeli.

"In Israel, even more than in any other society," observes Baruch Kimmerling, "the past, present and future are intermingled; collective memory is considered objective history." One important element of this commingling is the once universal belief, still held in certain religious circles, of "a miraculous, messianic return to the Holy Land at the apocalyptic 'end of days.'"[31]

Israelis must contend perennially with the contradictions presented by the secular messianism of the founders of their state (who subscribed to the notion that flaws and corruption in the world, and specifically "the Jewish situation," must be replaced by a new order), and the unyielding, murderous, even exterminationist opposition espoused, overtly or otherwise, by many of their neighbors. They seek respite from these opposing impulses through the projection of prodigious military deterrence, through resort to nostalgia, and through perennial low-grade anxiety over potential apocalypse.

For Israelis, engagement in apocalyptic thinking is no mere fear mongering or neurosis. Just consider the Holocaust, which functions as a cogent engine for this activity. In *Translating Israel*, Alan L. Mintz extols the work of lauded author Aharon

Appelfeld (1932–2018), whom he says "most unequivocally [took] the Holocaust as a field of imaginary activity," that is, speaking of the unspeakable.[32] Mintz asserts, moreover, that "if messianism, even misplaced messianism, is the 'positive' paradigm of the Jewish apocalypse, the Holocaust, both as an event and as a symbol, is its negative pole."

The notion of examining the extermination of two-thirds of European Jewry through the prism of SF/F may, as the late Israeli literary critic Gershon Shaked—a prominent figure among the gatekeepers mentioned above—once observed, seems grotesque. The fantastic, writes Gary K. Wolfe, "by its very nature violates the norms of realism that have dominated not only Holocaust texts but virtually the whole body of what has been received and taught as 'serious' literature for the past two centuries." Yet some British and American novels, such as Len Deighton's *SS-GB*, Philip K. Dick's *The Man in the High Castle*, Harry Turtledove's *In the Presence of Mine Enemies*, J. R. Dunn's *Days of Cain*, and Jane Yolen's *The Devil's Arithmetic*, as well as Lavie Tidhar's *A Man Lies Dreaming*, have done so innovatively, proving Shaked misguided, if not hidebound, though not as misled as those who argued that the only fitting response to the Holocaust was silence.[33]

If the Holocaust is to remain "a continuing confrontation with unimaginable evil," adds Wolfe, it must "be reimagined for succeeding generations on their own terms." Nonsurvivors find themselves at a particular disadvantage, since the Holocaust still remains, as Judith P. Kerman has observed, almost "too fantastic to contemplate." Which is why almost every account reports refusal by so many European Jews to believe the specific and generally accurate warnings they had received, even as they were herded onto the trains that transported them to the death camps and into the gas chambers that awaited them. "When the real is so fantastic, what literary effects will succeed in making it credible, and in helping the reader comprehend its human meaning?" she asks. And Jews outside Nazi-dominated lands simply refused to believe that such a thing could take place at all. In July 1943, for example, a gentile refugee from Poland, Jan Karski, arrived in Washington, DC, and was interviewed by Justice Felix Frankfurter, perhaps the most prominent Jew in the United States at the time. After hearing Karski's eyewitness report on what was going on in his homeland, Frankfurter said: "I am unable to believe what you have told me."[34]

The Holocaust was the first wholly industrialized genocide. Science fiction emerged as a response to industrialization and the impingement of science and technology on modern life. Nowhere has there been a greater travesty involving these three elements, bolstered, it should be noted, by the insidiousness of near faceless bureaucracy. It stands alongside the nuclear destruction of Hiroshima

and Nagasaki as one of the elementally apocalyptic events of our time. Polish-Is-
raeli author Mordecai Roshwald understood this intrinsically. So did firebrand
Amos Kenan, who described future Holocausts in *Shoah 2* (1975) and *Block 23* (1996).

One of the tasks undertaken by Israeli speculative literature has been to
expose both these dangerously juxtaposed motivations—an atavistic paganism
and, perhaps to a lesser extent, religious and secular messianism and romanti-
cism—that led to the Holocaust. Given the country's utopian origins and Hebrew
literature's unstinting examination of the Zionist enterprise and its fallouts, the
main burden for assuaging these anxieties has defaulted to the dystopian novel.
As Rovner declaims, "There is nothing new in Jewish literature about predicting
the end as a means of forestalling it." [35] Just read the Book of Jonah.

Dystopian literature serves as the main exception to the rule that most Israelis disdain the *fantastique*. It may not have proved as wildly popular in Israel as in
the contemporary West, where adults and youngsters alike thrill to the hyperbolic
drama in novels and films of cataclysmic *Hunger Games/Mad Max*ian continu-
ums. But as Rovner observes in his seminal study of Israeli end-time literature,
"nearly 40 years' worth of apocalyptic Hebrew fiction has in fact been translated
into English worldwide." Examples, several of which we address below, include
Amos Oz's novella *Late Love* (1975), Orly Castel Bloom's *Human Parts* (2004) and
Dolly City (2010), and Ari Folman's graphic novel adaptation of his 2008 Academy
Award–nominated film *Waltz with Bashir*. (Folman would go on to film a combined
live-action/animated version of the late Polish-Jewish writer Stanislaw Lem's
satirical SF novel *The Futurological Congress* (1971), released in 2013 as *The Congress*.)

This would seem to fly in the face of the trend among English-speaking Jews
(identified by Alan Mintz) to disengage from Israeli literature that does not reflect
their heroic idealization of Israeli society. "I would argue," contends Rovner, "that
the central reason these literary works were selected for translation [into English]
is precisely because they acknowledge that Israeli reality falls short of the Zionist
ideals of cultural rebirth and national security. To clarify further: what explains
the existence of these works in translation is that readers in the Diaspora seek to
reinforce the mythology of Israel's heroism and military prowess, while at the same
time they seek to retain a martyrology of Jewish victimization."[36]

Misgivings over past military actions going as far back as Israel's War of
Independence, incessant terrorism, the overwhelming shadow of the Holocaust
looming over Israeli imagination—and that cast by a fortress hillock overlooking
the crossroads linking Europe, Asia, and Africa in the heart of Israel—have also
helped bring apocalyptic tropes to the fore. Trapped between an unsustainable
longing for the halcyon days of what Israeli singer Arik Einstein nostalgically

called "Good Old Eretz Israel" and the imminent expectation of cataclysm, a significant portion of Israeli literature, Rovner says (referencing modern Hebrew literary scholar Arnold Band), is impelled by a "nostalgia for nightmare."[37]

Though wary of engaging in bouts of unfettered fancy, Israeli writers were certainly well aware that Orwell, Huxley, and Burgess had crafted their respective literary nightmares while incurring the wrath of the writerly classes mostly because of their political underpinnings, not just on the basis of genre. Doubtless they were protected both by their literary reputations and their seriousness of intent in issuing cautionary storm warnings.

It didn't hurt Israeli dystopianism that one of the first Hebrew books to dabble with some of its tropes was written by one of Israel's most respected authors. In 1971, Amos Oz published a novella, *Ahavah Meuheret (Late Love)*.[38] More psychological than classically prescriptive or cautionary, *Late Love* placed modern dystopian imagery and descriptors squarely on the map of contemporary Hebrew literature. Oz thereby reset the standard Zionist tableau, imbuing it with tropes borrowed and deployed, it sometimes seems, from dystopian and pulp science fiction. However distasteful to then-current Israeli literary sensibilities (and probably to Oz's own stated intent), neither this new vocabulary nor the novella itself could be ignored.

If Israeli dystopias eventually gained a measure of local acceptance, as Gail Hareven observes, it is because they had "a point, that [they had] some sort of connection to 'the burning reality of our life,' that [they examined] some fractured symbol or in short, as Gogol put it, 'that it benefit the country.'"[39] Indeed, even detractors of *1984*, *Brave New World*, and *A Clockwork Orange* clearly understood that these books did not merely offer fanciful jaunts into the future but were in fact very much about the imminent realities of the day.

This did not assuage all literary concerns. One of the editors of this book (S. T.) interviewed author Amos Kenan in 1984 about his novella *The Road to Ein Harod*, a near-future political thriller. Kenan bridled at the presumption that this book, though awash with SF/F tropes, qualified in any way as science fiction. "Look outside," he barked. "This is documentary journalism."

It comes as no surprise that two of the best received and most enduring examples of Israeli dystopias—Kenan's *Ein Harod* and Binyamin Tammuz's *Pundako shel Yirmiyahu* (Jeremiah's inn)—should have been published in 1984. That year's advent, after all, provided cause for worldwide reflection and stocktaking. Israel, moreover, remained mired in the morass of its ill-conceived invasion of Lebanon in 1982, which was to defy extraction or hoped-for results for years to come. Its official title, Operation Peace for the Galilee, was as brazen an example of Newspeak as anything Orwell ever devised.

The First Lebanon War profoundly embittered Israelis and Jews in the Diaspora, many of whom recognized it as an adventurist folly that had little to do with its stated aims. Misgivings over then Defense Minister Ariel Sharon's scheme to reconfigure the entire Middle East, outrage over Israel's inadvertent culpability in the Sabra and Shatila massacre, the perennial sense of helplessness and vulnerability pervading Israeli society, the emergence of the first suicide bombers, the intimations of a tottering power structure culminating in the never-officially-explained abdication of Prime Minister Menachem Begin—all these found voice in dystopian visions.

A generation later, *Ein Harod* begat an Arab-Israeli response in Sayed Kashua's Hebrew-language novel *VaYehi Boker* (*Let It Be Morning*, 2004).[40] This book is set in the Arab-Israeli columnist's hometown of Tira, to which the unnamed protagonist, who nevertheless shares much of his biography with his author, retreats after being terminated by a left-wing Israeli newspaper in Tel Aviv. Where once he waxed nostalgic, now Kashua, one of the small number among Israel's 1.7 million Arabs who enjoyed an urban, middle-class existence, confronts his alienation from the narrowness, parochialism, and despondency of traditional Arab-Israeli hometown life. His protagonist's sense of entrapment increases severalfold when the town is surrounded by a military force bearing orders to shoot anyone trying to cross their lines.

The reader may be excused for interpreting this predicament as a metaphor for, or even a symptom of, the fraught Israeli Arabs' condition. But Kashua, whose earlier book, *Aravim Rokdim* (*Dancing Arabs*, successfully adapted for film in 2014) earned acclaim in Israel and abroad, is never obvious or hidebound. The book concludes with the protagonist's discovering, to his horror, that the encircling army belongs to a Palestinian Authority engaged in a land swap with the Israelis as part of a final peace settlement.

Tammuz's *Jeremiah's Inn* took a different, and to some Israelis no less alarming route to the apocalypse: an Ultra-Orthodox takeover of the nation.[41] The plot transpires in an Israel temporally farther afield: one dominated by an array of warring fundamentalist rabbinical courts headquartered in a physically, religiously, and socially fragmented Jerusalem. At once hilarious and horrifying, the book is written as a pastiche of rabbinical parables. While certainly readable by anyone literate in Hebrew, it is befittingly written in parts in the archaic Hebrew style traditionally (as well as currently) used in rabbinical circles for religious discourse. As this style has no equivalent in English (nor, perhaps, in any other language save Ecclesiastical Latin), the prospects for an English-language translation are not favorable.[42]

In 1987 author, playwright, and television host Yitzhak Ben-Ner published *HaMal'achim Ba'im* (The angels are coming), a novel, inspired by his 1977 short story "Aharey haGeshem" (After the rain),[43] that melds elements of *Ein Harod* and *Jeremiah's Inn* with Burgess's *Clockwork Orange*. Ben-Ner depicts a Jewish state buckling under the boot of a fundamentalist government that enforces its will by directing pogroms against the secular residents of Tel Aviv and other coastal environs. The fantastic tropes incorporated into the text include a pair of imaginary dwarves; a policewoman of extraterrestrial origin; a protagonist who emerges from a severe beating with new healing powers brought on by the slow appearance on his forehead of a blue Star of David; a country no longer threatened by Arab animosity, but which has subsequently turned upon itself; and a high-tech sector that colludes with or deliberately ignores the centrifugal forces tearing society apart.

The reception extended to Ben-Ner's opus is illustrative of the Israeli literati's nearly implacable abhorrence of SF/F tropes. Initially, Gershon Shaked, already mentioned above as a primo literary gatekeeper, had touted Ben-Ner's talent for "crafting of realistic plots and the accurate presentation of human situations." But then, in 1987, Ben-Ner subverted his literary standing with *HaMal'achim Ba'im*, a hard-core science-fiction dystopia, leading to considerable wringing of writerly hands and gnashing of teeth. "How much longer will our readers . . . put up with the pranks of our writers?" asked one put-upon pundit. "Is it not time to turn our backs to a literature that treats us this way?"[44]

It would take years for this attitude to change, as an increasing number of books garnered greater public attention and acclaim. In 2008, for instance, Assaf Gavron published *Hydromania*, an ecothriller (translated into German, Dutch, and Italian) set in 2065 and depicting a desperately parched and dramatically truncated Jewish State facing imminent destruction by invading Arab forces. The book offers a handy example of the notion that Israelis are more open to genre forays if these address societal concerns. The Italian newspaper *La Stampa*, for example, observed that *Hydromania* "captures and unfolds the two fundamental obsessions of the country: the fear of being crushed by the immense Arab world and the fear of dying of thirst."

In 2013, to offer another example, Yali Sobol, son of renowned Israeli playwright Yehoshua Sobol and lead singer of the prolific Israeli band Monica Sex, published *Etzba'ot shel Psantran* (A pianist's fingers). The novel, yet another variation on the by now standard leftist Israeli dystopian theme—this one following the advent of yet another war—envisioned the tormenting by thought police of artists, Post-Post-Zionists, leftist columnists, kibbutz remnants, and the last remaining subscribers of *Haaretz*.[45] For leftist columnists, kibbutz members, and *Haaretz* readers observing the country's inexorable shift to the right, such scenarios bespeak very real anxieties.

Orly Castel-Bloom's novel *Dolly City* (1992; translated in 1997) presents another, albeit more extreme, case. Dolly City, a nightmarish stand-in for Tel Aviv (named for the book's eponymous protagonist-murderess), "the most demented city in the world," is a singular creation. Here, explains Castel-Bloom—in a stripped-down style that many claim changed (some would say diluted) the tenor of Hebrew literature forever—everyone is on the run. And "since everyone is running, there's always someone chasing them, and since there is someone chasing them, they catch them, and when they catch them, execute them, and throw them into the river."[46] Dolly, a surgeon, spares her son this fate, but only by inoculating him with poisonous microbes, carving a map of Israel on his back, and relieving a German baby of his kidney for transplant into her hapless boy. In no uncertain terms she strives to imprint her own Israeli nightmare on his still maturing flesh.

Castel-Bloom's Grand Guignol gives way to what at first appears to be a more sober and less flamboyant engagement with the purely dystopian in *Halakim Enoshiyim* (2002; translated as *Human Parts*, 2004).[47] The book appeared ten years later, during the Second Intifada, when Palestinians armed with explosive belts regularly rendered Israeli civilians into unidentifiable mounds of bloody flesh at the push of a vest button. In her scenario the government proves unable to contain the carnage, the prime minister collapses, and the cabinet succumbs to paralysis. Suddenly, the country falls prey to a triple-whammy: an outbreak of the "Saudi flu," eight-foot snowfalls, and hailstones the size of baseballs. The weather, it turns out, was caused by an undersea volcanic eruption; the outbreak of disease, by an Arab biological assault. As ocean liners careen down Tel Aviv avenues (an image that would later resound in Lavie Tidhar and Nir Yaniv's surrealistic novel *The Tel Aviv Dossier*), the country teeters on the brink of dissolution.

In 2010 the acclaimed Israeli poet and novelist Shimon Adaf published a novel, *Kfor* (Frost), set in a far-future Tel Aviv in which a group of yeshiva students portentously begin to grow wings. Author and editor Nick Gevers applauded the novel's "vivid description of life in Israel as well as . . . its subtle, incisive treatment of the fantastic as a phenomenon and as a literary genre." Adaf is represented in the present volume with the story "They Had to Move," selected from the commemorative thirtieth anniversary issue of *Fantasia 2000*.

Perhaps the most sustained exploration of the nexus between Israel and the apocalyptic, however, can be found in Gail Hareven's accomplished SF/F collection *HaDerech leGan Eden* (The road to heaven), published by Keter in 1999. In "Lir'ot et ha'Nolad" (literally, "to behold the newborn," a Hebrew expression used to describe foresight), for example, a far-future society cognizant of impending end-times projects youngsters approaching their majority to near the end of human existence, where, it is hoped, they will witness glimmers of the causes of disaster and survive long enough to return home with useful intelligence. Gail Hareven is the most accomplished, and one of the few unabashedly genre savvy, of those mainstream Israeli authors to have discovered the promised land of SF/F.

Israeli theater has proved particularly amenable to representations of apocalypse. Literary scholar Zahava Caspi argues that this is because the stage is adept at showing the symptoms of the profound existential traumas that Israeli society has suffered since the Yom Kippur War of 1973.[48] The sense of redemption that emerged from the 1967 Six-Day War, and the sense of despair that followed the Yom Kippur War so soon afterwards, created an opening for messianic attitudes, in particular. Overall, theatrical representations of the apocalypse, especially during the 1970s, offered an outlet for what some might construe as a prodigious case of societal PTSD.

Caspi identifies two waves of apocalyptic theater in Israel, one corresponding to the Yom Kippur War near-defeat and the other to the Lebanon War and the First Intifada during the 1980s. Notable examples included Shmuel Hasfari's 1982 play *Tashmad* (the Hebrew date corresponding to 1984), about a plan by Israeli settlers to destroy the Al Aqsa Mosque and replace it with a new temple; Motti Lerner's *Hevlei Mashiah* (Premessianic tribulations), in which such a plan comes to fruition, sparking a regional war; Yehoshua Sobol's 1988 *Syndrome Yerushalayim* (Jerusalem syndrome), which portrays Jerusalem's destruction in AD 70 as an analogy to the situation in the occupied territories today; Hanoch Levin's *Retzah* (1997; translated as *Murder: A Play in Three Acts and an Epilogue*, 2005), which depicts an endless procession of violent actions and reactions in the Middle East; Shimon Bouzaglo's 2002 production of *Geshem Shahor* (Black rain), which ends with Israel under atomic attack; and Tamir Greenberg's *Hebron* (2007), in which the earth denies burial to children killed in the conflict, spewing forth their bodies in a gallery of flames that engulfs the town of Hebron.

Nava Semel's *And The Rat Laughed*,[49] which deals directly with questions of the Holocaust and specific memories of that event, was afforded an operatic adaptation by the Tel Aviv Cameri Theatre with the Israel Chamber Orchestra, staged in April 2005. The narrative transpires after a "Great Ecological Disaster" inaugurates a cybernetic society in the micro-nation of TheIsrael at the onset of the twenty-second century.

Israeli author Savyon Liebrecht, also well known for her preoccupation with the Holocaust, creates an equally harrowing scenario in her novella *A Good Place for the Night*, which we include herein. Adam Rovner classifies the story as "futuristic Holocaust fiction." If these stories present a variety of Israeli necropolises, Etgar

Keret's Tel Aviv, insofar as it figures in his 1998 novella *HaKaytana shel Kneller* (*Kneller's Happy Campers*), is Limbo. A multivalent variation on Keret's theme can be found in Ofir Touché Gafla's 2003 Geffen Prize–winning tour de force *Olam Basof* (*The World of the End*). In it, a ghostwriter who cannot abide the death of his wife follows her into the afterlife. Michael Weingard of the *Jewish Review of Books* describes the book as *"Orpheus and Eurydice* meets *Alice in Wonderland."*[50]

Another recurring theme in Israeli speculative literature, alluded to above, is that of the alternate (or counterfactual) history. Literature itself is inevitably counterfactual by nature. As Rovner observes, "It represents possible worlds rather than a description of real states of affairs. Literature's figurative language employs the creative potential latent in everyday language in order to open a horizon of new possibilities. . . . Gifted men and women marshal the incantatory power of words to vitalize the imaginary and render phantasms substantial."[51] The Arab-Israeli conflict as actually played out was never really foreordained. "No sequence of events ever is. Matters could always have turned out otherwise. . . . Inevitability is a chimera, a product of organizing contingencies into a narrative that elides the haphazardness of existence."

A number of allohistorical accounts have been published in Hebrew. Fans of Pulitzer Prize–winning American writer Michael Chabon, the author of *The Yiddish Policeman's Union*, winner of the 2008 Hugo and Nebula Awards, may be surprised to learn that Israeli novelist and playwright Nava Semel covered similar, though certainly not identical, ground four years earlier in her own novel, *Isra-Isle*. In Chabon's opus the remnants of a defeated Israel settle temporarily in a small autonomous region of Sitka, Alaska, in 1941, where they live in various degrees of disharmony with the local Inuit and Native American populations. In Semel's novel, they live in upstate New York on an island settled by Native Americans. Both narratives, not incidentally, rely heavily on the conventions of detective fiction, SF, and alternate history.

Following on Semel's consideration of a Territorialist solution to the Jewish problem, Yoav Avni considers the fortunes of a Jewish state based on the so-called Ugandist solution tabled by the British colonial secretary Joseph Chamberlain in 1903. The story, its original title *Herzl Amar* ("Herzl said," the Hebrew equivalent of "Simon said"), transpires in a Jewish republic in East Africa whose problems in 2005 seem quite au courant with those of present-day Israel. For example, the Jewish state is planning a withdrawal from Maasai tribal territories while dismantling two of the country's oldest Jewish settlements, threatening a civil war. The book's protagonists, meanwhile, are completing their tours of duty in the IDF, intent upon backpacking to the Middle East, and specifically to the eternally moribund Holy Land, a magnet for post-compulsory-service pilgrims and transients.

In *A Man Lies Dreaming* (2014), Israel's immensely prolific and preternaturally peripatetic author Lavie Tidhar presents us with Hitler as a hack private eye after decamping to Great Britain following his failed 1923 Beer Hall Putsch. In *The World Hitler Never Made: Alternate History and the Memory of Nazism*, Gavriel D. Rosenfeld says of his first encounter with a Hitler-victorious counterfactual, Robert Harris's *Fatherland* (1992), that while the conceit startled him, the book itself was hardly a tour-de-force. At best, he attests, it was entertaining, a common descriptor of Len Deighton's *SS-GB* and other such work. We may say much the same for former Israeli left-wing politician Yossi Sarid's aforementioned novel *Lefichach Nitkanasnu* ("Accordingly, we are here assembled," a memorable phrase from Israel's Declaration of Independence), another bestseller in Israeli terms.[52] The book begins in 1948 and extends in year-long-segments well into 1967. What, Sarid asks, might have happened had the Zionist establishment extended a more complete and fitting welcome to Jewish refugees from Arab states who began to show up in 1950 after expulsion by their Arab neighbors? What, moreover, if they had been treated not as an unwelcome afterthought deserving of across-the-board underclass status, but of the same material assets and support afforded German and European Jewry? The what-ifs go on and on.

Themes and motifs aside, you will find in *Zion's Fiction* a cornucopia of good to great stories. Generally speaking, these may be divided into two categories: stories written by mainstream and genre authors. Among the former you will encounter Gail Hareven's superlative story "The Slows," the only Israeli SF story ever published in *The New Yorker* (getting any SF/F story into *The New Yorker* is no mean feat, even in an issue dedicated to the genre). Others authors of the same ilk include Savyon Liebrecht, Nava Semel, and Shimon Adaf. But the majority of the stories were written by authors who grew up, in the literary sense, within SF/F, including Rotem Baruchin, Yael Furman, Guy Hasson, Keren Landsman, Eyal Teler, Lavie Tidhar, and Nir Yaniv, to mention but a few. Like so many genre authors worldwide, they were fans first, published writers later on. Their emergence and their impressive output are the reasons that made us offer this anthology to the wider readership they deserve.

One final point we wish to make concerns Russian-language SF/F writers now living in Israel. The Russian immigrants are reputed to supersede their native-born compatriots, no slouches themselves, in their consumption of books. And of all the kinds of books Russians love to read, SF/F ranks pretty highly. Highly enough that many of them view Israeli reticence over speculative fiction, indigenous or otherwise, as inexplicably *nekulturny*—"uncultured," one of the worst insults in the Russian vocabulary.

For the moment, most of them still prefer to remain ensconced within a Russian-speaking milieu. Their SF/F fanzines, journals, and live-action role-playing clubs operate largely under the Israeli radar. The majority of Israelis have absolutely no intimation as to how this hidden literary geyser will soon erupt as their progeny swap Russian for Hebrew, and, should their parents' literary predilections endure, change the nature of Hebrew belles lettres forever.

"I think the proportion of Russians to Israelis remain[s] roughly the same since the Great Aliyah of the 90s," says the Ukraine-born Israeli scholar and writer Elana Gomel (whose story "Death in Jerusalem" we are delighted to present in this volume). "But I have no doubt that it has already significantly increased the appreciation of, and interest in, SF in Israel. The growth of festivals like ICon . . . the number of young Israelis who read/write SF (interestingly enough, often in English, even though it's not their mother tongue), the emergence of Israeli comics, etc. In my classes on SF about half the students are 'Russians' (even though many of them grew up or were born in Israel)."

For them, we wait. And with them, we dream.

Notes

1. First coined by M. F. Egan and subsequently espoused by Lloyd Arthur Eshbach and Robert A. Heinlein, the term *speculative fiction* was generally intended to deemphasize the technological aspects of a great deal of earlier science fiction. Heinlein defined the term as a subset of SF involving extrapolation from known science and technology "to produce a new situation, a new framework for human action."
2. Horror, currently referred to as dark or weird fantasy, is a rarity in Israeli speculative fiction, although a few, among them Asaf Ashery and Orly Castel-Bloom, have valiantly tried their hands at it. Many Israelis will argue that they live with enough daily horror to avoid subjecting themselves to additional, imaginary torments.
3. Quoted in Michael Weingrad, "Riding Leviathan: A New Wave of Israeli Genre Fiction," *Jewish Review of Books*, Winter 2014, http://jewishreviewofbooks.com/articles/602/riding-leviathan-a-new-wave-of-israeli-genre-fiction. Yanai would subsequently set matters aright with the publication of two unabashed fantasy novels, *HaLivyatan MiBavel* (The leviathan of Babylon, 2006) and *HaMayim shebein HaOlamot* (The water between the worlds, 2008).
4. Danielle Gurevitch, "What Is Fantasy?" in *With Both Feet on the Clouds: Fantasy in Israeli Literature*, edited by Danielle Gurevitch, Elana Gomel, and Rani Graff (Brighton, MA: Academic Studies Press, 2012), 13.

5. Adam L. Rovner, *In the Shadow of Zion: Promised Lands before Israel* (New York: NYU Press, Kindle Edition, 2014), Kindle Location 161 of 8224, retrieved from Amazon.com.

6. Gail Hareven, "What Is Unimaginable?" in *With Both Feet on the Clouds*, 45.

7. Usually, this is rendered in English as "If you will it, it is no dream." Herzl, however, used the German word *Märchen*, fairy tale.

8. Leon Uris's protagonist, Ari Ben Canaan (*Exodus*), was a feeble caricature of this idealized image.

9. See Jeff Vandermeer and Jeremy Zerfoss, *Wonderbook: The Illustrated Guide to Creating Imaginative Fiction* (New York: Abrams Image, 2013).

10. Some cases in point for this kind of bowdlerism include a 1938 translation of Lawrence's *Lady Chatterley's Lover* with no sex scenes and a 1924 translation of Wallace's *Ben Hur* from which all references to Jesus and Christianity (including, of course, the subtitle, *A Tale of the Christ*) were carefully expunged.

11. Nachman Ben-Yehuda, "Sociological Reflections on the History of Science Fiction in Israel," *Science Fiction Studies* 13 (1986): 75.

12. Quoted in Oren Tokatly, *Mediniyut Tikshoret beIsrael* [Communications policy in Israel] (Tel Aviv: Open University Publishing House, 2000), 85.

13. Elana Gomel, "What Is Reality?" in *With Both Feet on the Clouds*, 33. The term Mizrahi applies to Jews from Middle Eastern countries, many of whom are able to trace their lineage to the Babylonian dispersion, not to be confused or conflated with Sephardic Jews, whose forefathers had lived in Spain and Portugal for centuries prior to their expulsion in 1492 and 1496, respectively, and who generally dispersed southward and eastward. In fact, these are two distinct subcultures.

14. Ioram Melcer, "Why Doesn't It Rain Fish Here?" in *With Both Feet on the Clouds*, 194; Gomel, "What is Reality?" 32.

15. Robert Scholes, *Structural Fabulation: An Essay on the Fiction of the Future* (Notre Dame and London: University of Notre Dame Press, 1975).

16. Baruch Kimmerling, *The Invention and Decline of Israeliness: State, Society, and the Military* (Berkeley: University of California Press, 2001), 8; Elana Gomel, "What Is Reality," 33–34; Diana Pinto, *Israel Has Moved* (Boston: Harvard University Press, 2013), 1.

17. Dan Horowitz and Moshe Lissak, *Trouble in Utopia: The Overburdened Polity of Israel* (New York: SUNY Press, 1989).

18. Very early on, the Zionist movement was almost split by a conflict between two opposing views: the so-called Territorialists held that the Jewish Problem required an immediate solution and were willing to accept any territory that may be offered, notably British Uganda. The Zion's Zionists faction, on the other hand, insisted on the Land of Israel as the only possible place in which the desired solution could be implemented. Herzl himself initially supported the former view but then yielded to the Zion's Zionists to prevent the dissolution of his fledgling movement.

19. Hareven, "What Is Unimaginable?" 46. This, however, has not stopped allohistorical speculation on the matter, as in "What If Frank Had Immigrated to Palestine," in Gavriel D. Rosenfeld, *What Ifs of Jewish History* (Cambridge: Cambridge University Press, 2016), 187–214. Larry Niven quote from a panel discussion on the Doomsday Asteroid at the Weizmann Institute, Rehovoth, Israel, March 20, 2007, according to editor E. L.'s recollection.

20. Rachel S. Harris, "Israeli Literature in the 21st Century: The Transcultural Generation: An Introduction," *Shofar* 33, no. 4 (Summer 2015): 1–14, 200, quote from p. 1, retrieved from Proquest electronic database. Post-Zionism refers to a sense that by restoring Jewish sovereignty in the State of Israel, the Zionist movement has fulfilled its destiny and may therefore be designated as complete, hence obsolete.

21. Sheldon Teitelbaum, "Out of Science Fiction, a New View of Contemporary Reality," *Los Angeles Times*, January 17, 1988.

22. Hareven, "What Is Unimaginable?" 45.

23. "About CyberCozen," http://www.kulichki.com/antimiry/cybercozen.

24. Oren Soffer, *Mass Communication in Israel: Nationalism, Globalization, and Segmentation* (New York: Berghahn Books, 2015), 2.

25. Gomel, "What Is Reality?" 36.

26. Quoted in Soffer, *Mass Communication*, 14.

27. Shlomo Errel, *Undersea Diplomacy* (Tel Aviv: Maariv Books–Hed Artzi Publishing, 2000); Amnon Rubinstein, *The Sea above Us* (Tel Aviv: Schocken Publishing House Ltd., 2007); Yossi Sarid, *Accordingly We Are Here Assembled: An Alternate History* [in Hebrew] (Tel Aviv: Yedioth Ahronoth Books and Chemed Books, 2008).

28. Keren Omry, "SF 101," *Science Fiction Research Association Review* 306 (Fall 2013), retrieved from author's website.

29. Gurevitch, Gomel, and Graff, eds., "Introduction," *With Both Feet on the Clouds*, 9.

30. Omry, "SF 101."

31. Kimmerling, Invention and Decline, 16, 23.

32. Alan L. Mintz, Translating Israel: Contemporary Hebrew Literature and Its Reception in America (Syracuse, NY: Syracuse University Press, 2001), 50.

33. Gershon Shaked, "Facing the Nightmare: Israeli Literature on the Holocaust," in *The Nazi Concentration Camps* (Jerusalem: Yad Vashem, 1984), 690; Gary K. Wolfe, "Introduction: Fantasy as Testimony," in *The Fantastic in Holocaust Literature and Film*, edited by Judith B. Kerman and John Edgar Browning (Jefferson, NC: McFarland & Company, 2015), Kindle edition, loc. 137 of 4490.

34. Judith B. Kerman, "Uses of the Fantastic in the Literature of the Holocaust," in *Fantastic in Holocaust Literature and Film*, loc. 325 of 4490. Felix Frankfurter quote from Stanford University News Service, News Release, March 7, 1995, http://web.stanford.edu/dept/news/pr/95/950307Arc5338.html.

35. Adam Rovner, "Forcing the End: Apocalyptic Israeli Fiction, 1971–2009," in *Narratives of Dissent: War in Contemporary Israeli Arts and Culture* [e-book], edited by Rachel S. Harris and Ronen Omer-Sherman (Detroit: Wayne State University Press, 2012), 209.

It is very interesting to note that a similar trend can be discerned now in the Arab world, where "a new wave of dystopian and surrealist fiction [emerges] from Middle Eastern writers who are grappling with the chaotic aftermath and stinging disappointments of the Arab Spring. Five years after the popular uprisings in Egypt, Tunisia, Libya and elsewhere, a bleak, apocalyptic strain of post-revolutionary literature has taken root in the region. Some writers are using science fiction and fantasy tropes to describe grim current political realities. . . . 'There's a shift away from realism, which has dominated Arabic literature,' said the Kuwait-born novelist Saleem Haddad. . . . 'What's coming to the surface now is darker and a bit deeper.'" ("Middle Eastern Writers Find Refuge in the Dystopian Novel," *New York Times*, Books Section, May 29, 2016.) A notable example is Iraqi writer Ahmed Saadawi's *Frankenstein in Baghdad: A Novel* (Arabic, al Kamel, 2013; English translation, Penguin Books, 2018).

36. Rovner, "Forcing the End," 206, 209.

37. Ibid., 99, 206; Arik Einstein, *Eretz Yisrael haYeshana vehaTova*, Phonodor album 13038, 1973.

38. Amos Oz, *Late Love*, in *Unto Death*, translated by Nicholas de Lange (New York: Harcourt Brace Jovanovich, 1975).

39. Hareven, "What Is Unimaginable?" 30.

40. Sayed Kashua, *Let It Be Morning* (New York: Grove Press, Black Cat, 2006).

41. Compare Robert A. Heinlein's *Revolt in 2100*, in which the United States is a theocracy ruled by a self-proclaimed Prophet.

42. Not that this would stop similarly themed novels from Amit Godenberg, *Ir Nidachat* [A city withdrawn], 2015; Yishai Sarid, *Ha'Shlishi* [The third one], also 2015; or Dror Burstein, *Teet* [Clay], 2016.

43. Yitshak Ben-Ner, "Aharey haGeshem" [After the rain] (Tel Aviv, 1977).

44. Gershon Shaked, *Gal Ahar Gal baSipporet haIvrit* [Wave after wave in Hebrew narrative fiction] (Jerusalem, 1985), 168; Avraham Hagorni, "A Dwarf and a Half" [in Hebrew], *Davar*, November 20, 1987.

45. Yali Sobol, *Etzba'ot shel Psantran* [A pianist's fingers] (Tel Aviv: Kinneret Zmora Bitan Dvir, 2012); Weingrad, "Riding Leviathan."

46. Orly Castel-Bloom, *Dolly City* (Dalkey Archive Press, 2010), 76–77.

47. Orly Castel-Bloom, *Human Parts* (Boston: Verba Mundi Books, 2004).

48. Zahava Caspi, "Trauma, Apocalypse, and Ethics in Israeli Theatre," *CLCWeb: Comparative Literature and Culture* 14, no. 1 (2012): 3.

49. Nava Semel, *And the Rat Laughed* [*Tzhok Shel Achbarosh*] (Proza, 2001; English translation, Melbourne, Australia: Port Campbell Press, 2008).

50. Savyon Liebrecht, *A Good Place for the Night* [*Makom Tov La'Laila*] (New York, Persea Books, 2006); Rovner, *In the Shadow of Zion*, 215; Etgar Keret, *HaKaytana shel Kneller* [*Kneller's Happy Campers*], from the collection *Ga'agu'ay leKissinger* [*Missing Kissinger*] (London: Chatto & Windus, 2007) and adapted for film in 2006 as *WristCutters: A Love Story* and as the graphic novel *Pizzeria Kamikaze* in 2005; O. T. Gafla, *Olam Basof* [*The World at the End*] (2003; translated in English, New York: Tor, 2013).

51. Rovner, *In the Shadow of Zion*, 215.

52. Lavie Tidhar, *A Man Lies Dreaming* (London: Hodder & Stoughton, 2014); Robert Harris, *Fatherland* (Billings, MT: BCA, 1992), 372.

The Smell of Orange Groves

Lavie Tidhar

On the roof the solar panels were folded in on themselves, still asleep, yet uneasily stirring, as though they could sense the imminent coming of the sun. Boris stood on the edge of the roof. The roof was flat, and the building's residents, his father's neighbors, had, over the years, planted and expanded an assortment of plants, in pots of clay and aluminum and wood, across the roof, turning it into a high-rise tropical garden.

It was quiet up there and, for the moment, still cool. He loved the smell of late-blooming jasmine; it crept along the walls of the building, climbing tenaciously high, spreading out all over the old neighborhood that surrounded Central Station. He took a deep breath of night air and released it slowly, haltingly, watching the lights of the spaceport: it rose out of the sandy ground of Tel Aviv, the shape of an hourglass, and the slow-moving suborbital flights took off and landed like moving stars, tracing jeweled flight paths in the skies.

He loved the smell of this place, this city. The smell of the sea to the west, that wild scent of salt and open water, seaweed and tar, of suntan lotion and people. He loved to watch the solar surfers in the early morning, with spread transparent wings gliding on the winds above the Mediterranean. Loved the smell of cold conditioned air leaking out of windows, of basil when you rubbed it between your fingers; loved the smell of shawarma rising from street level with its heady mix of spices, turmeric and cumin dominating; loved the smell of vanished orange groves from far beyond the urban blocks of Tel Aviv or Jaffa.

Once it had all been orange groves. He stared out at the old neighborhood, the peeling paint, boxlike apartment blocks in old-style Soviet architecture crowded in with magnificent early-twentieth-century Bauhaus constructions, buildings made to look like ships, with long, curving, graceful balconies, small, round windows, flat roofs like decks, like the one he stood on—

Mixed amongst the old buildings were newer constructions, Martian-style co-op buildings with drop chutes for lifts and small rooms divided and subdivided inside, many without any windows—

Laundry hanging as it had for hundreds of years, off wash lines and windows, faded blouses and shorts blowing in the wind, gently. Balls of lights floated in the streets down below, dimming now, and Boris realized the night was receding, saw a blush of pink and red on the edge of the horizon and knew the sun was coming.

He had spent the night keeping vigil with his father, Vlad Chong, son of Weiwei Zhong (Zhong Weiwei in the Chinese manner of putting the family name first), and of Yulia Chong, née Rabinovich. In the tradition of the family, Boris, too, was given a Russian name. In another of the family's traditions, he was also given a second, Jewish name. He smiled wryly, thinking about it. Boris Aaron Chong; the heritage and weight of three shared and ancient histories pressing down heavily on his slim, no longer young shoulders.

It had not been an easy night.

Once it had all been orange groves. . . . He took a deep breath, that smell of old asphalt and lingering combustion engine exhaust fumes gone now like the oranges, yet still, somehow, lingering, a memory-scent.

He'd tried to leave it behind. The family's memory, what he sometimes, privately, called the Curse of the Family Chong, or Weiwei's Folly.

He could still remember it. Of course he could. A day so long ago, that Boris Aaron Chong himself was not yet an idea, an I-loop that hadn't yet been formed. . . .

It was in Jaffa, in the Old City on top of the hill, above the harbor. The home of the Others.

Zhong Weiwei cycled up the hill, sweating in the heat. He mistrusted these narrow, winding streets, both of the Old City itself and of Ajami, the neighborhood that had at last reclaimed its heritage. Weiwei understood this place's conflicts very well. There were Arabs and Jews, and they wanted the same land and so they fought. Weiwei understood land and how you were willing to die for it.

But he also knew the concept of land had changed—that land was a concept less of a physicality now, and more of the mind. Recently he had invested some of his money in an entire planetary system in the Guilds of Ashkelon games-universe. Soon he would have children—Yulia was in her third trimester already—and then grand-children and great-grandchildren and so on down the generations, and they would remember Weiwei, their progenitor. They would thank him for what he'd done, for the real estate both real and virtual, and for what he was hoping to achieve today.

He, Zhong Weiwei, would begin a dynasty here in this divided land. For he had understood the most basic of aspects, he alone saw the relevance of that foreign enclave that was Central Station. Jews to the north (and his children, too, would be Jewish, which was a strange and unsettling thought), Arabs to the south, now they have returned, reclaimed Ajami and Menashiya, and were building New Jaffa, a city towering into the sky in steel and stone and glass. Divided cities, like Akko, and Haifa, in the north, and the new cities sprouting in the desert, in the Negev and the Arava.

Arab or Jew, they needed their immigrants, their foreign workers, their Thai and Filipino and Chinese, Somali and Nigerian. And they needed their buffer, that in-between zone that was Central Station, old South Tel Aviv, a poor place, a vibrant place—most of all, a liminal place.

And he would make it his home. His, and his children's, and his children's children's. The Jews and the Arabs understood family, at least. In that they were like the Chinese—so different from the Anglos with their nuclear families, strained relations, all living separately, alone. . . . This, Weiwei swore, would not happen to his children.

At the top of the hill he stopped and wiped his brow from the sweat with the cloth handkerchief he kept for that purpose. Cars went past him, and the sound of construction was everywhere. He himself worked on one of the buildings they were erecting here, a diasporic construction crew, small Vietnamese and tall Nigerians and pale, solid Transylvanians, communicating by hand signals and Asteroid Pidgin (though that had not yet been in widespread use at that time) and automatic translators through their nodes. Weiwei himself worked the exoskeleton suits, climbing up the tower blocks with spiderlike grips, watching the city far down below and looking out to sea and distant ships. . . .

But today was his day off. He had saved money—some to send, every month, to his family back in Chengdu, some for his soon to be growing family here. And the rest for this for the favor to be asked of the Others.

Folding the handkerchief neatly away, he pushed the bike along the road and into the maze of alleyways that was the Old City of Jaffa. The remains of an ancient Egyptian fort could still be seen there; the gate had been refashioned a century before, and the hanging orange tree still hung by chains, planted within a heavy, egg-shaped stone basket in the shade of the walls. Weiwei didn't stop but kept going until he reached, at last, the place of the Oracle.

Boris looked at the rising sun. He felt tired, drained. He had kept his father company throughout the night. His father, Vlad, hardly slept anymore. He sat for hours in his armchair, a thing worn and full of holes, dragged one day, years ago (the memory crystal-clear in Boris's mind) with great effort and pride from Jaffa's flea market. Vlad's hands moved through the air, moving and rearranging invisible objects. He would not give Boris access into his visual feed. He barely communicated anymore. Boris suspected the objects were memories, that Vlad was trying somehow to fit them back together again. But he couldn't tell for sure.

Like Weiwei, Vlad had been a construction worker. He had been one of the people who had built Central Station, climbing up the unfinished gigantic structure, this spaceport that was now an entity unto itself, a miniature mall-nation to which neither Tel Aviv nor Jaffa could lay complete claim.

But that had been long ago. Humans lived longer now, but the mind grew old just the same, and Vlad's mind was older than his body. Boris, on the roof, went to the corner by the door. It was shaded by a miniature palm tree, and now the solar panels, too, were opening out, extending delicate wings, the better to catch the rising sun and provide shade and shelter to the plants.

Long ago the resident association had installed a communal table and a samovar there, and each week a different flat took turns to supply the tea and the coffee and the sugar. Boris gently plucked leaves off the potted mint plant nearby and made himself a cup of tea. The sound of boiling water pouring into the mug was soothing, and the smell of the mint spread in the air, fresh and clean, waking him up. He waited as the mint brewed, took the mug with him back to the edge of the roof. Looking down, Central Station—never truly asleep—was noisily waking up.

He sipped his tea and thought of the Oracle.

The Oracle's name had once been Cohen, and rumor had it that she was a relation of Saint Cohen of the Others, though no one could tell for certain. Few people today knew this. For three generations she had resided in the Old City, in that dark and quiet stone house, she and her Other alone.

The Other's name, or ident tag, was not known, which was not unusual with Others.

Regardless of possible familial links, outside the stone house there stood a small shrine to Saint Cohen. It was a modest thing, with random items of golden color placed on it, and old, broken circuits and the like, and candles burning at all hours. Weiwei, when he came to the door, paused for a moment before the shrine and lit a candle and placed an offering—a defunct computer chip from the old days, purchased at great expense in the flea market down the hill.

Help me achieve my goal today, he thought, help me unify my family and let them share my mind when I am gone.

There was no wind in the Old City, but the old stone walls radiated a comforting coolness. Weiwei, who had only recently had a node installed, pinged the door, and a moment later it opened. He went inside.

Boris remembered that moment as a stillness and at the same time, paradoxically, as a shifting, a sudden inexplicable change of perspective. His grandfather's memory glinted in the mind. For all his posturing, Weiwei was like an explorer in an unknown land, feeling his way by touch and instinct. He had not grown up with a node; he found it difficult to follow the Conversation, that endless chatter of human and machine feeds a modern human would feel deaf and blind without, yet he was a man who could sense the future as instinctively as a chrysalis can sense adulthood. He knew his children would be different, and their children different in their turn, but he equally knew there can be no future without a past—

"Zhong Weiwei," the Oracle said. Weiwei bowed. The Oracle was surprisingly young, or young-looking, at any rate. She had short black hair and unremarkable features and pale skin and a golden prosthetic for a thumb, which made Weiwei shiver without warning: it was her Other.

"I seek a boon," Weiwei said. He hesitated, then extended forward the small box. "Chocolates," he said, and—or was it just his imagination?—the Oracle smiled.

It was quiet in the room. It took him a moment to realize it was the Conversation, ceasing. The room was blocked to mundane network traffic. It was a safe haven, and he knew it was protected by the high-level encryption engines of the Others. The Oracle took the box from him and opened it, selecting one particular piece with care and putting it in her mouth. She chewed thoughtfully for a moment and indicated approval by inching her head. Weiwei bowed again.

"Please," the Oracle said. "Sit down."

Weiwei sat down. The chair was high-backed and old and worn—from the flea market, he thought, and the thought made him feel strange, the idea of the Oracle shopping in the stalls, almost as though she were human. But of course, she was human. It should have made him feel more at ease, but somehow it didn't.

Then the Oracle's eyes subtly changed color, and her voice, when it came, was different, rougher, a little lower than it had been, and Weiwei swallowed again. "What is it you wish to ask of us, Zhong Weiwei?"

It was her Other, speaking now. The Other, shotgun-riding on the human body, joined with the Oracle, quantum processors running within that golden thumb. . . . Weiwei, gathering his courage, said, "I seek a bridge."

The Other nodded, indicating for him to proceed.

"A bridge between past and future," Weiwei said. "A . . . continuity."

"Immortality," the Other said. It sighed. Its hand rose and scratched its chin, the golden thumb digging into the woman's pale flesh. "All humans want is immortality."

Weiwei shook his head, though he could not deny it. The idea of death, of dying, terrified him. He lacked faith, he knew. Many believed, belief was what kept humanity going. Reincarnation or the afterlife or the mythical Upload, what they called being Translated—they were the same, they required a belief he did not possess, much as he may long for it. He knew that when he died, that would be it. The I-loop with the ident tag of Zhong Weiwei would cease to exist, simply and without fuss, and the universe would continue just as it always had. It was a terrible thing to contemplate, one's insignificance. Human I-loops saw themselves as the universe's focal point, the object around which everything resolved. Reality was subjective. And yet that was an illusion, just as an "I" was, the human personality a composite machine compiled out of billions of neurons, delicate networks operating semi-independently in the grey matter of a human brain. Machines augmented it, but they could not preserve it, not forever. So yes, Weiwei thought. The thing that he was seeking was a vain thing, but it was also a practical thing. He took a deep breath and said, "I want my children to remember me."

Boris watched Central Station. The sun was rising now, behind the spaceport, and down below robotniks moved into position, spreading out blankets and crude, hand-written signs asking for donations of spare parts or gasoline or vodka, poor creatures, the remnants of forgotten wars, humans cyborged and then discarded when they were no longer needed.

He saw Brother R. Patch-It, of the Church of Robot, doing his rounds—the church tried to look after the robotniks, as it did after its small flock of humans. Robots were a strange missing link between human and Other, not fitting in either world—digital beings shaped by physicality, by bodies, many refusing the Upload in favor of their own, strange faith. . . .

Boris remembered Brother Patch-It from childhood—the robot doubled-up as a moyel, circumcising the Jewish boys of the neighborhood on the eighth day of their birth. The question of who is a Jew had been asked not just about the Chong family, but of the robots, too, and was settled long ago. Boris had fragmented memories, from the matrilineal side, predating Weiwei: the protests in Jerusalem, Matt Cohen's labs, and the first primitive Breeding Grounds, where digital entities evolved in ruthless evolutionary cycles:

Placards waving on King George Street, a mass demonstration: No To Slavery! And Destroy the Concentration Camp! and so on, an angry mass of humanity coming together to protest the perceived enslavement of those first, fragile Others in their locked-down networks, Matt Cohen's laboratories under siege, his rag-tag team of scientists kicked out of one country after another before settling, at long last, in Jerusalem—

Saint Cohen of the Others, they called him now. Boris lifted the mug to his lips and discovered it was empty. He put it down, rubbed his eyes. He should have slept. He was no longer young, could not go days without sleep, powered by stimulants and restless, youthful energy. The days when he and Miriam hid on this very same roof, holding each other, making promises they knew, even then, they couldn't keep. . . .

He thought of her now, trying to catch a glimpse of her walking down Neve Sha'anan, the ancient paved pavilion of Central Station where she had her shebeen. It was hard to think of her, to ache like this, like a, like a boy. He had not come back because of her, but somewhere in the back of his mind it must have been, the thought. . . .

On his neck the aug breathed softly. He had picked it up in Tong Yun City, on Mars, in a back-street off Arafat Avenue, in a no-name clinic run by a third-generation Martian Chinese, a Mr. Wong, who installed it for him.

It was supposed to have been bred out of the fossilized remains of microbacterial Martian life forms, but whether that was true no one knew for sure. It was strange having the aug. It was a parasite, it fed off of Boris, it pulsated gently against his neck, a part of him now, another appendage, feeding him alien thoughts, alien feelings, taking in turn Boris's human perspective and subtly shifting it. It was like watching your ideas filtered through a kaleidoscope.

He put his hand against the aug and felt its warm, surprisingly rough surface. It moved under his fingers, breathing gently. Sometimes the aug synthesized strange substances; they acted like drugs on Boris's system, catching him by surprise. At other times it shifted visual perspective, or even interfaced with Boris's node, the digital networking component of his brain, installed shortly after birth, without which one was worse than blind, worse than deaf, one was disconnected from the Conversation.

He had tried to run away, he knew. He had left home, had left Weiwei's memory, or tried to, for a while. He went into Central Station, and he rode the elevators to the very top, and beyond. He had left the Earth, beyond orbit, gone to the Belt and to Mars, but the memories followed him, Weiwei's bridge, linking forever future and past. . . .

"I wish my memory to live on, when I am gone."

"So do all humans," the Other said.

"I wish . . ." Gathering courage, he continued. "I wish for my family to remember," he said. "To learn from the past, to plan for the future. I wish my children to have my memories, and for their memories, in turn, to be passed on. I want my grandchildren and their grandchildren and onwards, down the ages, into the future, to remember this moment."

"And so it shall be," the Other said.

And so it was, Boris thought. The memory was clear in his mind, suspended like a dew drop, perfect and unchanged. Weiwei had gotten what he asked for, and his memories were Boris's now, as were Vlad's, as were his grandmother Yulia's and his mother's, and all the rest of them—cousins and nieces and uncles, nephews and aunts, all sharing the Chong family's central reservoir of memory, each able to dip, instantaneously, into that deep pool of memories, into the ocean of the past.

Weiwei's Bridge they still called it in the family. It worked in strange ways, sometimes, even far away; when he was working in the birthing clinics on Ceres or walking down an avenue in Tong Yun City on Mars, a sudden memory would form in his head, a new memory—Cousin Oksana's memories of giving birth for the first time, to little Yan—pain and joy mixing in with random thoughts, wondering if anyone had fed the dog, the doctor's voice saying, "Push! Push!" The smell of sweat, the beeping of monitors, the low chatter of people outside the door, and that indescribable feeling as the baby slowly emerged out of her. . . .

He put down the mug. Down below, Central Station was awake now, the neighborhood stalls set with fresh produce, the market alive with sounds, the smell of smoke and chickens roasting slowly on a grill, the shouts of children as they went to school—

He thought of Miriam. Mama Jones, they called her now. They had loved each other when the world was young, loved in the Hebrew that was their childhood tongue, but were separated, not by flood or war but simply life and the things it did to people. Boris worked the birthing clinics of Central Station, but there were too many memories there, memories like ghosts, and at last he rebelled and had gone into Central Station and up and onto an RLV that took him to orbit, to the place they called Gateway, and from there, first, to Lunar Port.

He was young, he had wanted adventure. He had tried to get away. Lunar Port, Ceres, Tong Yun . . . but the memories pursued him, and worst among them were his father's. They followed him through the chatter of the Conversation, compressed memories bouncing from one Mirror to the other, across space, at the speed of light, and so they remembered him here on Earth just as he remembered them there, and at last the weight of it became such that he returned.

He had been back in Lunar Port when it happened. He had been brushing his teeth, watching his face—not young, not old, a common enough face, the eyes Chinese, the facial features Slavic, his hair thinning a little—when the memory attacked him, suffused him. He dropped the toothbrush.

Not his father's memory, but his nephew's, Yan's: Vlad sitting in the chair, in his apartment, his father older than Boris remembered, thinner, and something that hurt him obscurely, that reached across space and made his chest tighten with pain—that clouded look in his father's eyes. Vlad sat without speaking, without acknowledging his nephew or the rest of them, who had come to visit him.

He sat there, and his hands moved through the air, arranging and rearranging objects none could see.

"Boris!"

"Yan."

His nephew's shy smile. "I didn't think you were real."

Time-delay, moon-to-Earth round-trip, node-to-node. "You've grown."

"Yes, well. . . ."

Yan worked inside Central Station. A lab on Level Five where they manufactured viral ads, airborne microscopic agents that transferred themselves from person to person, thriving in a closed-environment, air-conditioned system like Central Station, coded to deliver person-specific offers, organics interfacing with nodal equipment, all to shout Buy! Buy! Buy!

"It's your father."

"What happened?"

"We don't know."

That admission must have hurt Yan. Boris waited, silence eating bandwidth, silence on an Earth-moon return trip.

"Did you take him to the doctors?"

"You know we did."

"And?"

"They don't know."

Silence between them, silence at the speed of light, traveling through space.

"Come home, Boris," Yan said, and Boris marveled at how the boy had grown, the man coming out, this stranger he did not know and yet whose life he could so clearly remember.

Come home.

That same day he had packed his meager belongings, checked out of the Libra, and taken the shuttle to lunar orbit, and from there a ship to Gateway, and down, at last, to Central Station.

Memory like a cancer growing. Boris was a doctor; he had seen Weiwei Bridge for himself—that strange semiorganic growth that wove itself into the Chongs' cerebral cortex and into the grey matter of their brains, interfacing with their nodes, growing strange, delicate spirals of alien matter, an evolved technology, forbidden, Other. It was overgrowing his father's mind; somehow it had gotten out of control; it was growing like a cancer, and Vlad could not move for the memories.

Boris suspected, but he couldn't know, just as he did not know what Weiwei had paid for this boon, what terrible fee had been extracted from him—that memory, and that alone, had been wiped clean—only the Other, saying, And so it shall be, and then, the next moment, Weiwei was standing outside and the door was closed and he blinked, there amidst the old stone walls, wondering if it had worked.

Once it had all been orange groves . . . he remembered thinking that, as he went out of the doors of Central Station, on his arrival, back on Earth, the gravity confusing and uncomfortable, into the hot and humid air outside. Standing under the eaves, he breathed in deeply, gravity pulled him down but he didn't care. It smelled just as he remembered, and the oranges, vanished or not, were still there, the famed Jaffa oranges that grew here when all this, not Tel Aviv, not Central Station, existed, when it was orange groves, and sand, and sea. . . .

He crossed the road, his feet leading him; they had their own memory, crossing the road from the grand doors of Central Station to the Neve Sha'anan pedestrian street, the heart of the old neighborhood, and it was so much smaller than he remembered as a child—it was a world and now it had shrunk—

Crowds of people, solar tuk-tuks buzzing along the road, tourists gawking, a memcordist checking her feed stats as everything she saw and felt and smelled was broadcast live across the networks, capturing Boris in a glance that went out to millions of indifferent viewers across the solar system—

Pickpockets, bored CS Security keeping an eye out, a begging robotnik with a missing eye and bad patches of rust on his chest, dark-suited Mormons sweating in the heat, handing out leaflets while on the other side of the road Elronites did the same—

Light rain falling.

From the nearby market the shouts of sellers promising the freshest pomegranates, melons, grapes, bananas; in a café ahead old men playing backgammon, drinking small china cups of bitter black coffee, smoking narghiles—sheesha pipes—R. Patch-It walking slowly amidst the chaos, the robot an oasis of calm in the mass of noisy, sweaty humanity—

Looking, smelling, listening, remembering so intensely he didn't at first see them, the woman and the child, on the other side of the road, until he almost ran into them—

Or they into him. The boy, dark-skinned, with extraordinary blue eyes—the woman familiar, somehow, it made him instantly uneasy, and the boy said, with hope in his voice, "Are you my daddy?"

Boris Chong breathed deeply. The woman said, "Kranki!" in an angry, worried tone. Boris took it for the boy's name, or nickname—*kranki* in Asteroid Pidgin meaning grumpy, or crazy, or strange. . . .

Boris knelt beside the boy, the ceaseless movement of people around them forgotten. He looked into those eyes. "It's possible," he said. "I know that blue. It was popular three decades ago. We hacked an open source version out of the trademarked Armani code. . . ."

He was waffling, he thought. Why was he doing that? The woman, her familiarity disturbed him. A buzzing as of invisible mosquitoes, in his mind, a reshaping of his vision came flooding him out of his aug, the boy frozen beside him, smiling now, a large and bewildering and knowing smile—

The woman was shouting, he could hear it distantly, "Stop it! What are you doing to him?"

The boy was interfacing with his aug, he realized. The words coming in a rush, he said, "You had no parents," to the boy. Recollection and shame mingling together. "You were labbed, right here, hacked together out of public property genomes and bits of black market nodes." The boy's hold on his mind slackened. Boris breathed, straightened up. "*Nakaimas*," he said, and took a step back, suddenly frightened.

The woman looked terrified and angry. "Stop it," she said. "He's not—"

Boris was suddenly ashamed. "I know," he said. He felt confused, embarrassed. "I'm sorry." This mix of emotions, coming so rapidly they blended into each other, wasn't natural. Somehow the boy had interfaced with the aug, and the aug, in turn, was feeding into Boris's mind. He tried to focus. He looked at the woman. Somehow it was important to him that she would understand. He said, "He can speak to my aug. Without an interface." Then, remembering the clinics, remembering his own work before he left to go to space, he said, quietly, "I must have done a better job than I thought, back then."

The boy looked up at him with guileless, deep blue eyes. Boris remembered children like him, he had birthed many, so many—the clinics of Central Station were said to be on par with those of Yunan, even. But he had not expected this, this interference, though he had heard stories, on the asteroids and in Tong Yun, the whispered word that used to mean black magic: *nakaimas*.

The woman was looking at him, and her eyes, he knew her eyes—

Something passed between them, something that needed no node, no digital encoding, something earlier, more human and more primitive, like a shock, and she said, "Boris? Boris Chong?"

He recognized her at the same time she did him, wonder replacing worry, wonder, too, at how he failed to recognize her, this woman of indeterminate years suddenly resolving, like two bodies occupying the same space, into the young woman he had loved, when the world was young.

"Miriam?" he said.

"It's me," she said.

"But you—"

"I never left," she said. "You did."

He wanted to go to her now. The world was awake, and Boris was alone on the roof of the old apartment building, alone and free, but for the memories. He didn't know what he would do about his father. He remembered holding his hand, once, when he was small, and Vlad had seemed so big, so confident and sure, and full of life. They had gone to the beach that day; it was a summer's day, and in Menashiya Jews and Arabs and Filipinos all mingled together, the Muslim women in their long, dark clothes and the children running shrieking in their underwear; Tel Aviv girls in tiny bikinis, sunbathing placidly; someone smoking a joint, and the strong smell of it wafting in the sea air; the lifeguard in his tower calling out trilingual instructions—"Keep to the marked area! Did anyone lose a child? Please come to the lifeguards now! You with the boat, head towards the Tel Aviv harbor and away from the swimming area!"—the words getting lost in the chatter; someone had parked their car and was blaring out beats from the stereo; Somali refugees were cooking a barbecue on the promenade's grassy area; a dreadlocked white guy was playing a guitar, and Vlad held Boris's hand as they went into the water, strong and safe, and Boris knew nothing would ever happen to him—that his father would always be there to protect him, no matter what happened.

The Slows

Gail Hareven

The news of the decision to close the Preserves was undoubtedly the worst I had ever received. I'd known for months that it was liable to happen, but I'd deluded myself into thinking that I had more time. There had always been controversy about the need for maintaining Preserves (see B. L. Sanders, Z. Goroshovski, and Cohen and Cohen), but from this remote region I was simply unable to keep abreast of all the political ups and downs. Information got through, but to evaluate its importance, to register the emerging trends, without hearing what people were actually saying in the corridors of power was impossible. So I can't blame myself if the final decision came as a shock.

The axe fell suddenly. At six in the evening, when I got out of the shower, I found the announcement on my computer. It was just four lines long. I stood there, with a towel wrapped around my waist, reading the words that destroyed my future, that tossed away a professional investment of more than fifteen years. I can't say that I'd never envisioned this possibility when I chose to study the Slows. I can't say that it hadn't occurred to me that this might happen. But I believed that I was doing something important for the human race, and, mistakenly, I thought that the authorities felt the same way. After all, they had subsidized my research for years. Eliminating the Preserves at this stage was a loss I could barely conceive of, a loss not only for me and for my future—clearly I couldn't avoid thinking about myself—but for humanity and its very ability to understand itself. Politicians like to refer to the Slows as being deviant. I won't argue with that, but as hard as it is, as repulsive and distressing, we have to remember that our forefathers were all deviants of this kind.

I confess that I passed the rest of the evening with a bottle of whiskey. Self-pity is inevitable in situations like this, and there's no reason to be ashamed of it. The whiskey made it easier for me to get through the first few hours and fall asleep, but it certainly didn't make it any easier to get up in the morning. As if to spite me, the sky was blue, and the light was too brilliant. As often happens in this season, the revolting smell of yellow flowers went straight to my temples. When I pulled myself out of bed, I discovered that the sugar jar was empty, and I'd have to go to the office for my first cup of coffee. I knew that at some point during the day I would have to start packing up, but first I needed my coffee. I had no choice. With an aching head and a nauseating taste in my mouth, I dragged myself to the office shed. I opened the door and found a Slow woman sitting in my chair.

Despite the security guards' repeated instructions, I tended to forget to lock doors. Our camp was fenced in, we all knew one another, and the savages entered only during working hours, and then only with permission. How had she sneaked in?

Years of fieldwork had taught me how to cope with all sorts of situations. "Good morning," I said to her. I didn't even consider reaching for the button to call the guards. True, there had been occasional attacks in other camps, but for all sorts of reasons there had been none in ours to date. Besides, as I always said, the people most likely to be attacked were the policemen and the missionaries, not me, so I had a logical justification for bending the rules a little.

The savage woman didn't answer me. She leaned over to pick something up from the other side of the desk, and immediately I became afraid. The fear spread rapidly from my legs to my chest, but my brain kept working. So the rumor was true: they had got their hands on a cache of old weapons. To them, perhaps we were all alike after all—policeman or scientist, it didn't matter much from their point of view. But then the woman turned back to me: she was holding a human larva strapped into a carrier, which she laid on the table.

"You promised you wouldn't take our babies from us," she said in the angry, agitated voice so typical of the Slows. As my adrenaline level fell, it was hard for me to steady my legs. The savage woman fixed me with her black eyes and seemed to see this. "You pledged that you wouldn't take them. There are treaties, and you signed them," she spat out impatiently. I was always amazed by how fast news reached the Slows. It was clear to anybody who worked with them that they were hiding computers somewhere, and perhaps they also had collaborators on the political level. The nearest settlement of Slows was a half-hour flight away. They weren't allowed to keep hoverers, and there were no tracks in the region, so to get to our camp she had to have set out the evening before. It seemed that she had known about the decision to close the Preserves even before I did.

"Those treaties were signed many generations ago. Things change," I said, though I knew that it was silly to get into an argument with one of them.

"My grandmother signed them."

"Is it your baby?" I asked, making a point of using their term, as I gestured at the human larva on my desk.

"It's mine." Luckily, the larva was asleep. Fifteen years of work had more or less inured me, but at that hour of the morning, and in my condition, I knew that my stomach wouldn't be able to stand the sight of a squirming pinkish creature.

"Do you have others?"

"Maybe." The female Slows don't usually give birth to more than three or four offspring. Given the way they are accustomed to raising offspring, even that many is hard work. This savage woman was young, as far as I could judge. She might have concealed another larva somewhere before coming here. There was no way of knowing.

"You can't break the agreements," she said, cutting into my thoughts. "No. Listen to me. You've violated almost every clause. Every few years you renege on something. When you forced us into the Preserves, you promised us autonomy, and since then you've gradually stolen everything from us. From hard experience we've learned not to trust you. Like sheep, we kept quiet and let you push us farther and farther into a corner. But now I'm warning you. Just warning you: don't you dare touch the children!"

Many people will think this strange, but over the years I've learned to see a kind of beauty in the Slow women. If you ignore the swollen protrusions on their chests and the general swelling of their bodies, if you ignore their tendency to twist their faces wildly, with some experience you can distinguish between the ugly ones and the pretty ones, and this one would definitely have been considered pretty. If her grandmother had really signed the treaties, as she said, she might have been one of their aristocrats, the descendant of a ruling dynasty. It was evident that she could express herself.

"Will you agree to have some coffee with me?" Fieldwork often involves long hours of conversation. With time I had got used to the physical proximity of the Slows, and sometimes, when their suspicions subsided—when they accepted that I wasn't a missionary in disguise—they told me important things. The new decree had put an end to my research, but I might still be able to write something about the reaction of the savages to the development. Attentiveness had become a habit with me, and, besides, I was not yet capable of packing up the office.

"Coffee," I repeated. "Can I make some for you?" Since she didn't answer and just stared at me with a blurred face, I said, "You've certainly come a long way. It wouldn't hurt me to have a cup, either. Wait a minute, and I'll make some for both of us." The Slows had grown used to harsh treatment, and when they encountered one of us who treated them courteously they tended to get flustered. Indeed, this dark-eyed woman seemed confused, and she kept her mouth shut while I operated the beverage machine.

No doubt the savages were a riddle that science had not yet managed to solve, and, the way things seemed now, it never would be solved. According to the laws of nature, every species should seek to multiply and expand, but for some reason this one appeared to aspire to wipe itself out. Actually, not only itself but also the whole human race. Slowness was an ideology, but not only an ideology. As strange as it sounds, it was a culture, a culture similar to that of our forefathers. People don't know, or perhaps they forget, that when the technique for Accelerated Offspring Growth (AOG) was developed it wasn't immediately put to use. Until the first colonies were established on the planets, the UN Charter prohibited AOG. It's not pleasant to think about it now, but the famous Miller, German, and Yaddo were subjected to quite a bit of condemnation for their early work on the technique, all of it on ethical grounds. In a society that had not yet conquered space, AOG was viewed as a catastrophe that, within ten years, was liable to cause a population explosion on Earth, which would exterminate life through hunger and disease. The morality of the Slows had an undeniably rational basis under those conditions. We may be revolted by the thought, but the fact is that Miller, German, and Yaddo had all spent the first years of their lives as human larvae, not unlike the one that was now lying on my desk; they, too, had been slowly reared by savage females, just like the one who was waiting beside me for her coffee.

"We have to talk," she said as I placed the cup on the desk and glanced for just a split second at the creature sleeping in the carrier. "There's no reason for you to use power. There's no point, because you have all the power anyway. We're no threat to you."

I knew something that she didn't know, because it was a secret that hadn't been publicized on the networks: in one of the colonies on Gamma, far from the Preserves, there had been an outbreak of Slowness. This was probably why the decision had been made to close all the Preserves at once—to eliminate any possibility of the infection spreading.

"It's possible to compromise on all sorts of clauses," the savage woman said, "so why not compromise with us? We'll die out on our own in a few generations anyway. There are less than ten thousand of us left."

The problem isn't one of numbers, I thought, but I didn't say it to her. The problem is that in many people's eyes you are not a remnant but a gangrene that could spread and rot the entire body of humankind. Even I, with my interest in your way of life, can't say for certain that the politicians are wrong about this.

"We've thought of all kinds of possibilities," she said. "Since we have no choice, we'll agree to let your missionaries into our settlements. We'll guarantee their safety and give them complete freedom to talk to whomever they wish. We'll agree that one parent's consent is enough in order for a baby to be surrendered for accelerated growth, and we'll make sure that parents obey that rule. What else do you want? What else can you demand? In the end, without wasting any more energy on us, you'll get everything you want anyway."

"Not this one," I interjected, pointing at her larva. A tremor twisted her face and made it ugly. I drank the coffee and noticed that the larva had opened its eyes. The coffee was sour. The machine was apparently not working properly again. But there was no point in calling in a serviceman when I had only a few more days to spend here.

"Don't take them away from us," she whispered, and her voice shook. "I need at least a few years. You must allow us that. Why do you hate us so?"

The ardent possessiveness that savage parents—especially the mothers—display toward their offspring is the key to understanding the Slows' culture. It's clear that they don't love their offspring the way we love ours. They make do with so few, and, at the rate they rear them, at best they get to know only their children's children. Whereas even I—who have spent years away from civilization in barren camps like this one—have managed to produce seventeen sons and daughters and a lineage of at least forty generations. Still, they talk constantly about their love for their offspring, and its glory.

"Hate?" I said to her. "Hate is a strong word."

The human larva turned its head and gaze toward the savage woman. Her eyes clung to it, and her chin quivered. She had pretty eyes. She had put on black and green makeup in my honor. A week or two of body formation would have made a good-looking woman of her, in anyone's opinion. She trusted me, apparently, knowing who I was, having heard about me or made inquiries, and perhaps she hoped that, as a researcher, I would agree to represent her side. She had put herself in jeopardy by sneaking into my office in this way. Someone else in my place might have panicked, and an unnecessary accident might have taken place. Through her grimaces you could see a face that wasn't at all stupid. She had certainly taken my well-known curiosity into account, and my composure. She knew that all I had to do was reach out and press a button, and they would come, chase her away, and take the larva from her. I wasn't about to do that, but sooner or later, no matter where she hid, it would be taken.

In all my years of work I'd refrained from saying anything that would identify me with the missionaries, but now, seeing the tremble of her chin, I heard their words of consolation coming from my mouth. So be it. In any event, my work had come to an end.

"I know what you think, what they've told you. Lots of misunderstandings and rumors circulate in the Preserves. Listen to me, I promise you that no harm will come to the children."

"Do you mean that you won't take them?" the savage princess asked in a soft, strange voice. "That the decision has been revoked?"

"Decisions aren't my field. People like me don't make policy. What I want to explain to you is another matter. Maybe you think that accelerated growth will shorten this offspring's life. Believe me, woman, that's a mistake. Whoever told you that was either wrong or lying. Our life span is no shorter than yours. Actually, the opposite is true: progress gives us a longer life. If your son is ultimately given over to AOG, he won't lose even a single day. On the contrary, he can enjoy all the years before him as an independent adult. You'll see your son's children, and your descendants will inherit the planets."

The savage woman twisted her jaw to the side. "You think we're stupid."

The Slows have manners of their own. You can't expect them to behave like us. Still, in her present situation I would have expected her to make an effort. But the very fact that she wasn't making an effort held my interest. Perhaps this was an opportunity for me to hear something new. Usually they were so cautious when speaking to us and behaved evasively, even with me.

But just at that moment the larva started to bleat, and the savage woman instantly lost her impertinence.

"You may do it," I said to her. "Pick it up. I've been in the Preserves for years, and I've seen such things."

Without looking at me, she freed the larva from the carrier and held it to her chest. I observed six of my offspring during the process of accelerated growth, and the distress of the first weeks, before they reached decent maturity, comes back to me every time I'm forced to observe a human larva up close. There are times in a person's life that are meant to be private, and the state of infancy is certainly the most pronounced of these. The larva was silent for a moment, then it started to bleat again.

"How old is it?"

"Eleven weeks." The most horrifying human larvae are the big ones, which already look like people but lack the stamp of humanity. At least this one was similar in dimensions to our offspring. Nearly three months old. He could have been a productive adult already. Footsteps could be heard outside, and the sound of two people talking. The savage woman's eyes widened. She put her hand first to her mouth and then to the larva's open mouth.

"Don't worry. They won't come in here. They know that I hold interviews." The touch of the woman's hand on the creature's lips increased its discomfort, and now it raised its voice, screeching until its wrinkled face turned almost purple. Someone was liable to enter after all. The savage woman stuck a finger into the larva's mouth, but it turned its head away and looked for something else.

"Don't you feel sorry for it?" I asked, but she seemed not to hear me, cradling the larva in her arms and also turning her head here and there with an unfocussed look in her eyes.

Human beings as we know them are excited by every development in their offspring, because what purpose is there for the hard labor of parenthood if not to send forth an independent, productive adult who can satisfy his own needs? But the Slows appeared to enjoy the helplessness of their larvae—the lack of humanity, the deplorable fervor of the little creatures, their muteness, their mindless appetites, their selfishness, their ignorance, their inability to act. It seemed that the most disgusting of traits were what inspired the most love in savage parents.

The screeches stunned me. I was so riveted by the sight of that wriggling caterpillar that I almost missed the moment when the woman started talking again. "If we knew how much time was left for us. . . ." So she didn't know everything: the invasion would start that day; it might already have begun. "If we knew that we had another year or two, if you would only tell us how much time there is, people could prepare themselves." Had she come as a spy? If they greeted the police with violence, they'd only bring disaster down upon themselves. A few spontaneous uprisings were to be expected. After all, theirs was a volatile culture. But an organized attack would be a kind of stupidity that was hard to fathom.

"I'm asking for so little," the savage woman said. "Just this—to know how much time remains for us. Listen to me. I know you're different from them. You're not a missionary. You know us. You're merciful, not like them. I feel it. You could have called the guards when you saw me here, but you didn't do it. Maybe you once also had a baby you loved."

The larva arched its body backward, and the woman unconsciously fingered the opening of her shirt. Suddenly I knew what she wanted to do, and with that thought the sourness of the coffee rose in my throat. To give it her milk bulges—that's what she wanted, that's why she was plucking at her shirt. When I was a student, I was forced to watch a film about ancient nutrition customs. It was for a course restricted to advanced students, but none of us were advanced enough to view that sight without a sharp feeling of nausea. From close up we watched the ravenous face of the larva and the swollen organ thrust into its wet mouth. It was a rather large larva, at least thirteen pounds, and the depraved sucking noises that it emitted mingled with the female's bestial murmur. White liquid dripped down its chin, and the woman tickled its lips with her gland, holding the organ shamelessly between finger and lustful thumb. I still remember the strong protest voiced by three women students, which was understandable.

"If you'll just answer me that," the savage woman said, and her voice shook with feeling. "Just that."

The emotionality of the Slows had the strange characteristic of clinging to me like a stain. As sometimes happened after a few hours of conversation with one of them, I began to feel polluted. "The good of the children is the only thing that we consider," I said finally. "Do you want a cup of water? I see that you haven't touched your coffee."

When I got up and went back to the machine, the woman bent her body over the larva, almost concealing it under a black curtain of hair. The cold water refreshed my mouth, removed the traces of yesterday's drink and the bitterness of the coffee, dislodged the clinging feeling. I drank two cups. It is sometimes possible to identify rational thought among the Slows, but their emotional exaggeration dilutes it. Though I had hoped to calm the savage woman, at that moment it was clear that there was no point in trying.

When I returned to the desk with a cup of water for her, I saw that she was rocking slowly on the chair, moving the larva rhythmically back and forth. It was tired from so much screeching, and its voice was growing weaker. She was so deeply immersed in her drugged movement that she didn't notice me. I watched the two tired bodies moving together, and knew that soon, very soon, there would be an end to their suffering. The larva would become a man in control of his body, and she would accept it and smile. With clarity I saw that image, and, as though to transmit it to her, I reached out and placed my hand on her shoulder. All at once, like an animal, the woman recoiled, raised her head, and bared her teeth. The sudden movement jolted my body backward, and for a long moment we were frozen, twisted in mid-movement, looking into each other's face.

"Don't touch me!" she spat out, as though at an enemy. Her face was transparent, and I could read everything in it, all her distorted thoughts. She believed that what I wanted was to hold her soft body, to curl my fingers and grasp her flesh, to press it against mine and rub, blind and hopeless, against her milk glands. Her eyes, like snakes, penetrated my thoughts and fed them her abominable vision, the visions of a lower animal. For nine years I had been in the Preserves, and never had I experienced such a defilement.

"No one's touching you," I pronounced with difficulty, turning toward the door and putting my hand out to press the button. By the time the alarm went off, and the sound of the larva's weeping reached me, I was already in the light—in the bright, bright light outside.

Burn Alexandria

Keren Landsman

The sound of the bell woke me up.

"Don't take it," murmured Yonit out of her slumber.

"I have to take it," I said, but she was already fast asleep again. I rubbed my eyes and found the switch in the darkened room.

"We have a five-seven-twenty. Still closed. Military's deployed. Waiting for us," said Shir at the other end. I coughed. He waited, and when I didn't reply, he sighed. I know exactly how he looks when he lets out that sigh. "Invasion. You, of all people in the Universe, should remember that—"

"I do remember that everything beginning with a five means invasion, and that this instance does not require urgent intervention," I interrupted him. "But what's with the twenty?" Shir had this talent for memorizing protocols in far too many details than our ordinary work required.

Shir sighed again. I knew he sighed again because he kept silent, and when he finally spoke, his voice was half-a-tone lower, and he was distinctly stressing each word. "Seven – twenty. Seven – twenty."

"Seven – twenty," I mimicked him.

"Multiple hits. But a single location, so far."

"Shit." Now I was fully awake.

"As I was saying." He hesitated for a moment. "You're coming, aren't you? I don't have to alert . . . the Others?"

"No, of course not. I mean, yes, I'm coming. You don't have to alert anyone else." Neither he nor I wanted to call our Superiors in the middle of the night. We never got any help worth a damn from them, and even just reporting things could have serious consequences.

"Sending you a bubble." Shir hung up.

When I went out, Yonit opened half an eye and murmured, "Take care," hogging the entire blanket.

The white bubble stopped outside our house and opened to my touch. Inside, the screen was showing the movie of the month, and the sound system played calming Muzak. I would have been happier if I could link up with the Office and download data rather than listen to a selection of identically senseless tunes, but I don't have the budget for a secure download, and the Office doesn't have the budget to send me a coded private bubble. Instead of linking up with the Office, I connected with the Cloud and downloaded instructions for knitting a complicated scarf.

The bubble stopped jarringly in a black, open square surrounded by blocks of darkened buildings. This was the new construction zone, not yet occupied. A network of reflectors pulsed light around a sphere of darkness. I left the bubble, which flew off immediately to take the next passenger. There were no other bubbles there. The network of reflectors turned out to be a cordon of soldiers. They were whispering when my bubble disappeared. One beam of light approached me, coming off a band around Shir's head. He was dressed eclectically, like the rest of us, distinguished only by a white tag bearing the letter *S*.

"You're scaring all these aliens away," I said, stepping forward.

The beam turned toward me. Shir grinned. "I wish it were this easy. . . ."

I smiled in reply, took out my headband, and put it on. The soldiers stood at ease. I gave them a nod. You couldn't see their faces in the darkness.

"Did you know that Fraud Division has light implants?" Shir gestured at the darkness.

"That's because they're not as elegant as we are." I waited for the implant to synchronize with the headband. The light was just an excuse. The really important part of the band was the add-on that interfaced directly with my nerve center. Space spread out in front of me, shining in various electromagnetic wavelengths, giving darkness shape and form.

Beside me Shir took an orange-red hue. The pineapples embroidered on his dress lay dark against his body. The air he breathed in became dark blue inside his chest, then turned red before it was exhaled. The line of soldiers pulsated in green. Their guns were totally black, except for the stocks, which were red where warmed by their hands. The buildings were painted violet, in threads. I could see where rooms were sprouting up at the tops of these buildings.

Between the buildings, in the space in front of me, lay darkness—a large, dark sphere, not radiating in any wavelength our headbands could identify. I ran a basic analysis. It came back empty. You could see the patch of ground touched by the sphere.

"They reported multiple hits," Shir said quietly.

"Obviously." I breathed in. The air smelled of burnt gasoline and fertilized soil. "Buildings were damaged," I said. Buildings had to be grown and cultivated, at immense expense. We were a by-product of the planet, nothing worth preserving.

Shir crossed his arms over his chest. "Someday they'll realize how important individual lives are."

I patted his shoulder. "And then they'll destroy the lot of us."

He grinned, nodding toward the dark sphere. "Shall we take samples?"

"I'd like to send a query . . . ," I started.

Shir raised his hand to stop me. "Already checked. Analysis came back empty. No similar reports in the past, the Superiors don't know what the external shell is made of, and it's definitely not an alien we know of."

I shut my mouth.

"Took you a lot of time to get here." Shir shrugged. "I got bored."

I shook my head. "We really ought to find you some hobby."

I switched off my band. It sucked up too much energy and added no information. I removed it, put it in my jacket pocket. Shir did the same. I moved in across the cordon of soldiers, got down on one knee, and touched the ground with my hand. Analysis came back as ordinary soil, and I felt nothing unusual. Half a meter away from me, there was blackness. I pulled at the top of Shir's cowboy boots. "Come here, tell me what you can feel."

He knelt beside me and put his hand next to mine. His sensory interface was better than mine, more advanced. He turned his face to me.

"Feel anything?"

He nodded. "Something." Shir dug deeper with both hands. "It doesn't feel compacted." He sniffed. "And the smell is ordinary," he added.

"Nothing burned or destroyed. I don't think it crashed here."

Shir nodded, slowly, and stared at the darkness in front of us. "It grew up here?"

His processing interfaces were better than mine, but my intuition was much better than his.

"Appeared," I said, quietly, "and swallowed up everything around it."

Shir stopped breathing.

"This is a space-warp field," I said. He nodded. I could almost hear his memories reappearing. We both had memories of all those invasions since the very first one, which also began with a warp field. Only that one had appeared in the middle of the ocean, split into dozens of smaller fields and spread all over the planet within days. While this sphere just . . . stood here.

Shir pulled his hands out of the ground. "Do you want to call . . . Them?"

"No," I replied in a hurry, before he could send a query to Central. I pulled my own hands out of the ground and shook off the dirt. "And neither do you."

Shir shook his head and said, not looking at me, "I don't. But if it's another invasion. . . ." He looked at me. "Too late to transfer to Fraud Division?" He smiled.

"You really fancy their light implants, don't you?" I gave him a hand. He took it and I pulled him up.

"Plus the fact that they don't have to charge off into unidentified alien spaceships."

I nodded. "How old is your backup?"

"Twenty-eight minutes, after I disconnected from the bubble."

I patted his shoulder. "Well, then everything is alright."

Shir rolled his eyes. "You really like reconstructing, don't you?"

Instead of answering him, I sent a data cluster to my backup, turned around, and gestured, "After you, Assistant Regional Inspector Ben-Yair."

Shir smiled and offered me a sloppy salute. "Affirmative, Deputy Regional Inspector Potashnik, Ma'am." He started walking towards the darkness. "Congratulations on your promotion, by the way," he said, stopping one step away from the sphere. "Didn't have time to say this day before yesterday."

"Yes you did." I stopped beside him. "And congratulating me twice won't change the fact that you owe me a cherry pizza for getting ahead of you."

"It's abominable and I won't have it!" Shir was saying the right words, but his voice was too strained for the quip to work. He hated reconstruction as much as I did, or even more so, because no one was waiting for him in the house he was returning to.

The soldiers had moved into attack positions, following an order I couldn't hear. One of them saluted us. Shir and I interfaced for a joint countdown and started a simultaneous data streaming that went directly into our backups as well as to the other members of our unit. We breathed in together, breathed out together, laid our hands on the sphere together. The hard shell moved under my hand and softened in response to my touch.

Data exploded into my interface. I sent out as much as I could. I remembered how it felt. Just as it did in the Superiors' invasion. Then we hadn't been fast enough, and our reconstructions lacked data. We have changed our procedures since. Come the following invasions, self-destruct was timed so that as much information as possible will have been sent out before we were destroyed.

I engaged self-destruct.

I was waiting for the pain, smashing and sharp, and then a first breath and opening my eyes in a darkened room. On my right-hand side, future replicates of myself, on my left, just empty pods. In front of me, Shir's replicates, senseless, unconscious. I had counted the empty pods once, then deleted the information and left an instruction for myself never to do that again.

I stopped breathing and closed my eyes. The pain didn't come. Neither did the awakening in a darkened room. Data streaming continued. I opened my eyes. Shir was standing beside me, looking every bit as flabbergasted as I felt. I ran a self-analysis. Destruction sequence had not been initiated. The analysis pronounced the sphere safe.

The soldiers never reacted. They were not part of the countdown. All they knew was that they had to shoot at anything coming out of the sphere.

"If we disconnect...," I whispered.

Shir nodded but did not reply. Something had stopped our physical destruction.

The surface of the sphere quivered and dissolved. Shir and I stumbled directly into it. As we crossed over, I felt a small vibration in my consciousness, a vaguely familiar one. I wanted to send a query to the Cloud, but communication was blocked. The surface of the sphere closed tight behind us.

Shir turned to me. "We can initiate self-destruct. Destroy this thing from the inside."

Before I could reply, everything lit up around us. We found ourselves in a huge room, larger than any hall I've ever been in. In front of us a spiral wooden stairway materialized, and all around us there were shelves full of books, measurement instruments, statuettes, and potted plants. Beneath the stairway an old-fashioned globe materialized, showing the continents as they were ten thousand years ago. A man in a white robe smiled at me. "Salutations, O messengers of culture!" he said.

I tried to communicate with Shir subvocally, but all my outgoing frequencies were blocked. I could only scan things and collect information, not transmit.

"This is just a hologram," said Shir, scratching his head.

"I know." I studied the man. The details were near perfect. "But why should an invading species mimic Humans?"

"Distraction?" Shir clenched his fists.

I looked around. "But whatever for? We're isolated. No command could breach this sphere."

"To delay us?"

I shook my head. "It doesn't make sense. None of the previous ones ever tried to use the basic command. They don't even know about it." I put my hands on my hips. "Maybe to download data ahead of an invasion?"

Shir scratched his head again. "I don't sense any data download."

I searched. "Scan you?"

Shir shook his head. "I scanned you. Nothing connected, at least so far as I can sense."

The hologram stood frozen in front of us. Shir stepped forward. The hologram moved and indicated toward the stairway behind it. "Well met, O seekers of knowledge," it said.

Shir turned to me. "An interface that responds to users' movements," he said. He snapped his fingers absentmindedly. "But why should an invasion begin with a responsive interface? Why don't they just burst out and kill everyone?"

A smallish woman came out from among the shelves. "Sorry, sorry, excuse me, I'm sorry." She was pulling on a white robe, similar to the hologram's, as she came running straight at us, right through the man's image.

"I truly am sorry, it took me some time to adjust the translator to the vernacular." She stopped in front of us, breathing heavily. "You really should start cataloging your dictionaries correctly. I had to go through fifty zetta to get at the right terminology, all from separate sources."

I scanned her. She was Human. Or at least the closest imitation of a Human my scans could identify. Shir let out his breath. I assumed his scan results were the same.

She was dark-haired and short, armed with eyeglasses and a scolding stare. I felt Shir cringing where he stood. The woman put out her hand. "Head Librarian, Alexandria, version eight."

I didn't offer my hand, and she withdrew hers. "Alexandria version eight?" I repeated, slowly. My access to the Cloud was blocked, and I couldn't use our databases.

The woman waved her hands. "Well, they've kept coming up with more and more libraries that called themselves 'the Great Library of Alexandria,' and each and every time they were destroyed, or forgotten, or just became bureaucratic monstrosities that no longer stored any information. And there was also the one they filled with fireproof paper," she snickered at a private joke, "as if leaving things on paper could ever be a good idea. But people are a sentimental lot, you know, and eventually. . . ."

"Just a moment." Shir took a step forward to stop the flow of chatter. "I don't understand. Who are you?"

"Nuphar the Literate." The woman smoothed down her robe. "I am the Head Librarian of the Great Unified Consolidated Library of Planet Earth, from Alexandria, 3067 by the common calendar." Nuphar gestured in the general direction of the hologram. "I needed to have someone occupy you while we downloaded information. I apologize for taking so long to get here."

Shir and I exchanged looks. He nodded in the direction from which we had entered, just a slight, hardly perceptible nod, followed by raised eyebrows. We've known each other long enough for me to interpret this, and I nodded in reply. Even if we could have left, it was our duty to stay and find out what's going on. The woman facing us was a Human Being. This time we were not dealing with an invading species. It was . . . it was. . . . I didn't know how to comprehend what it was.

Nuphar cleared her throat. "But I am here now. So . . . we can begin."

"Begin?" I echoed.

Nuphar nodded in the affirmative. "Begin. We'll have a round of introductions, and then you may call in the rest of your delegation." She sent a look behind my shoulder. "You are part of a delegation, I hope? We've left very clear instructions." She didn't even stop for a breath of air. "Don't worry, you are in a time bubble. No time is passing outside, so you'll have ample time to invite them."

A time bubble. This explained the space-warp we were in, and why we couldn't send messages out.

"There is no delegation." Shir shifted his weight from one foot to the other. He looked plain against the elegance surrounding us, dressed in his hodge-podge of fabrics, exactly like me.

Raising her hands, Nuphar sighed. "I can't believe this is happening again!" She said. "I just can't believe it. What's wrong with humankind? We bring you knowledge, and culture, and . . . and. . . ." She adjusted her glasses and passed her glance between Shir and myself. "Well, never mind, let's do it properly." She pointed at herself. "I, as I said, am Nuphar the Literate. And you are . . . ?"

Shir and I exchanged looks again. He raised an eyebrow, tilting his head in Nuphar's direction. I nodded. Once. She was Human, and we had the strictest orders regarding Human Beings. Shir tightened his lips, and I imagined I could hear the sigh he would have made, had we been in a place where he could afford to sigh.

"Oh, don't tell me this stupid belief—that vouchsafing your name to a stranger allows someone to steal your soul—has survived to your time." Nuphar was talking fast, and a lot, and I could hardly find my way among the words that were piling up atop each other.

Shir's internal processor was faster than mine. "I am Shir Ben-Yair," he pointed at himself, "Assistant Regional Inspector, Silence Unit, Northern Region." He pointed at me. "And this is Romi Potashnik, Deputy Regional Inspector, Silence Unit, Northern Region."

"Silence Unit?" Nuphar frowned. "Is this a librarians' thing? Sounds offensive, really. Have you considered a name change?"

Shir laughed. Briefly. "Librarians." He turned to me, tilting his head toward Nuphar. "Did you hear that? Do you want to be a librarian?"

I smiled. "Sounds like fun. What do librarians do?"

Nuphar gave me a searching look. "You don't have any librarians?"

I shook my head.

"Who points book-lovers at the books they could love? Who cross-files information? Who keeps the records straight?" Nuphar was stressing each and every word now. "Who takes care of the libraries?"

This one I could answer. "Each person takes care of their own, of course. If you're very close to someone, you can join your libraries."

"And even then, not everything," said Shir, quietly. I took care not to look at him. This was too personal. Yonit was still with me. Shir had lost his entire family before complete backups of them could have been created. I knew he used to go out from time to time to look at what was left of them, torn pieces of consciousness floating in a container that was unable to reconstitute them properly.

Nuphar turned her eyes from me to Shir, then back again. "But you don't have places, physical places, to go to in order to find specific kinds of knowledge?"

We both shook our heads in unison. Nuphar looked through me, at the back wall, and sighed. I felt like I'd failed a test. She returned her eyes to me and straightened her back. "Very well. Come along, and I'll show you what you're missing," she said, and the brightest smile I've ever seen appeared on her face.

The Great Unified Consolidated Library of Planet Earth, from Alexandria, 3067

by the common calendar, encompassed anything imaginable in mazes so complicated they could hardly be mapped. Papyruses locked in exquisite time-bubbles,
shards of pottery preserved in climate-controlled rooms, figurines of ancient
deities, shrouds, paintings, clothes, musical instruments, and dance simulations.
And books. Lots of books. This was a full, complete record of Human history.

Nuphar was striding along, her robe swirling around her legs, occasionally
exposing the colorful garments she wore underneath. It seemed that fashion
in whatever place Nuphar came from included phosphorescent rhomboids and
purple leggings. "We stop every three hundred years, give or take, and collect
anything that needs to be documented. This is a compromise between our desire
to document everything and the fact that it's simply impossible to document
everything," she said. She pointed to a room full of animals, frozen in a variety
of positions. "There were supposed to be people outside, waiting for us with
your documentation, but seeing as you never got our instructions. . . ." She left
the rest of it hanging.

Shir slowed down. I pulled his arm. We had to keep up with Nuphar.

He cleared his throat and whispered in my ear, "How do they contain all
these rooms?"

I shrugged. "Space-warp? We know they enclosed their ship in a time-warp
field."

Nuphar smoothed her hair with one hand and tucked a tuft of it behind her
ear. She said, not looking at us, "We are not here at all. Just the vestibule is here.
I mean, at your place. Meaning, in your space-time. As soon as we left that room
we moved into my space-time."

Shir cleared his throat. "Which is. . . ?"

Nuphar stopped in front of a featureless round door and smiled again. "The
Eighth Library of Alexandria. Established 3067, in existence for one hundred
fifty-seven years now."

Shir and I stopped in our tracks. I looked at Shir swiftly, noticing a slight grin
showing in the corner of his lips. She brought us back in time. That explained
everything. The hologram's archaic speech, the strange globe in the vestibule, even
the sumptuous décor. We could prevent the invasion. We could warn Humankind.
We could fix the future in which we blow up again and again just to rise again
in backup and continue to defend Earth from invasion, in the only way we had
been able to devise.

I felt a similar grin stretching my own lips.

"We are inside a gigantic structure. Well, not one structure really, more like
a collection of museums and libraries interlinked by bridges. All wrapped up in

a single space-time bubble, and time here is disconnected from your time, but we do move forward in time, although at a different pace. And it is possible to come out, but only forward, to the time in which the vestibule is located." Nuphar made a little bow. "I am a sixth-generationer. But we do have some who joined from the outside, not born here."

"Born here. . . ." said Shir. I felt a little better realizing that he too couldn't follow her. All I could figure out was that we didn't move back in time. We were in an isolated time-bubble, and we shall reemerge to the time from which we came. At least, I hoped this was the correct interpretation. We had little knowledge about space-time fields.

Nuphar nodded. "At the Library. It is too gigantic to be kept entirely out of the space-warp field. We only come out on stoppage duty, like now. Well, not exactly like now. Now you came in, but I didn't get out, not yet. But I shall, and we'll collect information about the current civilization. Let's hope at least some of your information is properly cataloged, otherwise it will take us years, and then we'll renew the instructions." She turned back to the door and opened it, murmuring to herself, "I'm sick and tired of having to renew the instructions on each stoppage."

Nuphar moved away from us, unaware that we didn't enter through the doorway. This door she now opened led to an enormous hall, larger than the vestibule, but rather than plush stairways and holograms of bookshelves, this one was full of longish desks with green-shaded lamps. On both sides of these desks, filling the room, there were people. I saw seven hundred and twenty-four persons of various ages, wearing various garments that looked as if they were taken from the halls we'd passed through. Some were bent over books, others were conversing in whispers.

I stopped breathing. Shir grasped my hand. His hand was moist. I squeezed it. I have never seen so many Human Beings in one place. Not since the days of the first invasion. And even then, all those Humans were crowded in underground cellars, wearing rags, starving.

"Romi," Shir whispered. He cleared his throat and said again, "Romi."

I was afraid to use the scan. I didn't want to find out that this too was a hologram. I heard Shir sniveling. I looked at him. Tears were running down his cheeks. My eyes too felt watery. I used my free hand to wipe away the teardrops. I should have made a quip, or asked him to pinch me, or done something else to relieve the tension. But nothing came to mind. No quip, no gesture. Just the thought that hundreds of Humans were sitting there in front of me, and none of them looked sick, or injured, or. . . .

Nuphar came back. "Enough," she said. "Don't you take it so hard." She looked at the people on their benches and then back at us. "I know they are talking to each other," she said quietly, "but I can assure you, they are alright, on the whole." She shrugged. "You know how that is; after such a long time, discipline becomes loose. Even among librarians." She gestured towards the other end of the hall. "There are some more things I have to show you; we shouldn't waste time."

Shir looked around him. "I thought we were in a time-bubble."

Nuphar rolled her eyes. "Time is not passing outside. In here, it does. I'm getting old while you stand there staring at some people making a little noise in a library."

She was right. Humans do get older. Shir started to smile, and his smile infected me, and then we were both giggling uncontrollably. A room full of Humans who grew old in a perfectly natural way.

Nuphar frowned and put a finger to her lips. "Silence!" She said. "This *is* a library, after all."

We made the effort and fell silent. Holding each other's hands, we crossed the room, not daring to stare at anyone for any length of time. I photographed whatever I could and filed it for future viewing. I was still afraid to scan these people, but the smell of all these crowded bodies—sweat, soap, and some perfume—was very clear. No hologram could mimic reality so accurately.

Nuphar never stopped chattering since the moment we'd left the great hall. She led us to the places where they grew their food. She explained about caloric calculations and birth control, and I recorded everything she said because I knew I wouldn't be able to register all of it in real time. Shir's hand became drier as we went along. He was even able to talk to Nuphar from time to time, and get some necessary information out of her in those rare moments that she stopped to take a breath.

"Normally there are people who are supposed to prepare everything we need to scan and document," Nuphar sighed. "I don't understand why it never happens the way we ask. It is for the greater good, after all." She sighed again. "So I'll need from you a representational list of extant cultures," said Nuphar as we walked past a display of jugs in various sizes, from a few fingers' width to several meters, "and references to mapped areas. We can refer you to locations that used to be important once, for us to document the changes that have taken place there."

Shir cleared his throat loudly, to stop Nuphar's flow of words. "When have you last visited the outside?" He asked.

Nuphar stopped and scratched her head. "Three . . . no, two hundred and seventy years ago, external time."

Shir and I exchanged looks. I turned my eyes back to Nuphar. "There's been a lot of changes since," I said.

Nuphar raised her hands. "But of course. It *has* been two hundred and seventy years. Civilizations rise, civilizations fall. It's fascinating!"

"Yes." Shir paused for a while. "Fascinating," he repeated quietly.

Nuphar smiled. "I *knew* you'd like it!" She turned back and kept walking, pulling Shir and me behind her. "I'll give you the full tour later. First it's important that I get you to the Information Center, make reader cards for you and all that red tape." She stopped, adjusted her hair, and turned to face us. "We've been able to create a complete reconstruction of all influential civilizations, so that all future scholars will be able to predict the course of events or learn more about the past," she said, spreading her hands as if to embrace the entire library. "And you will be the first ones in two hundred and seventy years who'll get to see this!" She raised a finger. "But first things first. Reader cards."

She opened another door that led to a small room lit by spheres hovering near the ceiling. It contained one desk and three chairs. Nuphar sat at the desk, raised her hands in the air, and a keyboard materialized in front of her.

Shir and I exchanged looks and sat down in the chairs facing her.

"I programmed this keyboard," she smiled at us, "based on old blueprints."

She typed our names and titles on the holokeyboard, then raised her head. "We must plan our expeditions. Even if your world is in war, there are always historians who want to get to the Library, and we're extraterritorial, independent of any nation or period of time." She was frowning and licking her lips as she typed.

Shir leaned forward and laid his hand on the keyboard. Nuphar looked up at us. "Don't do that," she said, frowning even more.

Shir cleared his throat. "We have something . . . There's something you should know." He looked at me furtively.

I knew what he wanted me to do. I was senior, so I had to take the lead. I took a deep breath. There was an oath. A short one. We'd recorded it dozens of years ago. I hadn't dared look at it since. "Can we connect with your screen system?" I pointed at her desk. "Something small, we don't need an entire hall."

Nuphar looked at Shir, and again at me. "Is it important?"

I nodded.

She frowned. "Well, we'll return to your reader cards momentarily." She typed, and connection instructions floated in my vision.

Shir laid a hand on my shoulder and squeezed it slightly by way of encouragement. I laid my hand on the desktop and made contact with the central computer. It was old software, but I managed to fit one of the protocols to my own software and broadcast.

An old me, thirty-four years of age, in tattered uniform, with blood stains on my face, looked straight at Nuphar. Nuphar looked at me, and returned her eyes to the figure that used to be me. I activated the simulation.

"I, Romi Potashnik, being of sound mind, do hereby put my consciousness and my body in the hands of the Supreme Generator," said my projected self and took a deep breath. It wiped its eyes and added: "We shall never stop, we shall never cease, we shall never desist."

The simulation ended. Shir put his hand beside mine and his oh-so-young image appeared above the desk. "I, Shir Ben-Yair, being of sound mind, do hereby put my consciousness and my body in the hands of the Supreme Generator. We shall never stop, we shall never cease, we shall never desist." He saluted, and the image froze.

Nuphar looked at us. "Is this for the record?"

"No." Shir gave Nuphar a direct look, capturing her eyes. "This was recorded one hundred nine years, four months, ten days, and three hours ago."

Nuphar looked like she was about to smile, but her smile vanished before it could reach her lips.

"This is my last recording as a Human Being," I said, and Nuphar shifted her glance to me. "I don't know how many times I've been reconstructed since."

"You aren't. . . ." Nuphar's eyes moved back to Shir. "Both of you . . . ?" She bit her lip and shook her head. "No, of course you aren't," she whispered. "Your facial expressions, your gait, the way you understand each other much too well." Now she directed her glance at me. "Are you telepathic? Do you have a way of broadcasting your thoughts to each other?"

I opened my mouth to reply, but Shir was faster: "No." He loosened his clenched fist. "We can broadcast subvocally, but that's not possible in here."

Nuphar's giggle was a brief one. "All frequencies are blocked in here; we don't want to disturb our readers," she said.

We smiled in reply. This seemed like the correct response. Nuphar's smile froze and disappeared.

"But you *do* look human. Our scans identified you as human beings." She closed her eyes. "Metallic skeleton and human skin?"

"Of course. All over our bodies." I cleared my throat. "Otherwise we couldn't have penetrated space-warp fields."

"Of course not," she repeated. Nuphar opened her eyes and looked at me. "Explain. Now." She spread her fingers, and the keyboard rematerialized underneath her hands.

"It would be faster if we downloaded all our knowledge directly into . . ." began Shir, but he fell quiet as Nuphar turned her eyes to glare at him.

"Listen, kid." She straightened her back. "I am a Librarian, a sixth-generation Librarian. I've been doing this since before you were born. Or created. Or assembled in a lab."

"Grown in culture," said Shir.

Nuphar raised her hand. "I couldn't care less. I've been doing this many more years than you can imagine, so don't you tell me how to prepare information for cataloging. We'll download everything to the Library's memory, of course. But first I want your story in general outline, so we can determine how to start processing the new information by subject headers."

Now she looked at me. "Proceed, for future generations."

I wanted to tell her that there won't be any future generations, at least not on Earth, but Shir made a coughing noise, and I started telling her. About the invasion, about our inability to prevent the aliens' taking over our planet, about lost technologies, about the relentless slaughter. About the moment we found out that what they really wanted was the Moon, and that they came to Earth just to rid it of vermin that might have interfered with their designs. About the deal that sealed the fate of all the members of the Silence Unit. I did leave out the sense of loss, the physical pain that came with each explosion, and the mental anguish when memories started flowing to newly activated backups. As well as the need to go on functioning even though everything we were meant to defend was gone.

Space-warp fields know how to seal themselves against anything mechanical and protect whatever they surround from external detonations. But they are sensitive to living matter and can recognize intelligence. Our combination of living tissue and intelligence can confuse them long enough for us to detonate the charges hidden inside us. The first invaders got the Moon, and Humankind remained on Earth to protect it from repeated invasions by other aliens who coveted exactly the same resources.

"But humankind. . . ." Nuphar did not complete this sentence. She looked at Shir, at me, back at him. "But why? Whatever for? If there are no more human beings. . . ."

"Because this is our destiny," I replied. "We need to defend Earth."

"The Prime Directive says, defend Earth for Humankind," added Shir.

"But there is no humankind anymore," said Nuphar again, tearfully. "No more human beings. Whatever for . . . why . . . ?" She raised her hands from the keyboard and buried her face in them. Her head remained between her palms, her hair hid her face from us. Her shoulders were trembling.

Shir raised his eyebrows and tilted his head in her direction. I nodded. We are not capable of genuine compassion.

Nuphar sighed and raised her head. Her eyes were red. I made a note to add this item to the programming of my next backup. She sniffled, put her hands on the desk, and the keyboard reappeared beneath her hands. "Go on," she said. "Dates. Locations. Major battles. How many invasions there were. Go on."

We didn't reply. Nuphar raised her voice. "Come on, robots, start talking."

I cleared my throat.

"And don't make this noise." Nuphar straightened up. "You don't have to breathe. You're just a machine in a humanlike bag."

"But we do breathe,' said Shir. Despite his stiffened body, his voice was calm. "We have pain fibers. We feel and behave like Human Beings."

"But you are *not* human beings," Nuphar raised her voice again. "You're just . . . just . . ." Her voice broke. She snuffled again. And again. But this time she didn't lower her head or shift her glance. I looked at her.

"If we weren't here, you'd have had nowhere to come back to," I said.

"We're not coming back," Nuphar interrupted me. She wiped her nose. "There's nowhere to come back to. We'll seal the Library and move on, like always, and stop again in three hundred years to see if anything may have changed."

"Nothing will have changed." Shir sat very straight. "We'll go on exploding, and when you come back you'll find Earth still . . ."

"Full of machines," Nuphar completed his sentence for him, and there was a sting in her voice. She glared at me. "Do you wish to make a protest also?"

I nodded.

"So come on. Proceed." Nuphar spread her fingers over the keyboard.

"I just think," I said quietly, "that this decision is not up to you."

She did not answer. She just looked at me.

"There are more than two thousand Human Beings in here. As you told us yourself. You explained that you live in an organized anarchy. The decision whether to stop, move on, or come out must be made by all. Otherwise you'll be trampling all over their rights."

Nuphar continued to stare at me. I returned her gaze. My internal programming said that after ten seconds I must blink, and after thirty seconds I must lower my eyes. These intervals were set by Romi Potashnik when she created the very first backup.

After half a minute, I lowered my eyes. I waited. The room was silent.

Nuphar sighed. "Okay," she said finally. I raised my head. She removed her fingers from the keyboard.

"I'm going to call a general meeting." She bit her lower lip. "And you will not interfere." She hesitated for a moment. "This is an order, hear?"

We nodded. She could not change our programming, but we knew we'd better not point out her mistake. Romi and Shir had programmed us, inputting the spectrum of permitted responses to Humans and specifying the chain of command. They had not known that Humankind was going to be wiped out in its entirety three hours after they completed their programming and that these reactions would become redundant, since there would not be any Humans to obey.

The meeting hall was crowded and noisy. I was unable to figure out the rules by which this was organized. Some shouted, some stood up on the desks and stomped their feet, some sat by and only made comments. Nuphar did all of the above, sometimes standing on a desk, sometimes stomping her feet, sometimes heckling speakers, sometimes doing all at the same time. Nobody ran the discussion or controlled it.

We sat at the side of the room, ignored by all, having done our job. I was worn out and couldn't follow the discussion anymore. My internal counter said it was more than twelve hours since we had entered the sphere. I needed food and sleep. Shir, on the other hand, looked livelier. His programming said that the later the hour the more alert he will be, except for those five hours and twenty minutes he spent restlessly turning over in his bed each night.

Shir turned to me. "They're about to wrap it up," he said.

I raised my eyebrows.

"Noise is abating." He pointed at my head. "You really should upgrade your decibel counter."

"Then it's decided." Nuphar's voice got louder, and everybody shut up. "We stay here. We'll cut short the next waiting period, and in the meanwhile we'll see whether we can create weapons or some means of defense for the Silence Unit."

There were scattered cheers and a few clapped their hands, especially the ones who stood on their desks. Nuphar turned to us. She was all sweaty and her face was flushed. "You can go back home now." She smiled, but this time the corners of her eyes did not move when she stretched her lips sideways. "We thank you for everything."

"We are not going back home." Shir's voice was quiet, in comparison with the hubbub that surrounded us just a few moments before.

"So go back to your pods," said Nuphar, her foot drumming on the top of the desk where she stood. "What's important is that you get out of here."

Shir spread his hands. "We do have homes. We live in a way designed to make the Superiors believe Earth is still populated." He added, pointing at me, "Romi has a live-in partner."

Who had remained in bed and asked me to take care. This was my only rec-ollection of her. I never knew if Romi kept all other memories of Yonit to herself deliberately, or maybe this was all she had managed to upload to her backup. She didn't even create Yonit. I created her, from the limbless body that waited for my first backup to come back home.

"Excellent." Nuphar folded her arms on her chest. "Then go back home."

I stood up, and Shir stood behind me. "We can't go back home. We must destroy the vestibule."

Noise exploded in the room. Shir made a face. "That's why I don't upgrade my decibel counter," I whispered in his ear. He only nodded.

Nuphar raised her hands. "Silence!" she shouted. After her third attempt, the room grew a little quieter. She put her hands on her hips. "What do you mean, destroy the vestibule? The vestibule connects us with this Earth of yours. If you ever want to see humans again. . . ."

I shook my head. "That's too dangerous. We must defend Humankind."

"Which means you," Shir completed my sentence for me, gesturing at the room. "If anyone could penetrate the vestibule, they would be able to destroy the lot of you."

Nuphar straightened up. "Only humans can. . . ." she began, but then fell silent. Her face grew pale.

"It won't matter at all," shouted a voice from the crowd. I turned to where it came from. The source was a man with a white beard, wearing a purple robe and a skirt. He stood up, straightened his robe, and addressed me. "This is what you're saying, isn't it? That after enough information-gathering stops, they will have figured out how to breach the vestibule and kill us all."

"Why should they?" Nuphar raised both her hands and her voice. "It makes no sense. Why should they attack us at all?"

"Because you are an invading species." Shir stepped forwards, swinging his glare all over the room. "You might decide you're interested in the Moon. Or Venus. Or Uranus."

I snorted. "Nobody's interested in Uranus. Miranda, if anything."

"We are *not* an invading species!" cried Nuphar. "We are human beings. This planet belongs to us!" Shouts of agreement from all around her. She folded her hands. "I refuse to surrender without trying. We shall fight. We shall defend ourselves."

"We shall defend you," said Shir. "This is what we're here for."

An older woman stood up, wearing a golden crown and holding a scepter in her hand. "If you destroy the vestibule, we'll never be able to come back," she said. "Our Mission will have become pointless." She climbed on her chair and pointed her scepter at us. "You will have destroyed humankind." The room thundered again.

Shir and I exchanged glances. He shrugged. It was no use talking to them. Anyway, once we'd be out of here we'd decide for ourselves what to do. Our programming said, defend Humankind at all costs.

We sat back. Nuphar climbed down from her desk. She came to us, sighed, pulled up a chair, and sat down in silence.

The white-bearded man spoke louder now. "They want to bury us here." He raised his hands. "They want us to remain in this Library for good."

Waves of discussion swept the room like a thunderstorm, splitting and rejoining again. Someone offered to give shelter in the Library to all of our kind before the destruction of the vestibule, as a reward for saving Earth, and was immediately shouted down in protest: the Library was for Humans only, and we were most definitely non-Humans. A voice cried out that by the same token they could invite the aliens in. Shir cringed where he sat. I laid a hand on his knee in encouragement. He laid his hand on mine.

Nuphar grew rigid suddenly and looked at me. "How did the aliens discover the space-warp field?"

I shrugged. "We don't communicate with the Superiors about anything beyond immediate defensive measures."

She moved her eyes to Shir. "And all these invading species, are they the same kind of aliens?" she asked.

Shir shook his head. "The data systems passed on to us by the Superiors indicate different biologies, with no evolutionary connection."

Nuphar's face blanched. "And they all started arriving during the past two hundred years, more or less?"

I nodded.

"And you've never asked why? How come they all arrive at the same time to the same place?" She sighed. "Whatever happened to curiosity? Your bosses didn't program you for it?"

Shir straightened his back. "Curiosity, that's what killed Humankind. This is what made those first people enter an alien spaceship rather than destroy it as soon as it was discovered."

Nuphar turned her eyes from Shir to me and back again. She nodded, slightly, and stood up. She climbed onto the desk, raised her hands and cried out, "We've reached a decision."

My throat constricted. I didn't want to leave. There were Humans here. There were the smell, and the warmth, and a sense of Humanity. But I had to leave. Shir grasped my hand. I didn't have to look at him in order to realize that he felt the same.

"The problem with robots," Nuphar made a gesture in our general direction, "is that they only obey preset programming. They don't ask why. They don't know why aliens are attacking Earth. They don't know why aliens are mining the Moon. They don't even know how come so many aliens developed, at the same time, a space-warp that yields to human tissue." She turned to us and spoke more softly. "They defend us without realizing that it was *we* who destroyed humankind."

The room fell silent all at once.

Nuphar bit her lower lip. She was speaking only to us now. "A time-warp field works exactly like a space-warp field, except that instead of existing everywhere simultaneously, it exists everywhen simultaneously." Her voice steadied a bit. "Last time we were here, we left clear instructions about the date and location of our return. Obviously, parts of those instructions must have leaked out, away from Earth."

"No." Shir got to his feet, dragging me with him.

"And that's why the aliens are coming. They want to complement their space-warp fields with time-warp as well." Nuphar smoothed her robe using both hands.

"But information travels at the speed of light." I folded my hands on my chest. "Your instructions could have spread out for two hundred light-years at the most."

Nuphar mimicked me, crossing her hands over her chest. "Our instructions were warped by the field, and the fields are in synch everywhere, everywhen."

There was silence in the room. I heard the sharp, rugged breathing of the crowned woman. A roomful of people, all of whom comprehended this faster than I did.

"Once the Founding Fathers set up the original field, it warped space. Not just time." Nuphar lowered her voice, as the room was completely quiet now. "I am so sorry." She sniveled. "But what happened was that areas of space became warped all across the Universe, broadcasting our instructions further and further."

"And they are coming here looking for more know-how?" I closed my eyes. More and more invasions? Forever?

"Just a moment!" Shir snapped his fingers. "If all fields are in synch...."

Nuphar nodded. "Destroying any one of them will suffice to destroy them all."

"But we keep destroying them!" I nearly shouted.

Nuphar shook her head. "We are still here." She moved a tuft of hair behind her ears. "So long as the original field is here, those fields can't be destroyed."

I was trembling.

Nuphar addressed the crowd. "Those aliens won't stop, for as long as their warp fields work. They won't stop trying to get the know-how we have here. We know how science can be used for destruction. It is our duty to make sure this won't happen ever again."

People were wiping their eyes. The crowned one buried her face in her hands. Nuphar looked at us. "Does Earth have the resources to support two thousand four hundred thirty-five human beings?"

We nodded as one.

Nuphar nodded in reply. She turned to address the crowd again. "I propose a declaration: Mission accomplished, immediate evacuation." She fell quiet then.

There was a moment of alarming silence, then the white-robed man stood up. He said nothing. He just stood there, looking at Nuphar. The woman beside him stood up, and two children, too. One minute later the entire bloc they were with stood up, then the rest of the room.

Shir and I exchanged looks. He turned to Nuphar. "I don't understand," he said.

Nuphar came down from her desk and approached us. "Our Mission was to document human civilization, as much of it as possible." She shrugged. "We're the only humans left. The Library's work is done." She laid both her hands on Shir's shoulders. "Thank you."

She looked at me and said, "The original field surrounds the entire Library. Destroying it means destroying the Library."

I was trembling. Again.

Nuphar smiled at me. "Not to worry, we too have backups. Everything is either scanned or hologrammed. We shall lose the original stuff, but paper, that's a stupid way of saving information anyway." She moved her eyes to Shir. "Perhaps we shall build a new Library outside?"

Shir smiled and nodded. As did I.

Emerging from the vestibule, we found the night as we'd left it. The soldiers were frozen in the same positions they were in when we'd entered the sphere. I sent out a stand-down order, and they shouldered their guns. I went to their leader. "We need an evacuation, but there will be no use of the Web. Your trucks still here?"

He nodded.

"Summon them."

He frowned.

"Now," I said, louder.

He saluted, and sent some troopers to bring in the trucks.

Shir entered the sphere and returned almost immediately, but the stubs on his chin were half a centimeter longer. "At long last, they're ready."

I came closer. "How much time passed inside?" I asked quietly.

Shir shook his head. "Don't ask."

I smiled. He smiled in reply. Things will be alright now. I knew they will. There will be Humans again on Earth, and this time we'll be able to protect them as should be. We'll destroy the Library's field and use their know-how to improve our offensive tactics. For the first time since the original activation of my first backup, I felt the sensation Romi defined as "relief." Shir had an identical smile on his lips.

People started coming out of the sphere. I saw the soldiers tense, but then their faces were flooded with emotions. One of them cried openly. The librarians came out with suitcases, backpacks, wheelbarrows, large spheres floating above them, jars on their heads. The soldiers escorted them to the trucks. I made sure no transmissions came out. We didn't know for certain whether the Superiors were listening, but we didn't want to take any chances.

There were more people than trucks. Some soldiers went out to get extra bubbles. Nuphar came out last; her cheeks were smeared with tears.

Shir approached her first. "You forgot your gear," he said.

She shrugged, and wiped her nose.

I joined them. "Do you need any help?"

Nuphar snuffed again. "We have a problem," she whispered. She cleared her throat and repeated, quietly, "We have a problem."

I straightened my back.

"We have no explosives." Nuphar wiped her eyes. "I thought we had, but when I came to the room where they were stored, I saw that they were not kept properly, and now they are useless." She looked straight at me. "We have no way to destroy the fields." She bit her lip and added, "The Library . . . is very large. It seems that you two won't be enough."

Shir patted her shoulder. "Don't worry, Nuphar, we've done this any number of times." He grinned. "We are Earth's greatest experts on field demolition."

Tension drained out of her shoulders all at once. "I didn't know how to ask," she said quietly.

I shook my head. "This is our destiny." I laid a hand on her shoulder and tried to mimic the way she'd said it earlier, "Not to worry, we have backups."

Nuphar smiled. "So . . . this is not a suicide mission?"

Shir pointed at his chest. "Human tissue and a mechanical body, that's a stupid way of storing consciousness anyway."

Nuphar let out a giggle. She handed me a chip. "This is the floor plan for the entire Library. To make sure you hit the right places."

I accepted the chip. "You'd better go get your things. We'll do it as soon as you come out."

She nodded and went back to the vestibule.

I downloaded the data. Nuphar came back, wearing new clothes, with a bluish robe on her shoulders and a hat made out of some thin metallic stuff on her head, holding a three-legged suitcase and a floating balloon. "I'm ready," she said.

I ran the data. The Library was humongous—bigger than any field we've ever tried to destroy. There must have been a solution hidden in there, but it eluded me. I stretched my hand to Shir. "I need help with the calculations." I didn't want to broadcast the pattern to him.

He raised his eyebrows, but then laid his hand on mine. We interfaced. He repeated my calculations. When the results came in, he clenched his fist and looked straight at me. He nodded. A small nod, imperceptible to others.

"What's going on?" Nuphar moved her eyes between us.

I cleared my throat. "We need some help."

"Sure. Whatever you'll ask for." Nuphar patted her hat.

"Not from you," I said, trying not to sound disdainful. "From a few more of our backups."

Nuphar raised her eyes to Shir. "Is the Library too large for the two of you?" she asked.

Shir raised one hand. "It's okay, we can handle this. Not to worry," he smiled. I sent out a short burst of information to my backups. Enough to wake them up, not enough to arouse suspicion, if the Superiors happened to be listening. I knew Shir was doing the same.

"You can get on one of these trucks." Shir pointed at Nuphar's suitcase. "Need help?"

Nuphar shook her head. "I'll wait here. I know your backups will be the same as you two, but I want to see you off on your last journey." She let out a small giggle. "Sounds awfully dramatic. How does it go, your phrase?"

"We shall never stop, we shall never cease, we shall never desist," we said together, quietly.

Nuphar nodded and laid a hand on her suitcase, which stood there beside her. "It's a good phrase."

She waited, but we didn't reply, and she turned her glance to the trucks.

I felt the quiver of my consciousness waking up in a darkened room. I remembered this sensation from the earlier times I've woken up there, although it was always accompanied, those times, by crushing pain and then nothingness. Beside me, Shir stopped breathing.

I close my eyes against the vertigo I felt as my backups woke up one by one. I looked through the eyes of one of me, to the right-hand side. The backup to my right looked back at me. I blinked once. I blinked back. I felt myself awakening all along the line, more and more, glancing right and left, but instead of seeing empty pods on my left-hand side I saw more copies of me, all waking up, blinking, looking from side to side, in a growing whirlpool of sensations. I waited until the last one of me looked to my right. On my right-hand side there was just the wall. All of me looked straight ahead, at Shir's replicates.

My nerve center couldn't handle that much data. I had to shut down unnecessary, memory-consuming activities. The line of Shirs woke up. My pod opened and I stepped forward, the first thud on the ground repeated by all my extant replicates.

The entire line of Shirs stepped out of their pods, too.

"It's the first time I know how many of me there are," we said in unison. "I'm glad you reached the same conclusion as mine."

Shir Prime nodded, a uniform wave repeated along the line. "I was afraid we should wake up alone one day."

In the dark square I reopened my eyes. "Come along." I looked at the single Shir standing beside me.

"We're coming." He looked at me, expressionless. We invested too much of our processing capacity in the effort to keep all our bodies in synchronized motion. Nothing was left for routine maintenance activities.

I shut my eyes again to block unnecessary input. Got my backups out of our room and marched us up the stairs, into the cold air. Shir got his backups out, stepping beside me. We were twenty kilometers away from the sphere. We didn't speak, didn't send out needless messages. Ran along at a uniform pace, keeping quiet. My feet were injured by stones. I blocked out the sensation of pain. Shir ran beside me, keeping up.

Dawn came, and the world grew gray.

We arrived, together. I saw myself standing, eyes closed, beside an empty sphere. Textureless, colorless. A hole in the middle of existence. Beside me was Shir, his eyes closed too. Nuphar looked at me. Her face grew red.

"You are naked," she said to the version of me standing beside her. My facial-expression-reading subroutine wasn't working.

The I by the sphere opened my eyes, and control reverted to me.

"I know." I straightened my uniform, a tweed jacket and a hijab. The line of my backups stood in front of me. "Enter," I ordered. Shir opened his eyes, and his backups marched forward.

We sent each one of the backups the locations assigned to them. They moved into the sphere.

"How can you tell they'd found the right places?"

I looked at Nuphar, and all my backups still outside looked at her with me. "This is our Destiny," we said, and kept on marching.

One of my backups saw how shaken Nuphar was. Another one noticed how she turned her eyes away. I didn't bother to catalog those facts.

Nuphar kept silent, but she did turn to Shir after nine minutes and thirty-seven seconds: "How many backups do you have here?"

"Enough," said all Shir backups as one.

She turned to me. "Are you sure you can hit everything?"

"Yes, we worked out our optimum dispersal." I concentrated on assigning my backups to the appropriate locations. Some of me noticed that the bubble trucks started leaving the square. As more backups were swallowed by the sphere, my processing capacity increased.

After the last backup had entered the sphere behind me, I was able to assemble a full answer: "We've computed the necessary force, and we are sure we'll be able to destroy the entire field."

We turned our backs on her and moved into the sphere. We didn't have communication inside, but I knew my backups were in place. There were red footprints on the floor wherever we went. The old man's hologram stood frozen, pointing at the nonexistent stairway behind it.

"I've sent instructions in case we won't succeed," Shir broke the silence.

"Won't succeed?" Nuphar had reentered the sphere, and now was looking around. "Is there a chance you won't succeed?"

I hadn't expected her to reenter. We had to get her out. My subroutine determined that Humans need to be calmed down in order to let us do our work properly. I shook my head. "Shir always worries too much," I said, smiling at Nuphar.

"A lot of your backups went in." Nuphar removed her flashy hat. "I came in to ask how many backups are left."

I didn't answer her. She turned to Shir. "How many backups of yours are left?" She raised her voice.

Shir looked at me.

Nuphar stamped her foot on the floor. "Answer me, you robots, how many backups of yours there are?"

"None," Shir replied quietly. "We are the last ones."

Nuphar straightened up. "Then call in someone else from your unit. I won't allow you to destroy yourselves." She waved her finger at me.

Shir smiled at her, looking more Human than ever, as far as I recalled. "We're already inside. There's no communication with the outside."

"Then get out." Nuphar waved her hand at the wall behind her. "Call somebody else. Do something."

Shir just stood there, his hands down the sides of his body. "The Silence Unit was created after the first Superiors' spaceship had swallowed everyone Romi and Shir knew. Everyone sent out to communicate with them and offer an exchange of information. They'd built us in order to save the rest of Humankind."

"You've already told me all this." Nuphar squeezed her hat, looking directly at me. "You have a partner. You can't leave it alone."

I held her shoulders. "We've been repulsing invasions for one hundred and ninety years. We've died and been reconstructed again and again for one hundred and ninety years. We're tired." I softened my voice. "There are other members of our unit; they'll protect you. They have all our knowledge but none of the memories of pain."

Shir came closer, looking into her eyes. "Please. This is our chance."

He waited, but Nuphar never answered. She wiped her eyes and nodded. Shir leaned forward and hugged her. Nuphar's shoulders were trembling. He stepped back. Tears ran down Nuphar's cheeks. She turned to me. I hugged her too, allowing her to rest her head on my shoulder.

When I loosed my hug she wiped her eyes again. "I'll never forget you." She moved her hair back. "I'll document everything."

Shir smiles. "The Ninth Library of Alexandria. Established 15,534, in existence for four and a half seconds now."

Nuphar nodded, turned back and moved away from us, out of the sphere.

We breathed in. We breathed out.

Shir smiled.

There was pain, and then there was nothingness.

The Perfect Girl

Guy Hasson

The bus is full, but when it stops at the Indianapolis Academy only I get off.

I'm sweating in my bra, and it's not even hot. My panties are too tight in one place and too baggy in another. My dress is too conservative. They're going to know.

I watch until the bus disappears behind a turn and a hill. I wait a couple more seconds, take a deep breath, and turn around.

It's like there's a huge gate in the middle of nowhere, with a seven-foot wall stretching in both directions, deep into Indiana country. To one side of the gate is a small booth with an armed guard.

"Hi," I say, coming closer, being cute.

He steps out of the booth. "You're new." All business.

"Yes." I'll bet he knows everybody's faces.

"ID, please."

I shuffle a bit in my purse and then give him my ID. He puts it in some portable computer thing; it bleeps; he pulls out my ID and hands it back to me. His hand accidentally grazes my finger as he does so, and I get a small sense of him. He's not a telepath. He's attracted to me. God, I hate myself.

He goes back to the booth, presses a button, and the gate slides open.

The Academy is inhumanly large, a twentieth-century architectural construct, meant to look like it was built in the seventeenth century somewhere in Europe. I feel as if I've shrunk to half my size.

"Good luck," he shouts after me.

"Thanks," I call back.

I put on my gloves.

The gate shuts behind me. God, I hate myself.

The lecture hall is built for three hundred.

I get there first, which is oh-*so*-joyful.

I pick a place somewhere in the middle.

One by one, they come in. And as each of them enters, they all sit in the front row. A minute before eight, I pick up my things and join them.

Professor Bendis comes in at eight on the dot.

Ancient. Smart. Godlike.

He takes his time getting to the podium and looking at us.

He can read my mind. I cross my legs.

He lowers his chin, looking down at us. "There are six students," he begins without preamble, "in the class of '14. One of you will probably learn that this is too tough, that this isn't for him or her, and will drop out within the first month. If this does not happen, we will expel one of you after two months.

"After your freshman year, one of you will be dropped out.

"After your sophomore year, one of you will be dropped out.

"After your junior year, one of you will be dropped out.

"Of the two that are left, only one will graduate. Only those who graduate will be free to return to civilian life. All those who are dropped will be sent to our *sister* institution." He looks at us all. Yes, we all know what that means. "We do *not* take our talents lightly. They are new, few, and far between. So far. We must learn to police ourselves and behave responsibly before the government sees fit to step in any more than they have and police us."

He looks at us all. "Good luck to all of you." He leans back. "Now, to your first lesson."

I am *way* over my head here.

"In this class, in our profession, we deal with *truth*. The *whole* truth." Professor Parks is only ten years older than I am. I'm ten yards away from her and I can *sense* her strength. Jeez.

"During your first year here," she continues, "you will become intimate with each of your fellow students. I am not talking about physical intimacy. I am talking about a greater intimacy. You're going to let each of your fellow students into your head. For an entire year. You will analyze each other to the core. You will bore out the truth. You will touch on complexes, truths, hates, fears, loves, and secrets. And you will *have* to *share* everything that's in your mind or you will be kicked out of the Academy.

"There will be no running from the truth here. There will be no hiding the truth. There will be no secrets.

"It will be the hardest thing you have ever done. It is the most basic act we require of you.

"In being truthful with others, you will be forced to be truthful with yourselves."

I've only known these people for three hours, and I already know one's a whore, one's a gasbag, one's socially inept, and I don't know anything, yet, about the other two except that they scare the daylights out of me.

They're going to know this.

They've already judged *me*.

Freshmen get the sleazy duties. Each student, in his or her own turn, went into the office and came out looking as if someone had just pulled their teeth.

I'm the last one. I go in.

A black-haired Adonis sits behind a table. He's probably a senior. "Alexandra Watson?"

"Yes."

"You're. . . ." He looks closely at his list. "Ah." He raises his eyes from the list and looks at me. "You're in the morgue."

I swear my brain freezes for a second. "What? I'm sorry, what?"

He just looks at me. He knows I didn't mishear. My vision becomes spotty. "The morgue? But this is an academy. It's an academy for psy—"

"We have a morgue," he cuts me off quickly. "People have been donating their bodies to science for decades. We're a new science. People advance scientific knowledge by donating their bodies to us."

"But what good is a—"

"You can still read a man's mind after he's dead."

"What!"

At least for a while. Doctors autopsy bodies. We autopsy personalities. For our own safety as well as for the safety of innocent bystanders, the Academy is maintained by as few people as possible. We all have to chip in. We all have to pull our shifts at the morgue. I did it. Everyone in your class will do it. Right now, you're doing it. You will report there now. Three floors down."

"There are five horizontal refrigerators for five bodies. At the best of times we only get one, so there's no danger of us being overbooked."

The woman briefing me hates the way I look, and she doesn't mind beaming that emotion at me while she talks.

"You get a body, you get it off the gurney, you put it in the fridge. Okay so far? Great. If someone wants to use the body, you pull it out . . . like so. When people are done with it, you put it back, make sure this door is closed . . . see? Then you leave the room and lock it. Understood?"

I nod.

"The room temperature must always be kept at ten degrees Celsius or bad things happen to the bodies. It must be kept at that temperature even when the freezers are empty, in case a body comes in. This is the keypad responsible for this.

"You are accountable for this room. You are responsible for anything that happens to it even when there are no bodies in it. Times like right now, when we have no bodies—which is most of the time—you keep the room clean, you keep the temperature steady, and you let no one in. Someone comes in and does something—even if someone breaks in—it's your responsibility.

"When there's a body here, this is what you do. If anyone wants use of the body, if a class comes in, they need permission from you. They need you to open the doors for them and to roll the body from the fridge to this room. Only the dean has the other key, and he makes it a point to *never* use it.

"You watch the class come in, you watch them leave. Anything happens to the body or the room, it's your responsibility and your ass. There are no set hours in which you're supposed to be here. Just make sure you maintain this place. Is everything understood?" She smiles at me when she asks, but I clearly hear the word *bitch* in my head. My god, she's good. She's not even near me.

"Yes," I say. My voice sounds weak.

"I'm going now. You'll need to stay."

"Why? I can just lock the—"

"We just got a call thirty minutes ago. A donor's heading this way. Passed away this morning."

"What?"

"You will wait here till the ambulance comes. The man will come and give you papers to sign. You will sign all the papers. And I do mean *all* of them. The man will leave. You will put the body in the fridge, and then you will lock up. Understood?"

I've been sitting in the morgue for three hours, now, waiting for the body.

There's been nothing. There's no phone here. Even if I used my cell, I wouldn't know who to call or who to ask. I don't even know the name of the student who gave me the instructions. I sit here waiting, imagining, remembering every horror movie I've ever seen. I have ghosts on the brain, zombies, dead people coming back to life, dead children, animals rising from graves, knives in showers, blood spilling, curses, even my own body on the slab.

Who would give their minds to science? Who would allow their memories, their emotions, their entire lives to be explored, raped, pillaged by total strangers? Why would anyone do that?

The steel doors swing open, and I jump ten feet in the air.

A fifty-something orderly wheels a body on some kind of pushcart. The body is zipped inside a black bag.

"Special delivery," he smiles at me.

"I—"

"Hey, hey," he almost touches me. "You're turning green. Oh, god, I love first timers. Look," and suddenly he's all friendly again, turning back to the body. He's trying to tell me through his actions that there's nothing to worry about. "I'll show you how it's done, so you'll know for next time, all right? Just don't throw up on me." Another smile.

I nod.

"What you do is, you take the body out of the bag," he unzips the entire thing, revealing a woman's body. "You move her to this gurney." I can't take my eyes off her, disgusting as this is. She's around my age. Unspoiled, naked body. Beautiful face. "Like this," he continues. "Then you take a sheet from here, and you cover her with it." He does so. "After all, you telepaths are going to remove the sheet to touch her, aren't you? Then you shove her into the freezer." He closes the freezer behind him, turns to me, and flashes his most disarming smile. "There. All done. Now sign this," he produces a form from his shirt pocket, unfolds it, and puts it in front of me.

It's to acknowledge receipt. I sign the form wordlessly and get to keep a copy. I notice the name. The body is Stephanie Reynolds.

"Excellent," he repockets the paper. "Now where's your form?"

"What?"

"Where's your form?"

"I just signed it."

"No. Where's *your* form?" I look at him blankly. "They told me you signed it."

"Signed what?" But a shiver begins to run up my spine. She had said to sign *all* forms, and she had enjoyed that moment in particular.

He goes to one of the drawers, full of different forms, and pulls out one. "This. They told me you signed this."

I look at it. "What is it?"

"Anyone who works here, anyone who goes to the Academy, signs this. It says you consent to donating your body to science, to this. After all, you guys need to help yourselves, don't you? They usually send me all the paperwork a couple of weeks into the semester, once they've threatened you a bit. You're going to sign it anyway. So you can sign it now, if you want."

This was what she'd emoted at me when she left. Perverse pleasure. And the knowledge that if I don't do this I'm out of the Academy, looking at a forced, life-long military career with no way back into civilian life. And I can't afford to be . . .

I don't think my voice is even audible when I say, "I'll wait. Thank you."

He shrugs. We both know I'm going to sign it eventually.

It's eleven p.m. when I get to my dorm room for the second time today. For the second time ever. In the morning, I had just enough time to throw my bags on the floor before I had to go to first period. The rest of the students in my class are down the hall. We each get a huge suite with a bedroom, a small living room, and a bathroom.

I crawl onto the bed. Showering can wait. Unpacking can wait.

I want to cry.

Later. Later. Please. Later.

I wake up in the middle of the night, my heart beating: I forgot to set the alarm!

I stumble off the bed, drowsy, everything spinning.

The light's on. I slept in my clothes. My mouth is dry. My alarm clock is still packed.

I need to pee. I go to the bathroom, and a glance at the mirror makes me gasp. What the—!

My face! My face is smeared with red-and-white toothpaste!

The door—I didn't lock it.

Did they touch me, even for a second? Did they invade my thoughts? Did they invade my dreams? Did they read me?

Was it my class? The older students?

I hate this place. I hate these people. Dammit!

I sit on the edge of the bathtub and cry and cry and cry.

"When we die," Professor Bendis begins his lecture at eight on the second, "although there are no thoughts, the neural paths remain. The memories remain. Identity remains. The emotions of the past, the complexes, remain. They are all inactive. We can search them, navigate through them, without resistance from the subject. And thus we can probe and learn. Undisturbed, not afraid of harming anyone's privacy.

"It takes roughly seven days for the 'mind' or the 'personality' to deteriorate and disappear beyond our capability of probing it. As my own professor used to say, 'Our personality dies seven days after our body does.'"

He slams his hand on the podium. "There's a fresh body in the morgue. We have less than six days to analyze the subject's mind. Until further notice, class will be held there. Ms. Watson, you have the key on you?"

"Yes."

"Then we shall go."

I open the freezer and wheel out the body.

The class holds back a gasp. I can feel their collective need to run away.

Professor Bendis ignores them. He walks up to the body, removes the sheet enough to reveal her face, and touches her forehead with a finger. Five seconds later, he breaks contact and looks at me.

"Ms. Watson, do you know her name?"

"Stephanie Reynolds, sir."

He nods. "Do you know her middle name?"

I blank out. Then I see the form in my mind. The slot for middle name was empty. "No," I say.

"Touch her," he says. "And tell me her middle name."

I come closer, standing right beside the body. Why did he have to pick *me* first?

I touch her, searching.

There's nothing.

I raise my eyes. "Professor Bendis, I'm not sensing any thoughts or emotions."

"Of course not. She's dead, Ms. Watson. She hasn't had a thought for approximately twenty-four hours."

"Then how—"

"But the neurological patterns are there nonetheless. The memories of thoughts and emotions she's had are still stored in the physical connections inside her brain. *You* have to think for her. *You* have to *create* movement. You will have to move from one pathway to another. And you will only be able to move down emotions or thoughts or memories she's had before and that have been etched into her mind. Your movement will be through her memory."

Hesitating, I touch her again.

Nothing.

I will her thoughts to move.

Nothing.

I look at him. "But to move I have to start from someplace. There's no place to start."

"To get a starting point, you have to think a thought she'd already had. You have to find a place that already exists in her memory. That's not as difficult as it sounds. Try this. Put your finger on her, and think 'mother.'"

Without noticing, I think "mother" a split second before I touch her. Automatically, my mother's image is in my head, especially the way she's starting to look her age. I have her height, I have her build, I have her face. I know that's what I'm going to look like when I'm old.

And there's an image of my mother, tired, and for the first time I can see that she's fifty. And suddenly I understand that whenever I look at her, I see the image of who she was when I was five. I haven't seen her real face in years.

She's shorter and smaller and older than I am. And worn. She's worn. You can see the fight on her face. I don't want people to see how hard it was to get to this place. Please don't let me be as wrinkled—

No, that's not me. That was Stephanie. Stephanie's mother. Stephanie's thoughts. I look up at Professor Bendis. Her thoughts fade into nothing, even though I'm still touching her.

"From there on," Bendis says. "You move to a place that is 'linked' in some way to this memory. For example. You can easily move from 'mother' to 'father.'"

Mother, tired, for the first time I can see that she's fifty—

—Dad is fifty—

I see his fiftieth birthday. Dad sits on the sofa, watching television, while Mom frets over the spread-out dinner table.

I see it in his eyes. I've seen in it in his eyes all day. He claims he doesn't care, but that number hits him where it hurts: he still thinks he's young. He still thinks he's twenty-two. Dad thinks he's Peter Pan.

He thinks he still *looks* twenty-two just because he weighs the same.

The doorbell rings. Mom looks up—

"From there," Bendis continues, "you can move to 'mother and father fighting.'"

The doorbell rings. Mom looks up, and I can feel the pressure, the sweat. She's not ready—

—Mom shouting at Dad, I think—

"It's inconsiderate," Mom is practically shouting.

"But it doesn't make any sense!" Dad's tone becomes even calmer than it was a second ago. "I never notice if people are making a noise when they chew. You're being unreasonable."

"It doesn't matter if it makes sense to you. I find it disgusting. I find it abhorrent. That's what I feel. You know it makes me feel bad, and you're still doing it."

"But there is no reason in the world why it should bother you. You're being hysterical for nothing." So cool, I sense Stephanie's thoughts, dipped in disgust. So ignorant of feelings. Why can't he understand her? Why does he do that? Why doesn't he understand?

"Understand her!" Stephanie wants to shout. "Just for once, understand—"

"From there," the professor's voice breaks into Stephanie's emotions, "to 'Will I fight like this with *my* husband?'"

"I want a man who understands me," Stephanie says. She's lying on the bed—I can sense the location in her mind and feel the covers on her stomach. Margaret is lying beside her, also on the stomach, resting on her elbows. And although I didn't pick it up from Stephanie, I can see from Margaret's face that these two are now more or less sixteen. They're alone in the house. I know that.

"He has to be kind," Stephanie goes on, and I feel in her what that emotion means, how nice it would be. "And considerate." Yes. "And he will love me." Yes. "And give his life for me." Yes. I feel exactly like that.

"From there to 'Marriage is not for me.'" The professor's words, although calm, land on me like a wall of bricks. Stephanie's mind vanishes to me.

Of course marriage is for her! I just felt it! She was ready for marriage and she was only sixteen!

The professor is looking at me. "Problem?"

"No."

"From there," he continues, "to 'Marriage is not for me.'"

I close my eyes, preparing, knowing I'm looking for something that does not exist.

"—Kind. And considerate. And he will love me—"

—Marriage is not for me—

"When I finally find a man, a man I'm ready to settle down with and who is ready to settle down with me, I will not let him marry me." She's lecturing Margaret. I can't see the buildings, but the gyro inside all of us says that they're at the university. This is probably a couple of years ago. *"Marriage is an institution that started out in barbaric times. Women were slaves at worst and cheap labor at best. When I find a man—"*

—Did you find a man? I ask her—

Her emotions run away from me and I lose her. She's gone.

It takes me a second to realize you can't ask dead people questions. I need to find the right thought in order to—

"You see?" The Professor notices my concentration has lapsed. "Unlike our own minds, the minds of the dead are open books. All you have to learn to do is to navigate. Do you understand, Ms. Watson?"

"I think so."

"Good. Then tell me her middle name."

I look at him and I don't understand.

"Her name, Ms. Watson. What is her middle name?"

I concentrate and touch her again. "My name is . . ." I think.

"My name is . . ." Stephanie stands in front of the class. Her inner gyro puts her at first period in Mrs. Craig's class. She's in the first grade. This is her first day of school. *"Stephanie Jean Reynolds and I live in 1421 North Shadeland Avenue."*

"That's enough," Mrs. Craig says. *"Thank you, Stephanie."*

Stephanie nods and sits down.

I break my touch with her and look at Professor Bendis. "Her middle name is Jean, sir."

"All right. Very good, Ms. Watson. Step back."

I nod, and move back.

Professor Bendis calls on another student and puts her through the wringer. And then another, and then another. He asks each of them a different question, he guides each of them through a different set of memories. But he doesn't touch Stephanie again, not even once. In the five seconds he touched her, he accessed more information than all of us did in two hours.

And through all of this, Stephanie's immobile face rests there, unmoving, still perfect though dead, while the rest of the world frets around it. I watch it rock slightly, only a millimeter in every direction, when someone touches it. Everyone touches it at a different spot.

Mark touches her on the cheek. Suzy on her shoulder. Greg hesitates, and touches Stephanie's temple.

And Stephanie jiggles ever so slightly whenever someone pulls his fingers away, as if her face and the finger were glued together.

The class is done after two hours. We're all in a hurry to get to the next class. Professor Bendis reminds us that tomorrow we should reconvene here and not in class.

While they leave, I have to put the body back in the freezer.

I move as slowly as possible, waiting until they're almost all out the door and their backs are definitely turned to me. As I slip the sheet over her face, I touch her for only a second, making it seem like an accident. And as I do so, I concentrate on the flutter you get when you're in the beginning of a relationship, the butterflies in the stomach you feel when it's the real thing, when . . .

Stephanie sits there, alone in her bedroom, her cheek squished against the wall. Her gut burns, physically burns, with what I know to be fear and insecurity. Her feet—now in socks—feel as though they're a hundred times more sensitive than she's used to. Her feeling of butterflies in the stomach is ten times stronger than mine.

She thinks about yesterday, about the kiss they had, the buzz it gave her, and it feels like blood actually fills her eyes and blots her eyesight. She slides her cheek down the wall of her bedroom slowly, playing that kiss again, exhilarated, fearful.

I can't help myself, and I surf to that memory, to that "yesterday" in his apartment—

I am in the kiss. I am feeling Michael's tongue, Michael's lips, on mine. I see only his eyes, wild, blue, innocent, lovely eyes. I close mine as I kiss him, and he slips his hand down my shirt. His warm fingers on my breasts feel like—

The contact is broken, and I'm back in the morgue. I hadn't even broken stride. I wheel her a few more seconds, then look behind me, at the door.

Professor Bendis is standing there, looking at me. His face is expressionless, but he saw me. I know he saw me. And I know he knows what I did.

He doesn't move. Either out or back in, he doesn't move.

I turn around, certain my face is red, and finish wheeling her into the freezer. I put her in, and close the door. I check its temperature. I fiddle with it, to create an impression that I'm very busy. I recheck the freezer door. I open it and close it again. I look at the temperature again. There's nothing more I can think of, so I finally turn around.

He's not there. Probably hasn't been there in quite a while.

I hate myself.

I lock the morgue and head for my next class. My heart is hammering. It won't stop.

I don't know what this feeling is. Is it the excitement? Is it the butterflies? That kiss?

No, it's the feelings of blood blotting the eyes, love pumping through her, stronger than her, stronger than me.

My heart won't stop hammering.

I walk into Professor Willis's class, and sit down.

The other students' heads turn to the door. I follow their gaze. It's Professor Parks.

"Alexandra Watson," she says.

Oh, what? "Yes."

"Come with me."

Everybody's looking at me now. I stand up slowly, looking down. I make my way to the door. Why did I have to sit so far away?

She leads me out and shuts the door to the class. We're standing in the corridor.

"Did I do something, Professor Parks?"

"No. I need your key to the morgue. Open it up for me," she says.

I realize I've been staring at her blankly for a few seconds longer than I should have, when she says, "Let's go."

I follow her down to the morgue. I look at her from the back as she walks. She dresses exactly as she looks: Controlled, powerful, smooth. I'll never get to be that.

We reach the door. Half her class is already there. No, my mistake. They're juniors. Half a class *is* their class.

I put my key in the lock and realize I can get to touch her again.

Did he love her? Are they still together? I mean, *were* they still together when she died? Did she find someone better?

I stand over the fridge without remembering getting here. I open the door, and just as I wheel her out, just as I'm figuring out how to touch her accidentally, I see that the students and Professor Parks are looking at me. They're like Bendis. If I touch, even accidentally, they'll know. They're telepaths. They know what a touch does.

I act businesslike. I don't touch. I stand back and let Professor Parks stand over the body. Professor Parks approaches the gurney and removes enough of the sheet to reveal her face.

"All right," she begins, addressing the class. She then stops and turns her attention to me. "Thank you, Ms. Watson. You can go back to your class, now."

What? "But. . . . I'm not supposed to leave it unatten—"

"We'll take care of it," she dismisses me. "We've all done this before. We'll put her back in the freezer and close the door behind us. You can go. Come back when class is over and lock the morgue. There are no vandals here."

"Now . . ." she turns her attention back to her class as I begin to walk out ". . . if you think that what you did last year when autopsying the dead was exploring the mind . . ." I open the door, and let myself out. ". . . you're about to learn that it was child's play compared to what we're going to do n. . . . " I shut the door behind me.

I go back to class.

Once class is over, I run down to the morgue and go inside. The room is empty. The light is off. Stephanie's in the fridge.

I wonder—

I could lock the door from the inside. . . .

No.

I leave the room and lock it behind me.

I go to the cafeteria. All my class is sitting together. A weight on my shoulders just got heavier. I buy some food and sit with them.

"So who's going to read who?" Greg says, his eyes gleaming.

"What do you mean?" Megan sits opposite him. She's attracted to him.

"They're going to set us up in pairs, you know. And then the pair is going to read one another's mind all year long, just like Parks said."

"Don't be stupid. One of us is leaving. We'll be an odd number."

"So what do you think is going to happen?"

"Everybody is going to read everybody." Rebecca says it like it's obvious.

We catch ourselves looking at each others' faces.

Greg laughs and shrugs. "Maybe they'll do a mirror thing. I always wanted to try that with another telepath."

"What's a 'mirror thing?'"

"Well, for example. Alexandra reads my mind, and sees what I think of her." He smiles at me and winks. He's coming on to me. God, this is shit. "Then I read Alexandra's mind and see how she *perceived* what I thought of her. And then she reads my mind, and sees how *I* perceived *that*. And so on. And so on. And so on. And the more times it happens, the farther it will be from the original thought. I always wanted to try that."

"Hmm . . . ," Rebecca says calmly. "I don't know why you have to do it just on how someone perceives you. You could do it on every thought, on every image we see, on every sound we hear."

"Which one of us do you think will be the one to make it?"

"Me, of course," Rebecca says immediately. She smiles, but she beams at us, *I've never failed in my life.*

Greg laughs, amused. "Actually, it will probably be me. The only thing I've failed at in life is failing. Boy, I've tried to fail, I've tried to get myself kicked out, and I keep getting the best grades." He laughs again, and he doesn't care that no one thinks that anything he said is even amusing.

For the first time, I look around me.

All the rest of the students are here. One or more of them came in last night and smeared me with toothpaste. Was it the ones looking at me? The ones not looking at me?

I hate this place.

Going over to next period, I get called to the morgue again. During the day, I get called one more time. One for each year, I guess.

The classes over, I head back to the dorm. I stop. I look at the entrance.

Jeez, what's the matter with me?

I should go to my room.

Fuck this. I'm going to make sure Stephanie's okay.

I lock myself inside. I keep the lights off. I walk, as silently as possible, to the freezer.

Feeling things with my hands, I pull her out. I move aside most of the sheet. I touch her.

And I'm smack inside the kiss, the same kiss I've been living in since I touched her seven hours ago. It's stronger here. It's stronger in her dead mind than it is in my live one.

—*How did you meet him?*—

Her thoughts disappear.

I delve into the kiss again, and surf from there backwards, until they are no longer touching—

I move forward, my movement creating her thought, surfing through an existing memory—

She's sitting on the floor, leaning on the sofa, looking at her notebook. Her inner gyro says that this is night and that she's in Michael's apartment.

Michael is behind her, on the sofa, looking over her head.

"Oh, man, this is uncomfortable," Stephanie says. She wiggles her back. Then, after she convincingly seems uncomfortable, she shifts her position and moves aside, in-between Michael's legs, her back still turned to him.

"There. Much more comfortable."

He's shown interest in her before this. She's shown interest. She's been manipulating things all night, so that he hardly has to do anything to make the first move. But he still has to do it. He has to want her enough.

She asks him about a question in the notebook she had placed on her knees.

He leans forward, trying to read it. He obviously realizes now how close he is to her, and suddenly he looks at her. He smiles, and she smiles back. He almost laughs, and her body sends out a buzz of pleasure. And suddenly the hand she can't see caresses her far cheek. She leans her face into his hand, the world forgotten. And his lips are on hers, and they are in that familiar kiss, and her body goes wild as most of it grows alive with pleasure. Everywhere he touches, everything he does, is perfect. It's like her brain is melted and all she is is her body and her skin.

All right. All right.

I take my hand away. Her face more than jiggles this time. She almost stuck to me.

Did it get hotter in here since I came in?

I could go back to the moment any time I want. I just . . . need to calm down a bit.

Wow.

Someone else's touch has never had such a powerful effect on me.

I look down at that face.

Wow.

Who are you, Stephanie?

I caress her cheek.

All I see is the ceiling, but Michael's hands are all over my naked body, and they are inside me, and the pleasure blots out all other senses. The pleasure comes in waves and waves and waves that spread out, that annihilate the rest of her mind. It makes her body one. It nulls her mind.

I break contact.

I look at her. More. More. More!

I run it over and over and over again, the waves that continue even when he no longer touches her.

All right. All right. I should stop. I should do something else. After all, her entire life is there, behind that face. Everything she ever thought, everything she ever dreamed, everything she remembers. Everything.

How like me are you, Stephanie?

Her face does not answer.

When were you betrayed, Stephanie? Were you ever betrayed?

I caress her again.

"Don't you understand how bad it makes me feel!" Stephanie is screaming at the top of her lungs at her mother. Stephanie is sixteen and in her living room. Can't you get it through your head! Do I have to scream at you every single week about the same thing?" Stephanie's mother has agreed to another family meeting at Grandma's, when Stephanie

has tried to establish time and time again that she would go any other day but Sunday, that Sunday was her day, her private day for herself. "Can't you see—can't you see—how bad it makes me feel!" And the tears come out. "Do you like making me cry?"

"Stephanie, how can you react like this when all we're doing is going to see Grandma?"

"It's not Grandma; it's the fact that it's Sunday."

"But it's just a few hours."

Something sinks inside Stephanie. A helplessness. "This is how I feel, Mom."

"Well, then you should do something about that. Change the way you feel. You're being ridiculous."

A wave of incredulity washes over Stephanie. "Mom. What about all those times, all those arguments with Dad? That he doesn't understand you. That you can't help what you feel. You should know. You should get what I'm saying. This makes me feel bad.

"We're going to see your Grandma. You love her and she loves you. Why are you giving me such a hard time?"

And suddenly it dawns on Stephanie that every time her mother complained about Dad not getting her, not being considerate, that was her trying to get her way. When the shoe is on the other foot, she makes everything about her. That's how she gets her way. For Stephanie's entire life, Mom has always made it about her. And Stephanie fell for it. And all the work Stephanie ever did, and all the times she put herself aside to help Mom, all the times she sacrificed her time, her precious time, to do what Mom wanted and to make her feel good—that was for nothing. She has never appreciated it, has never noticed that Stephanie was helping. All she wanted was more, more, give me more, Stephanie.

Her mother is inconsiderate, blind, deceitful, and, worse than that, she has ignored Stephanie all her life, ignored who she really is and everything she's done.

I stop.

I need to stop for five minutes.

I sit beside her and look at the rest of her body. There is something gruesome about this. There is something unfair in having such a great body even though you're dead. There's something beautiful in having someone lie there, prone, ready to reveal all her secrets.

What secrets are you hiding? What deep, dark secrets can you tell me?

"I only care about myself," she tells Margaret. They're both fifteen, sitting outside Margaret's house. "I don't care about other people. Everything I do, everything I ever say or do is just a show. Sometimes I forget, I get carried away, and I actually believe what I'm faking."

"Are you faking it with me?" Margaret looks at her, vulnerable.

"No," Stephanie touches her cheek. "I think you're the only person who understands me. I think you're the only person I really love. No one knows that I'm just a phony."

—Another "secret"—

"Jee-zus," Margaret is saying. They're both in her dad's car. Stephanie is driving, her heart is racing. "Am I glad you're driving. I would have hit the dog."

Stephanie missed the dog on the road, but a memory flooded through her mind. Her "secret."

That first day she drove alone in the car, and she ran over a cat. She had seen the cat run into the road and she had swerved. And then she had felt that horrible bump. She hit the brakes and had stopped in the middle of the road.

I see it now—

She steps out and looks back. The cat's head is squished, and the rest of its body keeps trying to walk in the air, jumping, turning, while its head is glued to the road. Five or six other cats gather in the middle of the road, and look at it, not understanding.

The cat's body spasms in place. And it is her fault.

She gets back into the car and drives away.

Fifteen minutes later, she comes back. The cat was is now a piece of meat on the road, having been run over many times now. Even its friends had forgotten it.

She never told anyone. She hated herself over that.

No. These were not as dark as I had hoped. I need to find the right emotion, the right memory or thought that will give me access to the really deep places.

I need to think about this for a day.

All right. That's enough for today. Still. I just want to see one more thing. I just want to see—

—Michael—

—*Michael*—

—*Naked*—

He stands there, naked. I'm sitting in bed, curled up between his sheets, as he gets up to go to his apartment before he goes to his job.

"Michael," I say. Stephanie says. Stephanie.

He looks at her. "Yeah?"

"Before you get dressed, give me my glasses." She points to the table.

He reaches for the table, and I see the folds in his stomach, the ribs stretch. He stops halfway, and looks at her.

"You want to see me get dressed?"

"Yes," she says. Playful. God, she's so happy.

He smiles back. He likes it. He gives her the glasses.

His image becomes clearer still. It didn't look hazy before. Stephanie's mind must have embellished intelligently, accurately, and unconsciously.

He dresses, now turning this into a mock striptease show, teasing her, dancing with his clothes as he slowly gets dressed. He's having a riot. He's so funny.

Once he's dressed, I replay this. As slowly as I possibly can without having her thoughts dissolve into nothing. It's not just the way he looks, it's what she feels, too. It's so amazing. I feel what she feels. As slowly as I possibly can.

Once that's over, I surf to another time, another place, and see him getting undressed, and another time I see her practically ripping his clothes off. I play that slowly as well.

I surf to each spot I can find, to see his body from all possible angles. I see him above her, as they're halfway through sex.

I see him lying down.

I see him getting out of bed, on the way to the bathroom. She checks out his ass, the way his legs look from behind. I see what they look like from the front.

I see her examining him while he sleeps. His hair rumpled; his face even more trouble-free than usual; his eyebrows with a single grey hair; his nose, his nose, his button of a nose; his mouth squished by the pillow; his chin needing a shave; his neck and the wrinkles she sees he'll have in ten years. She pulls away the covers to reveal his chest, smooth and hairless like a nine-year-old's. She peels the blanket from him softly, going down and down and down his body, until she examines his every appendage, his every hair, even his little toes. She takes care to put the cover back on each spot she's through with, so that he won't be cold.

I don't know how much time all of this took, but I have to see one thing. One more thing before I go back to my room.

I want to see her.

I see her standing in front of the mirror before she goes into the shower. She looks at her thighs, checking for fat. She looks at her stomach. She turns around and looks at her behind. She plays with her breasts, moving them to one side, then to another. They're uneven. Everyone's are uneven, but she doesn't like the way one is leaning, lopsided, looking dead. She has no idea how perfect she looks.

But looks change. I surf to other showers, to other times she took off her clothes.

And for some reason, I now center on her face. Every morning, when she wakes up, the first thing she does is go to the mirror to look at her face. Every time she's alone and goes by a mirror, she looks at her face. How tired does she look? Can you see the fight on her? Can you see how hard it is?

No, you can't.

I find a time when she goes on a date, that even she believes herself to be presentable and good-looking. I play her face slowly, looking at every flaw, at every inch, at every . . . at everything. I burn her face into my memory.

—No, you don't look tired, I tell her—

And everything vanishes.

Yeah. Can't talk to her. That was stupid.

I look at the time.

Oh, my god. Oh, my god. Oh. My. God.

Ten minutes to eight. Professor Bendis's class is about to start. I stayed here the entire freaking night, and I'm going to be late for his class. As quickly as humanly possible, I put Stephanie back in. I can't believe I did this. I shut the freezer door and take the key out of my pocket. The entire night! I open the door, go out, shut it, and—Bendis is standing there—I almost scream.

"Ah, Ms. Watson," he says in his calm voice. Oh, shit, I forgot. Class convenes in the *morgue!* A few more minutes, and everybody would have been here. "Working extracurricularly. Excellent."

Bendis turns around. I follow his gaze. Greg is coming. Bendis turns back to me.

"No reason to wait outside," he says. "Let's go in."

Greg looks at me as I follow Bendis.

"What?" I say.

"You're wearing yesterday's clothes."

Oh, god.

"Did you get *lucky* last night?"

Oh, god.

"Ms. Watson."

"Yes, sir?" I just wheeled her back out of the freezer.

"Do you know the name of her childhood friend?"

"Margaret, sir."

"That's right. She believes her father has what sort of complex?"

"Peter Pan, sir."

"That's right. Step back. We won't cover anything you don't know today. Mr. Willis, step forward."

Bendis doesn't let me touch her again during the entire two hours, but the truth is that they do cover things I already know.

The rest of the day I go through the motions all day, doing my best not to fall asleep. But when the last period's over, I go to my dorm room.

I lock the door twice, and put a chair behind the handle to make it impossible for anyone to come in without waking me.

I finally get out of these clothes and take a shower.

I'd like to see Stephanie again. Her emotions are so powerful inside me.

But I'm dead tired.

I collapse in my bed, cover myself with the blanket, and fall asleep.

"Ms. Watson," Bendis's voice is like a hammer. We are all standing over Stephanie's body.

"Yes, Professor Bendis."

"How did this girl die?"

My heart withers under his stare. "What?" It's never crossed my mind.

"You knew so much about her yesterday. Can you tell me how she died?"

How *did* she die? She's around my age. She can't be more than twenty-four. "No, sir."

Bendis looks at the rest. "Anyone?"

Rebecca behind me, raises her hand.

"Yes, Ms. Anthony."

"She committed suicide."

What! I turn to look at her. It's ridiculous!

"That's right," he says, and I spin my head to look back at him. She can't have! Her life is so perfect. She's so. . . .

"How do you know?" Bendis says. "Did you go through the actual moment with her?"

"No, sir. I didn't see it when I was in her head."

"Then how?"

"Her hands," she points to the hands that are now covered. "She slit her wrists. I saw it yesterday, when Alexandra removed the sheet."

What!

"Very good. Sometimes we lean on our abilities too much and forget to look at the physical evidence. There's a lot to be learned just by looking and reasoning." He looks at the entire class again. "Did anyone else notice this?" Silence. "Has anyone gone over any moment from her last days?" Silence.

I can't believe she killed herself. It's just not possible.

"Well, barring incontrovertible telepathic evidence, does anyone have any ideas how this happened to her, just from the physical evidence before us?" I look at the body, and then I notice that Bendis hasn't removed the sheet from her body, on purpose. We can't even see her face.

"Slitting your wrists," I hear Megan behind me. Bendis looks at her. "Sir," she amends herself. "If I may. Slitting your wrists is usually a . . . I heard that it's a cry for help, sir. There are easier and more effective ways to kill yourself."

"That's right. It *was* a call for help. Unfortunately, as we see before us, no one heard it in time." He purses his lips. "Each of you has been in her head at least twice, now, on two different occasions. You had your free roam of her mind. And not one of you saw a problem, a call for help, a deep depression, a hint of the event that ended her life." There's silence, again. "Today we are going to learn to look for signs of trouble, for calls for help, for tendencies toward extreme emotions.

"Ms. Watson!"

"Yes, sir."

He uncovers Stephanie's face. "Tell me how she died."

I look at her face. I take a breath, and take off my glove.

"What are you going to do?" Professor Bendis interrupts just as I'm about to touch her.

"I . . . I was going to look at her last days."

"How?"

"What?"

"How are you going to find her last days?"

"Um. . . . I don't think I have a pain or a feeling that I know corresponds to wanting to take your own life, so I thought I'd take the worst moment I've seen till now in her life, and try to expand on it."

"Which moment?"

"I . . ." I look at him and I don't want to say it.

"Do it."

I cover my eyes. It's not exactly true what I told him. In fact, I'm going to do the opposite.

I touch her.

—I replay the instant in which she had multiple orgasms, in which the pleasure overwhelmed her. And then I reverse it, searching for a lack of it—

She can't breathe, her heart-rate doubles, and it's dark.

What the hell! Her inner gyro says she's in her bedroom, and it's the middle of the night. Her parents are sleeping in the next room.

The scene she's just reacted to happened in her head. Michael's leaving her for good. This would explain his behavior over the past few weeks. Michael's leaving for good.

And for an instant, in her mind, it's true and inevitable.

Her world is so dark. There is no hope. There is no reason to live. There is only pain.

But this isn't it yet. It's not what Bendis wanted. I take the feeling and multiply it a thousand-fold.

Her pain takes my breath away.

And suddenly I see her from the outside. There's no one in the room but us two and she's not covered. I see her naked. I see her guts. I see her soul, her passion, her greatest desires, her pain, oh, how beautiful her pain is, bottomless, perfect, amazing. This pain opens her up to me in ways that couldn't exist if she were alive.

I surf her blackness. It is endless. There is nothing about her I can't know. She's giving me all her secrets. To me. I love her.

More, open up more for me.

The pain multiplies by a multitude. Michael is there, saying "Yes," and suddenly a wave of —of—of—of—of—

of—of—of—of—of—

of—of—of—of—of—

I'm on the floor, pain shooting through my elbow. Rebecca is holding me, half helping me up. I must have fallen.

"What happened?" I whisper.

"Bendis yelled at you to break contact," she heaves me up, then adds, "And when you didn't, he slapped you."

"Are you all right, Ms. Watson?"

"Yes, sir. I'm sorry. I don't know what happened."

"Keep your distance from the body," he says. And I notice I almost grazed her.

"Yes, sir."

"You saw Michael before it happened, didn't you?"

"Yes, sir."

"When Michael said what you saw him say, Stephanie's brain short-circuited from the pain. The same thing almost happened to you, Ms. Watson. She had to live with it. You don't. You weren't even ready.

"Sit the rest of the class out." He points to a chair. "That's enough adventures for one day, Ms. Watson. You'll be fine." Almost in the same breath, he looks aside, and I'm forgotten. "Mr. Crowley, step forward."

"Yes, sir."

"Same assignment. Find what led to her death."

"Yes, sir."

"And Mr. Crowley?"

"Yes, sir?"

"Try not to short-circuit your mind. This is just an assignment."

"Yes, sir."

"Ms. Watson, a word," he says once class is over.

We're all alone. I still have to put the body back in. "Yes, sir."

"You're not hurt." There's no question in his voice, but he's right. The ordeal was over as soon as I sat down.

"Yes, sir."

"This happened because you're identifying with the subject, Ms. Watson. You mistook her feelings for your own, instead of being an observer. That's dangerous with a young woman who killed herself. During our next lesson, we won't be going forward to her last few days. We'll be going *backward*, trying to understand the seeds of the emotions that led to such pain. You're not ready to see her death. Do not try it alone. Do you understand?"

"Yes, Professor."

"Good. Lock up." He walks toward the door, then stops and looks back at me. "By the way, Ms. Watson."

"Yes, Professor?"

"Are you really fine?"

"Yes, sir."

"Good. Then I should tell you . . . I'm gay." So I should stop fantasizing about him. He probably hears me drooling every time he walks into the room.

"Yes, sir." Should I . . . ? Should I tell him? Damn it, yes. "I know, sir."

He smiles, impressed. He knows I got it from his mind and not from physical evidence. "Very good." And he walks out.

That only makes you more attractive, sir.

I rush to Professor Parks's class. I sit through an entire hour and a half, and it's like sitting on a geyser. Once her class is over, I rush out. We get thirty minutes for lunch, but I almost run to my dorm room.

I shut the door, double-lock it. I run to the bathroom, lock *its* door, put down the toilet's lid, and sit on it.

Suddenly my throat constricts and I have to gasp for air.

Stephanie's feelings overwhelm me again. But I'm not touching her, so it's diffused, less powerful than it was. It was a pain worse than loss of hope, worse than loss of a loved one. Her future vanished, and it was as if she had vanished. No, it was even worse. There was no reason for her to live. It was the most basic emotion I have ever felt in a human being. There was no internal reason for her to exist. She ceased to exist at that second.

That was the emotion. Carried to the power of ten.

I didn't see all the events that led to this when I was in her mind. I had to hear it from the class during the rest of the lesson.

Michael has been growing apart, keeping his distance, never initiating a call, but always sounding fine when she called. They hadn't met in weeks. Stephanie had ignored it for as long as she could, but eventually she confronted him. He waffled and stammered, so she said, "Are we through?"

He said, "Yes."

That instant she saw in his eyes how long he had wanted her to know. And she knew she had lost him forever.

And for her, it touched on something primal and ancient. A key turned inside her and the world turned white.

I saw more, though. I felt more before Bendis slapped me. Something in between the whiteness. Something. . . .

I replay the feelings I felt. Piece by piece, I separate some of the emotions. Despair. The return of the ability to think. Walking home. Sinking into bed and out of life. And there are some actual moments in my head, some very clear moments from her last day.

Stephanie was lying on her stomach, face buried in the pillow, hardly breathing, all darkness. The inner gyro says it was her bedroom and that it was after seven p.m. It was dark outside even though she hadn't seen it.

Her mother's voice comes from behind, annoying, unbearable—she's been talking for a while, now.

"I don't know," she says, "what you're going through, or what's so bad. But if you're even thinking about killing yourself" and a shot of electricity goes through Stephanie's spine—she's been thinking exactly that *". . . I want you to know . . . I won't have it. I'll kill myself. I won't have it."*

"Oh, gawd!" Stephanie shouts into the pillow, and her pain is unbearable. This is exactly like her mother. "This isn't about you! Not everything is about you! This is my pain! Stop making everything about yourself!" And she shouts so loudly that she becomes hoarse, having uttered just those words. And without words, she keeps shouting in her head: This is mine. Mine! Don't you get that?

I don't know how this conversation ended. I don't know how it began. But it was close to the end.

There's another memory.

Still in the pillow. Still dark. Later still.

Her father's voice behind her, more reasonable than ever, calmer than ever, "You will come to dinner and you will eat."

Stephanie rolls her eyes, even though he can't see her. Please, please, go away. You don't understand. Go!

"No one cares that you're depressed," he goes on with an emotionless voice. More emotionless than ever, he tries to show her what nothing should feel like. "Depression is a choice. A luxury."

She wants to cry. But it's her father. She worships him. She needs him to understand. "You don't know." Stephanie turns around on the bed, looking at him, her voice plaintive like a six-year-old. "You have no idea what depression is. Or you wouldn't say that. You don't know."

"Ridiculous. I feel as depressed as the other guy. But I do not let it bother me, because I cannot afford to."

"Dad," she bursts into tears, feels the hopelessness of explaining emotion to him, but needing him to get it. "You don't feel as deeply." It's the first time she's ever said this to him. "You don't know what depression is. You don't know what it does to me."

"Depression . . ." his voice grows even colder " . . . is an indulgence, nothing more. Any reasonable person can put it aside."

That's all there is of that memory. I break down into tears.

Her pain is in me. Her pain washes over me and I bathe in it and I can't stop crying and I don't want to. I know that pain. I love that pain. I need that pain. Stephanie understands me. Anyone who feels this understands me.

An hour later I'm still crying, and now I can't stop.

I missed one class. I can't go to the other, even if I do stop crying.

That exhaustion you have after you've cried a lot, they'll feel it, they will all feel it. And see it on my face. And hear it in their heads. I can't go.

I'll stay here, with Stephanie.

Her emotions are better, clearer, stronger, more powerful.

She can handle those emotions that are greater than mine. But not me. I can't even handle my own, stupid world.

This isn't good. It isn't healthy. I . . . I need help.

There's no one to turn to, though. There's no one who will understand. There's no one who. . . .

I walk over to the morgue and unlock the door. I pull her out.

Stephanie. Stephanie. . . .

Have you ever been as alone as I am now?

My hand hovers a few millimeters from her cheek, almost touching.

Have you ever been as desperate?

I almost touch her.

Have you ever needed someone to love you so desperately?

My finger doesn't touch her, but something in the air is—

She collapses on the bed, feeling violated.

My finger wavers in the air and the contact is broken.

Jesus. I need to breathe.

That was like staring into an emotional mirror. She is everything I'm not, and yet she is everything I am, only more. Her emotions are more powerful than my lame ones. She has unreachable depths, whereas I only travel in the shallow end. She has an ability to deal with pain, while I . . . I don't even know who I am.

Help me, Stephanie. Help me!

The door creaks when I open it. I can hear my breath. My chest is tight. Her back is turned to me. She's typing on a computer.

"Professor Parks?"

She swivels in her chair. "Ms. Watson?"

She stands up, extending her hand. I practically jump backward, belatedly realizing that she is wearing gloves.

She pulls back her hand and sits back down. "How can I help you?"

"I . . . It's not important."

"I didn't ask you if it was important, I asked how can I help."

"I . . . I have a question."

"All right."

"I . . . uh." If I ask her, she'll know I'm unstable and kick me out. But if I don't, I'll go crazy, and she'll kick me out. But if I ask her, she'll know I'm unstable. But if I don't, I'll go crazy. But if I ask, she'll know I'm unstable. But if I—

"Ms. Watson?"

"Yes, ma'am?"

"You had a question?"

"No, no, I don't. Thank you."

"Trust me, Ms. Watson," she puts her hand on the table and stares into my soul. "You *had* a question."

"Well, I did, but it's not important now."

"Still. I want to hear it."

Oh, damn.

"Ms. Watson?"

"Well, see, if I ask it now, it'll be magnified and it'll seem like this huge thing, when it's this really, really small question."

"I see. That's fine." She swivels back, and starts typing again. "You have a question for me, Ms. Watson, and you're not leaving this room before you ask me a question. I don't care if it's the question you came in here to ask or another question. But you're going to ask me a question." And on she types, not looking at me.

"I have another question," I say.

"All right." Her back is still turned. She's still typing something on her computer. "Ask away."

"It's a theoretical question."

"Good."

"Is it possible . . . ?" Something in me sinks. She's going to know.

"Is it possible?" she reiterates.

Just plod on. Just plod on. Just plod-plod-plod on. "For someone. . . ."

"For someone," she repeats softly, as she searches for a function key. She finds it and presses it, "A-ha!"

"To become the person you're. . . . To have her thoughts overtake you?"

Parks swivels on her chair, looks at me, and says simply, "No." She turns back to the screen. "There. You're free to leave now, if you want."

"Thank you." She's all right.

I'm near the door, when she says, "Alexandra?"

Alexandra?

"Yes, Professor Parks?" She's facing me, leaning closer. I can feel that her mood is soft and smooth.

"It's like this. Your brain is your own. You cannot become a different person. When we feel someone else's thoughts or emotions, we simply find the corresponding thoughts or emotions in us. If it doesn't exist in us, then we can't feel it. Everything goes through *your* mind, and every emotion is actually yours. That's why even with telepaths we don't know that the pain someone else feels is the pain you feel. We still don't know if we see the color red in the same way. Because when we read someone's mind, we interpret it through our own mind and emotions. So, no, it's not possible to become someone other than yourself. It is possible, however, that you need a gigantic hug."

I laugh and look down.

"Well, I'm not allowed to hug you." She stands up. "But I *am* allowed to feed you." I look at her, surprised.

"I'm on my way out to the city. There's a fantastic fish restaurant there, my treat."

"But . . ."

"I'm not going to touch you. I'm not going to read your mind. I'm not going to delve into your business. I am going to *feed* you." She saves her document and turns off her screen. "And anything we say . . ." she turns off the light in the room and leads me out ". . . will not be held against us. All right?"

"I . . . I don't. . . ."

"Say 'yes.'" She likes me. I can feel it.

"Yes."

"Good. Let's go."

She's got a ten-year-old Mazda that smells new.

Inside the car feels like outside the Academy. I lie back and sink into the seat. She drives us around the Academy and toward the gate.

The same guard that let me in that first day is there now. He opens the gate as we approach.

I look at him. I don't think he can see me through the tinted glass.

We are outside the Academy. We are outside the Academy.

I shut my eyes and melt into the soft cushions.

Bright lights. The smell of smog. Young men and women walking the streets in immodest clothes. Civilization. It's like I've been in the jungle for two years.

The restaurant is full of people, but there's still room inside and outside. I ask Professor Parks to sit outside. I want to soak in the atmosphere.

"You have no privacy when you're a telepath," Professor Parks says after we've ordered. "Normal people can relish in not knowing. We can't afford that luxury.

"When your boyfriend makes love to you, he touches you, and you see everything he feels and everything he thinks about you. It's never as perfect as you would like. It's ugly and spotty and sketchy. When you're insecure, you touch him and you know he doesn't like you as much now as he did yesterday, and that if you tell him what you know, he'll like you even less. You see the parts about you he can't stand, and you see the parts he can't get enough of. You know what he fantasizes about you, and you know when he fantasizes about someone else. And when he makes love to you, you see your body while you're doing it, and you know that your right breast looks strange, that you gained two pounds, that your legs don't look flattering from most angles, that you need to shave again, and what your breath smells like. And you know that what he really likes about you is that you remind him of the buxom sixteen-year-old babysitter he used to have when he was a kid, and that, even though he doesn't know it, he's still in love with his first girlfriend, with whom he's never been able to get along.

"And the hard thing is to learn that it's always like this. Even 'as good as it can possibly get' is like this. You have to learn that this is the truth and that this is normal. You have to abandon the lies when you're a telepath and start living in the real world."

A waiter brings our drinks. She thanks him and he walks away.

"We have to face each mask and make it vanish. We have to clear everything. All the subterfuge we feed ourselves with. We have to dig under all the tasks we set for ourselves, under all the complexes and falsehoods and false reactions we have set up while we were growing up. We have to learn to clear everything away. Sometimes it feels like you're wiping your entire personality away. But then you realize—you have to realize—that whatever's left, that's you, that's really you.

"If you go through it, Alexandra, if you go through the entire four years—and

I know you can—you wouldn't believe the person you'll become. You wouldn't believe the strength that comes from having no secrets, from knowing so much about yourself. From knowing that when you speak, you don't lie.

The waiter brings in the food. The Professor has sea scallops and I have Alaskan king salmon. On her. She recommended it.

"Thank you," she tells the waiter. Then, as he leaves, she makes a face and drops her fork. "Bathroom." She smiles at me. "Be right back."

I nod.

I take the opportunity to look around and look at the people in the street. Shirts made of nets, crazy tattoos, wild haircuts, teenagers younger and younger, looking older and older.

Two minutes ago, the couple behind me got up and left. The couple in front of me, behind where Professor Parks sat, is getting up now. We're going to be just the two of us outside. It's getting cold. But I just want to keep looking at the people, to feel the whiff of haphazard thoughts whenever one of them gets too close. To look at what they're wearing.

Michael almost bumps into the couple that's leaving on his way out of the restaurant. That was awkward. He smiles his usual worry-free smile, and—huh?

Michael?

Those same features, that same face, that—

I never thought of him as alive. But of course he's alive. Of course he's real. They're all real people. Everyone's still alive, except Stephanie.

I stand up. Michael keeps his back to me, makes sure the woman is fine, and exits the restaurant. Once on the sidewalk, he comes in my direction. As he passes near me, I get a perfect view of those clear, lovely, baby-blue eyes. The eyes that shine "happy" at you when you wake beside him in the morning.

He looks at me then looks past me.

He didn't recognize me. But why should he? I sit back down. I won't look back. I won't look back.

Professor Parks returns.

"So," she says. "Can I tell you something about myself?"

We get back into her car. It's twenty minutes till we're out of the city, another ten until the scenery becomes green again, and another ten before we're at the Academy's gate.

We don't talk much.

The gate opens automatically for her.

"Wait," I say. She looks at me. "Can I get out here?"

"What?"

"Since I'm *out*, I'd like to go see some people I know."

"Are you sure?"

"I have a few dollars on me. I can get around. Just drop me here."

She thinks about it for a second, then says, "Sure."

I let myself out. "Thank you," I lean back in, the door still open. "Thank you."

She smiles and crinkles her eyes. Then she looks forward, and says, "I'm tired. See you tomorrow."

"Thank you," I say again and close the door.

She drives through the entrance, and the gate slowly rolls shut again. The guard looks at me, but keeps his distance.

I look around. I don't have a cell on me, and I don't know the number of a cab company.

I walk over to the guard. "Excuse me," I say. "Can you call me a cab?"

"Where are we going?" the cab driver says.

"Back to the city," I say. "1421 North Shadeland Avenue." Stephanie's home.

I ring the doorbell. No, no, I should go. Go, I should go. Just go, just go, just. . . .

Someone touches the handle on the other side of the door. Fuck me. Fuck me. Fuck, fuck, fuck me.

The door opens slowly. I put on my best smile.

I see Mom's face in the doorway, looking up at me, wrinkled, old, the way Stephanie couldn't see her. She literally has half Stephanie's face, something Stephanie never noticed.

She looks up at me, with her green eyes, and they've almost lost all of the shine and softness they had when she was in her late twenties and Stephanie was only a kid.

"Yes?" she says. Her voice is a rasp. Did I wake her? No, she doesn't go to sleep before midnight.

"Yes?" she says again.

My mouth is dry. I lick my lips. Help.

"Who are you?" she says.

"I . . ." I'm sorry, Stephanie's Mom. I'm sorry.

"What's your name?" Her voice grows more suspicious, and it's back to sounding like the voice I know. "What's your name, girl?"

"Alexandra Watson."

"What are you doing here? It's late."

"I'm . . . I'm . . . Stephanie!"

Her eyes dim at the mention of her name. "What?"

"Stephanie. I. . . ."

"You knew Stephanie?"

"Yes." Yes! "I was . . . I was her friend. I was her best friend."

Something happens to her mom's eyes that Stephanie doesn't recognize. Does she see the lie? It's the truth. I'm sorry. "I'm sorry." I *am* sorry.

"Come in," she says.

"I was in New York. I just got back to Indianapolis a couple of minutes. . . ."

"Come in," she says and moves aside, clearing the way for me.

Jesus. I know this living room. I know its smell. The memories give the living room a claustrophobic feeling, hemming me in on all sides.

She grew up here. I've seen the walls change over two decades, I've seen the room shrink as she got older. The wallpaper was ugly green when she grew up, until her mom replaced it with elephants, and later still with brown geometrical shapes. I've seen five different television sets where the current one sits.

"Charles," she says. And he turns around.

And Charles, Stephanie's dad, sits there on the sofa in front of the television set. He looks at me. Perfectly shaven. Not typical for this time of day. They must have had guests.

They had. Obviously they had. They're in mourning.

"This is Stephanie's friend," Sylvia introduces me. "Uh. . . ."

"Alexandra, sir."

I offer my gloved hand. He shakes it.

"You're . . . Stephanie's friend?"

"Yes, that's right."

"From the university?"

"Yes, yes. We took communication studies. We had the same classes, and we just. . . ." I blank out. I just shrug, "You know." Her mother nods in understanding. Her father is looking at me. "She told me everything about you two. Charles . . ." he nods ". . . and Sylvia."

"She told you everything about *us*?" she asks.

Oh, no. "She told me everything about everything. We talked for hours." Sylvia looks around, wiping her moist hands on her clothes. Oh. She didn't catch me in something, she was making it about herself again.

"Would you like. . . . Would you like something to drink?" Sylvia asks. "We have tea, we have. . . ."

"Tea would be great, thank you. With nothing in it."

Sylvia turns and goes to the kitchen.

"There were a few people here earlier," her dad says. "But they're gone. I'm not sure what we can offer you. . . ."

"Oh, Charles," her mom shouts from the kitchen. "She just flew in. We're not going to drive her out. . . ."

"I'm not saying that. I'm just saying I don't know what we can . . ." and I can see that he changes his mind in mid-sentence, and says something else, ". . . talk about." He breathes deeply and turns around. "We have a few albums of her over here," he points. "And . . . her friends did some sort of a shrine in her room. It's . . ." he points ". . . through there."

I look up. That familiar small corridor that leads to Stephanie's bedroom on one side and to her parents' bedroom on the other. "Can I look at the albums?"

"Of course."

He leads me to a little stand near the TV, filled with albums. I sit on the floor and take an album. He sits back on the sofa, and mutes the television. I take an album and look at him again. He's still watching TV, he just muted it.

I open the first page. Stephanie at seven days, I've seen this picture a million times. She's as cute as can be, the perfect baby.

Baby Stephanie breastfed by her mother on the porch. Oh, my god, look at Sylvia. She's not even my and Stephanie's age; she's younger. She's a little kid. In a couple of years, when Stephanie will have clear images of her mother in her memory, she'll be this huge giant of a grownup. We'd never seen Sylvia like this.

Four-year-old Stephanie running through the tall grass. I remember the day they took the picture. Mom kept telling her to run and run, and Stephanie did, chasing after a butterfly she made up, performing for her mother. She's so carefree, so happy. I'll have to check with Stephanie, later, and see what changed, how could she have grown up and had the happiness sucked out of her.

Stephanie's first bike. I remember the day Dad took the training wheels off and had to run after her for an hour.

The entire family at a beach in San Diego. Look at Dad. He's like he's a different person. Pretty handsome, too. His legs were like elephant-legs to Stephanie. She used to run in between them as if they were a tunnel.

Sylvia's coming closer. I turn around and look up. She's holding a cup of hot tea.

"Thank you," I take the hot tea.

Sylvia sits on the edge of Charles's couch, looking at me.

"How did you two meet?"

"I met her during our first day as freshmen. On the way to western lit."

"You became friends?"

I nod. "She was an amazing woman. She was my best friend."

"Did you.... Did you know about.... Did you know she was going to...." She trails off.

"I know about Michael," I say. And she looks into my eyes. Oh, my god, she's asking me if I could have stopped it. "But.... By phone. And.... All I knew was that it was big. I didn't know that it was *this* big."

She sits by me. I sip the tea. It's too hot. I want to look at the album, but she's looking at me expectantly. She always gives this look when she has something to say but would rather force the other person to ask her what it is.

I look at her for a few more seconds, and when she says nothing, I turn back to the album.

I can't take it. I can't take her looking at me. I can feel her desire to say something. I can feel her pain all the way over here.

"Um...." I face her again. "Can I go to the bathroom? I'm a bit...."

"Sure," she stands up. "Through there."

I put the cup down, get up, and walk through the corridor.

My hand hangs on the handle, and I look around. They can't see me from here. Behind me and to the other side is Stephanie's room. I can say I made a mistake, that I didn't know where the bathroom was.

I shut my eyes.

Who cares? *I* don't.

I walk to the door of Stephanie's room and open it slowly.

Oh, god. It feels like her. It smells like her. It's slightly bigger than I thought, but that's because I'm shorter than her.

That smell. Slight draft of dust from the bookshelf mingled with a whiff of Margaret's perfume. She was here recently.

Her bed is to one side. I can still see stuff under Stephanie's bed, a hint of the teddy bear she'd had since she was a kid. I bend down and look. She dropped it there a few hours before Michael broke up with her. After Michael broke up with her, it didn't matter.

I bend down, and pick it up. It's tattered, but still soft and familiar and friendly.

I put it back in its place.

"The bathroom's over there," I hear Sylvia at the door.

"I know," I turn around. "I just saw the room. I had to come in."

She walks in and sits on Stephanie's bed. "You remind me of Stephanie."

"I do?"

"Something about you looks like. . . ." Oh, gee. "Oh. You blink like her."

"I what?"

"You blink like her. No, it's not that. It's when she was embarrassed, she always blinked to cover it, and crooked her head, just like you're doing now."

I catch myself. I never *used* to do that. I must have picked it up from Stephanie. And, more embarrassed than before, I do it again. I've been picking up the way she moves.

"I think I got it from her. It's easy to pick up."

Sylvia shrugs. "Well, it makes you look like her."

I feel myself going red. "Thank you."

I look around.

I can't look at the room when she's here. But I feel closer to her, now.

"Sit," she taps the bed beside her.

I sit next to her.

We just sit there, silent. I stare at a spot on the wall ahead of me, afraid to make a wrong move.

It's so silent, I can hear her breaths. I can hear that they're harder than they used to be. I feel the rhythm change in the way she breathes. I try to breathe as noiselessly as possible. The fridge in the kitchen kicks in again. Her father is turning on the television sound. I hear the sofa creak beneath him as he changes position.

"Well," Sylvia says.

I lower my eyes. "I'm sorry." It's the only thing I can think of to say. And then the tears come, "I miss her. I miss her."

And beside me, without touching her, I feel Sylvia's bitterness a second before the words reach me. "She did it to spite me."

My heart stops. "What?" And I look at her.

"We had an argument. That last day. A few hours before."

Oh my god.

"What. . . ." I can't say it, but I have to. "What was it . . . about?"

"She was depressed because Michael broke up with her. And I came in . . . to help. And she yelled at me. All the anger and pain she had for Michael, she took out on me."

"Sylvia, I mean. . . . She was depressed. Because of Michael." I find the most harmless way to phrase it, and I say it with the softest voice I have, "It wasn't about you."

"I knew she was depressed," her voice drops to a whisper, although there is no one else in the room. "I knew she had depressions. I thought. . . ." She bites her lips. "I thought she might kill herself." She waits for a response. I don't give any. "I told her how much it would hurt me. I told her that's not what you do to people you love. I told her how hard we would all take it." She grabs my hand and stares into my eyes. Thank god I'm wearing gloves. "And she did it anyway. She didn't reason, she didn't wait for it to pass. She did it anyway. I told her how much it would hurt me, and she went and did it. She did it to hurt me."

"No, Sylvia. I know Stephanie. She would never do anything to hurt you. This was about . . ."

"You know her from now. I've known her a lot longer than you. It was the same argument we've always had, only now she found a way to blame me and to keep on blaming me forever. She wants me to walk around blaming myself for the rest of my life. That would make her feel good."

No, no, you're getting it all wrong. "Sylvia," I gently caress the fingers that touch me. "We talked about you a lot." There's a flash of danger in her eyes. "No, nothing bad. She said nothing bad. She loved you, and I know—I know, Sylvia— that what she did, it wasn't meant to show you a thing. If anything, it was meant to show you that it wasn't about you."

"She wanted to hurt me . . . ," self-pity gushes out of her, ". . . and she did." Her mouth turns into a cynical smile. "Well done." It's still all about her. It's still all about Sylvia, and nothing about Stephanie, nothing about Stephanie's pain.

"Sylvia," I'm fighting myself to keep my voice soft and encouraging. "You're talking as if this was just another argument with you two, just a bigger one. But this is so big. Can't it be that it was about something else entirely?"

"You weren't here," she states emphatically. She turns her back to me and gets up. "Anyway, what does it matter now?" She straightens her clothes, and whispers. "I'll never forgive her."

I want to cry. She committed suicide—Stephanie gave her life—and you can't even hear what she was saying. It was in front of your face, and you're treating it like it's the same old same-old, damn you!

"What does it matter why she did it?"

We both turn around. Charles is standing by the door. He's looking at Sylvia, speaking to her, not to me. "It was the easy way out."

"The easy way out?" The words are out of my mouth before I realize I'm talking. "It was the bravest thing she ever did!"

Sylvia looks at me, shocked, but Charles, behind her, says, "Brave? It would have been brave to stay alive another day. She didn't. It would have been brave to go to the university again. She didn't. It would have been brave to strive, to survive. But Stephanie. . . . She ran away. From responsibility, from friendship, from pain, from facing her fears. She ran away. The way cowards do."

"But. . . . You don't know what a bad state she was in. You don't know what great pain she was in."

"How much pain could she possibly have been in? Her boyfriend broke up with her."

"To some people, that's life and death."

"I've known heartache. Trust me when I say you can walk away from it alive."

"When she went through it, Charles, her pain was so huge, it was so awful, that she killed herself. Otherwise, like you say, she would never have killed herself. The fact that she did take her life shows you how awful her pain was."

"No. She killed herself because she was a coward. It had nothing to do with her depression."

That bastard! He won't admit it!

"I really think we should not be talking about. . . ." Sylvia steps between us.

But I practically shove her aside. The man drives me so crazy. "You never believed she felt what she felt! You've been delegitimizing her emotions since she was a kid! She killed herself to show you how *strongly* she felt! She killed herself because her pain was so great that none of us could understand it!"

He snorts. "I thought you said she killed herself to show me how strongly she felt." He looks down, and I can feel how much he needs a smoke. He looks back up and says softly, "You don't know what you're talking about." God, how he needs a smoke. "She was weak. She was always weak. She always ran away from problems. She never had the heart to face them. That's what happened."

What the hell is this? The Spanish Inquisition to your recently dead daughter? It's like she died for nothing! It's like she lived for nothing! Weren't any of you listening when she cut herself and bled to death!

"Look." I hear tears in my throat. "She was the bravest woman I've ever met."

He shrugs. He doesn't care to talk to me anymore.

"Look," I force him to look at me. "Give me one time that she ran away. One incident!"

He half turns away. "What does it matter?"

"Because!" And it sounds like I'm speaking each word separately as I say, "You don't remember her right. You don't understand her. You have to remember . . ." and I almost lose my voice ". . . who she was!" I feel tears coming, and I can't stop them. "There's a great hole in the world, and it's shaped like Stephanie! She's gone and the world has changed and none of you can see it! She's gone and the world is different!"

"Alexandra. . . ." Sylvia takes a step toward me.

"The world is different," I back away, half-screaming, tears streaming down my cheeks, "but you're both the same! What's the matter with you people!"

"Alexandra. . . ." Sylvia gently brushes away a tear from my cheek. I get a whiff of paranoia—a fear so powerful it taints every image I see. I shove her hand aside quickly, and, backing away, I fall onto Stephanie's bed. The familiar sheets embrace me. The mattress bends to fit my body again. Sylvia takes a step closer. I turn around, and scream into the pillow.

"Leave us here," I hear Sylvia say.

The feeling I get from Charles grows distant. He's walking away.

"Take as much time as you need, dear."

She stays for a minute, her hand on the back of my shirt. Eventually, she stands up and walks away. She turns off the light and then shuts the door.

I take a huge whiff of the pillow and stretch out on the bed. I take the blanket, fork it in between my legs, just the way she used to, and hug it.

Stephanie! Stephanie will show them. She'll show them.

There are birds chirping outside, and light blinds me when I try to open my eyes.

Oh my god! I sit up, ramrod straight.

What's the damned time?

I almost choke. Five thirty! And I'm not even. . . . And I slept in my clothes. . . . And I slept in her room. . . . Hi, room. . . . And I yelled at her parents. . . . And I need to see Stephanie. . . . Dammit, I need to go.

I stand up and straighten my clothes. I straighten the mattress and the bed.

They couldn't possibly have left me here without looking in. Sylvia must have come in to check on me at least once and seen me asleep. She let me sleep in her daughter's bed. Jesus.

I don't want to see them again.

I cling to the door, trying to feel if anyone's there.

Nothing. I'm not getting anything. Either they're asleep or not home.

I straighten the mattress and the put the pillow back in the room. I look at the room.

Bye, room.

I open the door. Silence. I walk into the living room, and, as silently as possible, I call a cab.

I go past the guard at six fifteen a.m.

There's plenty of time. But I can't, I can't, I can't go to the morgue in the same clothes again.

I go to my dorm, take the quickest shower I've ever taken, get dressed, take my cell phone, and get to the morgue at fifteen minutes to seven.

I unlock the door as quickly as I can, close it behind me, and go for the freezer. I wheel her out and remove the sheet.

Oh, that face. I love, I love, I love that beautiful face.

I take off my glove and stare at her.

Show me they're wrong, Stephanie. Let's go through the end again. Show me how powerful your pain was.

I touch her, readying myself for the shock I felt yesterday. And. . . .

Nothing.

What? No!

I play another emotion in my head.

Nothing. She lies there, unmoving, beautiful.

Still touching her, I replay a memory I've gone through.

Nothing.

Dammit!

Bendis said we usually had a week, well, six days, and it's only been four! You can't do this to me!

I try again.

Nothing.

Please.

Nothing.

No! I didn't get everything from her! I didn't get her essence into me! I'm missing memories! I'm missing experiences! You can't disappear on me, Stephanie. You have to let me remember you. You have to let me carry on your memories forever.

I touch her again.

The coldness of her cheek hurts me. There is nothing.

There is nothing left of her.

Oh, god.

There's a hole in the world, and it has Stephanie's shape.

There's a hole in the world. There's a hole in the world.

I didn't get all of her. Oh, god, I didn't get all of her.

I leave the lifeless body in the fridge. I lock the door behind me and just stand there.

What time is it?

Seven a.m.

Maybe I should try again?

Leave her alone, she's gone.

My stomach tightens.

Parks. Yes. Professor Parks touched her, and she's my friend.

I walk up to her office.

It's closed. What time is it? Seven-oh-eight.

I'll wait.

There's probably a procedure about what to do with the dead bodies. As soon as the rest of them find out about her, I'll probably have to go with the wagon or burn the body or something.

Maybe I should try to touch her again?

Leave her alone. Leave her alone. Stephanie's not there anymore.

What time is it?

I sense Professor Parks coming from around the corner.

She appears around the corner, surprised to see me.

"Stephanie is gone," I tell her.

There's a flash of something in her eyes, but I can't detect what it is. She looks at me and, at length, says, "I'm sorry."

She takes out her keys and opens her office. She walks in. I follow her. She settles in the chair behind her desk.

"I need your help." I say.

She looks up at me, and I still can't sense anything she's feeling. "How can I help you?" she asks, her words deliberate.

"You read her mind."

"I did."

"And you probably read more of her memories than I did. You've seen more of her emotions. You read her more deeply than I did."

"It stands to reason."

"Please . . . I need to see who she was. I need to see her core."

She leans back, and as she changes into her teacher mode, she lets slip some worry. "What do you mean when you say 'her core?'" And her question is so cold that it's as if she asked for a definition.

"I mean her *soul*, the center of everything she was. The core that made her. . . . Her core."

Parks leans forward. "Sit down."

I sit down and lean forward, my right hand on her desk. She looks at my hand. "Take off your glove."

And suddenly I'm afraid she'll know about last night. But I have to do this.

I have to know. I do as she says.

"Put your hand back on the desk."

I put it on the desk.

She takes off the glove on her left hand. My heart hammers. I can't let her know! I can't!

"I'm not going to touch you," she says, as she slowly puts her hand down, fingers spread, a few millimeters from mine.

"From this distance, with my ability, we're safe. I only feel what you want me to feel, and you only feel what I want you to feel. Let's test it."

And suddenly I'm smack inside Stephanie's and Michael's kiss. I feel his tongue inside mine, I feel the buzz it gave her, and it feels like blood actually fills her eyes and blots her eyesight. She slides her cheek down the wall of her bedroom slowly, playing that kiss again, exhilarated, fearful.

And then it's gone. That was her.

Thank you! I send her waves of gratitude.

She ignores them and says, "What do you mean when you say 'her core?' Give me an example." And with her eyes she gestures at my fingers.

When did I feel it? When did I not feel it?

She's looking at her eyes in the mirror. So ugly, so disgusting, she thinks.

"It's the power of her emotion!" I say. "The way she hates hers. . . ."

"Don't use words," she says. "Give me another example."

"Oh, gawd!" Stephanie shouts into the pillow, and her pain is unbearable. This is exactly like her mother. "This isn't about you! Not everything is about you! This is my pain! Stop making everything about yourself!" And she shouts so loudly that she becomes hoarse, having uttered just those words. And without words, she keeps shouting in her head: This is mine. Mine! Don't you get that?"

Did she see? I look into Parks's eyes. There's something noble in the pain. Something so deep. . . .

It slips out of me before I can finish my sentence—

She looks at her body before she dresses for the date with Michael, checking for spots, blemishes, new fat, old fat, each depressing her more, each an impossible hurdle. Will he notice? Will he still like me?

Beyond my control, faster than I can think—

I'm sweating in my bra, and it's not even hot. My panties are too tight in one place and too baggy in another. My dress is too conservative. They're going to know.

I pull my hand away. "I'm sorry. That was mine. I'm sorry."

"That's all right. I think I understand what you're saying. Put your hand back in place. This time it will be my turn to transmit." I put my hand back on the table, a millimeter away from her fingers. The part closest to the tip of her closest finger is slightly warmer, but I feel nothing else.

"Tell me if I have it right," she says.

And suddenly I'm Stephanie, again. It begins slowly—Parks is giving me a chance to look around.

Stephanie is nervous because of Mrs. Wright. She's been ordered to stay after school to talk to her about her behavior. We're in the eighth grade, now. Stephanie is thirteen.

Before Mrs. Wright got a chance to bawl Stephanie out, her cell phone rang, and she answered it. Her boyfriend is breaking up with her.

Events speed up to normal. Mrs. Wright is still talking to her boyfriend.

"No, come on." She glances at Stephanie in fear, then turns her back to her and lowers her voice. "Let's talk about this later, but let's not decide until we talk about this." And Stephanie felt the pain in Mrs. Wright's voice.

"Come on, Steve. . . ." And in Mrs. Wright's cracked voice, Stephanie recognized her own feelings. Too many of them. Mrs. Wright is like a future Stephanie. It made her want to cry.

And it disappears.

I look up at Professor Parks. "Yes!" I whisper at her. "That was it! That was the same emotion! Right there at the end. . . ."

Professor Parks purses her lips, and—

Stephanie is home, again. I have time to feel the inner gyro. She's almost seven. Mom and Dad are—

"I don't want a clown!"

"But clowns are fun and funny and you wanted a birthday just like everyone else," Dad reasons calmly. Mom and Dad are standing over her, telling her what they have planned for her seventh birthday.

"I don't want a clown!" Can't they understand how sad clowns make me feel? "I don't want a clown!" They make me cry! Can't you see? Don't you believe me? And in frustration, she begins to stomp the ground with her feet and shout, out of control and in tears: "I don't want a clown! I don't want a clown! I don't want a clown!"

And it's gone. That was the emotion. It was the precisely the same emotion that came at the end of the last incident. Without Parks I would never have thought to look in places like this, but that's not why she showed this to me.

I look into her eyes. I think she's taking me back in time! I think she's taking me down to Stephanie's core!

And suddenly Stephanie is four years old and she's at eye-level with Mom's bed. Mom is lying on the bed. There is sun outside. It's almost noon. Mom is lying there, on her stomach.

"Mom, let's go outside! Let's do a picnic! Let's sit in the sun!" And that emotion is

here again! She feels pleasure and fun and joy. No, that's not true. She's faking it. She wants her mother to feel that.

Mom lifts herself slightly and gives Stephanie a questioning look, her face mooshy from sleep.

"Come on!" Stephanie tries to excite Mom. "It's such a great day!"

Events zip in fast-forward, at Parks's behest—

I see Mom getting up, and setting up a picnic outside.

Parks slows down events—

Mom is hugging me. "You are so pretty and lovely. You're the best and wonderfulest little girl in the world. What would I do without you to keep me sane?"

And suddenly events zip back, in quick rewind—

Before the picnic, before Mom got off the bed, before Stephanie woke her up, before Stephanie walked into the room—

Stephanie stands in front of Mom's closed bedroom door, about to come in and wake her. Something is wrong. Something is wrong with Mom again. No: Mom is in pain.

She looks at the door, and chooses to go in.

Stephanie decides to go in. She shoves everything she feels aside, and puts on her cute face. She opens the door. . . .

And it's gone.

"There were hundreds of these incidents all through her childhood," Parks says. "Stephanie's mother was deeply depressed. When she congratulated Stephanie the way she did she made Stephanie responsible for her happiness. Stephanie felt she bore responsibility for her mother's good mood. And, eventually, for everyone's good mood."

I look at her. "But . . . that wasn't it."

She smiles. "I know." She leans closer and her smile grows wider. "That's the point. Watch."

"I don't want a clown!" They can't understand how sad clowns make me feel. (The pain hits her. I can distinguish it better the second time around.) "I don't want a clown!" They make me cry! (Pain!) Can't you see? (Pain!) Don't you believe me?

"I (Pain!) don't want a clown! I don't want (Pain!) a clown! I don't want (Pain!) a clown!"

And it's gone.

"Was that the same thing you felt before?" Parks asks me.

I crinkle my eyes. "Yes."

"Did you see it more clearly now?"

"Yes." What does she want from me?

"Did you see the pain?"

"Yes."

"Did you recognize it?"

"No."

"All right."

She blinks and—

"Oh, gawd!" (Stephanie shouts at her mother. We're back to the day she died, again.)
"This isn't about you! (Pain!) Not everything is about you! (Pain!) This is my (Pain!) pain!
Stop making everything (Pain!) about yourself! (Pain!)" And she shouts so loudly that she
becomes hoarse, having uttered just those words. And without words, she keeps shouting
in her head: This is mine. (Pain!) Mine! (Pain!) Don't you get (Pain!) that?

And the scene changes—

She looks at her body (Pain!) before she dresses for the date with Michael (Pain!),
checking for spots (Pain!), blemishes (Pain!), new fat (Pain!), old fat (Pain!), each carries
its own series of these pains. Will he notice? (Pain!) Will he still like me? (Pain!)

"Wait," I move my hand away.

She looks at me patiently.

I recognize the pain. When four-year-old Stephanie opened the door, when she shoved her emotions aside, there was a feeling of loss at losing yourself, at pushing yourself aside. That was the pain that was flooding her all the time now, in her grownup life.

I look at Parks. I want to ask her to play it again for me. But I don't need her for this.

"Oh, gawd!" (Stephanie shouts at her mother. We're back to the day she died, again.)
"This isn't about you! (Pain!) Not everything is about you! (Pain!) This is my (Pain!) pain!
Stop making everything (Pain!) about yourself! (Pain!)" And she shouts so loudly that she
becomes hoarse, having uttered just those words. And without words, she keeps shouting
in her head: This is mine. (Pain!) Mine! (Pain!) Don't you get (Pain!) that?

Stephanie's pain, her great pain, that great, bottomless depth it had—it dissolves before me now, made of smaller, completely trivial pains.

I look at Parks, my hand wavering out of her reach. "Wait," I say. "Wait."

Let's try something else.

"Stephanie," her mother says. "How can you react like this when all we're doing is
going to see Grandma?" (Pain!)

"It's not Grandma, it's the fact that it's Sunday."

"But (Pain!) it's just a few hours." (Pain!)

Something sinks inside Stephanie. It's that sense of feeling the door, replayed. She has
to shove herself aside, she has to put herself on hold. She is so helpless. "This is how I feel,
Mom." And she is in greater pain because she knows her mother will never understand.

Because inside she knows her mother will need her to put herself aside again.

It can't be! Her pain was so important to her! It defined her! It defined her personality! It was there every second of her life!

No. I run everything I've seen of her in my head, and everything is different now.

Stephanie was wrong.

Everything she understood was wrong. Everything she felt was wrong. Everything she had felt was so trivial, so ridiculous. It all boiled down to nothing.

But. . . .

"Professor Parks . . ." And she looks at me with patience. "Professor Parks, Stephanie's pain, the reason I liked it so much . . . I also have it. I also have that same pain. *All the time!* Are you saying that everything *I* have, everything *I* feel is *wrong?*"

Professor Parks looks at me for a second, and then she smiles graciously. "Welcome," she says, "to the Indianapolis Academy."

God.

"It's not true!" I scream. I am so weak. "I am *not* dust! I am not *nothing!*"

Professor Parks doesn't move.

That's it. She's done with me. She just sits there and looks at my face. Why would she even talk to me? Why would anyone love me?

But someone does love me. Or at least he did love me. I have to call him. I have to see him. I have to feel his touch again.

Not even looking at Professor Parks, I run out of her office and into the hall. I run through the corridor as I take out my cell phone and dial his number.

I press "Send" only once I'm out of the hall, on the grounds, alone.

It's ringing.

"Yeah," he answers, always sounding the same, always sounding cheerful and carefree.

"Michael," my voice breaks. I'm not sure he heard me. "Michael. It's me."

"I'm sorry, I don't recognize the voice."

"I, uh, I'm sorry. It's me, uh, uh, uh, Alexandra. I'm . . . Stephanie's friend."

And the temperature drops on the other end of the phone.

"Yeah," he says, his voice different.

"I need to meet you. I need to talk with you about something. Now." He hesitates for a split-second, so I push on. "John's Café?" Five minutes from the university, where he teaches.

"I'm giving a lecture in an hour."

I can't tell anything from his voice. Which probably means that he really doesn't want to do this. I have to see you! "Thirty minutes, then?"

Slight hesitation. "All right."

"Good. Thank you." And I hang up immediately.

I am *not* nothing!

I see him coming into the café.

He looks around. I've seen you naked, guy. I could pick your body from a police line-up.

Now he looks for women sitting alone. There's only me. He's coming over.

Suddenly I realize I have nothing to say to him. There is nothing I could say.

He stops beside me. "Alexandra?"

Quickly, I remove my gloves underneath the table. I stand up and offer my hand. He takes it.

And I am inside him. I don't care what he feels or what he thinks right now. All I care about is finding an image of Stephanie—There!—and replacing me with her image.

For a second, he's stunned at seeing Stephanie in front of him. But he doesn't let go of my hand.

And I use that to see . . .

Stephanie—

Stephanie!—

Naked—

And I see him watch Stephanie take off her clothes for the first time. The way her legs go all the way up, the way there's a little fat, just as you reach the crotch. He loves that small ring of fat so much, finds the space between that and her panties, that space through which light gets through from behind, so appealing.

And I feel how badly he was attracted to her then. And I make him feel it again, now, for me, standing in front of him.

"Hug me, Michael." I cling to him. "Hug me. Hug me." And he does. Tightly, so tightly.

And his cheek touches my forehead.

I surf to the moment he first saw her, sitting among five other women he didn't know. And her image practically leapt at him, touched him, showing something in her even from afar that he liked. At first sight.

I am not as beautiful as she was.

"*Stay," she says. They're at his apartment. It's the middle of the day. He has to go teach.*

"*I have to go." He puts on his pants.*

"*Stay," she purrs, and curls on his bed like a cat. He can see, underneath her playfulness, how desperate she is.*

He puts on his shirt.

She grabs it, her mood changed, and looks at him. The desperation in her eyes grows. She's afraid that if he leaves the apartment she'll never see him again.

Oh, my god. I remember this moment. I've seen it in her head. But I don't . . . feel it anymore. I was never as desperate as this.

I make Michael hug me tighter, and I search for a memory of her later in their relationship, his strongest memory.

"Yes," Michael says. *They're in the corridor where she cornered him, outside his apartment.*

Stephanie stands in front of him, and it's as if everything inside her changes. Something in her eyes changes, something in her cheeks falls, her face freezes, and she collapses into a ball on the floor.

It's as if she is dying in front of him.

She *did* die that instant. But something in me doesn't feel for her as much as I used to. I am not as depressed as she was. I am not in the same pain as she was.

I look up at Michael. I am not in love with him. I am not attracted to him.

I step back, and it feels like pieces of who I am fall to the floor.

I am not as beautiful as she was. I am not as desperate as she was. I am not as depressed as she was. I am not in the same pain as she was. I am not in love as she was. I am not attracted to Michael as she was. I am not as crazy as she was.

I am not Stephanie. And I am not Parks. And I am not Bendis. And I am not my parents.

I am not dust. I am not nothing.

And it dawns on me that I am . . . something.

I am me, for once. I am different now. I am strong. I am as strong as Parks. I am stronger than Parks, and she knows it. I am aware of my thoughts. I am free. I am without fear. I am ecstatic. I am in love . . . with no one. I am in need . . . of no one.

And I am through with this.

I let Michael sit, and I walk off. He'll be confused for a couple of minutes, but he'll be all right.

I call a cab.

When we get there, I see a sign above the gate I failed to see before: "Welcome to the Indianapolis Academy!"

That's right. Because we deal with truth.

Hunter of Stars

Nava Semel

The night all the stars winked out, I was born. This is why nobody in our family paid any attention to what was going on outside, why none of them witnessed this world-changing event. They were all busy waiting outside the delivery room for my first scream, and Mom claimed I wouldn't stop screaming, as if I'd already known that the world I was coming into had become completely dark.

Mom and Dad, and Grandpa, and my two spinster aunts, none of them rushed, crazed, into the streets or fields, like all the other people in the world, to see a sky that went completely black all at once; none of them cried out for the stars to come back.

Except for them, there's not a single person in the world who can't remember what they were doing at that terrible moment, which is called in history books the Obscuration of the Minor Lights. Until this very day—ten years have passed

126

since—people are holding massive rites; even a special prayer was devised for the return of the lost lights. I remember nothing of that night, of course, 'cause a tiny little baby can't tell day from night and knows nothing about stars or heaven. All this I was told by Grandpa, who also found out only the next morning that the world had turned upside down just as they were naming me.

Neri, that's what they named me.

Mom, who breast-fed me with inoculation-enriched milk, said that I wouldn't stop screaming for days on end.

The world got used to it. At first people cried, then they didn't cry so much, and Grandpa says that people get used to bad things just as they get used to good things. In school we were taught that this was an ecological disaster no scientist had anticipated, and unlike those who claim that this was God's curse, Grandpa says that this was people's curse. All those toxic gases they were releasing into the atmosphere for centuries had made the air lose its clarity, and now no starlight can penetrate the black tire that surrounds us. And even though all means of transportation are driven by solar energy nowadays, the air is still sick, and the scientists have found no way to repair this heavenly short-circuit.

My science teacher claims that what happened to our planet was in fact a blessing, because now it is clad with a defensive shield preventing evil aliens from discovering and hurting us. But if earthlight can no longer spread out into the distance, I'm afraid that if God should happen to look for us from high above, He won't know we exist.

On every birthday, before the annual rite for the return of lost light, I go out on the balcony and whisper to Him, so that no one else can hear: "We are still here. Do not forget us."

Even on ordinary days, I keep nagging at Grandpa: "How did the world look with stars?" And he sits down in the special old folks' armchair, tailor-made for his one-hundred-twenty-two-year-old body, that delivers healing currents, and tells me how when he was a kid he always waited for a shooting star to make a wish. Once he even saw a meteor shower, but I'm not sure he didn't invent this one.

Even if these stories are the products of Grandpa's wild imagination, I envy him 'cause he got to live in a star-spangled world, for now even the moon is rarely seen—a dim patch, you really need to make an effort to see it—and only when it is full.

Its picture as a thin crescent, rocking in the sky like a hammock—Grandpa calls it "a light banana"—can be seen only in natural history museums or at the planetarium.

Today is my birthday. On the cake Mom had baked before she left with Dad for the annual rite of prayer, my best friend Sheli arranged candies to look like the constellations Big Dipper and Orion the Hunter, and at the edge of the cake she stuck Polaris, the northern star that used to accompany Grandpa in navigation hikes when he was young, in the army—believe it or not, we used to have a military once—and the northern star always showed him the way.

Sheli is short for Shalhevet, "flame," and she knows by heart the entire star chart, which only select astronomers get to see through their most advanced telescopes. I find it sad that most people chose to forget this chart, and for them the stars are like the dinosaurs that got extinct millions of years ago, or like those peoples mentioned in the Bible—the Babylonians and the Assyrians and the Amalekites; they, too, ceased to exist a long time ago. For them, that's how things are, and if the Universe keeps changing anyway, the time has come for the stars to disappear as well. So long as the sun is still there, says Sheli's mother—and never mind if its light is drab and grayish. What's important is that its rays are there, and we can go on living.

Sheli and I have studied together since our first teaching day, when we were three. Most kids study on their own, facing the computer wall that connects them with their study groups, what used to be called in Grandpa's old days a class, but Sheli and I persuaded our parents to allow us to be in the same room so we can talk face-to-face, not just through the computer. Every morning we take our hoverbikes and go either to her home or mine, and what I like most of all is to hear her whisper "Neri" in my ear when she asks for help in her homework.

On our common screensaver we are met every morning by Orion the Hunter in a picture taken from an ivory bas-relief created thirty-two centuries ago. At the back of this relief there are eighty-six slots, which is the number of the days of a woman's pregnancy, and someday I'm going to count them one by one, when I'll go to see this bas-relief at the Beijing Observatory.

Sheli is fond of the ancient legend about Artemis, the moon goddess of Greek mythology who'd fallen in love with the brave hunter, so much that she'd forgotten to light up the moon. Her brother Apollo, the sun god, got mad at her and decided to kill the hunter. He made her shoot an arrow at him by mistake, and Orion was killed. Poor Artemis placed her lover in heaven beside her, and this is how he lives forever, and since the days of Greek mythology, Orion's light was the brightest in the sky. When Grandpa was a kid, it could be seen from everywhere on Earth. On my birthday cake Orion doesn't look like the shiniest hunter in the world, but I forgive him, 'cause you can't copy everything using candles.

We were waiting for our guests. Grandpa was napping in his special old folks' armchair, and we promised to wake him up when the guests arrive for the party, but nobody came.

"Why are they so late?" I asked Sheli, hiding from her my fear that someday everyone I love will disappear suddenly, just like the starlight.

I put on the phosphorescent shoulder pads that always make us seen in the dark, and I put on the phosphorescent headband we also have to wear at night, and we went out to the balcony.

Sheli tried to encourage me: "Perhaps this will be the night when all the stars decide to light up again?"

From Tel Aviv's artificial seaside came to us the noise of the crowds as they were stirring, and we could hear them praying all together: ". . . and bestow light for blessing on all the face of the earth."

The sea looked like a blank tabletop made out of marble on which nothing was reflected, and from the balcony my birthday cake looked like a forgotten block of basalt. I was so disappointed. I thought that they forgot my birthday because of the annual rite.

We were leaning on the balustrade, watching the Heavenly Body Substitute Searchlight that lit up exactly at midnight to swing its mighty beam across the empty dome above us.

I asked, "Sheli, do you think that maybe on another planet there are two kids like us wondering where Earth has disappeared to?"

Sheli replied that she was sure that the universe was full of curious kids, even if they didn't look like us. Alien children—that's what she said—have hearts, and even if they cry without tears, they are just as sad as we are and just as happy, and they too discover ancient heroes up above and tell legends about them.

We almost fell asleep on the carpet when they finally arrived, Mom and Dad and my aunts, one of them with a new boyfriend, and some more friends from the Horsehead Nebula neighborhood where we live. Around Orion, on the cake, they stuck ten candles plus one, and I tried not to blow them out all at once so that some light could remain.

Then I opened my presents. Mom and Dad gave me TriDi spectacles that simulate the entire Milky Way galaxy, and one spinster aunt got me bedsheets with a Big Dipper pattern, and from Grandpa I got a phosphorescent soccer ball you can play with in the dark, and Grandpa promised me that we were going to score many goals with it. And from Sheli I got a computer game in which I'm an astronomer, discovering a lot of new stars and naming them. The first one we discovered she named after me, "Neri's Star."

Only my other spinster aunt gave me a massive book about extinct rhinos in Africa, saying shrewishly, "You're a big boy now, Neri. It's time to grow up. Enough already with your fascination with the stars. A whole lot of good they were, one should think. Just a decoration, that's what they were."

Auntie had met her new boyfriend at a demonstration of the Movement against Star Worship. Her headband bore a sticker with the inscription "Stars belong only in movies."

Grandpa was a bit miffed with his wayward daughter and made a wish for me that on my next birthday all the stars will light up again, and he felt certain that I won't miss that moment. He also wished that he, too, will still be with us then.

If it won't happen on my next birthday, then maybe on the following one.

When all the birthday leftovers were cleared, Mom and Dad sat together with Grandpa, and my two spinster aunts with their new friend went to sleep. I went out to the balcony again, this time without my phosphorescent shoulder pads and headband. I was swallowed by darkness. Sheli came out after me, and we reached out and held hands.

I whispered into the black sky: "Orion, my shining friend, I will always follow you. Like you, I will be a hunter of stars."

The Believers

Nir Yaniv

In God's Name

The old woman in the grocery store stares at the floor and doesn't look up. She examines the date printed on a chunk of cheese, and her hand shakes. She turns around, and the cheese drops from her hand into one of the two carts nearby.

It's the wrong cart, and a small child sees the cheese fall, then hit a pack of frozen chicken legs. There's a terrible tearing noise, and the old woman is split in two. Blood and stomach and intestines spray all over the place, and then there's a gargling noise, and then silence.

Everyone ignores this, each keeping his or her head down. Except for the little boy, who's waiting patiently with his mother in the line in front of the cash register.

He still doesn't understand the need to lower one's head. His mother covers his ears and eyes with her hands, but it's too late. It's oh so late. From somewhere in the air comes the sound of the beating of wings.

Next Tuesday I'm going to have a meeting with a machine that will change my life. My head will be put inside a big gray plastic egg, wires and tubes protruding out of its top. I'll spend an hour like that. When I get out, I won't be the same person that I am now.

I will not be the only person to be changed like that. There are many others. Or maybe just a few.

I don't know, I'm not supposed to know, I don't want to know. I know just this: maybe when we all are changed, we'll be able, at last, to kill God.

Today, when I think of it, I understand that the incident at the grocery store was the first time that I saw the Hand of God. Until then my life seemed pretty safe, and I had no clue of what could happen to anyone who is careless about anything to do with the divine. Which is, after all, everything.

God took mercy on the children, of course He did. God never punishes the young ones—but only because He needs a steady supply of adults.

God examines kidneys and heart, but not those of everyone at the same time. Not because He can't, but because He's bored by it. Or maybe it's just laziness. Some of us consider this good fortune, and the rest prefer to believe that He knows exactly what they think of Him and does whatever He feels like doing, just let them stop pretending and fulfilling the commandments.

Those people have a problem. All of us have a problem. Because God has a terrible personality.

If I think about this too much He'll notice me. Let's change the subject. Here's a subject that is, paradoxically, rather safe: belief.

This reminds me of my first argument with Gabi, when he told me about his underground movement, the Atheists.

"I fail to understand how you can disbelieve something that exists," I said. "Especially when it's something as explicit as God."

"And we fail to understand how you can believe something that doesn't exist," Gabi said. "Like the way God was until a few years ago."

Several dozen years, but who's counting.

"And also," he added, "after we finish with Him, He won't exist anymore."

I didn't answer. I didn't want to draw attention to myself by thinking about it. I think that I'm thinking too much about this right now.

Change of subject.

Here's how we met: I sat on a stone bench in the public garden, by the fountain, too close to it. The spray hit me from time to time. It didn't matter. Nothing mattered. On other benches, mothers sat with their children, a herd of coifs and hats and children's toys. No one wanted to sit near me. No one but Gabi, who popped out of somewhere, sat by me, and said, "I know."

"What?" I said.

"I know exactly how you're feeling."

He didn't smile.

"You have no idea," I said.

"Look at me," he said. "Raise your head and look."

I did that, and I saw. The absence. The emptiness, huge, engulfing, drowning, whining. The soul, perforated, defiled, that will never be the way it was. I saw the vast hole in it, gaping, and I knew that it was just like mine.

"Go away," I said. I wanted to hold him, to hug him, to merge with him. I added, "Leave me alone."

"Just like I told you," he said. "I know how you feel. And I have a solution."

"Please," I said. "Please, go away."

He did, but only in order to return.

The young boy and his mother stand by the table. Two candles for the Sabbath, fresh Sabbath bread, covered. The mother reaches out for the prayer book, the Siddur.

"Mother," the boy says and points with his finger, "Mother, no, it's not right, wait a moment," but it's too late.

It's always too late. It has always been too late. And now, just a moment after the sound of sucking and pumping and pulling and absorbing, the dried body of the mother, sans blood and bones and flesh and tendons and cartilages and mucus, drops, very slowly, paper-thin, hovers down dreamily to the floor, then rests.

God's first appearance occurred before I was born. I have heard old people tell tales of life before it, the way the world was set. Some of them—most of them—remember it fondly. Some say that it was horrible, everyone doing whatever they wanted to, Sodom and Gomorrah, impurity, abomination, sin, chaos. All of them, always, miss it. That was before I was born. I miss it too.

"You want me," Gabi said.

"You know the punishment for male inter. . . ."

"Don't say it," he said.

I didn't understand what was going on inside me. Yes, I "wanted" him. To be with him. To touch him. The idea had never occurred to me before. On the contrary: the mere thought of . . . deviants—that's the safe word at the moment, the word that won't attract His attention—nauseated me. Undoubtedly God felt that way too. And then Gabi appeared, and. . . .

"I don't want to make it hard on you," he said. It took some time for both of us to catch the double meaning. Yes, the punishment for the forbidden intercourse is death. As are most punishments, these days.

But when it comes to this particular sin, the reaction is particularly quick and harsh. And I thought to myself, maybe I'm not really interested in Gabi. Maybe I just want to die. Maybe I'm just aiming for the most horrible possible death. How far from the truth can you be?

I had a girlfriend once. A long time ago. We couldn't hold ourselves back. We never thought of getting married, or even engaged. We knew, of course we knew, but the urge was too strong. We slept together. We took pleasure in each other. Exhausted, sweating, happy, we fell asleep.

A weird smell woke me up in the morning. Just beside me, in bed, a gray-red-purple sack, moist, dripping, wet. Still twitching. Fluttering about. My girlfriend, turned from the inside out.

A Jew who believes in God doesn't believe that God exists. Existence is a matter for God's creation, not for God himself. Attributing existence to God means lowering Him to our level, the level of the stone and the bush and the animal and the man and the rest. Unfortunately, God has never heard of that. And if He has, He has never shown any interest.

A young man bumps into a girl in the library. In his hands there are several forbidden books, which he found on one of the shelves in the back, a place forgotten by the censors. She clutches in her hands a thin booklet, "Dreams of Angels."

Her face is small, delicate, drawn in thin, sharp lines. They both apologize, smiling shyly. The next day they have dinner together. The next evening they sit in his apartment. He fights the urge, and the guilt—he still remembers his previous girlfriend's death.

She, without delay, gets out of her clothes. He says, "No!" She smiles, spreads two white wings. She, or he, no gender, no guilt. An angel.

The young man discovers a new form of attraction. He cannot stop looking. The angel is his whole world now, his whole life. Without the angel, his existence is meaningless. And the angel, without gender or guilt, and as the future will show, without any particular meaning, approaches, grows, touches. Penetrates.

It's impossible to explain what happens to you when an angel penetrates you.

It's not physical—you wish it was, for then at least you would be left with something of your own. No, your body remains untouched, unfelt, unnoticed, even pure, while the angel penetrates the only place that really matters. You feel it swelling and widening and expanding within you, and then you're gone.

Superficially, you're still there, imprisoned in your corporeal body, but it is your mind that has been defiled, and your self isn't there anymore, and the person you were will never be anymore. And when the angel departs it leaves a hole in you, an empty space, a place that it occupied and that you can never, ever fill again. All of us, all of the people who will visit the machine next week, have such an empty space in the place where we used to have souls.

Know All Tuesday, twice blessed, I walk slowly on my quest, my mind deliberately at rest. Every step gets me closer to the address I was given, an abandoned warehouse in the old industrial zone. I wonder who, of all the people around me, I will meet there, if any, and then silence the thought. The sun shines, it's a nice day, and those, if I manage it, are going to be my only thoughts till I arrive.

"What are you going to do?" I shouted. "How exactly are you going to fight . . . ?"

Gabi reached out and covered my mouth with his hand, then hugged me. "I fight no one," he whispered, "but there are more people like us. And, you don't understand this yet, but there's something unique about us."

I pushed him away. "I feel this uniqueness all the time," I said. "I'm not impressed by it."

"Oh, it's not only what you feel. We have other qualities. I . . . I don't fully understand it myself, but there's someone who does. We call him the Know All."

"And that person, did he explain to you everything about those 'qualities' of ours?"

"Not in any words that you or I can understand. But that doesn't matter. He's building a machine that will set us free. In several days there'll be a meeting, and you'll be able to listen to him for yourself."

I didn't answer. It sounded too ludicrous. Some mad scientist builds a silly contraption from springs and coils in his basement laboratory, and a bunch of retards dance around him, hoping for salvation. How pathetic.

I agreed to go anyway. Never underestimate the power of hope, ludicrous as it may be.

We saw from afar the pillar of cloud and pillar of fire. When we arrived at the street, it was already clean. Not much was left of the machine or the Know All, or of the building in which they had once resided. Gabi was desperate to get closer, to look for remains, but I held him back and forcibly dragged him away.

That night we almost committed the deadly sin. We felt suicidal. It was Gabi who saved us, at the last moment.

"No," he said. "This can't be the end. The Know All was smart enough to know that this could happen to him."

I wanted to say that it didn't sound very smart, losing your life like that, but the sarcasm got stuck in my throat.

"Get up," Gabi said. "Get dressed. We're going out."

We went to a place I didn't know, a safe house in which, so Gabi said, some of the Atheists' meetings and some of the Know All's famous speeches had taken place. One small room, without a bed, without chairs, just one desk, and on it a stack of papers, and on the top one a title: "The Tower of Babylon."

And under it—diagrams, drawings, descriptions.

"I knew it," Gabi said. "I knew it."

"What's the meaning of this?" I asked. "What's this about the Tower of Babylon?"

"I don't know. Let's take it home and figure it out there."

And the whole Earth was of one language, and of one speech, in the land of Shinar; and they dwelt there. And they said one to another, Go to, let us make brick, and burn them thoroughly. And they had brick for stone, and slime had they for mortar.

And they said, Go to, let us build us a city and a tower, whose top may reach unto heaven; and let us make us a name, lest we be scattered abroad upon the face of the whole earth.

And the Lord *came down to see the city and the tower, which the children of men built. And the* Lord *said, Behold, the people are one, and they have all one language; and this they begin to do: and now nothing will be restrained from them, which they have imagined to do.*

Go to, let us go down, and there confound their language, that they may not under-stand one another's speech.

So the Lord *scattered them abroad from thence upon the face of all the earth: and they left off building the city. Therefore is the name of it called Babel; because the* Lord *did there confound the language of all the earth: and from thence did the Lord scatter them abroad upon the face of all the earth.*

"What does that mean?" I asked.

"You didn't know the Know All," Gabi said.

"He never said anything directly. Always clues or parts, or both. I think I know what he wanted to say here. Think of it, Raphi. Read it again. To scatter. To *scatter!*"

"But even if you somehow manage to build the machine, you'll get just what he got."

"Not necessarily. The Know All had a problem—he knew. We, on the other hand, don't know. This may have been his intention from the start."

"He killed himself deliberately?"

"I think," Gabi said, "that he died for the sake of the machine."

Then came the days in which each of the Atheists received a packet of pages, diagrams, drawings, descriptions.

Each of them built or found, or found someone else to build or find, the part, the component, the ingredient that was described and diagrammed in his or her own packet. No one had any idea about the function of any one part, much less the whole, and those who could make an educated guess tried to avoid thinking about it, or asked for someone else to take on the chore.

And I, while they were slowly bringing this enormous task to completion in this or that abandoned warehouse, lay days and nights in bed contemplating a sin that would destroy me without pain. And Gabi wasn't there to stop me, for he was the one who had the hardest task of all—that of putting all of those parts together.

Who knows what I'd have done to myself if it hadn't occurred to me that giving in to the machine was a sufficient sin in itself?

And curiosity, of course. Even for someone like me, who has already paid a considerable mental sum for it.

And then there was a note in my mailbox: "Come."

And on Tuesday, twice blessed, walk slowly on my quest, my mind deliberately at rest, I'm getting closer, closer, closer to the nest.

The Tower of Babel

The door is unlocked, and I step inside. There are no windows in the warehouse, but it's not dark. The walls glow. I don't understand how or why.

In one corner, darkness. A big gray plastic egg, wires and tubes protruding out of its top. It hums, or maybe I'm just imagining this. I go there and sit under it, on the floor, and pull the egg over my head.

Darkness. I sit there for quite a long time. No sound is heard, no indication is given, no activity is visible. Maybe there is none, and I'm sitting inside a piece of dead junk, waiting in vain for salvation or a quick death. I don't move. Maybe I even fall asleep, there in the quiet and darkness.

Minutes pass, or maybe hours, or maybe days. Nothing happens.

I remove the machine from my head and stand up. The light is blinding. The walls are ablaze with light. I see, now, that they are mirrors. And in those mirrors I see my face, and I say to myself, I know that face. Where do I know it from? Small, delicate, drawn in thin, sharp lines. Not the face I was born with, but that which has been mine since . . . since . . .

Since that girl, in the library. Since the angel came and took and went away. Went away in my own body, leaving me alone. Only now can I see that.

I spread my wings and fly.

Fly, through the ceiling, through the top floors, through staircases and elevators, through the roof, fly out. And over the roofs around me, dozens of Atheists, glowing, radiating, winged, hovering.

Down on the street there's no commotion, no notice. No one sees the angels gathering. Gabi flies over and says, "We've been waiting for you."

I try to hug him, but he moves away.

"Later," he says. "We're flying." He raises his hand, points at the sky, and smiles.

"That's the true meaning of it. The tower of Babel. We go up to the sky."

I smile back, but something within me is rotten. This is not the way it should be. And the hole in my head, the place where my mind should have been, is still there, still not filled. Nothing has changed.

"After me!" Gabi roars, and everyone takes off, a squadron of angels, the soft murmur of wings, the sun shining upon the beautiful, glowing things.

They rise, higher and higher, further and further from the gray, dirty city under the clear, bright sky, from the filth, from the sin. And from me.

I land on one of the nearby roofs, sit on the dirty whitewash, lie down, look straight at the sun. Waiting in the light, just like I waited before in the dark.

The angels, above me, become smaller and smaller, fade out. I notice anger within me, scorching anger, beneath the intolerable calm of the hole in my head. Anger at God, of course, and at the angels, but mostly at Gabi and at myself.

Why didn't I join them? Jealousy? Fear? Or maybe I'm just lethargic with the disappointment of still being alive?

The sun moves in the sky, slowly, as usual, then faster and faster. Something is askew. Something is wrong. And if I want to die, why haven't I flown with them? And maybe my absence is the small factor that has decided the battle against them.

The sun moves in a great arc towards the sea, and I get up, stand erect, hover, fly—up and up, higher and higher, and the sun moves lower and lower and already I can't see the city below me, and the light diminishes.

Up and up. A glow comes out of the fogginess above me, white lightning, and a great noise rings in my ears, or maybe in my mind, screams over screams, and I think I notice, among them, one particular tormented voice, which may or may not be Gabi's. I will never know.

Because at that moment there's the sound of tearing, and the sky above me opens, and I find myself passing like an arrow through a rain of angels.

Burning.

Boiling, bubbling, melting, twisting, shedding skin and innards and bones and feathers.

Dropping. I slow down, change direction, try to fall with them, hurling like a bullet toward the faraway ground, but they fall even faster. Compared to them I feel like a falling leaf, floating gently down, without hurry.

I try harder, push down faster, but in vain. The city appears, grows up with terrible speed, but not as terrible as that of the remains of the angels hitting it like bombs, clouds of some and fire of others marking the places where they smash into the ground and the buildings. I don't bother slowing down.

I hit a roof and some walls and then the ground, then I realize that I'm going through them all. I feel nothing. I find myself alone on the face of the earth.

The day before yesterday I tried sleeping with someone, a young guy I met at the park. He melted the moment I laid a hand upon him.

Yesterday I went to the supermarket, took some meat and squashed a carton of milk into it. The building burned and went up in a flame, and only I was left, alone.

God has cursed me. I am not alive and I cannot die, and I am not punished for my sins, though others are. And maybe that was, after all, the plan.

Because tomorrow, just after the sun rises, I will go out and fly up, up, and away, over the clouds, through the great fogginess, straight into the citadel of God, and I shall stand in front of Him, and He shall be punished for His sins, and if not for His—then for mine.

I have always believed in God. It's about time that He started believing in me.

Possibilities

Eyal Teler

The memory will haunt me until my death—not long now. Fifty years could not erase the image of that old man, the feeling of my fists meeting his face. I can still see him standing there, taking my blows without protest, then crumpling to the ground. No cry, no blood, just a helpless body. Funny how this is what I remember—killing myself. The rest is too fantastic to contemplate: the time machine, Ray introducing me to myself, asking me not to become that man, not to go to Korea, to war.

The death—the death is real. Ray might have taken the body back with him, but the memory remains: killing a helpless old man, without reason, in a bout of madness. It is a cancer. Much like the one the doctors diagnosed, it eats me from inside. For many years I had used my writing and my success to block it, but the memory has won—no stories come to me as I'm lying on this hospital bed.

Thoughts that had played in my mind long ago, before I decided there was nothing but madness in them, are now coming back—questions about the reality of it all. How could Ray get a time machine, in that other reality? Just having me go to war couldn't change reality so much, could it? It would be hubris to think so. And my actions, my words, that killing—they didn't make sense.

Yet it couldn't have been a hallucination. The only drug in my life had been my cigarettes, and my mind had always been sound enough—even when I suffered from depression. Besides, that time machine left a mark on the asphalt—I checked for it the next day.

I wish I had had the courage to find out what really happened on that day. I've never told anyone about it. Only once, about twenty years ago, did I try, halfheartedly, to find an answer.

"You must be Simon," she said. It sounded so conclusive that for a moment I was tempted to turn back from her door. After all, if I could only be Simon, a specific, well-defined Simon, what use was there in seeing her?

"And you have no choice but to be Sedef, I guess." I wondered, though. I hadn't expected a short, round-faced girl, nor that broad smile in response to my dry joke. But her soft voice, with a hint of foreign accent, was as I remembered it from the phone.

"Come in," she said, and I followed the path that her hand traced in the air to a brightly lit room with landscapes and a kitten picture on the walls. She motioned me to sit on the beige sofa, but I just stood, feeling as if I had happened to walk onto the set of the wrong movie.

"What did you expect, candlelight and voodoo accessories?"

Was I that transparent? What had I expected? An older woman, perhaps, with an air of mystery—a fraud—not someone my wife's age, about half my fifty years. It was just a silly cliché, of course, and I wouldn't have dared using it in a story. Funny how easy it was to use it in real life.

She looked more like a grade-school teacher than a seer, with her open, gentle, not-too-sharp face. Maybe it was fitting, in a way. We were all just gullible kids, those of us who came to her. Sure, Ray said that people swore by her. But then he also said that we should remain kids at heart. He may be my friend and mentor, but that doesn't mean we have to agree on everything.

How had I managed to convince myself to visit a woman with a power I didn't believe in? It was probably not too late to fix that mistake. I decided to turn around and leave.

The sofa was comfortable.

"So, Sedef, what can you tell me about that power of yours?"

She smiled. "Is this an interview?"

"No." I preferred not to think of it that way. Interviews were intrusive and tiring, and my seeds of dislike for them had long ago grown into resentment. "Just curious. I never met anyone who claimed they had a power to see alternate realities."

She giggled. "Will you stop calling it a power? Any more of this and I'll have to start wearing spandex outfits. I don't think I have the body for them." She didn't. Not that the flowery dress she wore looked that great on her.

"My talent, or 'gift,' if you wish, is the ability to see what might have happened had you made a different decision at some specific point in your life. I can tell you the most likely path that your life would have taken in that case. I don't really know how I do it, and, no, I can't really prove it, but people always tell me that it feels right, that they really would have done things that way." Of course they would, if she was a good enough con.

"So, tell me what would have happened had I gone to war. I mean, to Korea."

"Sorry," she said, "I need to get more of a feeling for you first. Like, what do you do for a living?"

I didn't know whether to feel insulted that she didn't know me or happy that I didn't have to deal with yet another mushy encounter.

"I create dreams." My futuristic dystopias could perhaps be more correctly classified as nightmares, but it was the more lighthearted contemporary fantasy, the kid stuff, that had made me a household name. The wonders of commercialism. Not that I complained—it had been nice to take those vacations in fantasy lands.

She gave me a vacant stare.

I showed her. I liked telling tales. I loved the moment of conception, the minute or two when the idea was born, still ugly and unclean but with its inner beauty already showing. I told her a story set in a world where everyone had her power and knew the results of their choices.

"Wow!" The look she gave me could only be described as awe. My stomach turned.

"You liked my story?"

"What? Oh, it was fine. It's not that. It's just that your power of suggestion is so strong! You must be a great author!"

What a good performance; I nearly fell for it. Obviously she had known all along who I was. Still, I decided to play her little game.

"What do you mean?"

"Well, everyone affects the possibilities, you know. Not just choices affect them, but also wishes and dreams and desires. Authors, they don't just think of ideas—they develop them, research them, let other people share them. Their words are like magic—they can change the world. Even the impossible can become possible this way. I once went with a friend to a writers' conference. I could feel the possibilities change all around me. Not a lot, but it was still a little frightening.

"But you, you just told a story, without thinking about it a lot, without sharing it with lots of people, and I could feel the world changing. I could feel my power ... damn!" She laughed. "Now I'm calling it a 'power' myself. I could feel it grow a little stronger, like this world was becoming more like the one you told me about. It's like you're changing the possibilities directly. I don't know any famous writers, but I don't think it's normal."

"I'll try not to write too many alien invasion stories then." Yeah, right. Trying to convince me she had a power was one thing. Telling me I had a power was just too much. "So, can you do your reading now?" Better get this charade over with.

"Yeah, I think I have enough feeling for you now. What war was that?"

"Korea."

"Wow, that's old! Sorry, didn't mean it like that. It's just that most people come to me to validate some recent decision they've made, not to ask me about something that happened thirty years ago. Don't know how easy it'd be. Hell, I was just a little baby in Turkey at the time." She was older than I had thought. "But I'll try."

Her eyes lost focus and looked up, and her forehead creased, as if she were trying hard to remember something. Then her hand went to her chin, her fingers brushing her lips. She reminded me of a female version of Rodin's *Thinker*—but with clothes on, which made it somewhat less interesting.

I waited. I thought how to spin the tale I had told her into a publishable story. A better point-of-view character and some plot complications suggested themselves—enough material to pursue back home.

Sedef was still in thought, so I got up, curious to see what titles she had on her bookshelves. She didn't have anything of mine. Several shelves strained under the weight of reference books—many of them about medicine. The rest were mostly classics and assorted poetry. She seemed to like Frost.

I glanced at my watch, then looked at her and wished she would stop. She could have at least made the show less boring—she could have mumbled or something.

"You know . . ." Her words startled me. I half imagined that she had fallen asleep in that posture. "There's something very strange here. Some . . . barrier.

I've never felt anything like it. I may be able to see through it, but it will take me some time. Could you tell me perhaps why you didn't go to war? That might help."

What could I tell her, that I had murdered myself for no reason, as if I had been possessed? That since that day I've kept fearing that I'd kill the people I loved? It had been too much for a boy of nineteen to think about. I was declared unfit for duty, of course, due to my mental state. I shut myself in my room and stopped seeing my friends. I wrapped myself in my writing and hoped that the stories would help me forget. All I wanted was to forget. Why did I come here to stir up these memories?

I made a show of glancing at my watch. "Oh, I'm sorry, I forgot an appointment. I have to go. It's probably for the best. You'll be able to look into my other possibility at your leisure, without pressure. Don't worry, I'll pay you for your time. Here." I pushed a hundred into her hand as I picked up my coat and made my way to the door. "I'll come back another day."

I went out quickly, but I think I heard her say: "But I don't take money. . . ."

Lying in this hospital room, where day and night fade into a half-waking sameness, the memory makes me long for those days gone by, for the sound of words forming on a page in my typewriter, for conferences, even for signings—yes, I half miss even the company of people, of fans, and of Carolyn, to whose arms and tall, athletic body I returned that day; Carolyn of the intoxicating smell. I had overlooked her indiscretions, as she had for a while overlooked my mistress and true love: my writing. After our divorce the gossip columns told me that she had decided famous actors were easier to deal with than famous authors.

Those had been busy days—too busy to go back to see Sedef, or so I'd told myself—busy enough to push the memory back into its lair and take the thought of her with it. Once, some ten years ago it was, I think, I saw her on TV, on 60 *Minutes*. She was a physician. "Miracle doctor" they called her—one whose diagnosis was always on the mark. She had been offered work at ROI, a big research firm. I was tempted to find her again, to have her finish the reading. It didn't matter if she was a fraud. If she could have come up with some plausible explanation, something to help me close that painful subplot of my life, that would have been enough.

I laugh inwardly and cough outwardly. It hurts—my punishment for being such a skeptic. I've seen and done strange things in my years on Earth, not the least of them killing an older version of myself, and still I don't give her the benefit of the doubt, even though she had told me of a special barrier. She couldn't have known enough for that to be a trick.

I found out where her lab was, but I didn't go. She'd be too busy to do a reading for a silly author, I was sure—excuses were always my strong suit. Perhaps she didn't even do readings anymore, being a famous and busy doctor. My wish to meet her remained just that—a wish. I still wish for it now, but it is too late. Even picking up the phone is too hard for me now.

There's a knock on the door—a futile gesture. Weak as I am, the mere thought of saying "come in" makes me feel tired. I hear my thought echoed by the gruff voice of an orderly. There's some argument about nobody being allowed to see me, but it's settled quickly.

The door opens gently, and the tapping of low heels approaches my bed. I wait until she gets within my view—no use wasting my strength on turning my head. I wonder who she is and what she wants. I don't get many visitors—Ray is the only one, in fact. I made sure the press was kept out.

"Hello, Simon," she says. The voice startles me so that for a moment I forget my weakness and turn my head, and I see her sad smile. "I'm Sedef. You once came to me for a reading."

As if I could forget. Yet the shock adds to my weakness and I can't even tell her that. I can't even smile back at her. I think of that old man that I hit—how silently he fell.

She has aged a lot since last I'd seen her. At last her looks seem to have caught up with her age. She looks rounder, and her hair, black touched with gray, is more orderly now. Perhaps she has a daughter named Pearl who is combing it for her, I muse—creating background details is a hard habit to break. Her clothes are more elegant, and I think the suit suits her—I find the pun amusing.

The joke eases the shock, and at last I manage to straighten my fingers—a feeble gesture of hello. She notices it and smiles. I'm glad now that the blanket is not over my hand, even though my arm feels cold.

She sits by my bed on the chair that up till now has been reserved for Ray, on his infrequent visits. She takes my cold hand in her warm one. It's a good feeling, to have someone warm touch me. Her smile is warm, too, and there is warmth in her eyes. I find that I'm a little uncomfortable with all that warmth, even though I've often wished for more warmth, both for my body and for my heart. I don't complain, though—I let her keep holding my hand.

"You know," she says, "I was really insulted when you left me, twenty years ago, and even more when you didn't come back. I decided to put you out of my mind, but I couldn't. I met no one like you, with your power to alter the possibilities, and that strange barrier in your past. When I found out who you were, I was even more intrigued. You couldn't have thought that the other path would have made you more successful. So why were you interested in it?

"I tried quite a few tricks to see your other path. I even researched you and read some of your books to get a better feeling for you. You know, some of them are quite disturbing. I liked the Lilian series, though. It's more humorous and optimistic. It helped me forget the insult and think that perhaps there was some good in you after all.

"Anyway, I finally discovered that to move through the barrier I first had to move a little farther back in time. I didn't even know I could do that, before. It then became easier than any other reading. It was as if your other path was the natural one, and I had to get back on it and then continue. It still doesn't make any sense to me. Still . . . ," she pauses and smiles, "I guess I must thank you for all that practice. It really helped me understand better what I could do. It helped me help people better. Thank you." It feels bad to get thanked for being selfish, but her gentle "thank you" warms my heart nonetheless.

"You had a very interesting life in that other possibility. Once I saw all I could see, I continued to follow you, day by day, in that other life. I can't see the future, you see, even in another possibility, so I spent a little time each day finding out what you were doing. Then you died there, and I thought that if you were still alive here. . . . I guess I'd better start from the beginning.

"Let me tell you the story of a young man," she says. "He left his home, his parents, his sister, and went to war. It wasn't easy for him to leave, and worse still was the war itself. Many of his friends died, people he cared a lot for. When it ended, he couldn't face going home. He felt that it wasn't right for him to live, with his friends dead. He started taking foolish risks, learning sports like cliff diving and bull fighting. Perhaps he was even disappointed that he was good enough at them to escape dying for years and years.

"It was in his days in Spain that he met a young woman from Turkey. He didn't want to be her friend, but she always came to see him fight. She saw something special in him. Once, after he was injured pretty badly by the bull, she happened to see him being brought to the hospital where she interned. It wasn't easy for her to get to see him, as he was quite famous, but she managed to pull a few strings and visit him." She smiles. "I guess it's the kind of thing she does.

"He talked to her then. He told her that he was sorry the bull hadn't killed him. He said that he had friends waiting for him in another world, where life was beautiful and there were no wars.

"Then he talked to her about wars. He talked about them for hours and hours. He would only go to sleep when the doctors made the woman leave his side and would continue talking when she returned. 'Soldiers are dreamers,' he said, 'and when a soldier dies, there is a little less dreamt beauty in the world.'"

I understand now what she had told me about how people react to her readings. That really felt like me, when I was younger and naïve.

"He talked about the dreams of his friends and how these dreams came to an end. And he talked about the dead of the enemy. He described the horrors of the ones unfortunate enough to survive, without parts of their body, or without a place to live or things to eat. When he came to the end of what he had seen with his own eyes, he talked of the wars he had heard about, the horrors he could only imagine.

"Eventually he finished talking and slept for an entire day. When he woke up, he said that perhaps it was good that he hadn't died. He had a gift for stories before he went to war, he said. Perhaps if he could put all those horrors on paper, to show people what war was like, then he could do some good and make his friends in heaven happy.

"But the woman had a special gift. She had heard his war stories, and she had sensed something, and so she told him no. 'You are special,' she said. 'Whatever you tell becomes more real, more possible. Don't tell stories of war; tell stories of peace.'

"And he did. He told her stories of ending conflicts, of age-old feuds becoming forgotten through acts of love and kindness; of tyrants falling and of religious tolerance. He told of the Koreas healing back into one country, of Turkey and Greece ending their differences, of peace in the Middle East, of Europe joined. She was his only audience. 'People don't want stories of peace,' he used to say. 'They want conflict, action.'

"They moved in together, into a small apartment on the outskirts of Madrid. She worked at the hospital while he took care of their children and thought of new stories to tell. She would come home exhausted, and he would read stories to her while she slept. Around them the world blossomed. It took years and years, but they could track the change. Those stories that he typed they kept together with the news clippings from the papers when they became true. They could not be any happier, with each other, with their children, and with the world.

"And then he fell ill. The doctors found lung cancer, too advanced to be cured. They tried, the doctors. He tried. He told stories of doctors finding cures for cancer, and I know that they did, but they were too late to help him. He died in hospital, a few days ago. He did so much good for the world, but he couldn't do himself a favor and quit smoking, the silly man." Her voice breaks at the end. She squeezes my hand and falls silent.

It couldn't have been. She must have gotten it wrong. "I . . . ," I gasp, "killed . . . me."

"Huh, what?" Her thoughts return to me from elsewhere.

"Ah . . ." I start to say, but my voice betrays me. I force my head to my right, to the stand where my laptop sits. I'm not sure if I truly thought I'd write any stories here, or whether I just enjoyed the disapproving looks from Ray, who likes to act as if computers are demons taken form.

When it boots, and the word processor opens, she helps guide my feeble hand over the keys, "i killed me," I write, "time machine." Could I have helped create one with my stories, in that other reality? Did I really have that much power to change the world?

She thinks for a while, probably trying to decide if my illness had made me delirious.

"Well," she finally says, "It sounds rather fantastic, but a time machine could explain why the other path felt more natural. It would take something that could really warp reality to change the natural path of someone's life. But I still don't understand what you mean by 'I killed me.' You mean literally?"

I don't answer her. I'm too weary to make a sound or even nod.

"Simon, I'm sorry. I've tired you with my story. I guess I'll come back later, after you've rested a little."

She gets ready to let go of my hand, and I force my fingers to tighten around her. I know that there's no way I can hold on, so I'm grateful that she stops and sits back down.

"Simon," she says, and I can hear the humor in her voice, can almost see her smile. "It's about time you didn't let go so easily." She pauses, probably smiling again. I open my eyes, and sure enough, there she is, smiling and looking into my eyes. Her smile grows wider. "Good," she says.

"I know you're tired, but I'll tell you what we'll do. I'll ask you questions and you can squeeze my hand for the answers. One time for yes, two for no. No, bad idea—wouldn't want to tire you. Nothing for no, then. I'll just wait enough to make sure." She smiles again. "Okay, let's see if I get this straight: the older you, from the other reality, came back in a time machine to the time you were about to go to war, and you ended up killing him. Is that what happened?"

I hesitate for a second, then squeeze her hand feebly.

"That's what I thought. Not that it makes any sense. I'm quite sure now that the possibility I followed was your natural path, and you never got near a time machine there. There probably never was one to be near. So it must have been something else. But what? I wish you could tell me more. Maybe after you've rested."

No way. I'm not letting her go. I have to finish this now. There might not be another day. What was the signal for "no"? Nothing—no, that's no good. I guess I'll just have to squeeze "yes."

"Yes? So you want to rest?"

I guess that saying "no" now would be okay.

"No? Or are you just resting? Not a very smart signal scheme I came up with, is it?" She smiles. I smile back, which probably looks grotesque, with half my face paralyzed.

She smiles a big smile back. "Well, if you can smile a big smile like that, I guess you don't need to rest. So, you want to continue?"

I squeeze "yes."

"You want the computer?"

No. I just need to think.

"You need some time to think?"

Hey, she didn't tell me she has ESP too. I smile in my thoughts and squeeze her hand.

I think back to that day, fifty years ago. My memory is as sharp as ever, but emotions still cloud my view. I push past them, try to see the scene as I saw it then: two men stepping out of a strange contraption that hadn't been there a moment before. One of them old, feeble, and unfamiliar; the other, Ray, old but recognizable. I remember him telling me the other guy was the old me, and I then saw myself in him. I nearly freaked out then.

There's some detail here, some buried realization that I must uncover. I stop thinking and let the scene take over, as if it were part of a story, as if these were characters of my own creation that I'm trying to get to understand.

Obviously, Ray was the protagonist. He was the one who talked to me, the one who acted. The old me did little. What did Ray want? He asked me not to become that guy. He wanted me to continue writing. He brought that guy to show me what I would become, and then took his body away. Yet Sedef says that I died in hospital. Perhaps he snatched me from there, then returned me back, dead. Did she miss that moment? She probably couldn't follow every moment of my life—that would have left her no time for her own.

No, that doesn't make sense. That old me looked old and muddled, but he didn't look like he was dying. How did he look? I try to picture that guy—his face like mine, but wrinkled, gaunt; his body thin, shriveled. That's nothing like me, even after the cancer started taking its toll. I might have imagined this to be me, fifty, even twenty years ago, but not now. Could I have aged differently in that other reality? I find it unlikely.

Ray, the bastard! Did he hire an actor to impersonate me?

"Ray!" I cry. It comes out as a croak. I look to my laptop. When she gets it for me, I type, "Can you check him?"

I wait.

"Ray ... Bradbury; the writer, right? I remember now. You knew him before you went to war. You don't meet him again in the other possibility, but I remember that my research of you mentioned him. I guess you're friends here. Now that I think of it, I saw him interviewed once. He thanked you for putting science fiction in the limelight. That stuck in my mind."

It was really Ray who deserved the fame. He was the real artist, with his prose that was poetry. I've always thought it unfair that it was my straightforward style that won people's hearts. Ray never agreed with me, of course. "Simple people need a simple style," he used to say. It was enough for him that they were reading.

"So Ray had something to do with the time machine? And you want me to check his alternate life?"

I squeeze "yes" to both questions.

"I'm not sure I could follow someone else's life based on your decision. I do have some feeling for him, from that interview and what I saw in your own life. . . . I guess I'll just have to try."

I find it funny that she uses the same Rodin posture that she did twenty years ago. She does have nice lips, I notice when her fingers brush them. I wonder if she has anything of mine on her bookshelves now.

I imagine her mind flying from the east coast to the west, finally settling on Ray's house, dropping down to the mess he calls a basement to see him sitting among his books, writing his next story on his old typewriter.

A touch on my arm wakes me up. "Simon, are you asleep?" I open my eyes, and I see her smile. "Not a very clever question, is it?

"I'm sorry," she says, "but I couldn't really see Ray. I did find something. It jumped into my mind when I tried to look for Ray in that other possibility. I guess I could see it because it had something to do with you. He wrote a story about you, you see. He even got it published very recently, so I guess we're lucky that I'm just checking for it now. Wouldn't have been able to see it before."

"What ... was ... it ... about?"

"I didn't see the exact details—just a second, I'll see what I can get. My God! It was about him taking your old you to the past to convince you not to go to war. Would you believe it? Did he really do that? No, of course not. Oh, I see. It makes perfect sense now!

"Ray is a good writer, right?" I know an understatement when I hear one. "He probably waited for you to come back, all these years. He thought about you, he even got a story published about you. He finally did it—he changed the possibilities; he changed your past! That's some power."

The time machine, the encounter—they were part of a story? He probably didn't even realize what he's he'd done. I certainly hope this doesn't mean that book burning will become true one day. But I don't really care. It all makes sense now—my irrational behavior, the killing—it was just a story. I didn't kill me! I didn't kill anybody! It's like the stone has been raised from over my grave, and I can breathe again. I smile, and Sedef smiles back at me, her brilliant smile amplifying mine.

Ray didn't have to make me kill myself. But I guess that's just the way he is. I smile again, imagining how I'll give him a piece of my mind in the next life. There must be one—enough people believe in it. I might have to wait for him a few years, though—he doesn't seem too willing to let go of this life. I, on the other hand, will soon be looking at new vistas. I hope that heaven isn't based on the most mundane of human dreams.

I look at Sedef one last time. She takes my hand, and I close my eyes, lose all sensation but her warmth. No more pain, no more queasiness. It seems so right to have her by my side as my consciousness slips slowly away. The warmth becomes sunny, and I'm surrounded by light. A tunnel beckons me. Of the world of my life, I carry only one thing with me; one thing, as if sketched by Lewis Carroll—a smile.

In the Mirror

Rotem Baruchin

On Thursday, Mika, who was my cat, mine and Liron's, got killed. One of us, we didn't know who, left her carrier open on the way to the vet, and in one moment Mika busted loose, bolted out of the cage and onto the street. She was run over immediately.

When we got home, Liron headed straight to the sink to do the dishes. There were no dirty dishes in the sink, so she got all the nice dishes from the top shelf and scrubbed them. After that, she went on, working through the bottom shelf, even though the bottom shelf dishes were sparkling clean. She emptied the saltshaker and washed it. She cleaned all the spice jars and the egg tray in the fridge. She washed the dishes for two and a half hours, crying the whole time.

Mika was originally Liron's cat, not mine. When we moved in together, I adopted her, and Liron used to say that "now she has two mommies." Mika liked scaring us to death by sneaking into bed between us and by licking our toes during breakfast. She loved toppling glasses from the edge of the table. She loved playing with Liron's chains until they got completely tangled. She loved being petted behind the ears and scratched under the chin. She loved attention of any kind.

Liron went to the nearby hardware store and came back with the expensive salad serving bowls I wanted to buy last week before she had said, "Danielle, we don't have three hundred shekels, and we hardly ever eat salad." It was only when she unpacked them and started washing them with hands already red and wrinkled from water that I realize that I would have to crack the mirror.

The thought made me feel tired. The last time I cracked the mirror was only two years before, and it took me over a week to get over the terrible fatigue. I lay in bed with red eyes, staring at the ceiling, getting up only to go to the bathroom. Fortunately, Liron didn't see the cuts on my hand. It took her physically carrying me to the doctor's—I was too weak to walk—and his not finding anything wrong before she could be persuaded that all I needed was some rest.

When night fell, and Liron's weeping from the den finally died down, I stood in front of the mirror, trying to delay the inevitable while examining the oh-so-smooth spotless surface, the ancient gilded frame, my own familiar reflection.

Liron hated the mirror. She thought it was ugly and old fashioned. I didn't like it either, for completely different reasons. At first I loved looking at it, especially after cracking it. The first time I did it I was ten years old, after destroying—in a fit of rage—the doll Nana Chana left me, the only thing she gave me other than the mirror. Now, I wouldn't crack the mirror for something as silly as that. I did it then, and for months after I would sit in front of the mirror holding the doll, enchanted, looking at the other Danielle who put the fragments in a small jug by her bed and would occasionally take them out and touch them. Once, she cut her finger on one of them. When she grew up and would look in the mirror, I would study her reflection, comparing it to my own. Same red hair, same green eyes, but something in the eyes was different, and it wasn't just that she couldn't look right back at me.

I stopped watching that Danielle. I had thought she would grow up to be much like me, and it would be boring to look at her. But things turned out differently. She went to a different high school, studied nursing, and married a doctor. A man. I stopped looking at her because I could no longer see myself in her cold eyes when she put her hair up in a tight bun every morning. It bothered me, seeing how different from me she became over such a small thing. I didn't look much at the others, either, since I had Liron.

Liron, I reminded myself. I'm doing this so Liron won't be unhappy. I thought about one more minute, gathering my strength. And then I made a fist. I hit the mirror hard, concentrating on Mika, thinking about her fur, white with gray spots, about her quivering whiskers, a soft purr under the blanket. The mirror cracked. The sudden pain in my hand followed the sharp sound of breakage. But the little crack didn't stay on my side. It faded into the mirror. And then a different Danielle looked at me from the other side. Yet she wasn't looking at me, but at the small crack in her mirror. Her hand wasn't bleeding, and there was a confused expression on her face. She was wondering what had happened, I knew, wondering what she is doing there. And then she heard Liron cry louder again from the other room, confusion turned to sorrow, and she left the mirror and went again to hug and comfort and pack.

On my side, Liron had stopped crying, and a small white cat with grey spots stood for a moment in the door, licking herself before making her way to the bed. I looked at her for a long moment, smiling, until Liron appeared in the doorway. I quickly hid my bleeding hand.

"Whatcha doing?" she asked, coming up behind me. She put her arms around my waist and looked at our reflection in the mirror. She didn't see what I saw on the smooth surface—the empty room, the sounds of crying and begging from the other room, followed by shouts, a door being slammed shut.

"Looking at my pretty girl," I answered, and turned into her hug, turning my back on the mirror. Liron smiled against my lips. "Flattery won't get you anywhere. It's your turn to do the dishes."

I would spend more time looking before Liron became mine. I was curious to know if the mistakes I fixed, the errors I erased, were justified for me. I looked at them often, as if to make certain, with evil satisfaction, that they were miserable, so that I could be happy. I would look at the Danielle who made the mistake of choosing biology instead of communications as her major in high school, so she never ended up getting close to Shiri Rosenstein, never kissing her on the lawn. She lived with a man and would often look at the mirror to avoid looking at him. He hugged her at night while he slept and she would lie awake, looking at the mirror, and I knew that she couldn't understand why she wasn't satisfied. I would look at the Danielle who decided to study gender instead of literature. She was a little plumper than I and lived with an angry woman who'd shout at her. I would look at the Danielle who had refused the job offer at the new publishing house because she was afraid it would be too big a risk. She, like me, met Liron, but Liron left her six months later after yet another fit of rage. She would edit, mostly at nights, sitting bleary-eyed in front of the computer, drinking a lot. I was certain that she would get fired soon.

The need I hated in myself, to always make sure the other Danielles were unhappy, disappeared when Liron came into my life. It was a month after we moved in together, and right after we hung a sign with our names on it over the door, she wouldn't stop complaining about it. "Why do we need a mirror in the bedroom?" she complained. "Why this mirror? It's so ugly." I told her that it was a family heirloom and that it had sentimental value—which was true, so I felt only slightly guilty.

On the evening when she broke the mirror, Liron waited for me in the kitchen when I got home, and when I saw her face, I immediately knew she did something to the mirror. But she was so pale and frightened that I also knew that it wasn't on purpose. Liron said that she tried to get some cardboard boxes she realized she would never unpack onto the top shelf, and one of them fell, hit the mirror, and broke it. "The broken remains are there," she said. "I didn't know whether to clean . . . maybe you want, I mean, to patch it up . . . or maybe keep them in a box and put a new mirror in the frame. I'm sure we can fix the frame. . . ."

My suspicion was confirmed when we entered the bedroom. The mirror was on the floor, next to the cardboard box that had broken it, where it fell. It was intact. There were no shards on the carpet and not a single crack on its smooth face, which reflected Liron's astonished expression. She looked at me, confusion and fear on her face, and rubbed her eyes. Her hands went, on their own, to wander on the mirror's smooth, perfect, surface.

"You must have only thought you broke it," I tried.

"No, no. . . . I'm sure, it was here . . . and there were shards all over the floor." She pointed, afraid. "And the frame, it was here, in two pieces. . . ."

"You dreamed it."

"I did not dream it."

It took me a long time to calm her down.

At night we lay with Mika snuggled between us, her back to my belly, her soft paws resting on Liron's chest. Liron claimed that was uncomfortable. "I have scratches on my boob," she complained, inspecting her body in the mirror in the morning. I smiled when she went to shower and I went to examine myself in the mirror. The weakness was not as bad this time—Liron barely noticed, but I still saw the unnatural pallor of my skin, the fatigue in my motions. Pain still pulled in my hand. Liron bandaged it earlier—I had to break a plate while washing the dishes to explain the cut. Cracking the mirror took so much energy. I hoped I wouldn't have to do it again soon.

A need I didn't understand led me back to the other Danielle, the latest one. She was standing in front of the mirror, looking at her expression with eyes red with tears. The bed was made—apparently, Liron had not come back that night. Suddenly, I felt the full weight of the guilt, as I have never felt it after cracking the mirror. I didn't understand why I felt that way. She was just another Danielle, a mistake. And it was my right to fix my mistakes. It wasn't my fault Liron wasn't with her now. "There are so few people who can change their lives, choose their options," Grandma said when she gave me the mirror. "You should be proud to be one of them."

I touched the mirror, its perfect smooth surface, looking at a crack that only existed on her side. "Sorry," I said, even though I knew she couldn't hear me.

I sorrowfully turned my eyes from the other Danielle, who kept looking at the mirror. Suddenly my back tingled, and I froze, turned around slowly. The other Danielle wasn't looking at her reflection. She was looking at me. I was sure of it. Her eyes focused on me with pure hatred. I stared at her, frozen, stunned, trying to understand how she could look back at me. Her look was cold and furious, and she balled her hand into a fist. Fear suddenly ran in my veins, and I reached out to stop her, screaming, "No!"

She was smiling at me while she broke the mirror.

Liron lies so close, but there's a wall between us. Her back is to me, stiff and upright. She's been so cold to me since Mika, and I can't help but wonder whether one day she'll look at me again with love in her eyes. We don't know which of us left the carrier open, but I know she blames me. I want to hug her and erase the pain she's feeling, to be happy and to make her happy. But instead I cry silently, and my tears fall on the sheets, soak into the mattress, disappear into the night.

And as I stop looking at her and turn around, refusing to sleep facing the frozen back, I wonder if it all could have been different. If only I could change it, the brief, stupid moment when the cage opened and Mika darted out of the cage and into the street. I think about it as I fall asleep, while my eyes rest on the crack that suddenly appeared, only two days ago, on the old mirror that my Grandma left me.

The Stern-Gerlach Mice

Mordechai Sasson

kept on falling even though I had regained consciousness, falling way, way down. I screamed like crazy and opened my eyes to find myself in a hospital bed. But the sensation of falling persisted. Worse than that, I could hear thoughts. Hear, not read—I perceived people's thoughts through my sense of hearing. For half a day I kept pleading with doctors and visitors to stop the yammering inside their heads. People sitting beside me kept emitting an incessant, enervating babble of noises. I had to shout when I wanted to talk to them; otherwise I couldn't hear myself. To make things worse still, my visitors shouted back at me, assuming that I was suffering from a loss of hearing.

I finally realized that this mind-hearing thing had a lot to do with distance—inverse-square, or some other exponent. The further the persons who did the thinking were from me, the quieter their thoughts became. My pleadings finally made people sit as far away from me as possible, and then we *really* had to shout at each other. So all this talk about reading minds and broadcasting thoughts is bullshit. Old wives' tales.

Old wives? What about my Nana? Yes, they assured me. She's alright.

The police officer who came to question me asked if I had been injured by the mice. I told him that a sophisticated mouse-made weapon had been used against me. The policeman wanted to know how I could tell it was mouse-made. I said that the weapon was totally mousy, was designed to be operated by a mouse. The disgusting rodent had used its tongue to manipulate it.

"Lucky for you, the Tin Beggar saved you," said the policeman.

The officer's thundering thoughts told me how upset he was. First there was all this imbecilic biogenesis thing in the Judean Desert, with an outbreak of evolution so wild it ought to be called a revolution; then there was this American lady who came from outer space down to Jerusalem, after the Thirteenth Shock that had left her lethally disturbed. And now the mice were making their appearance on the troubled and troublesome stage of homeland security.

I could hear how disgusted he was with the forthcoming war. He didn't think it's such a glorious deal, fighting mice. His thinking became too noisy, and I had to shout at him to stop it, just stop thinking and let his mind rest, let me rest as well.

The sensation of falling lasted the whole day, even though I was awake, and because of this I was afraid even to move a finger. I lay stretched out like a wounded rubber sheet, pale as death itself, nausea churning inside me. My tongue lolling, I held tight both bedsides so as not to tumble in my nonexistent plummet.

It took the entire day before I calmed down, ceased feeling that I was falling, and stopped hearing thoughts. The side effects of my injury slowly ebbed away. Now I could turn my mind to the war.

The mice had taken over Nana's street. Preserved in its old style as a Jerusalem heritage site, this street bordered on the religious neighborhoods. I didn't think it was such a big deal, taking over that street. It had been taken over by roaches a long, long time ago. And the mice held it for just a short while. The Tin Beggar, willing to sacrifice its metallic soul, bravely defended all those unconscious people and, specifically, saved me. The Tin Beggar also evacuated people from the street, for which it won an official citation from City Hall. Lucky beggar!

Then came the police, and later on the military. The military overcame the resistance offered by the mice and drove them away, devastating half the buildings in the street as collateral damage. The way I heard it, not a single house remained entirely intact. The Stern-Gerlach mice suffered seven casualties during the military's assault, that's all (I myself killed more than that), because of this ability of theirs to shift to microscopic size and evade direct hits. The military, on the other hand, filled a whole hospital ward with soldiers who kept begging those around them, as I did, to think *quietly*.

The Stern-Gerlach mice!

How did we get ourselves in such a mess?

All thanks are due to science's indefatigable efforts to uncover The Truth. Some smartass biophysicist had tried to measure the Stern-Gerlach effect produced by an electron beam (beta radiation) passing through living tissue. Except that the beta radiation was immediately absorbed by the tissue. So what did our clever fellow do? He drilled a hole in a cat's skull, attached an array of powerful magnets to the sides of its head, and beta-radiated directly into the cat's brain. The electrons were absorbed, of course, but an electromagnetic wave kept propagating as a pulse from the point of impact. Passing between the magnets, the pulse split, then split again when it passed between the next pair of magnets, and so on.

The biophysicist rubbed his hands in pleasure when the cat lost consciousness in a series of bizarre convulsions. The cat remained unconscious and slowly perished because its immune system could no longer recognize it and started attacking it.

Various animals were then beta-radiated directly into their brains, all of them responding with various ways of expiring, stranger and stranger yet. The form death took depended on the brain area radiated, and the length of time it took them to die proved to be species-dependent. And so, in this relentless pursuit of The Truth, the lab turned into an enormous slaughterhouse. All this bloody spectacle just to show that *something* happens when an exposed area of the brain is beta-radiated inside a magnetic field. Cleverness will get you anywhere!

The experiment would have been halted in short order were it not for this curious fact: mice that were beta-radiated into the right temporal lobes of their cortices insisted on staying alive. Furthermore, lo and behold, the electric activity in their brains was enhanced. These mice became smarter than their control group counterparts. They learned faster which were the right buttons to push. Their ability to find the relationships between cause and effect across a time interval improved—meaning, their time perception became more extended. They turned out to be the uncontested champions in running through mazes in search of bits of cheese.

This was all the biophysicist could discover. He wanted to try it on humans but was immediately told to shut up. However, one group of irradiated mice escaped the lab, multiplied, as mice do, and became Jerusalem's scourge. The media gave them their name: the Stern-Gerlach mice. It was nearly impossible to get rid of them. *You* try to trap or poison a smart mouse with a good memory. In addition, the mice started massacring the cat population, making the alley cat the first urban animal officially designated a protected species.

Despite all this, the Stern-Gerlach mice had never built tools, never shifted their size . . . until they took over Nana's street.

Three days after I had been injured, having recovered from all those side effects, I was released from hospital and immediately went to see Nana. Because this was how it all began. . . .

It all began when I came to see Nana at lunchtime the day before Tish'a b'Av, kicking crumbling pieces of pavement as I went along. A stubborn growth of Bermuda grass burst through the tough surface. I reached the heavily shaded corner, under Hasson's pear tree, that led into the alley. The sun made me sweat profusely, but it also made the pears on this tree plumper. At the end of the alley, in front of her open door, Nana sat talking with the rest of the neighborhood's old ladies. The biddies were chatting, occasionally bursting into laughter or stabbing their synthetic wool with knitting needles for emphasis, performing fancy fencing moves.

Among the yentas sat Orit, Yaffa's fat, unmarried daughter, making her best efforts to fit in with their Little Old Ladies world. The viciousness of her gossip, the poison in her words, and her habit of gloating were yet to be softened by age.

Coming closer, I allowed myself a tiny smirk at their gossipfest and then called out to my Nana. Her eyes lit up when she saw me. I bent over and kissed her cheek. I love Nana even when she dabbles in the sea of gossip, and my love renders this murky sea pure and clear. Nana is proud of me—her eldest grandson, the university student.

"My legs ache," she said to me, "so why don't you go in and warm some food for yourself? Think you can manage?"

"Sure, Nana."

I went in, ate some, then dragged out a stool and sat there facing the old ladies, smoking a cigarette as they amped up their vicious gossip, brazenly besmirching those not present, shamelessly fawning on those who were. Every once in a while Orit would aggressively stop her needlework and ask me a question, just to be nice, to keep in touch with hers, the younger generation. I answered indifferently because she was so damned ugly.

A sound of metallic crackling and rattling came from the mouth of the alley. Hearing it the old ladies stopped their chatter, exchanging glances critical of the world-at-large. It was all I could do not to laugh at their reaction.

"The Meshuga, a curse upon its soul, is back again," said Yaffa.

"Poor thing, if one more bit falls off it, it'll come apart," Nana said in its defense.

"But it's such a bore," commented Orit in what she must have thought was a mature manner, and squinted at me.

Avrum's mother, who looked like an Egyptian mummy and was probably as old, held up a fragile finger and cackled, "When I was young, there were no such things around."

"It says in the papers that they kidnap children," said Orit.

"No, come on, it's not kidnapping children," replied Nana. "Poor thing, this Meshuga, it's been in the neighborhood for years, and no child got kidnapped, ever."

"How true," lowed Odelia's toothless mouth. "It's all stories made up by the Bank. Damn the Bank, where does it get off harassing them?"

"Tomatoes!" Avrum's mother burst out nostalgically. "When I was little we used to buy tomatoes at a store, from a person who was actually selling them. A real person. Not like today: you stick the bank card in a wall, and out comes a kilo of tomatoes."

"Bank, schmank," said Nana dismissively. "There's the Meshuga. All painters have a few screws loose."

The rattling noise grew louder, and then the Tin Beggar made its entrance. It limped in a tight, precisely controlled, clockwork way. Its left shoulder was bent, the result of an old sledgehammer blow, its face covered with a blackened patina. One eye was missing, and from the empty socket colored wires dangled down its cheek. One knee crackled, two of its fingers were broken, and a few holes in its head suggested it was missing some nuts. Just a regular neighborhood tin beggar, whom the crones gave a disdainful name to tell it apart from others of its ilk, even though tin beggars have no real names.

"Here comes Chambalooloo!" said Orit, frowning. She poked a knitting needle in the air and prophesized: "Some day all this will end, and not in a good way! The papers say they're dangerous, I'm telling you!"

"The papers all belong to the Bank," I interjected to silence her.

She huffed but threw me a flirtatious glance.

"Ah!" snorted Flora, "Now it'll want to paint us for a handout. Who needs to be painted, who? Tell it that the Rebbetzin said we shouldn't accept paintings from tin beggars."

"But the Rebbetzin also said we must treat them nice!" replied Nana fiercely.

"Nothing good will come out of this one," claimed Orit, disappointed. "This is no real man, this one."

Her mother looked at her, sad and hurt. The old ladies' lips trembled in an attempt to hide their smirks. As for me, I turned my face up diplomatically to see whether there were any clouds in the sky.

The robot stopped in front of us and asked, "Madam, can you spare a gift of metal?"

Nana smiled, signaled for it to come closer, searched in her housecoat's pockets, and took out a large nail, rusty and bent. Smiling happily, she handed it to the Tin Beggar: "There you are, Chambalooloo."

"Another nail?" Holding it, the Tin Beggar looked utterly disappointed.

A long time ago Nana poked around in her shed and found a bucket full of large, rusty, bent, totally useless nails. Generously, she would give one to Chambalooloo every day, except on Shabbat. As I said, Nana lives near a religious neighborhood. The tin beggars learned to watch their steps on the holy day, since the time some metallic unfortunate started cleaning a street in Me'a She'arim as a gesture of good will. It was Shabbat, and the worshippers emerged from their synagogue to tear it to pieces, leaving behind only tiny bits of metal.

"Would you like me to paint your portrait, Madam?" the Tin Beggar asked Nana.

Amazingly, the chief occupation of tin beggars is art. They paint, they play music, they tell beautiful stories, all for metal handouts. But resolutions angrily adopted by the Writers and Poets Union, the Painters and Sculptors Union, and the Musicians Union declared that any painting, poem, story, or tune produced by a tin beggar is not to be considered a work of art (and for good reason, too: few humans can meet the impossibly high standards set by the tin beggars). Thus, the tin beggars were doomed to remain the makers of ephemeral, perishable art, since there was no one willing to preserve it.

"There's a rule against painting in this neighborhood," said Nana. "But my leg hurts. Can you just do us a favor and throw out the garbage?"

Hearing Nana's request, I could no longer keep a straight face and burst out laughing. How like Nana! For a rusty nail a day, she'd made the Tin Beggar her slave.

The robot's shoulders sank. It went into her home and came out again, carrying the garbage can in one huge hand. I got up and stepped into the kitchen to make myself some coffee. Returning to sunlight, I sat myself back on the stool, facing the old ladies. The Tin Beggar returned Nana's trashcan to the kitchen.

Upon emerging, it started rocking to and fro on its heels to draw Nana's attention while she was arguing with the ladies about the exact time of the Tish'a b'Av fast onset.

I smiled again. It was waiting to ask whether Nana wanted anything else. Knowing her, she would definitely ask it to do some more, like clean the windows, then sweep the floor, and if there was any laundry to wash, do that as well. Nana was not one to let such an opportunity slip by.

Finally, Nana addressed the Tin Beggar. "Did you throw out the garbage, Chambalooloo, apple of my eye?"

"Garbage disposed of," it intoned. "Will there be anything else, Madam?"

"Chambalooloo darling," Nana said charmingly, "my leg hurts terribly. There are a few dishes in the kitchen sink. Could you please wash them? If it's not too difficult?"

My grin grew wider as I observed how obsequiously this gigantic hunk of metal was bent to Nana's iron will.

"No, it's not too difficult," groaned the robot.

The metal giant took a step toward the kitchen, then froze.

"Madam," it said quietly to Nana, "there is a giant mouse in your kitchen."

"You didn't even enter the kitchen, so how can you tell?" Nana wondered.

"I can hear it."

Nana pursed her lips in annoyance and waved a finger at the Tin Beggar. "It's not so nice, shirking work like this. What did I ask for, anyway? Some help for five minutes, that's all."

"I am not shirking work. You have a giant mouse in your kitchen."

Now Nana became mad. "There are no mice in my kitchen! You tell me, am I treating you wrong, the way you treat me now? Don't I give you a nail every day?"

"You are treating me kindly, and you do give me a nail every day, and I'll do the dishes. But right now there is a giant mouse in your kitchen."

I covered my mouth to hide my grin, squinting at the crones. They looked like they were ready to rise and stab the Tin Beggar to death with their knitting needles.

"That's what I told you," Orit said sanctimoniously to Nana. "Nothing good will come out of this one."

"No, you're wrong," said Nana vehemently to Orit (as a show of good will indirectly intended for the Tin Beggar), "it *is* alright. Perhaps it got tired today. But for years I've been asking it to help me, and it's come through every time. Maybe it's just not feeling well today."

The Tin Beggar said miserably, "I am telling the truth!"

The professionals claim that robots have no feelings. But we Jerusalemites know full well they're sensitive, and they do have feelings.

"What truth?" said Nana angrily.

"There is a giant mouse in your kitchen."

Nana decided to check this out, and, being the shrewd person she was, immediately put the burden on someone else. "Ethan," she said to me, "you go see what's in the kitchen."

I got up from my stool, taking the empty coffee cup with me, and flashed a friendly smile at the ladies. Odelia returned my smile with her zipperlike mouth. Avrum's mother's smile reminded me of the Angel of Death. Orit's fat cheeks hid her beady eyes as she attempted another coy smile. Only Nana gave me a direct glare.

I went into the hallway with the Tin Beggar trailing me in its meticulous limp. The rooms were lined up along the hallway, the third door leading into the kitchen. There was indeed some noise in there, the sound of something heavy being dragged on the floor. I opened the door and looked in.

Astonishment nearly knocked me off my feet. By the sink, near the cabinets, there stood a mouse as big as a small donkey, a bit taller than the height of my hips, all gray, its whiskers thick as ropes. The mouse, aiming its snout at the shelves, was sniffing the condiment jars one by one. Its weight was too much for its skinny legs, so it leaned on its backside against the floor. Its breathing was a running gurgle indicating a superhuman, I mean a supermousy, effort. I stared stupidly at the long pipe that was its tail.

"It might be dangerous," said Chambalooloo behind me.

Hearing its voice, the mouse turned heavily toward us, and what it did then made me gasp in even greater surprise. It shrank to cat size. The transformation was fast, and obviously, the reduction in size gave it back its agility. It started skittering to and fro, squeaking angrily. Eventually it calmed down a little, squatted on its behind in front of me, drawing its body up like a hamster. I stared at it, my mouth agape. The mouse started squeaking again, waving its paws. Recovering from my surprise, I realized that there was some pattern to its tweeting, as if it was trying to communicate with me. Judging by the motions it made with its paws, it must have been an angry communication.

I screamed in disgust and threw the empty cup at it, following close behind with my foot up to give it a kick. As the cup was about to hit it, the mouse shrank itself further and vanished.

I looked the question at the Tin Beggar. "What was that all about?"

"A Stern-Gerlach mouse," it said.

"Stern-Gerlach mice? I didn't know they could size-shift."

The Tin Beggar made no answer. Instead it proceeded, in its meticulous limp, to clean up the cup fragments. Then it did the dishes. I went out.

"What were you up to, breaking a glass? Marrying Chambalooloo?" Nana asked, whether in anger or in mirth I couldn't tell.

"I tried to kill the mouse."

"What mouse?" Nana was astonished.

"A mouse as big as a donkey," I told her.

"You're crazy!" Nana stated. "You're like Chambalooloo. A mouse like a donkey?! And in my own kitchen yet? Come on, you crazy, you! Where do you get off, saying something like that?"

My face reddened, but I managed to check an angry response. Nana gets mad quickly, and she has a big mouth. Once she gets started, there's no getting away from her.

After a few minutes Chambalooloo came out, its metallic hands wet. "I'm through, Madam, if you . . ."

"Thank you very much, Chambalooloo," Nana interrupted. "Next time, feel free to tell me if you're tired."

Obviously, Nana didn't believe the mouse story.

Suddenly I heard a belabored grunt behind me. I turned around, jumped up, and nearly fainted. In the doorway there stood a mouse as tall as a donkey and broad enough to look like a sickly lion. Around its head there was a metal band made of glowing, buzzing cubes.

The old ladies yelped in surprise; Orit even screamed. I felt like my chest and arms were being stabbed. I growled like an animal, grabbed the stool, threw it at the mouse, and dived after it. The mouse size-shifted, but the stool hit it halfway through the transformation, in the middle of its back. The impact knocked it aside, and I reached it and stomped my foot against its head, once, twice. I lifted my foot for a third stomp . . . and then all hell broke loose.

From the corner of my eye I saw a grey blur flying at me. I tried to fend it off, but the mouse sunk its teeth into my arm, hanging on to it. From the rooms and the corridor there came out a flood of angry, screaming mice. Mice were nipping at my legs. Then a gigantic mouse popped up behind me. Hearing its disgusting grunt I turned around, and the monster hurled its weight against me. I fell, and a flurry of furious mice scrambled over me, biting. The giant mouse made a move for my head, its gaping mouth revealing teeth as big as daggers, so help me God! I slammed it ferociously with the stool, and it yelped and started shrinking. I pounded it again and again until it nearly shrank from view. Overcoming my panic, I started whacking at the other mice, methodically now, not blindly as before. After killing twenty of them I realized I was bleeding from numerous puncture wounds. I hurled myself out and slammed the door.

Nana was white as a sheet. "Wow, Ethan! I thought you were lying when you said there was a mouse there. Forgive me. Actually, I must beg Chambalooloo's forgiveness as well."

The Tin Beggar hissed electronically from the corner of its speaker, "They are all over the street."

Whole families were running out of their homes, shrieking in terror. (The official inquiry would later determine that the mice, some as big as donkeys, had suddenly appeared in all these houses at the same time, driving out their inhabitants. They must have been microscopic when they invaded, then expanded to their gigantic dimensions. The mice showed up when the men were at work. Only I, a student, could afford to lay about when everyone else was laboring.)

How long can you stay frozen in shock? I started swearing as mothers and daughters burst from their homes, carrying infants in their arms. Old men fled for their lives, waving their feeble fists, and old women scrambled after them, shrieking. The street turned into a cauldron of frenzied howls. A mouse emerged from one doorway, sat on its bottom huffing like a hippo, and started keening, exhorting its fellow combatants with frantic paw gestures. But it never got to the end of its speech. A furious woman slammed a sizable rock against its head. The mouse tumbled, dazed, and before it could issue another squeak, half the street swarmed it with planks and kicking feet. As big as it was, all that was left in the end was some mincemeat.

(A month later I was invited to Israel TV studios for an interview. A trio of reporters, who looked like a contingent of the Spanish Inquisition, insisted that the mice had just wanted to parley. But we, members of the uneducated classes that we were, just had to press the attack. They declared that as a person of some learning I should have sensed the rodents' yearning for peaceful coexistence and stopped the mob. Knowing that I had single-handedly killed more mice than the military by attacking the mice directly, they branded *me* the aggressor. I got mad and asked them what should a man do when confronted by monsters that can tear his head off in one bite? He defends himself, inhumanely if necessary. And if he senses an opportunity—as when the speech-making mouse started distracting its comrades—he moves in as aggressively as possible to remove the threat. The TV people didn't agree, so I stormed out of the studio midway through the ordeal.)

I suddenly remembered the mouse in the kitchen, how it counted jars with its snout, and cried in amazement, "Damn that bastard! It was taking inventory!"

Nana said resentfully, "And tomorrow being Tish'a b'Av!"

She got up heavily from her bench. "Let's get in the house."

"Your house is full of mice!"

"Then what should I do? Sleep outdoors?"

The crowd pulverizing the speaker mouse quickly dispersed. Seeing the torn carcass of their gigantic comrade, several mice began whistling excitedly at each other.

All of a sudden I could hear my heart pounding in my ears, its volume and pace growing unbearably. I covered my ears, trying to stop the infernal noise. All around me little old ladies, younger women, and children suddenly fell to their knees, their eyes glazed. By the time my heart reached a crescendo, the noise became indistinct. I lost my sense of balance, the world tilted, and the ground suddenly slapped me in the face. On my way down I caught sight of Chambalooloo sweeping Nana into its clanging arms and running to the end of the street. As I began regaining my senses, it came limping back. "I hope they won't accuse me of taking part in this occupation and let the Bank repossess me."

"I'll testify in your favor," I replied numbly.

"Wait here," it said. "Women and children first."

I cursed it, too, as it shambled away from me.

Chambalooloo picked up fat Orit, who screamed in horror, or perhaps delight, almost choking it. I turned on my back and saw a police hovercraft above the street.

Reaching the end of the street, Chambalooloo tried to shake fat Orit off it. Orit refused to let go. It gently undid her stranglehold with its broken metallic hands, and she let out angry screams at its receding back.

Then a new apparition towered over me, a mouse wearing a helmet fitted with various antennae, wires, flashing lights, sparkling bursts of energy, and whatnot. It was flicking its foul tongue over the control panel hanging in front of its face. A loud whistle pierced the air, nearly piercing me as well. My muscles spasmed and I started screaming. Darkness descended. I floated off.

I tried to reach out and grab at something in this awful darkness. "You are going to die," I heard in the emptiness.

Then I started plummeting, an endless fall into a horrendous awful emptiness.

When I came back to visit Nana after my release from the hospital, the neighborhood was in shambles. Where Hasson's pear tree had stood I saw just a stump.

I found out that Nana had quarreled with Orit, because Orit tried to seduce

Chambalooloo. (True, as I live and breathe!) Nana had made the Tin Beggar her protégé, insisting that Orit would only make trouble for it.

The Tin Beggar, indeed, looked brand new. It told me that City Hall had awarded its efforts with a complete overhaul. It was scrubbed and polished, its nuts and bolts were tightened, and missing parts were replaced—the works. They had even given it a new eye.

Nana had gifted the newly refurbished Tin Beggar a new toaster. You should have seen its robotic delight. What a laugh!

And the mice? Your basic cold war: threats, raids, woe to the lone person who falls into the hands of the Stern-Gerlach mice. And woe to the mouse that falls into human hands. In other words, the usual. Recently, I've heard, in certain circles there's talk of trying to parley with the mice.

Another thing. I've become a painter.

How, you ask?

Some arrangement I've worked out with the Tin Beggar, since I've had the leverage: I'd threaten to tell the authorities it had known in advance of the Stern-Gerlach mice offensive unless it gave me some of its work. Now it gives me paintings, which I sign. What a pleasure, being a painter without actually having to wield a brush. Chambalooloo gets a fair shake, too, because I award it with electronic appliances. Besides, it gets recognition by proxy as a distinguished artist. And I get paid handsomely.

And other than that?

Other than that, all is peaceful and quiet in the new Jerusalem.

A Good Place for the Night

Savyon Liebrecht

In the fourth year, the funnel of air passed frequently over the house, teasing, descending to the garden of wooden monsters where the child used to wander. Every few days, Gila would hear the distant whistle grow shriller, like the siren on the eve of Holocaust Memorial Day or on the eve of Memorial Day for the Fallen in War, and she'd run out and pull the boy home. She was almost late once, and at the last minute, as she grabbed him from the sucking flow, she saw the opening of the funnel up close for the first time, damp and quivering, like an elephant's trunk. And once she was late. The boy's arm had been sucked in, but he struggled, flapping at the mouth of the funnel, swinging his short legs and his free arm, moving away and rising, and Gila ran under him, screaming, until he was dropped on the other side of the fence into the area of the epidemic over which birds were flying in circles. He was caught in a tree, then fell to the contaminated earth along with some branches, bruised all over. Later, frightened and exhausted, he let her isolate him in his room for three days and smear his body with an ointment she made from the bark of a tree that burned the skin and its fruit, which was shaped like cats' heads. Sometimes, when he cried and Gila was too tired, the nun would come out of her room and lovingly tend to him. But when he'd recovered from his mysterious illness and grew calm, he insisted on going out again, especially to the garden of monsters, as if he were heeding the call of his parents beckoning him to their burial place.

When the boy was outside, Gila would coax and threaten and plead with him to come in, but he, recalcitrant and rebellious, his body sturdy for a two-year-old, would slip away from the windows to the garden of warped tree trunks, and she became accustomed to straining her ears for the sound of the whistling air that heralded the coming of the funnel.

Not until he was asleep in his bed and she was secure in the refuge of the house did she stop the constant straining to hear. Then she waited for the funnel with forbidden excitement, occasionally seeing objects fly past like lightning and remembering how she had once seen a remarkable spectacle. It was as if the funnel had decided to tease her—like a naked young girl in a dark window, waiting to tease a neighbor across the way. The streams of haze rising from the ground began to move slowly, drawn in a single direction to form a clear diagonal curtain, curled at the edges and with a long, hollow space in the center, and one end of it moving lustfully, seeking prey. A large tree complete with its roots appeared suddenly at one end of the channel of clear air, flew like a shot arrow to the other end, and disappeared instantly. She stood there terrified and enthralled by the haze that was now flattening, returning to its former state, as calm as an animal whose appetite has been satisfied.

But then, the boy had already been a year old.

The first time she saw the funnel, she still hadn't known the boy existed. As soon as she walked into the house with the man, even before they saw the five dead people, before they found the boy sleeping in his bed, they suddenly heard the noise of a storm, and a tube of bright air cut through the smoke that had already begun to darken outside. Inside the illuminated tube of space, stretched parallel to the horizon and twice the height of a person, numerous objects sailed around slowly, becoming entangled in gentle circles: stools and a bookshelf, babies' clothes, frying pans, a mattress, a straw lampshade, landscape paintings, a tapestry of harem women, a bouquet of flowers and the vase that had once held them, pillows embroidered with silver and purple birds, a blue enamel kettle, a carpet, a woman's purse, newspaper pages. Gila looked in horror at the contents of the ghost house hovering in front of her: not too long ago someone had read that newspaper and had drunk tea brewed in that kettle; a dog had lain on that carpet; a woman had worn the straps of that purse on her shoulder; babies had soiled those clothes. Where were they now?

The graying smoke had once again subdued the channel of air, but still she stood at the window, waiting, as if she had been told part of a story and wanted to know the ending. Then the man had come out of one of the rooms and said, "There are five dead adults here and one live baby."

Two of the dead people had been guests, an elegant couple of Indian descent sitting in the garden on a wrought iron bench, he smoking and she brushing her hair. The three other dead people had been employees of the inn: a very tall, thin young man doing accounts at a desk in the office; an older man with gray sideburns bent over the stove in the kitchen; and a girl wearing a frilled chambermaid's apron lying like a contortionist at the foot of a half-made bed in one of the rooms on the top floor.

Elated, Gila stood beside the sleeping baby's bed and recalled a children's story one of her little girls had liked and the other had loathed: the three bears come home after an evening stroll to find Goldilocks sleeping in the small bed.

The man scrutinized her, pondering, watching this unknown woman glow at the sight of the sleeping child, reach out and cover his exposed shoulder, take pleasure in something familiar amidst the chaos they had been thrown into, holding on to the temporary ordinariness of a child breathing peacefully in his bed.

Then they began a search of the inn together. Stepping noiselessly from room to room, they looked into the gleaming bathrooms, examined the beds, were drawn to the windows that looked out onto a landscape of thin columns of dust that covered the earth.

Once, when the child still obeyed her and didn't go out into the garden, the funnel of air stopped in front of the house and tossed a cloth-wrapped bundle onto the doorstep. From the window, Gila looked at the package of rags that had been spit out at the door and saw it begin to move. A head emerged from it, the head of a very old woman. The child, who had never seen such an old person, screamed in fright. This wasn't the first stranger he'd seen. Although he'd known the nun and the sick man from the time he was a baby, occasionally someone would stumble upon the house, speak an incomprehensible language, look pleadingly at Gila, and wolf down the food she offered. Sometimes the stranger would fall asleep in one of the armchairs, and the man would sit beside him holding a stick, and when he woke up, the man would send him on his way. Once, three wild-looking women appeared, their hair and their nails grown long. One of them reached out to touch the child, and he drew back with a cry. Then time passed, and no one came to the house until the funnel spit out the old lady. Gila went out to her and, her hand covered with cloth, looked for the signs but didn't find even one: the backs of the old lady's hands were not covered with brown spots, there was no swelling behind her ears and no pus leaking from her eyes. Gila dragged the old lady into the house, sat her down in an armchair, and gave her some water, which she drank slowly. The old lady sat in that armchair for three days, sipping water, taking bites of a biscuit, relieving herself in her clothes. The child stood beside her all his waking hours, studying her from every angle, imitating the sounds of her strange language. On the fourth day she spit up black blood and died. The child cried when they buried her in the yard where—this he did not know—his parents were buried along with the three employees of the inn.

One time, the child had been close to discovering his parents. Driving rain had poured down all night, washing away the dirt that covered the bodies and scattering fragments of skeletons over the yard. From his room the child saw the bones first, and the man hurried outside to rebury them. Gila watched from the window, recalling the beautiful Indian woman they had found dead in the garden, wearing an orange sari edged with gold embroidery. Even if she had been preserved whole in her grave, the child would not have recognized her. Gila would sometimes wonder, and ask the man, whether a four-month-old baby had memories, whether he might know that the people raising him were not the ones who had given birth to him, whether they would tell him one day about the circumstances that had brought the three of them together, whether they should wait until he himself discovered how different his appearance was from theirs.

They agreed that, one day, they would tell him the whole truth, they would show him his parents' passports and his name and date of birth written in one of them. Meanwhile, the days passed, one following on the heels of the other according to the clock, but never revealing the secret of time. From the first day and through all the years they were never able to unlock the secret of the changing seasons, and only the chart they kept of the days helped them mark off time. The weather seesawed from day to day like a bad-tempered person; the sun blazed not like a ball of fire, but like formless lava spreading like a puddle over half the sky; rain fell not in a downpour, but like an entire cloud being hurled down, exploding on the ground with a crash that made the tree roots quake. Sometimes it would be dark and stormy for days at a time; sometimes the primeval landscape was bathed in a blinding, phosphorous light that flooded the enormous desolation, as flat as a tray, devoid of forests, grooved with fissures that spread in straight lines to the horizon like the furrows of a plowed field, spitting jet-streams of transparent dust from its grooves—a magnificent and menacing stage set. But sometimes Gila would wake and see, as if it were an ad for a tourist site, the kind of pristine, clear, fresh world you see after the rain: bare trees exposed to the pleasant sun; and above them, a sky beautiful with baby blue clouds, as if it had not witnessed the scenes of horror that had raged under it on that cataclysmic day; and in the distance, in a uniform shade of green, pastures as smooth as lake water; and on the horizon, a row of trees with densely tangled foliage, a kind of tree she had never seen before. Her gaze traveled over the clouds, assembled like a mountain ridge, as if they were the repository of memories from other landscapes that had sailed onward over the flat, bright countryside, and she felt suddenly calm: the sky was in its place and the earth was in its place. It was impossible that, beyond the distant trees, there were no roads or cities of living people now planning their day, which had just begun.

"Do you think the train might be working again?" she kept asking those first few months.

The man would look at her, saddened that she had once again been carried away by the deceptive landscape and that she would once again have to travel the path to the knowledge that the world she knew had vanished while she was in the train's smoking car, and he said, "The train is stuck in exactly the same place."

On evenings reminiscent of summer, the three of them would go out into the garden, or walk, or ride their bicycles far from the house until they got tired, sometimes heading toward what had been the train station and sometimes toward the corpses of the railroad cars that, before the catastrophe, had crossed Europe. Sometimes they'd pass the charcoal shepherd and his charcoal flock and see the three skeletons in the station and the skeletons of the passengers crumbling inside their tattered clothes. From the day he learned to walk, the child, used to the sight, would go into the ticket seller's booth, move the skeleton that had once been the ticket seller to the edge of its chair, squeeze in beside it, and play with the equipment and the money, but Gila and the man gazed at the skeletons and remembered how they'd looked on the day of the cataclysm. Then the child, hoisted up to the windows, would look at the skeletons in the train, his glance lingering on the skeleton of the little girl holding the book he would know by heart in another year, *Alice in Wonderland*, a birthday present from her teacher, who had written in it the false prophecy, "To the talented Mary Jane, who will write books like this herself one day, when she grows up."

In her dreams she would relive the moment the car shook suddenly, like a ghost train in an amusement park, and she opened the door of the smoking car and saw the sleeping people who, an instant before, had been awake. The brazen young couple who had been making love on the bench across from her (the girl's panting had embarrassed the other passengers, who shot glances at each other) were embracing, deeply asleep—she arched backward, her hair hanging over the seat, and he bent over her, his face buried in her neck; the frenetic young man's head was pressed against the window, as if he were kissing the cracked glass goodbye; the older man who had been flashing surreptitious glances of longing at the couple making love was tilted back, his hands crossed on his groin, his gaze fixed on the ceiling; the two strangers who had become friends during the trip, one explaining that he had come from a conference of ecology experts, the other proffering pieces of choice tropical fruit wrapped in cellophane, were sitting mummified, staring at each other; the little girl who had been engrossed in reading *Alice in Wonderland* was bent forward as if bowing deeply, her forehead touching the open book. Many of the train's windows were shattered, and splinters of glass glinted on the dark floor; objects and packages that had fallen from the overhead rack were scattered in the aisle; one travel case that had not been completely closed was now open, and meticulously ironed shirts were spread around it as if they'd been arranged for display. A suitcase had fallen, burying a redheaded young man so that only a clump of his hair stuck out over the handle of the suitcase and a pair of new jeans showed at the other end of it.

From where she was standing at the end of the car, Gila's eyes darted about, taking in the sight with the utmost clarity in incandescent, diamondlike brightness. She felt a momentary stirring of the hopeful suspicion that the passengers had conspired to pretend they were asleep to see how she would respond, and the whole thing—the artificial light, the unnatural positions—had been staged for a television show that tortured people for the enjoyment of other people, and in a minute the famous director would suddenly appear and the sleeping people would open their eyes and delight in her embarrassment. But the astonishing silence in the car, broken by the strange sounds of the earth cracking and the bubbling flow of dust from outside gave her gooseflesh, and the scene visible through the windows completely ruled out the idea of a hidden camera. The flat surface of the earth was now covered with a thick veil that flowed from it and billowed up to the sky, as if the earth's belly were boiling.

She tried to get a sound out of her throat to wake up the sleeping people, and a low, unintentional croak emerged, like the sound made by a mute trying to scream. Nothing moved in the car, and she stood mesmerized, refusing to acknowledge what she saw, refusing to think about what lay behind what she saw. Her legs began to move of their own volition over the shards of glass and articles of clothing scattered in the aisle, and she pressed her handbag, which held her passport and the pearl rings she'd bought for her daughters in the art museum, against her body. The people in the next car were sleeping too. The headrests, which were not covered with white doilies—she could see through the glass of the door that was stuck halfway open in its track—gave away the fact that it wasn't a first-class car, but it appeared that the passengers who had bought cheaper tickets had seen a more splendid show: feathered hats, lacy shawls, colored scarves, fur stoles, and bridal veils that had fallen from the trunk of a troupe of actors were scattered over the people, the seats, and the aisle.

"Hello, hello," Gila shouted into the car, but nothing moved. "Is anyone here? Is there anyone here?" she added in English, in a braver, more desperate voice inflamed by the fear that had begun to creep into her mind, by the knowledge that she could not ignore for long what she was seeing, and that she was not dreaming, but witnessing a dreamlike reality.

Her ears, which had already adjusted to the sounds of the splitting earth and had accepted them as background noises, suddenly seemed to absorb a new sound in the distance, as abrupt as a dog's bark. She hurried to one of the broken windows, stuck her head out between the sharp peaks of glass protruding from the window frame, listened hard, and screamed to the smoke-filled world outside, "Hey! Hey! Hello! Hello!"

A very faint voice sounded from the depths of the thick whiteness, "Hey, where are you?"

"Here, inside the train!" she shouted toward the human voice and stretched her neck even further, putting it in danger of being slit. "Where are you? Where are you?" Her throat swelled with the effort.

"Here," a distant voice echoed.

"I'm inside the train," she shouted excitedly. There was no doubt: a man's voice. "Don't go in the wrong direction! Come this way!"

"It's okay." The voice crossed the diminishing distance, and now the owner of that voice could hear that hers was a woman's voice. "Wait for me. I'm coming in your direction."

"I'm waiting for you, I'm waiting," she called, her excitement overcoming her embarrassment. She was seized by a strange feeling, as if she were in a movie she'd seen a long time ago and now she herself was the heroine, calling to a man she didn't know, the hero of the movie, quoting lines from a script that bore some sort of insane similarity to the present situation.

"Where are you?" she asked, frantic with worry.

"I'm getting closer to you," the voice said. "Keep on talking. I'll find you through your voice."

Now she no longer doubted the reality of the voice, and as nervous as a girl about to go on a blind date, she wanted to impress the stranger and to recall a song she'd learned by heart in English class, to assure him that she was worth the effort.

"Hey, are you still there?"

"Yes. I'm waiting for you in the same place."

"Why didn't you say anything?"

"I'm trying to think of something interesting . . ."

"That doesn't matter, the important thing is to keep talking."

"I don't know . . ."

"Maybe you should sing something, that's easier."

The words of the Israeli anthem came into her mind automatically and she pulled her head back inside and started to sing, and as she did so, she straightened like the encyclopedia illustrations of the evolution of monkey into man, "Our hope is not lost, the hope of two thousand years. . . ." She sang standing tall, like an instructor in a youth movement standing before his charges and singing with them, her head held high and her heart threatening to overflow. The words of the anthem suffused her with a sense of brotherhood and strength, and she heard her clear, lone voice, separate from the host of sounds around her, "To be a free people in our land, the land of Zion and Jerusalem. To be a free people. . . ."

A man's head suddenly appeared under the window behind a thin covering that looked like a transparent scarf, his damp hair speckled with white dust, dark crescents under his eyes, and he asked, "What language is that?"

Panting as if she had asthma, she gave silent thanks to whoever had brought her that man, who looked robust and spoke sensibly, and said, "Hebrew."

He reached up to the window and she reached down through it, and their hands met, crushing the dust between them.

Many times afterward she tried to re-create that moment, the first touch of their fingers, and couldn't remember anything special that might have made it one of those moments whose fateful nature is perceived only after it has passed. He turned to come onto the train, tugged at the stuck door to open it, and stopped there, stunned by what he saw. Through his eyes—like a child seeing for the first time the amazing sights of his country through the eyes of a tourist—she saw the inside of the car, and before she could ask what had happened to the people in his car, he said, "We have to get out of here right away."

"Where to?" She didn't doubt for a minute that she had to go with him.

"We passed a station a few kilometers back. I assume there's a telephone there. The cell phones are dead."

On cold nights they'd sit in front of the fire, and the boy, from the day he began to speak, always asked to hear stories. They didn't tell him about their lives before they'd come there, leaving that for when he grew up and could understand. They spoke as if life had begun the moment the train stopped, and Gila—as if she could look into his mind—understood how the fairy tale was taking shape in his imagination, how it would be magnified as time passed and one day would be told as a creation story: the story of how the train had stopped at an unknown place between Odessa and Frankfurt; the story of reaching the inn, which was surrounded by a network of intertwined, bare branches like a malignant tumor entrapped by blood vessels, an inn whose frightening façade enclosed an amazing interior, as in the fairy tales of wanderers who enter a lost wonderland and find a child asleep in his cradle.

After they found the boy and discovered that the telephone was dead and the electricity cut off, they went to bury the dead. The back garden was burned, and beyond it was a garden of misshapen, severed tree trunks that had screaming, evil-looking faces and grooved tongues, roaring with pain or hunger, and beyond that were gaping, smoking pits and earth that seethed, as if to show that even sand could boil. Every time the man dug a hole to bury the dead in, Gila stood guard, facing the trunks as if she feared that malevolent spirits dwelling in the evil shapes were plotting to leap out and tear the dead and the living to bits.

Later, they sat down to eat in candlelight that illuminated and shadowed their faces. The bread, the cheese, the olives, the homemade jam lent things a deceptive air of normalcy, but she couldn't identify the sweet liquid in a pitcher whose flavor reminded her of a Columbian spread she had bought in the neighborhood supermarket during its South American Festival.

"Are you American?" she asked, as if now, after they'd been saved from the catastrophe and had walked half a day together and found the baby and buried the dead, the time had come for a personal conversation.

"Yes."

"I'm Israeli."

"You live in Israel?"

"Yes. And you?"

"Near New York. A little north."

"Where exactly?"

"Do you know the area?"

"I have a sister in New Rochelle."

"So we're neighbors. I live in Scarsdale."

"Ah—" She was speechless with surprise.

"Yes," he replied, as if he knew exactly what she meant.

"What happened today. . . ." Just as she had given the signal to start their personal conversation, she now gave the signal to stop it and realized that she didn't have a name for what had happened.

"A new kind of catastrophe," he said. "Probably radiation that decayed immediately."

"Did you see how it started, how it happened?"

"No. I was in the smoking car. . . ."

"I was in the smoking car, too!" The coincidence excited her, the discovery that within the incomprehensible reality surrounding her so inexplicably, like a nightmare, there was suddenly a certain order, and now she was beginning to catch on to its logic.

"The walls of the smoking car must have been made of a material that stopped the radiation. The window faces upward, and that probably has something to do with it, too. The boy was in a closed room, which is probably what saved him."

"It's like what happened in Chernobyl, isn't it? I once saw a TV program."

"This seems much worse than Chernobyl. But it might also be some kind of natural disaster."

"How long do you think it'll take them to get the trains moving again?" she asked, as if she hadn't heard the terrifying things he'd said.

He gave her a sideways look of astonishment, as if at that very moment, as she was carefully spreading cheese on her slice of bread, he'd learned something important about her.

"That'll probably take some time," he said cautiously.

"They must already know in Frankfurt that something went wrong. After all, the train didn't arrive on time, and they're very precise there."

"Maybe they don't know. Maybe things went wrong there, too."

"They'll send someone to find out what happened," she promised.

"Who will they send, your army?"

She seemed to be picking up a tone of derision, and she bristled. Over the last week she'd been hearing a lot of teasing about the Israeli army. "And why not the American army?" she shot at him, "We don't have any weapons that you don't have too."

He laughed. For the first time since they met so many hours ago, she saw him laugh. His laughter seemed strange to her, wolfish. "Why are you laughing?"

"Because this sounds like a conversation between generals," he said. "And besides, I like to hear women talk about the army."

She fell silent. Something new, a faint hint of courtship, the feeling of tension familiar from other places, infused his voice when he specified what he liked in women.

She was so embarrassed by the subject of the conversation that she changed it. "Do you think the baby is healthy?"

"There are things we'll be able to see when he wakes up, and there are things that might appear much later on," he said, the tone of his voice now restrained, as if it were a dangerous animal rounded up to be put back in its cage.

"What will we feed him?"

"I imagine his mother must have had a supply of food for him that would last a while. We'll find something." His voice was already as soothing as it had been earlier.

That night, lying on the sofa bed in the baby's room, wearing her underpants and the Indian woman's lovely nightgown, hearing the man in his double bed in the adjoining room, Gila was free to think about her home in Israel, which seemed as imaginary as a previous life viewed from the distance of the month she had spent in Odessa and the new reality that had assailed her that morning. Maybe they already knew about the catastrophe. She tried, in her imagination, to bring a picture of the house closer. Maybe, in the early evening, they'd called the hotel in Frankfurt she was supposed to be staying in and found out that she hadn't arrived. At this very moment her husband was probably making urgent calls to his brother, a brigadier general; his cousin, the ambassador to Switzerland; and her sister in New Rochelle, speaking in a whisper from his study, trying to keep his concern from the girls for the time being. Maybe the evening news had already reported on the train that had disappeared in an area where a mysterious catastrophe had occurred; maybe they'd listed the names of the Israelis who were on the train, her name among them. At a certain point, they would have to tell her parents. Her mother would get into bed like she had when told of the death of her son in Lebanon, pull the blanket over her head, and refuse to eat or drink. How happy they'll be when they find out she was one of the survivors! What a welcome she'd get, with flowers and a banner the girls would paint, covered with hearts pierced with arrows.

The baby suddenly began crying, and, thrust from the joys of the future to the nightmare of the present, she got up and groped her way to him in the dark. The touch of her hands or her smell, which were new to him, caused him to cry harder when she picked him up carefully, took him into her bed, held him close, and put into his mouth the nipple of the bottle she had prepared earlier according to the instructions on the box. And she said to the man who appeared in the rectangle of the door, "It's okay. This is how I used to calm my girls," and she didn't realize until after he'd gone that she had mentioned her daughters to him for the first time.

Right then, before she felt the movement deep inside her, as if her body alone had recognized it first, she reached down as she had when she was pregnant, and with her fingers spread she would draw circles, soothing the fetus that was moving toward the wall of her womb. She thought she felt a movement in her belly, and suddenly, a small limb bulged from her body like a sharp fin sent to take a quick look around and then withdraw immediately. She continued to move her hand, searching for the limb that was teasing her, scorning her efforts, urging her groping fingers in one direction, disappearing into her body in another. So she lay there in the dark, her heart pounding, and pressed the unknown baby to her body, one hand holding the bottle, the other lying in wait at the bottom of her stomach.

On the day after the catastrophe, when they went back to the train station, about an hour's walk from the inn, they met the nun who looked like a girl and the sickly, bad-tempered man she was tending to. On the previous day they had been too worn out to look around the station office and storeroom. As soon as they'd discovered that the phone line was dead, they had turned and walked in the direction indicated by the large sign advertising, in pictographs, a place to sleep and eat: a bed and an X formed by a knife and fork. On their way back to the station, they came upon a group of bronze statues: a flock of sheep, some of them pushed up against each other and some of them standing alone, and at the head of the flock, a shepherd with an army backpack slung over his shoulder. They didn't wonder what a piece of art was doing in that remote place. They knew that ten hours earlier the man and his flock had been living creatures, and now they were frozen in time in the smoky expanse. Gila stood motionless and let her eyes register the incredible sight, and she discovered that the sights she'd seen on the previous day had blunted her sense of amazement. He touched her arm and they continued walking, their eyes growing more accustomed to a new visual language.

They found the cashier sitting in his booth, squashed against the window, his eyes gaping. The woman on the bench was also sitting as she had been the day before, her face sunk into the fur of her coat, clutching her travel case to her chest the way a mother clutches her baby. Standing up, leaning against the wall as if he'd fallen asleep on duty was a railroad employee wearing an elegant uniform covered with buttons and buttonholes. A nun suddenly appeared at the door to the office looking like a child dressed up as a nun. Agitated, she hurried over to them, sentences in Italian pouring out of her mouth. She grabbed Gila's hand and pulled her inside the office, where an old man sat shrunken in a chair. He looked at them and cursed in German, and to the man's question, he replied that he spoke English, and promptly began cursing in that language.

At the beginning of the third year, when she'd stopped dreaming about her girls, Gila dreamed that the rusted cars had been removed from the tracks and a sparkling new train was waiting in the station, all its doors open invitingly, its flickering lights signaling that it was about to move. By then she was sleeping in the man's bed, and she awoke with a start. Once, she'd managed to slip out of the bed without waking him and left the house before dawn. She rode there on her bicycle, a part of her going over and over the news that the world had returned to its former state, a part of her already afraid of the moment she would part from the man. At the station, the woman stroking her tattered bag and the cashier's skeleton bent over, counting its treasures, were still there. On the train, two skeletons had already begun to disintegrate. The passionate girl was almost completely bald; the nose of the man who had hidden his genitals had fallen off. Gila stood at the door, opposite the skeletons, and was almost relieved: and if she did manage to leave the man, who knows what she would find at home when the trains were back in operation again. Maybe the Arabs, the former owners, had come back to reclaim the house with its turquoise shutters and open balconies where she had lived since her marriage. Seventeen years ago her husband had carried her over the threshold as if she were a baby, and five years after that, he carried their two baby girls into the house in the same way. Maybe the house was deserted and the turquoise shutters had rotted and her beloved family was sitting motionless like the train people. Yet here, in the haze, life was beginning to stabilize: within a ten-minute walk from the inn, they'd discovered a treasure of flints, and two days ago they'd found another well. The tree in front of the door had begun to bear sweet, figlike fruit, and the boy had succeeded in writing another three letters in Hebrew in a handwriting similar to the one that had filled her daughters' first-grade notebooks. On her way back to the inn, like someone who had been in a coma and had regained consciousness, she scolded herself: the house in Jerusalem was still standing, and her dear ones were alive and healthy and very worried about her.

Several months after the catastrophe, at night, panting into his neck after making love so passionate that it never ceased to surprise her, she would say to herself: this is real life. This is real life with the distinct feeling of a new kind of happiness, lived on the edge, as it sometimes is in childhood, with the intriguing sense of danger and the thrilling pulse of life that had been absent from her former life, the sort that stirs people to climb mountains of ice and race cars across the desert like a storm. But in the morning those trembling moments were forgotten, and she'd again ask him when the trains would start operating.

At the time, she regretted having taken the nun and the sick man to the inn. The nun secluded herself in her chosen room, rarely coming out and rarely eating, but the sick man, aggressive and quick to shout, would seek her out instead, lie in wait for her, taunt her. Later he would taunt the boy, too. He would draw her into conversations in which she found herself helpless, impelled to ask questions she hadn't intended to ask, giving answers she hadn't intended to give, as if she'd lost control over what she said; later on, he'd do the same with the boy.

"Will you miss me when they find us?" he asked her on one of the first days.

"I don't think so." She took the opportunity for revenge.

"But we'll never know!" The roaring laugh exposed his dark palate. "You'll never have the chance not to miss me!" He slapped his knees, "You know why?"

"Why?" Once again, she felt that helplessness of having fallen into an invisible trap.

"Because no one will ever rescue us. We'll be stuck here together."

"Till when?" the trap snapped shut around her.

"Till we slaughter each other." He threw his head back with the shrill laugh of an asthmatic.

"You'll slaughter each other" was also one of the things the Pole had said too, his eyes riveted on the nun, who had come out of her room for a moment.

One day, on the morning she'd seen orange water spouting from a hidden spring in the pestilent area paint a stripe of wild, orange grass on the scorched earth, Gila decided to tell the man about the limb growing in her belly. But that was the day the Pole came riding to the inn on a new bicycle, clutching a huge sack in his arms. Muscular and energetic, bubbling over with ideas and speaking broken but understandable English, the Pole infused her with sudden hope: here was the man who would put things back the way they had been.

He'd learned English, he said reluctantly, from his dealings with tourists. On the nature of those dealings he refused to elaborate, as if there was still a danger he'd be extradited by the authorities, but she guessed: speculating with foreign currency, maybe pimping prostitutes.

They were happy to see him, gave him food and sat down to listen to him. This was their first encounter with an English speaker who could explain to them where they were and describe what was happening in the surrounding villages. He'd been on the road for months, he said, going from village to village on his way to his own village to see what had become of his family. His home was five hundred kilometers from there. He'd covered most of the way on foot. He'd found the bicycle at the train station and he already knew, to his regret, that he would have to leave it behind because of the poor condition of the roads. Meanwhile, he'd passed through ten villages.

He got up suddenly, grabbed the sack he'd brought with him, spread its contents on the floor, and showed them a priest's robe, statuettes of Jesus and his mother, bouquets of flowers made of painted clay, boxes of incense, candlesticks—objects he'd found in ruined churches.

Gila wanted to know the name of the inn and pointed to the sign outside.

"A Good Place for the Night," the Pole said. "A very strange name." He pointed toward the pestilent area and told them that near a distant train station he'd happened upon an inn called Katarina. He'd stayed there until he'd finished the supply of food.

The man wanted to know the condition of the villages he'd passed through, and the Pole used hand movements in place of the words that did not exist in his vocabulary to describe what he'd seen: one village was sunk in mud up to the roofs of the houses; in other villages, most of the houses, made of wood, had been razed down to their foundations; in three villages, even the church, which was made of stone, had collapsed; in the fields and houses he found only dead people. On the second day after the catastrophe he'd heard a baby crying, but he couldn't get to it, and then the crying stopped, and once he saw a young girl, who ran away from him and disappeared among the ruins.

"No more," he spread his hands to the sides as if to encompass all the horizons, "No more people in the world."

"And animals?" the man asked.

"Animals there are." The Pole counted on his fingers: horses, dogs, cats, mice. All hungry, all dangerous.

"Where exactly are we?" the man asked.

"In Poland, near the Austrian border."

"But the people we met don't speak Polish," the man said. "Around here, they speak a different language. The people from the village speak . . ."

In the middle of the sentence the Pole froze. The nun had come out of her room and walked through the hallway on her way to the sick man's room.

"There is a nun here?" He rubbed his eyes.

"Yes."

"How many are you?"

"Five."

"And there are more women?"

"No. Only a sick man and a baby."

"I must go to my family," the Pole said, as if he were giving up the chance of a better life for the sake of his family.

They told him they hoped he would find his village still standing and his family alive, supplied him with edible leaves, a bottle of water, a jar of jam from the pantry, and accompanied him to the path. Outside, the Pole tied the sack, his eyes roving constantly from window to window searching for the nun, and then he mounted his bicycle and rode off, waving to them until he disappeared.

The first few days, which turned into the first few weeks, Gila was still expecting to hear the sound of a car or a motorcycle: a representative of the local authorities come to inform them that the train was running again; a representative of the UN sent to the area of the catastrophe who might perhaps bring some sign that all was well at home. But in the meantime, life began to take on the form of a routine. She stayed at home to watch the baby; washed clothes in the river (a five-minute walk from the inn), whose water was not good for drinking; sifted through the things they'd brought from the train; boiled leaves and roots the man brought; and then checked in a laboratory of sorts he'd set up in the kitchen. The man came back from his wanderings every evening like a man returning to his home in the suburbs to tell his family about his day in the city.

Despite the family pattern that was taking shape, throughout the first few months Gila and the man kept their previous lives to themselves. She knew he was a chemist, married to a musician, a harpist, and the father of a son who was also planning to be a musician; he knew that she illustrated children's books, that she was the mother of twelve-year-old twin girls, married to a businessman. She knew he had gone to Odessa to attend an international conference on ecology; he knew she had gone there to copy illustrations from an ancient book of legends kept in a museum.

The horror outside bound them together; within the cramped togetherness they maintained their independence. He put his shirts and pants on the pile of her clothes, which was separate from the pile of cloth diapers cut from sheets, but his underwear and socks he washed himself, as if he were drawing a boundary line.

Around the time the boy started to smile, Gila was once again seized by restlessness. For a few days now, she'd seen the funnel lower like a plane in an air force flyover, dipping and raising its nose, then mockingly disappearing in a climb, sending out unclear, anxiety-provoking signals.

One evening, before the nun and the sick man came down from their rooms, as she was eating a tasty new dish and the child was jabbering to himself in his cradle (which had probably been a gift to celebrate his birth from a relative he would never know), she suddenly asked the man, "Is it possible that the world's been destroyed? That we're the last people left?" And she herself was shocked at the question.

The man raised inquisitive eyes from the calendar he was making on a wooden tablet, as if he were assessing her ability to face the truth. But even before he replied, she understood—for the first time since she came out of the smoking car—that she might never again see her daughters or her husband or her mother or her childhood friends or the other people who had populated her life, from the woman who cleaned the stairwells to the elderly lady with the girlish braid who sold her flowers on the street corner every Friday, and for the first time she was struck with the profound awareness that her girls and her husband and all the other people in her life probably no longer existed, and she burst into tears, immediately smothered them with her hands, and lowered her head to her knees, her hands still covering her eyes. A picture flashed through her mind of her daughters standing shoulder to shoulder, waiting to be photographed, then switched rapidly into a picture of the girls sitting opposite each other at the dining room table, illustrating the invitations to their bat mitzvah party.

Feeling the man's warm hand sending currents of calmness along her back, she straightened up, and even though she knew that her eyelids tended to swell and redden when she cried, making her face ugly, she raised her head.

"It's because of my daughters."

"I can imagine," he said.

"I have no idea how this will sound to you," she dared to say, completely vulnerable, "but I'm so glad you were in the smoking car."

"It's mutual," he said.

And she thought that this was probably the new, flexible vocabulary that adapted itself to the time and the place and although what they'd said entailed no commitment, it nonetheless signaled a potential alliance.

"So what does it mean—the world has been destroyed?"—she repeated the incredible words. "That no one is looking for us, that there is no place to go back to, that we'll stay here forever without electricity, without water. . . ." Her voice emerged in a childish singsong, an intonation appropriate to the words, "without home, or books, or paintings. . . ."

He suddenly hugged her tightly, pulling her out of her chair and pressing her to him, burying her head in his chest, shielding her like a parent protecting his child from all the dangers lying in wait for her, dangers she cannot imagine, as if he were trying to compensate her for the things she would not have—the loss of which was only now beginning to seep into her awareness—a list of things that she had only just begun to enumerate and that would grow longer. She sank into the consoling embrace, trying to subdue her renewed sobbing—about the electricity and the water and the terror of the funnel of air and the fact that she would probably never know the fate of her daughters.

Suddenly she felt his hand resting inquiringly on her stomach, and she understood immediately that this was not the touch of a lover, but the pressure of a doctor's hand feeling some worrying symptoms in the body of a patient, and like an obedient patient, she let him lift her blouse and run his expert hand, pleasant to the touch, over her belly. The tips of his fingers felt the edge of the limb slightly above her navel, and in the momentary battle between the lump in her belly and his fingers searching for it from outside, she felt a digging movement as the limb flipped over and slipped away into the depths of her stomach like an agile diver.

She expected him to recoil from her, from her strange body in which growths were sprouting, but he did not pull his hand away, he simply held it there as if to soothe the troubled spot and said, "I have two of them."

Without a word spoken, she went to his bed that night and found him waiting. As she approached in the darkness, he lifted the blanket over the place he had made for her, and when she slipped in next to him, she was immediately trapped in his embrace, her face close to his. She stopped breathing, waiting for the first movement that would dictate the movements to follow, but he remained quiet and tensed, locking her in his embrace and still waiting. She reached up to his face, trying to learn the features she knew by sight but not by touch, which was strange and new, a treasure of surprises, and she ran her fingertips over his chin, stubbly because of the blunted razor; over his jaws, his cheeks, his eyes, which closed under her touch; over the side of his nose, his lips, which opened like a trap in the darkness and caught her thumb in his teeth. She drew back in alarm and he, as if his plan had succeeded, laughed gently and reached down to the backs of her thighs and raised her nightgown over her shoulders, her arms and her hair pouring out of the neck opening. Then he bent over and pulled her under him, and they both stopped for a moment, his stomach lying against hers, before he began to move. The memory of the limbs wandering about in their bodies flickered through her mind, and though she pushed it away immediately, it left behind a faint, persistent fear. Her movements became suffused with despair when, from beneath him, as if she were verifying their existence, she moved her caressing fingers over each part of his body: his nape, his shoulders, the long back, the line of his spine swallowed up by the rise of his buttocks, the muscles of his thigh down to the back of his knee at the farthest reach of her fingertips, all of which swayed together until the movement of their bodies took on a life of its own, absorbing currents from the ground that turned it into a timeless rocking, a reminder of the soothing rocking of an earlier life, until the sweeping, protracted moment of climax that sent ripples to the edges of the body, subduing the storm, also calming the untouched place where the quivering source dwelled, and she wondered as she always did about the mysterious riddle of the body's ability to forget and its ability to remember. And within that remembering—like everything that had happened from the moment she'd walked out of the smoking car—the echo of distant sensations rose inside her, reminiscent of the maelstrom that had begun in her body when the man entered her, and she fell backward like someone collapsing into an abyss, knowing that his body too had memories of other places that were stirring now and filling him with longing, knowing too that as long as there was the promise of this moment, always surprising in its generosity, it would be possible to bear the horror outside that bed.

Many days passed, and their life was channeled into a routine somewhat reminiscent of the routine of the life she had left in the previous world, and yet it did not resemble it at all.

Sometimes she heard distant voices that aroused a faint memory of a house bordered by pitango bushes, a guava tree that bore so much fruit in the spring that its heavy fragrance spread to the inner rooms, and an almond tree at the edge of the garden that dotted the earth with its fallen fruit; of a little girl building a Lego tower in her room, the walls covered with pictures of parents and two little girls, a host of parents and girls, and in another room, another little girl seen from the back, giving milk to a cat, and a man sitting in his room leafing through his papers. Sometimes the images vanished suddenly, as in a magic show, and sometimes the picture became so clear that she could dive inside it and see up close the fabric of the girl's blouse, the cat's whiskers twitching in the milk. The reincarnation of her previous life would alternately awaken in her and then become dormant. Sometimes a familiar smell would arouse it, sometimes a touch. Sometimes it was aroused by the light of dusk that would appear at a random moment, a faint, expectant light that even in her former life had stirred in her a mysterious longing for something unclear, a feeling of certainty that she had missed out on something, and she felt burdened by an oppressive helplessness. If only she knew what that feeling referred to, she would rally and act to change it, but her inaction and the knowledge of missed opportunity saddened her so deeply that she cried now, as she had then.

At the beginning of the second year, turbid water fell from the sky day and night, and Gila was filled with restlessness. Now that they had a roof over their heads, a constant supply of food, a clear picture of the near future, and now that her feelings for the man were growing stronger, nightmares assailed her. She woke at night in a bloodbath. Her two girls had drowned right before her eyes, and she herself, handless, had tried to get them out by pushing and poking at them with her head, then had dived in after them, kicking her feet to raise them up, but they sank into the dark water, and she watched with desperate eyes as their hips, their shoulders, their faces, the ribbons in their long hair vanished. Dripping blood, she went into her bedroom and saw the large light fixture fall from the ceiling onto her husband sleeping in the double bed, the copper prong of the fixture directed at his head like a spear, and to the sound of bones being crushed, she woke with a shriek and found the man leaning over her, brushing her hair away from her face, whispering, "Sshh . . ." the way she once had whispered to her daughters.

"Don't you dream about them?" she dared to ask him one peaceful night.

"I don't have to dream; I think about them all the time."

"All the time?" she asked, almost insulted.

"Yes. And I know that I'll never see them again. I hope that if they survived, they'll find good people the way I found you."

Astonished, she rebelled, refusing to accept his brand of mourning, and she kept having nightmares filled with feelings of rage and helplessness for many more days. But in the end, she surrendered, and a short while before the Pole returned, she could already think of the man as if he were her husband, even though the two were different in appearance and character, in their thoughts and actions, in the way they made love to her, and she taught herself to believe that everything she told him she could have told her husband if he had been beside her. Months later, she'd stopped dreaming about her girls and imagined them part of a large group of children their own age, studying and spending their days as if they were in the camp they used to go to every summer from the time they were eight, and becoming teenagers and young women and finding husbands as much like their father as possible. One day she noted with astonishment that her nightmares had become rare, and all of her strength was invested in worrying about the man's safe return from his searches and about the child wandering in the garden of wooden monsters, exposed to the ravenous funnel of air. She was amazed at how old forces continued to operate like a well-oiled machine forever and how the senses were now tuned toward new people, remembering their old movements, like ancient springs forging their way along a map of channels that had altered, struggling in the depths of the earth, bearing the memory of that earlier flow, directing it toward a place that had suddenly changed. And how, after a period of paralysis when certain functions of the body had stopped, they awaken like a tree sprouting buds and continue along their path, blind to what is going on outside the shell of the body, assailed by stirrings of desire as often as in the past, causing people to grope their way to each other to find refuge, shelter, and repose; to seek affection and grace in a child, the heart opening to him when he smiled or learned something new; taking pleasure in the warmth that rose at the sight of the nun, in the sweet friendship.

In the midst of this newly forming serenity, the Pole came back long after he had left, waving his arms in the distance like a voyager returning home, and brought turmoil with him. His wild eyes in constant search of the nun, his hands flapping every which way, he told them about the destruction he'd found in his village. In the direction of the sunrise, on the ridge, several buildings were still standing, probably a military base, strewn with rifles and equipment and soldiers' uniforms, but everything else was in ruins. The village was located high on the mountain—he waved his hand upward—chasms and a valley below. In the place where the church used to stand only blackened stones remained. And everything was shrouded in fog. He hadn't met another living soul on the road, only hungry animals. He'd stopped in other villages on his way back. In one of them he'd found an undamaged house, but he didn't take anything from it, "Except for this," he said and pulled an antique ring inlaid with stones from his pocket and put it on the table in front of Gila, then returned his hand to his pocket, took out a plainer ring, and put it down next to the first, "And this is for the other woman."

The church—he continued speaking as if he hadn't noticed that his gifts were not received with thank-yous—the church had collapsed and the wind had blown everything away, leaving only the foundation stones. His house and his brothers' houses had been swept away, trees had been uprooted, even corpses of people and animals had been carried off. He'd seen some of the dead lying on the mountain slope, unidentifiable. Those, he'd buried. The bodies that had been swept into the chasm, he was unable to reach.

Silence fell after the Pole stopped speaking, as tired as if he'd just made the journey again. Even the sick man didn't snigger. Then the Pole asked, his eyes blazing, whether anyone had come to the inn in his absence. The man told him about the old woman who'd been tossed out onto their doorstep and asked if the funnel of air had also reached the distant villages. The light in the Pole's eyes died when he heard the reply. Several times, he said, he'd seen the funnel. Once, it had almost thrown him into the abyss; another time, it almost snatched him up, but he flattened himself on the ground and held onto rocks; and three times he'd seen it from afar, twice completely empty and once sucking up a pretty, live girl, he said, fixing mesmerized eyes on the nun, who pressed her shoulders closer together, shrinking under his gaze.

The nun refused to touch the ring the Pole had put on the table in front of her.

The next day he blocked her way on the stairs and tried to kiss her, but her shouts summoned Gila, who came running and managed to push him down the steps.

Frightened that the Pole might attack her, too, Gila begged the man to send him away, but the man claimed that the Pole had apologized to the nun and that they really needed the help of another man. And in fact, the intrepid Pole, with his highly developed senses and knowledge of the secrets of the place, would sometimes discover treasures, and in the end his presence in the room he chose for himself, next to the child's room, was accepted as permanent. Again and again he'd offer the ring to the nun, which she refused, and because of that, or perhaps despite it, he would lie in wait for her, trap her in the pantry, where one day he managed to rip her dress, and one night he sneaked into her room and stroked her breast as she slept. The nun was terrified of him. For days after that night, she trailed after Gila like her shadow, barricaded the door to her room with heavy furniture, prayed out loud, murmuring the name Mary over and over again, and sought the nearness of the child, who would soon be three, sitting beside him as he studied Hebrew, writing square words on pieces of flat leaves that were as strong as cloth with a pipe stuffed with the peel of a black fruit, as hard as lead.

On clear mornings the two men would go out together, and whatever they brought back was received with cries of joy: wild chickens, edible fruit, a kitten they gave to the child as a gift that made him glow with happiness. Those days brought with them an awakening of new life, and Gila discovered in herself hidden desires she hadn't known before. They further helped to delineate the borders of her new world, and just as, in the past, she used to long for new clothes she saw in shop windows, she now longed for a hat she'd seen in the passenger car of the train lying in the aisle among the theatrical clothes strewn there.

One day a golden-tailed bird appeared and built a nest in one of the trees, and a few days later, two more birds arrived, one white with a crown that resembled a bridal veil and the other covered with blue spots. On mornings when there were wind storms, Gila stayed under the covers beside the man, luxuriating in the ordinariness and the tranquility of the birds' chirping, and she would feel her stomach and find the limb that had sprouted overnight, then shift her hand to the man's stomach and hear him say, "It's still there." Sometimes the child would squeeze in between them, and the three of them would lie together in a tangle of arms and legs. One day the Pole succeeded in igniting a large flame by rubbing two bits of metal together, and they immediately replaced the rare flints, which required expertise to kindle. When the wild wheat ripened, they refrained from touching it because it reminded the man of a poisonous plant, but the Pole explained that it was edible and they went out into the fields the way people did in biblical times, and Gila had a memory from her previous life, the story of Ruth and Naomi and a play in her elementary school in which she played the part of Ruth, for which her cousin had lent her an expensive white nightgown she'd bought in Paris. That memory, like so many others, no longer caused her severe pain or longing, but merely tugged gently at her heart, as if she'd received regards from a distant lover. And there was a joyous day when the man found a bush whose leaves were excellent for making cigarettes. He kept the process a secret but allotted a generous number of cigarettes to the others, and in the evening they sat together and smoked, all except the nun, filling the air with yellowish smoke that smelled as sharp as eucalyptus. And one day Gila and the nun walked as far as the strange trees at the edge of the plain and saw that they had turquoise orbs, like amulets against the evil eye, hanging from the tips of their branches, and they found wild berries. The nun taught Gila a children's song in Italian about children picking wild berries. The whole way they spoke in the new language they had created, a mixture of English and Italian, and before they reached home the nun had gotten Gila to swear twice that she would protect her from the Pole.

When the boy turned three, the sick man's condition worsened. Now it was difficult for him to climb the stairs, so they emptied out the office for him, and he slept there. The nun brought a tub of water there every morning and helped him wash and dress, as devoted as a daughter. The sick man spent most days sitting and looking at the back garden. On cold days he looked out at it from inside the house, and during warmer hours he sat in the garden with his eyes closed or else he stared at the mounds of earth that marked the graves of the dead. Gila would occasionally go out and sit down beside him, fearing conversation with him and fascinated by it. And he, aware of this, openly amused himself with her.

"What do you look at all the time?" she asked.

"The question is not what we look at, but what we see. You, for example, look but you don't see."

She knew he was talking about the man, whom both of them had once seen staring at the nun.

"What do you see?" She would not allow him to drag her where he wanted.

"The question is not what I see, but whether what I see actually exists."

"And how can we know?" She was still thinking about those looks.

"We can't. Kant asked whether our consciousness has the tools to decipher the reality outside of us. And what, in your opinion, did he think?"

"What?"

"That we don't!" He celebrated his victory over her lack of knowledge. "But Heidegger, yes, Heidegger thought that the question was irrelevant, that we are inside reality, we know it. Oh, Heidegger, I would love to know what he'd say about the reality here." He closed his eyes and cut himself off from Gila with deliberate cruelty, leaving her determined not to think about the man looking at the nun.

Later on, as if the Pole had infected everyone with his own delirium, came a time that was as feverish and overwrought, as strident and unpredictable, as adolescence. Something in the air signaled calamity, and even the child felt it, never leaving the woman's side throughout that time. The Pole tried again to attack the nun, and she managed to escape to Gila's room. The old man, overtaken by rage, destroyed the fence in the back garden before he calmed down. The man, Gila knew without his saying a word about it, thought constantly about the woman who played the harp and about the son who was planning to be a musician. Restlessness permeated the air, as if the era of unexpected disasters had passed and dozens of signs were heralding the arrival of the next disaster.

During one of their nocturnal conversations, her head on his shoulder and her eyes on the moon that linked the worlds of time, the man suggested setting up a place for prayer in one of the empty rooms, because it was now—after they had a place to sleep and bread to eat and they knew of the treasures and traps the world around them held—now that they might begin to ask themselves the questions the ancients had asked after natural disasters had occurred, about good and evil, about crime and punishment, and it seemed right to prepare a place where they could draw strength from God.

"But you don't believe in God," she said in astonishment. "And besides, what kind of God could we create that would be good for me and for the nun, too?"

"As a nonbeliever, it's clear to me what isn't clear to believers: that they all believe in the same thing. But we won't make a revolution, we'll split Him up. We have at least two Catholics and one Jew, and the child's parents were probably Buddhists."

She chuckled in the darkness, "Look, you've created a new religion."

The next day, the two women emptied out the small room with tiny windows, took down many of the paintings from the walls of the house, and hung them in the room as crowded together as if they were stamps in an album, next to each other and above each other, wall to wall and floor to ceiling. They put small tables in the corners and assigned a different religion to each. The nun, radiating an aura of light, put a picture of Jesus and the small wooden cross the boy had made for her on one of the tables and decorated it with flowers and leaves. Gila took off the chain and Star of David she had bought for herself on Rosh Hashana and put it on the table across from the Christian corner. The child put on his table one of the cars from his toy train, which had once belonged to a child who himself had been a passenger on a train. The old man, ridiculing the entire idea, put on the fourth table an empty pillbox and a cane that he hadn't used in months, and the Pole put the ring the nun had refused to accept beside them. Then chairs were brought to the room, and the child dragged them this way and that to form a circle.

After supper, everyone went up to the prayer room. Gila was excited by the smell of the boiled apple leaves and the special tranquility that reminded her of the synagogue on Rosh Hashana eve, permeated with holiness and splendor and the fear of God, who was looking into people's souls. And that spirit, she imagined, had wandered from the synagogue on the shores of the Mediterranean Sea to the inn whose owners had given it its name in a moment of prophetic inspiration, and the spirit pervaded the room with its two small windows, enveloping the random, everyday objects as if they were holy vessels. Gila looked at the cane and remembered the watercolor that had hung next to the blackboard in her first-grade classroom: a group of people and a flock of sheep led by Abraham, his expression determined, walking toward the Promised Land, and the walking stick in his hand was the cane lying on the table in front of her.

The nun began praying in a hushed voice. They joined her until she whispered "Hallelujah," to which they responded like a practiced, many-voiced choir, and all the while a splintered, striped light filtered in through the small windows, softening their features. Gila looked at the Pole, wondering if he was sorry for what he'd done to the nun, then shifted her gaze to the man and saw that he was looking at her. A flood of feelings rose in her, and for some reason she recalled the excitement that had made her knees weak on the day of her bat mitzvah, and she reached out to put her hand in his, which she found waiting and welcoming.

The old man watched them from the side, his malicious gaze fixed on their joined hands. For a moment she caught his glance, and he did not hide from her the laughter in his eyes.

"Why did you come to the room yesterday?" she asked him the next day.

"I couldn't pass up the entertainment."

"So you came to laugh at us?"

"I like to watch people. I'm interested in their need to look for a reason for something that has no reason."

"So what is all this," she waved her hand around at the evidence that stretched as far as the eye could see, "Isn't there a reason for it?"

"That is the external manifestation, not the reason."

"What's the reason?"

"No one knows, not even a scientist who studies it for a million years."

"But there has to be reason!" She fought for the last remaining bit of logic.

"No."

"So what is it the result of?" she persisted.

"A whim."

"Whose whim?"

"That's the whole point: no one's whim."

Once again, she was annoyed after the conversation with him, but she could see clearly that something had changed in the group from the minute they'd begun praying, joining them to each other with the force of destiny as she had been joined to the man in that miraculous moment she'd met him on the train of the dead. The man, like someone with a detailed plan who bases his actions on intelligent logic, said later, "The time has come to start thinking about the future."

"What do you mean, the future?" she asked, remembering how, in another world, she had been proposed to.

"I mean the next generation."

She looked at him in surprise. She had mentioned her infertility problems to him many times and had told him about the many years of treatment she had endured before she became pregnant with the twins. "And who will give birth to it?"

"Not you," he said as if it were a promise.

"But she's a nun!" she said, horrified.

"She's the only one who can do it. She'll have to understand."

"And who will the father be?"

"Whoever she chooses."

She needed a long minute to digest this new situation and also to absorb the fact that he had made his plan secretly, without including her, and the seed of suspicion planted in her by the sick man began to sprout.

"And if she chooses you?"

"Then it'll be me," he said like a soldier volunteering for a mission.

"Have a good time," she said, anger rising in her at his plot, his pretense. "And who's going to tell her about this interesting plan?"

"You, of course."

"Not me, and not of course," she said, revealing how offended she was.

But the idea insinuated itself into her until it gained a foothold and would not let go, and the thing she was supposed to be fighting ambushed her, and against her own wishes Gila set out to fight a new war—to convince the nun to have a child—a war that was lost before it began, where her victory would also be her downfall, where she might lose more than she possessed. But she didn't give in to logic, and in a short time she had thrown herself into her mission as if she were obsessed. Again and again, the image of a baby girl flashed through her mind, the image of her daughters when they were babies, a baby that was crawling on all fours around the furniture in the room, holding on to the back of the armchair and rising up onto her feet, rocking in her cradle, sleeping between her and the man in their bed; sleeping between the nun and the man in the very same bed, and Gila was shocked at the sight.

On one of their fruit-gathering walks, after scrutinizing her constantly from every angle, Gila asked the nun if she liked babies, and the young woman nodded happily. Gila asked if she wanted a baby of her own, and the nun looked at her inquisitively. Gila pointed wildly at the nun's stomach, and the nun looked at the feverish eyes in front of her, embarrassed and blushing deeply. Gila did not mention the idea again for several days; she let herself calm down, let the possibility sink into the young woman's awareness. One day, while they were preparing a meal in the kitchen, Gila looked at her and, as if the matter had been settled, asked which man she'd choose to make a baby with. The nun gave her a penetrating look, suspecting that her only ally was about to betray her, and Gila, as if the name Judas Iscariot had not passed through her mind, spoke the name of the man as if it were a question. The nun shook her head firmly, her eyes terrified, perhaps recognizing the signs of an evil spirit that had taken possession of the woman who had sworn to protect her, perhaps frightened by the menacing persistence and by what lay beyond the menacing persistence.

But the thought of the nun's pregnancy—sometimes separate from the man—gave Gila no rest, and a few weeks after the idea had first been raised, as if she were thinking logically, she convinced herself that there was no choice: the child was already three years old. In another fifteen years he'd be ready to be a father himself. Who could guarantee that he'd find a bride then? Now, now was the time to arrange for a wife for him with whom he could continue the next generation.

She schemed for hours about how to convince the nun how imperative the act was, to describe to her in simple words, in her basic Italian, that there was no choice and she had to choose one of the men because she was the only one who could guarantee that life would continue, and there was no doubt that both Jesus and his mother would understand and permit it, because after all, Jesus too was born in an unusual way. Over and over again, with growing excitement, she told the man of her musings and imagined she saw a look of amazement in his eyes. His look, like a mirror, made it clear to her that he had been a part of her life for only a few years, and that she would never know whether it was his desire for the nun that had spawned the idea. She pursued the relentlessly intractable young woman the whole month, kept the child away from her, punished her with prolonged silences, and did not soften even when she heard the sounds of weeping coming in from the nun's room at night. Every morning, in a voice that grew colder and colder, she asked again which man she would choose, and the nun again burst into tears that made Gila feel relief and also an unfamiliar wrath.

She would never remember who came up with the idea of giving her to the Pole. During moments of self-awareness or when she was on the verge of sleep and less able to keep secrets, she suspected that the idea had been born in her own brain, imagined that she remembered some hesitation on the part of the man, but she wouldn't allow the memory to come. She did remember—but perhaps it was only after he brought up the idea and she objected—that the man had suggested waiting until the nun matured and maternal feelings developed naturally in her, and maybe, in the meantime, a man would appear who didn't frighten her; or maybe another young woman would come in another few years who could be the child's bride. Gila remembered herself becoming furious, but perhaps that was only after he had planted the idea in her brain; no man the nun might want would suddenly appear, she had said heatedly. The girls who survived after the cataclysm had probably been devoured by animals or sucked up into the funnel of air. Finally, she told him angrily of her suspicion that he hoped the nun would choose him in the end and that he wasn't trying to protect the young woman, but to keep her from the Pole. Several weeks afterward, he grew tired and surrendered to the madness that had gripped her, and he agreed to her idea, not so he could implement his plan but to put an end to her suspicions. But she took as a good sign the fact that he agreed on that particular day, because that very morning it had occurred to her that the funnel of air hadn't been seen for quite a while. On the calendar they had marked, she counted forty days. A good rain was falling outside, the sign of a blessing, not a lashing rain and not a rain that uprooted bushes, but one that fell generously and quietly, fertilizing the earth.

Gila also began to prepare the Pole with hints, with movements he was quick to grasp, with a quick, conspiratorial smile he understood well, and inflamed by the fire burning in her, the passion that had already begun to wane in him ignited into a surprising blaze. One night, as if by chance, after she had quieted the child and the sick man with a fruit extract that would keep them asleep for half a day, she and the man went out to the wrought iron bench at the far end of the garden.

The distant slam of a door came first, and they fell silent, stunned, the way it sometimes happens when events are expected. The man withdrew into himself and dropped his chin down to his chest, a sign that she was familiar with. Then they both tried unsuccessfully to shut out the sounds that assailed their ears, sounds that seemed to be shattering bone and penetrating veins and poisoning the body from within; spreading over house, the back garden, the garden of monsters, and the pestilent area to beyond the row of trees in the east and beyond the low mountain ridges in the west; echoing to the edges of the horizon: first the shrill, surprised cries of fear, and then the determined attempts to regain composure, the wild, courageous but futile rebellion; then the horrifying, despairing comprehension and the beginning of the body's surrender, the shift to a stream of explaining, scolding, pleading words; and suddenly the sobbing, the screaming that shook the blood vessels, the persistent pounding that sought to break through the imprisoning wall, the continual weeping like a siren, the harsh sounds of scraping like iron combs plowing the walls, the animal groans coming not from her throat but from the depths of her loins, the desperate sobs and then the wailing, slashing shrieks, the choking roars that make the throat swell; then the sudden silence of choked breathing and the submissive, sinking whimpering, feeble grunting, the squeaking of the door to the Pole's room as it opened and closed when he went to his bed.

And then silence prevailed: deep, dark, full of fear and guilt. They did not go up to their room that night. From the moment they heard the sounds blaring from the house and restrained themselves for the sake of the future, they sat in silence, cut off from one another, looking inward, trying to formulate for themselves their individual stories about what had taken place. Even after the long, mournful sobbing subsided, they did not go to their bed but continued to sit silently until the sun, surprising in its splendor, rose over the heavy treetops and so generously illuminated the wide sky and the fields—made them gleam in the first light—and she suddenly remembered a school trip and the breathtaking sunrise that had turned the Judean Hills pink.

In the morning, wrapped in the sweetness of slumber, silent and sleepy, the child slipped between them, and they made room for him. "I dreamed that the nun was screaming," the child said.

"In dreams, everyone is always screaming," the man said and wrapped the child's small, bare feet in the edge of his shirt.

Gila stroked his disheveled hair and said, "Look, sweetie. Look at what a beautiful sunrise we have today."

Death in Jerusalem

Elana Gomel

The crowd is sprinkled with Arabs in galabieh, Orthodox Jews in dusty black coats, and young girls with navel rings. People jostle and push against each other. But Mor walks freely through the crush of bodies, buoyed by the roundness of her stomach, her gaily colored maternity dress glued to it by perspiration. People respect fertility in Jerusalem.

She is relieved when she reaches the old residential area of Rehavia. The ghostly echo of prewar Europe lingers in the narrow alleyways lined with unkempt gardens. She opens the gate into the small courtyard where a rusted bicycle rests in the meager shadow of an ancient wisteria. The heat is killing her. Leaning against the wall to catch her breath, she closes her eyes and tries to cool off with a memory of blue steel and frozen candlelight.

The evening is almost bearable. This is the blessing of hilly Jerusalem as opposed to humid Tel Aviv, where summer heat lies on the land like a rotting corpse. As the sunset fades to lilac, Mor takes a shower and gingerly lowers herself into the beanbag in front of the TV. Channels flicker in a litany of war, famine, and disease.

She goes to bed early. Stretching on her back, she holds her breath, waiting for the baby's kick, and falls asleep, still waiting.

The scrape of a chair and a man's voice saying: "May I?"

The morning was hot, cloudless and blue, as all mornings would be for the next three months. But the man who sat by her in the campus cafeteria smelled of rain and fog. He smiled: his teeth were white and impossibly even.

They talked until she was close to being late for her class. The language of their conversation was English, as it immediately transpired that "May I?" was the full extent of David's knowledge of Hebrew. He was from Toledo.

"I've been to Toledo," she said. "They make wonderful swords."

"Toledo, Ohio," he corrected. "I don't like cutting weapons."

Was he some sort of pacifist? A pilgrim? Just a tourist? Mor did not care. He was the most beautiful man she had ever seen. Just a millisecond before she absolutely had to rush to the classroom, he asked her whether she was free in the evening.

They met at Dizengoff Square, which is not actually a square but the wide pedestrian overpass above a perpetual traffic jam. Its revolving fountain wobbled in the grayish twilight, occasionally coughing up a thin jet of water. Pigeons and pedestrians thronged the overpass, but there seemed to be a magic circle of quietude around David.

After a couple of drinks in a bar, they walked along the beach promenade, the black, oily sea heaving beyond the fluorescent strip of sand. Moonlight dribbled from the tarry sky.

"I like your name," he said. "Mor. Does it mean something?"

"It's a kind of spice or incense mentioned in the Bible," she said, searching for the English word. "Oh, yeah. Myrrh."

"Really?" he sounded interested. "I thought it had something to do with death. You know, like *mor*tality."

"Mortality, morbid, moribund." She shook her head. "You are right; it does sound like it belongs with these. Funny. I never thought about this. But it's a different word. *Mort*, death in French. Just a coincidence."

Her mother wanted to name her Hanna, but Daddy objected. She insisted, and so there were two names listed on Mor's birth certificate, even though she never used the other one. Another item to add to the list of grudges against her mother; another drop of sweetness to flavor her hazy recollections of the big, burly man who had brought her to the kindergarten one fine morning and was dead of a heart attack in the afternoon.

The silence between them seemed filled with unspoken promises. Mor tried to think what to ask him next and could not. Job, family, politics? What difference did it make? She would be happy to walk with him in this velvety dark for an eternity, just listening to the roll of waves on the bone-white beach. But did he feel the same? He asked for her phone number but made no definite promise to call. When she drove him back to his hotel (which turned out to be the expensive Sea Crest), he politely thanked her for the perfect evening and left without as much as a peck on the cheek. She fought tears on the way back home and counted the crow's-feet around her eyes as she brushed her teeth. Next day, just as she resigned herself to another dating failure, he called.

When the phone vibrates on the kitchen counter, Mor stares at the flashing display and tries to remember who the caller is. Her memory is holed like cheese, some memories willfully expunged, some unaccountably gone. A school friend? A former colleague? Not a relative, certainly. She has none. An only daughter of an only daughter; and her mother's entire family buried in unmarked graves.

It does not matter. She needs nobody. She has her son.

Stroking her belly, she watches the phone quiver and jump like a living thing. When it finally calms down, she tosses it into the garbage bin.

They met every day for a week. Mor learned a little more about David—enough for her to decide he was the One. He was so reassuringly normal, untainted by the feverish madness of the Middle East. He was an accountant, he said, and indeed, he was very good with numbers. His parents were dead, his numerous siblings scattered over an amazing geographical range, and there was no mention of an ex-wife or significant other. He read all the right books and had all the right opinions. He liked gadgets. Mor, being an adjunct professor in the Department of Life Sciences, listened to his technobabble with an indulgent smile. The only negative she could find was that he was surprisingly indifferent to good food, despite the plethora of culinary temptations on every street corner. Rice-stuffed vine leaves, couscous, creamy hummus, freshly baked pitas, honey-almond cake—he consumed them as dutifully and apathetically as if they were medicine. Mor told herself that was a necessary counterpoint to her own indulgences that were beginning to show in her curves.

One day he told her his return ticket was for tomorrow. The despair she felt was strong enough to frighten her. Did she really need him so much? She had her life, her friends, her job. She might meet somebody local, get married, have a family.

She was thirty-five. All of her school and army friends were married, most had children. The future stretched before her: blank, lifeless, childless.

They ate at the most expensive restaurant in Tel Aviv. David had a lot of money and spent it freely, though never recklessly. He walked her to her apartment block and pecked her on the cheek as he did every evening. Dully, she waited for him to turn around and walk away as he did every evening.

"Can I come up for coffee?" he asked.

The darkened rooms were bathed in the inflamed glow of city lights. Her neighbor's cat caterwauled in the yard and fell silent. She tangled with her clothes, but his undressing was quick and tidy. Running her hand over his delightfully smooth chest, she was, again, struck by how cool his flesh was: like a porcelain bowl with sherbet inside. Mor felt embarrassed by the drops of sweat gathering under her armpits and in the hollow of her neck. But David's body remained immaculate. His kisses were sterile; his mouth tasted of nothing.

His regular breathing did not speed up until it suddenly stopped. David's perfectly groomed hair tickled her lips and pushed back her rising scream.

"I'm sorry," he said, "but I cannot die. Not even a little death. So that's all for me, but don't worry, I'm satisfied."

She could see him clearly. His body was glowing in the dark, a bluish glow like candlelight seen through a thick slab of ice. The translucent flesh molded itself around the geometrical beauty of curving ribs and elegantly strung vertebrae, shining with hard, steely light.

"Little death," she repeated blankly.

He sat up. Now on the left side of his chest, just above the nipple, she could see a neat hole surrounded by petals of flesh that stirred restlessly, opening and closing like a sea anemone. The wound bled more metallic light.

"Orgasm," he said. "The French call it *la petite mort*."

"And you . . ."

"I am Death."

In fact, he was only *a* death, one of many. Over the next couple of days he explained it again and again: gently, patiently, and reassuringly.

There were, he said, a number of deaths (he talked of them in family terms—brothers, sisters, cousins). New ones appeared from time to time and oldsters retired, though, of course, none died. Each death was responsible for a specific mode of mortality, though in emergencies (he was vague as to what those might be) they could take over each other's domains. David's own specialty was death by shooting.

How old was he? He did not know; could not remember. Had he ever been human? He did not know that either. Was there a God? This received a blank stare.

And in between these conversations they went for ice cream or swam in the sea or toured the labyrinthine alleys of Old Jaffa or made love. He brought her flowers every day. After a week he moved in, bringing his natty suitcase from the hotel. After two weeks he asked her to marry him.

This precipitated a crisis. She threw him out, yelling at him to go to hell. She cried for hours afterwards, only stopping when she realized that he might have done just that. Next morning he was at her door with a fresh bunch of flowers.

She could not say no. She was in love. And yet she could not say yes, either. She pleaded with him to give her more time.

"Why can't we just live together?" she cried.

He explained that it would not be right. He wanted her to see how committed he was. And unless they were legally married, he could not give her his wedding gift. She tried to push the thought of the gift away from her deliberations—she was not to be bought, she told herself and believed it—but the magnitude of it was not so easily overlooked.

One afternoon her cell phone rang. Her mother's officious neighbor Dvora called to tell her she was worried about Mrs. Shalev's state of mind. She managed to introduce a not-too-subtle remark about Mor's dereliction of her filial duties, with the unspoken "and the only child, too!" accompanying every word.

When her mother failed to pick up the phone, Mor drove up to Jerusalem. Just as she was rounding the last bend in the highway, the setting sun shone a peculiar golden-mauve light on the bare hills with their clusters of whitewashed dwellings. In such moments Jerusalem seemed not so much a city as a physical state: a lighting flicker of vertigo or a stab of pain.

Her mother was in the living room, softly crying. The usual half hour of useless recriminations followed, with Mor getting so angry with her mother's drab misery that she felt like slapping her lined cheek. But eventually Mrs. Shalev rallied sufficiently to make tea. Mother and daughter sat at the kitchen table with a bowl of homemade cookies pushed closer to Mor's side.

"*Ima*," Mor asked. "*Ima*, did you ever see Death?"

Mrs. Shalev, who was stirring her tea, froze and then glanced at Mor with a sly, conspiratorial smile as if they finally got to share a grown-up secret.

"My mother did," she said. "Your grandmother, God rest her soul! She told me about it. When they were bringing them in, in the cattle cars, she was just a child. They let her stand close to a window so she would not suffocate. There was snow outside. And there was a man standing on top of a snowdrift: an ordinary man wearing an office suit. In the depth of winter. The people pleaded and screamed, and he was writing something in his notebook. He never raised his eyes as the train passed by."

Mor reminded herself that David never wore office attire.

"But Granny survived!" she remonstrated.

"Yes," her mother agreed. "For a while."

Two days later Dvora called again. When Mor came to Jerusalem, she found her mother dead in her bed. The family physician called it a heart failure but privately admitted that an overdose of tranquilizers might have played a part.

They went to Cyprus to get married. Israel has no provisions for a civil ceremony. In her increasingly sleepless nights, Mor sometimes imagined a council of elderly rabbis solemnly deliberating whether a death may convert to Judaism.

After a brief honeymoon they returned home as a married couple. Now, said David, they should have a reception for his family.

"At home?" Mor asked faintly.

"We will rent a banquet hall," David reassured her.

A catered dinner, of course, he said casually, say, a hundred and fifty people. No, not including your friends, we can have a separate reception for them; money's not a problem. No, love, not in Jaffa, the seaside is very pretty, but it has to be in Jerusalem. They all dream of visiting the Holy City, you may count on it.

Will they show up riding pale horses, she wanted to ask, or in clouds of lighting and thunder? But she knew she was being ridiculous. They would stand in line for passport control like everybody else.

Candles burned on the tables. People with champagne flutes and plates of canapés laughed, chatted, embraced, and wandered out onto the jasmine-scented patio.

"Wanda, Zoe, Jerome, Ervin," David introduced them one by one even when they arrived as couples. "Mark, Yolanda, Ahmed."

Only the first names. Did it mean that they all had the same family name?

"Maggie, Ruth, Xiaowei."

How many? God, how many of them?

"Guido, Carl, Donna."

Good-looking people, all of them: youngish, healthy, smiling, well dressed.

"Liliana, Eric, George."

And properly diverse too: whites, Asians, blacks, and browns in roughly equal proportions. Mark was African American, and elegant Miranda looked like an Ethiopian model. Ahmed would blend into any Middle Eastern crowd. Susan, arriving on Roger's arm, belied her nondescript name by sloe eyes and café-au-lait skin.

"Kalia, Roman, Patricia."

"Nice to meet you!"

"Have a drink!"

"What a lovely place!"

They all spoke English, but some with exotic accents: silky French, heavy Eastern European, or guttural Middle Eastern.

"Reginald, Oscar, Victoria."

Strangely old-fashioned names, but nothing old-fashioned about their bearers. Women in Fendi and Prada dresses, men in Armani suits. Glitter of jewelry and expensive dental work.

"Mikhail, Gloria, Stefan."

Greeting them at the entrance, Mor tried to guess their identities but was defeated by their impersonal gloss. She found an answer when she started to mingle. One wall of the dining space was composed of mirrors. And in the mirror she could see her new family as they really were.

Liliana was the Plague. Seen face-to-face, she was a slightly plump woman with crinkly brown hair and laughter lines. She was reflected in the mirror wearing a blood-red cloak that dragged on the floor, leaving a dark stain behind. Her pleasant features were disfigured by open sores, lips split and oozing pus. Holding a wineglass in a festering hand, her reflection smiled at Mor with missing teeth.

The garrulous Stefan was reflected with ashy, hopeless eyes; his ingratiating smile, a rictus of pain; his neat tie, a twisted rope. Suicide.

Elegantly slim Ruth was a gaunt, ravenous creature. In the mirror, her diaphanous dress became a transparent shroud that clung to her protruding ribs and swollen stomach. Famine.

George, the only man in the room wearing a T-shirt with an Escher print under a sports jacket instead of a suit, incuriously glanced at his own image whose throat was slashed by a gaping wound. The Escher geometry was transformed into a chaos of bloody blobs. Murder.

Victoria's shiny blonde hair was a couple of gray tufts on the mottled skull. Old Age.

Mark was reflected as a walking mass of burns, bleeding tissue, and splintered bones. Accident, she decided.

Zoe—the others seem to defer to her, and seeing her in the mirror with the black leather harness molding her voluptuous body, her thrusting breasts like missiles, a bracelet of rusty iron splinters around her full arm, and her face covered by a helmet-like mask, Mor understood why. War was undoubtedly high on the deaths' social ladder.

There were, however, some visitors whose reflections left her puzzled. Maggie was one of them. When David introduced her, Mor saw a nice British woman, slightly older than the rest. When she walked by the mirror Mor glimpsed a strange scarecrow figure with stick-like arms and legs, her face painted with garish whorls.

Mor circulated among the guests, making polite remarks, feeling strangely detached (even curiosity was evaporating), when there was a commotion at the entrance. She saw David speaking to somebody whose only visible part was a pair of fluttering hands. She quickly went there as David stepped aside, muttering something about "bad taste." Mor found herself facing the late guest.

He was a short, pedantic man with sandy hair and blue eyes magnified by rimless glasses.

"Let me introduce . . . Daniel," David said with a tiny pause before the name. "Daniel is retired. He does not socialize much."

"I thought it was my duty to come," said the short man.

Mor offered him a drink and steered him toward the mirror. He went willingly, planted his feet wide, and stared at his image. It was exactly the same as the man. And then Mor knew who her last guest was.

"I'm sorry," said Daniel. "I know how you must feel. But I had to come."

"Do you know me?" she asked and her voice sounded like the squeak of a mouse.

"I know all of you," he said.

She looked around. Should she appeal to Stefan, Death-Suicide, who had helped her mother escape? Or to Plague, Famine, Accident, Cancer, even War? Any other death to keep her company but this.

"You see, I'm retired now," continued Daniel, "and looking at the whole business from a historical perspective, I can't blame myself. I only followed orders."

"Can't you come up with a better line?" she yelled. The sheer banality of it transmuted her dread into anger.

"But it's true. Think about it. You call the shots. You, humans. We only do what we are told. A human hand pulls the trigger or signs an order, and we mop up the resulting mess."

"How convenient! However, I see the others shy away from you. Could it be even they don't approve of your methods?"

"Sheer prejudice," said Daniel. "Envy too. There is a great deal of jockeying for power going on among us. You'll find out. You are one of us now, after all."

"Fuck you! Do you think I'm doing this to be your sister-in-law? I love David. And anyway, what are you doing here, in this city, attending a Jewish wedding?"

Daniel only smiled, unperturbed:

"I have attended a lot of Jewish weddings," he said. "And of course you love David. I have seen love sacrifices too. Eventually they tend to benefit somebody, though not always the party intended."

They moved into a bigger apartment in Tel Aviv which David paid for out of pocket, despite the insane housing bubble going on in the city. Mor kept her mother's house in Jerusalem. He suggested she stop teaching. There was no need, he said. She refused. She needed those hours on campus when she could pretend that life went on as usual—or better than usual. She was a married woman now. She had a diamond ring, a loving husband, and money in the bank.

She did not want to know what David was doing when she was away. Every time she came home, she was afraid he would tell her. But he never did. They watched Netflix and ate dinner. He went through the motions of eating conscientiously, even though it was a sheer charade. He did not need ordinary food, of course, and she soon realized that he was incapable of tasting it. Despite that, his cooking was excellent.

When they made love, David's body glowed like ice, like frozen steel, the bluish petals of the wound-flower over his heart opening wide to disclose the dark seed of the bullet inside. On the hottest nights when Mor's side of the bed was sticky with sweat, his body was cool and sleek. He was indefatigable, he was obliging, they would have sex for hours, until Mor would finally doze off and wake up screaming.

Once she asked him whether deaths dreamed. He said no. Mor was sure he lied. But it was true he never slept, even though he sometimes pretended.

They were to have a party for her friends (all of whom loved David). She sent him out with a grocery list, having decided to cook herself. The idea of letting other people eat food prepared by a death made her queasy. She was chopping lettuce when the knife slipped and bit deeply into her thumb. Mor watched dark drops of blood pool in the shallow cups of lettuce leaves. And then the bleeding stopped and the cut closed reluctantly like a disappointed mouth, the skin smoothing over, the pain receding—not into well-being but into a strange sort of numbness.

They had an Indian take-away for her party.

Once a week she goes shopping, and she always ends up with another colorful package among her drab plastic bags. She comes back home and tears the bright paper to reveal a miniature garment. The clothes are all in delicate colors: cream, lilac, forest green. Pink and blue are vulgar. She intends to give the child a unisex name, like her own, fit for either gender—or none.

Watching the TV, she takes out an armful of baby clothes and keeps on folding and unfolding them, stroking them with her fingertips, checking the zippers and the buttons, her eyes on the screen. She seldom takes out the same piece on two consecutive nights. The amount of baby clothes one can accumulate in two years is considerable.

The first time she saw her husband feed was on a bright and clear winter day. She had parked her car and was walking toward a campus gate when she heard a sharp crack, which, from her military training she recognized as a shot. People were running. A crowd was milling on the sidewalk. A man was being sick.

A boy lay among the parked cars, a gun by his side. The boy had no face.

The crowd buzzed with senseless words: "suicide," "accident," "terror." Mor stared at the tip of her shoe, dark-stained by the puddle she stepped into. When she lifted her head she saw her husband standing by the body.

Mor did not call out to him because she knew that he was invisible to everybody else. In the cold sunshine his nude body glistened with metal-colored highlights. His arms and legs looked melted down. But the wound-flower on his left side was alive, its fleshly petals moving hungrily. When he knelt down and dipped his fingers in the boy's blood, it flashed a deep crimson.

Mor was sitting in the university cafeteria, poking at her lasagna and wondering whether the cardboard taste was due to the new caterers or to her atrophying taste buds. She had become careless with her diet. Why not, since she was neither gaining nor losing any weight, no matter what she ate? But last night while she was mechanically putting potato chips in her mouth in front of the TV, one chip stuck to her palate. She took it out and discovered it was a piece of cellophane.

It was hot and muggy; the people in the courtyard were fanning themselves and wiping their foreheads. Her long-sleeved dress was spotless.

She sipped her coffee and had to look at the black liquid in her cup to make sure it was not water.

At least she no longer needed to fret about wrinkles and sun damage. Her face creams had been tossed into garbage, together with her tampons. Her gynecologist was concerned about amenorrhea and tried to send her to a round of tests. She did not go, of course. A death cannot die, nor can it procreate. And neither can a death's wife.

Somebody plunked a tray bearing a Coke and a sandwich on her table. Irritated, Mor looked up and froze. The man standing in front of her was Daniel.

"May I?" he inquired, seating himself. This was the second shock. He was speaking Hebrew but with a slight Yiddish accent.

"What are you doing here?"

"Traveling," he replied. "I'm retired, you know."

"I should hope so!"

He lifted a conciliatory hand:

"I'm on your side!"

"It'll be a sad day when I need you on my side!"

"You already do." He examined his sandwich and bit off a neat semi-circle of bread and hummus. His teeth, Mor noticed, were big and yellow, as if he used to be a smoker. "Look, Hanna. . . ."

"Don't you dare call me that!"

"I gave you that name," he said.

She stared at the table.

"You are like a child in a new school," said Daniel. "All those secrets whispered behind your back, old alliances, old loves, old hates, and here you are, a newcomer, and nobody to explain the ground rules to you."

"And you decided to be my guide out of the goodness of your heart, I suppose."

He shrugged: "I do have a different perspective, you know. First, I'm very young. I still remember my mortal days."

"Were you human once?" she asked, horrified.

"All of us were."

Seeing her expression, he laughed.

"See? You didn't even know that. Your husband is not being very informative, is he?"

"How do you become. . . . How do you become what you are?"

"All kinds of ways. Some of us just grow away from humankind until we discover our true vocation. It's a gradual process, you see. Kids who play with guns and explosives, this sort of thing. Some hear the call but cannot make the crossover and remain stranded on your side, pathetic failures in their own eyes, never mind how many body bags they send to the morgue. Ted Bundy and such...."

"Ted Bundy," she repeated numbly. "Serial killers."

He airily waved his hand.

"Quite a lot of those. They sense the vacancies."

"And the others?"

"Well, sometimes it is a sort of deathbed conversion, ecstatic experience, call it whatever you like. But it's going out of fashion. Most people on deathbeds nowadays are drugged out of their senses. And then, of course, there are such as you."

"Such as me?"

"Yes. Marrying into the tribe."

"Are you suggesting I will become one of you?" Mor managed to keep her voice down only because she recognized a couple of her students at the next table.

"Your husband promised you immortality, didn't he? Well, he did not lie, but neither did he speak the truth. Characteristic of him. You can only be truly immortal if you become a death yourself."

"Never!" Mor cried and the girls at the next table glanced at her.

"What else will you do? Plenty of your new relations are in-laws, so to speak. Stefan, for example, and Victoria. You should talk to her, by the way; she is a relatively new bride."

"Victoria? How can that be? Isn't she Old Age?'

Daniel nodded and finished his Coke in a single gulp.

"Then how.... I mean, people have died of old age since the beginning of time."

"Precisely. That's the point. Deaths do not procreate, but they die."

"How can a death die?"

"Never heard of John Donne?" asked Daniel smugly. "'Death, thou shalt die.' I thought you liked literature. Not *Christian* literature perhaps. In any case, a death can only be killed by another death, and that under very special conditions. That's why we have rather mixed feelings about each other. We get together out of solidarity and even affection of sorts. There is a sense of fraternity after centuries of gossiping. But we also need to keep an eye on each other. Not that it always helps. Victoria's predecessor was assassinated by Hunger and War, Ruth and Zoe, only they called themselves by different names then. We change names pretty often. I'm proud of my current choice. You're the only one to appreciate its meaning, really. Dani-el: 'God judged me.'"

"Oh, cut it out!" Mor sneered. "Cheap theology! Why would Ruth and Zoe do such a thing? What's the gain?"

Daniel beamed at her:

"A very Jewish attitude, if I may say so. Well, since there are so many of us, the only way to gain influence is to enlarge the sphere of one's activity. To some extent this does not depend on us at all. You humans are our real masters, even though most of us consider you mere cattle. But that's just the deplorable lack of education. Not many of us read Hegel or understand the master-slave dialectic. Anyway, once a new modality of death is discovered, a new . . . executive comes into being by a process which, quite frankly, we don't quite understand ourselves. The twentieth century was a fertile one. Have you met John? In the sixties he was about to crown himself King of Death, but after the demolition of the Berlin Wall he has been semiretired. Tending his garden, I assume, growing mushrooms."

"Mushrooms?" repeated Mor blankly. "Oh, I see. Mushroom clouds. And you?"

"I am a different matter," said Daniel evasively. "In any case we don't—quite—control the course of human history, but we can give a nudge now and then. Ruth and Zoe hoped that by eliminating Old Age they would enlarge their own respective domains. The political situation was favorable, too. What they did not count on was that Mark's demure little bride, whom everybody considered half-witted, good perhaps for crib death but nothing more ambitious, would blossom overnight into the queen of geriatric wards."

"Why are you telling me this?" Mor's voice rose again. "Are you grooming me to be your successor? If you think I'm about to take over the gas chambers. . . ."

"Please!" Daniel shook his head. "A little perspective! The gas chambers have been inactive for seventy years! No, Mor, I'm saying just the opposite. A death's existence is boring, devoid of pleasure, not fit for a woman like you. I don't need to tell you what our sex life is like. And no children, of course. Your husband has trapped you on purpose, for his own amusement. He cannot love you, being what he is, but he cannot even appreciate you. You are a fighter; you are resisting being assimilated. But what if the force of your resistance is such that you'll be forever stuck in that twilight state, neither a death nor a living woman?"

Mor looked at the wreckage of her lunch. And then she looked at the man in front of her.

"You have a proposition," she said. "What is it?"

The red-eye flight was ruined by a cramped seat and talkative neighbor. But she emerged into the terminal at five a.m. feeling no worse—and no better—than after a night in her own bed.

Guided by her cellphone, she was in Holborn by eleven. She walked down Great Holborn Street until she came to an arched entrance into a cobbled courtyard. There she had to press the button several times before the gate swung open.

The flat was cluttered with dusty Victorian junk. The brownish liquid in her cup was either coffee or tea; even with her taste buds intact she may not have known which. Maggie took out the ingredients for the beverage from an old fridge that was not plugged in, its interior choked with bundles of cobwebby herbs.

"Daniel thinks the world of you," Maggie declared.

In contrast to her place, she looked neat and very British in her twinset and pearls. As long as Mor only glanced at her briefly, the illusion held.

"How nice," said Mor dryly. "The feeling is not mutual."

Maggie only smiled indulgently.

"Dear Daniel! He and I have a lot in common."

"How so?" Mor asked.

"We are both retired. Well, no. I'm semiretired. I still do quite a bit of free-lancing, but it's nothing compared to what it was once. I pity Daniel; so much work, and so spectacular, in such a short period, and then he is kicked out. There were certain affinities, you know, between what he did and my own skills."

Mor felt her gorge rise as the brownish liquid in her cup suddenly took on the tint of clotting blood. She tried to hold on to her nausea, but it subsided.

"It is ironic," continued Maggie chattily. "I'm the oldest one and he is . . . no, I take it back, he is not the youngest one, even though none of the millennials is as talented as he is."

"Are you really the oldest?"

"Yes. I was the firstborn. Even before your kind was quite sure of its direction. I was there when Neanderthals scattered ochre around the skeletons of the eaten ones. I was there when shamans withered babies in their mothers' wombs and flayed men alive without even touching them. And I still enjoy the old art. There are people, right now, dear, who are sticking needles in voodoo dolls and calling my name. Some things never change. When all the computer-guided missiles crumble to dust, I will still be there."

Maggie was smiling sweetly throughout the speech, but it was not her pink-glossed mouth that spoke the words. It was the other mouth, squirming beneath her skin like a black worm: the slit in the whorl-painted visage of Death-Magic.

"But why here?" asked Mor. "Why London?"

Maggie shrugged: "This land is so soaked in history that it's beginning to rot like a bloated sponge. But this is not about my plans, dear. Daniel has asked me for a favor, and I see no reason to refuse. David and I have never gotten along. His modus operandi is far too mechanical for me. No spirit. So shall we start?"

Mor nodded and braced herself for the ceremony she assumed was about to begin. Instead, Maggie just took a more comfortable position on her sway-backed couch.

"Once upon a time," she said, "there was a boy who loved guns. His family was dirt-poor, and they could not afford the weapons that he wanted. His father had the only gun in the family, an old Colt Browning. One day the boy came home and saw his father sitting at the table, the top of his head blown off. He looked at his old man for a while. And then he picked up the gun lying in the pool of blood, turned around, and walked away."

Maggie reached under the torn cushion and pulled out a wreck of an antique gun, rusted and bent.

"Old tales are right," Maggie went on. "The only power stronger than death is love. When we become deaths, old loves shrivel and fall away. But just as our bodies still bear one mark of our lost mortality, so do our souls. In a dusty corner of each death's still heart the one true love of his or her life lies sleeping. If it's woken, the heart will beat once and stop forever. And the death shall die."

"David does not love anybody," said Mor.

"This gun is your husband's one true love."

Mor's fingers closed on the coarse metal. The rust stained them red.

They drove up to Jerusalem to spend the Sabbath in the Holy City. It had become a habit by now. Mor bought a bottle of red wine and a couple of fat candles, which she lit in the bedroom. In the candlelight, David's real face poked through his unconvincing flesh. She caressed the bone and thrust her tongue between the lipless teeth.

Their mock lovemaking died down, as it always did. She sat astride the skeletal thing.

"Don't you ever miss it?" she asked. "The little death, *la petite mort?*"

"Why should I?" he said. "I have the real thing."

"But not with me," said Mor. "And I'm your wife."

He laughed.

"I did not marry you for that!"

"You did," said Mor.

Her hand snaked under the pile of her clothes and whipped out the gun. Quickly she pressed the muzzle to the wound in her husband's chest and pulled the trigger. For a second, she thought it could not work. But then the body underneath her convulsed, and dark, heavy blood erupted from the wound, splattering her belly and legs. At the same time she felt a hot explosion inside herself. A single groan escaped her husband, the metallic bones of his face corroding and falling apart, the hard sleekness of his flesh growing soft and mushy, her fingers sinking into his arms and encountering only the pliancy of a child's bones that were snapping like twigs, while she was crying out, dying a thousand little deaths in one infinite moment of time.

When it was over, she found herself lying prone on the bed in darkness. The candles had gone out. She turned on the light. The bed was littered with a pitifully small handful of bone fragments. She was ravenously hungry. She took a shower and spent the rest of the night eating canned tuna and watching movies in Arabic.

At dawn she went out into the clarity of Jerusalem. So early in the day, the city looked empty and innocent, its buildings dissolving into pink shadows on the craggy hills. Mor drove to the mall in Talpiot and stood by the parapet, looking down at the glorious panorama of the Mount of Olives with the golden dome of the great mosque and the dark lines of trees crossing the valley of Gehenna.

She heard steps behind and turned. Daniel, looking fresh and dapper in a white shirt and jeans, smiled at her.

"Well done," he said.

She stared at him, incredulous.

Over the left nipple, his shirt was stained by fresh blood.

"Thank you, Hanna. You have given me a new lease."

"You?" she gasped."Coming back?"

"No, no. My old job is done. I have simply taken your late husband's vacant place. Nature—or whoever our manager is—abhors vacuum. I am too young to retire. I knew that when there was a job opening I would be the first on the list. I'm sure I'll significantly improve on David's performance."

"I should have known," she said dully.

"Don't blame yourself. You did not imagine this morning would see all the guns beaten into ploughshares, did you?"

The city was waking up. A car honked, a child cried, a long call drifted up from the mosque in the valley.

"Just tell me one thing," she said. "What was your real name?"

He shook his head.

"I don't remember. Perhaps I did until last night, but now, with my new position. . . . I remember some things. Piano playing, a woman with dark hair—my mother? Light on linden leaves in spring. But it's fading, memory disappearing. Like that, see?"

He rolled up his shirtsleeve. On the white skin Mor could see disjointed blue strokes—the remnants of a tattoo—that were being absorbed into the body even as she watched.

"We all have our badges," he said. "I shan't be sorry to let this one go."

Mor looked into his eyes and smiled.

"You have miscalculated, Daniel," she said. "Or whoever you are. Killing is a spur to breeding. You should have been more careful about murdering your own. And now what will you do, you and your fellow maggots, when death becomes fruitful and multiplies? What will you feed on when life starts feeding on you?"

He stared at her uncomprehendingly.

"I am pregnant," she said.

"You can't be! You're still. . . ."

"Death's wife. I know. But my husband died in my arms, and I am carrying his seed. I am not a pawn in your game, you smug bastard! I am the mother of the future King who will ride down this very mountain and call up the dead from their graves. He will mold ashes back into bodies and clothe burnt bones with flesh. And he will judge you as you deserve to be judged. My son is King of the living and the dead, and he will make each death beg for oblivion before he slays you all. And you, you will remember your name when you are called to his judgment!"

Daniel's right hand crept up, the fingers melting together, acquiring a metallic sheen, fusing into a small but deadly looking gun.

Mor laughed. "I thought immunity from the family was part of the bargain! Fool that I was, to trust a death! But I have better protection. Go ahead, shoot me! Do it! Why can't you? Could it be you are sensing your King? Could it be my baby is already stronger than you?"

Daniel dropped his hand, which resumed its normal appearance. There was fear in his eyes but also something else, something that looked like relief.

"Well," he said, "this was not planned. But this was bound to happen, sooner or later. And of course, this is the most appropriate place for it. The only place. I wonder what went through David's dull brain when he decided to take his Middle Eastern vacation. But even if he had a . . . guidance, this is irrelevant now. You are right, Mor. I cannot touch you. And I can feel the thing in your womb even though it is tinier than a mustard seed. But I wonder what it'll be like when it's fully grown. It's conventional to wish a prospective mother joy, but frankly, I wonder whether you'll have much joy in your baby. Think of your predecessors: they did not fare well with their kingly sons, who had broken their hearts before future generations bestowed upon the poor women heaps of silly titles. But in any case, Your Future Majesty, though I may be bound to obey your son, I am not going to welcome him with myrrh and frankincense. And though I may be the first one to be hauled before his judgment seat, I will maintain my innocence to the end. I only followed orders."

He turned and walked away, his back ramrod-straight.

Every Friday Mor goes to the Wailing Wall, slowly wending her way through the narrow, twisting lanes of the market, bright with tourist junk and fragrant with spices, coffee, and sweat. Some shop owners recognize her and offer her bright blue beads against the evil eye, which she willingly buys. At the familiar corner stall she rests her heavy belly, sitting on a scratched aluminum chair and sipping cardamom-flavored coffee from a tiny cup. She hears shots and glimpses a steely blue apparition disappear among the fluttering rugs. She is unmoved, and so is Ali, who continues his rapid monologue in garbled English and shakes his head when she offers to pay for the coffee.

The square in front of the Wailing Wall is beaten into monochrome whiteness by the glare of the noon. A couple of soldiers lazing about in their glass booth throw her an indifferent glance. The women's section of the wall is less crowded than usual; only some Orthodox heads hidden under untidy wigs are pressed to the eroded stones like a row of bushy little animals. Their men rock on the other side of the partition, their black coats soaking up heat. Mor picks up a modesty shawl from the stand to cover up her bare shoulders, walks to the wall, kisses the warm, powdery rock.

"Soon," she tells the unmoving weight in her womb. "Soon, honey."

At home she lights the Sabbath candles, fixes dinner, and sits in front of the TV, absorbing the latest litany of nuclear threats, military casualties, and political crises.

A breaking news banner appears at the bottom of the screen when Mor feels a sickening pang in her lower abdomen. She sits up, breathless, the dinner tray pushed aside. Yes, no doubt of it, the beginning of labor, just as she had been taught in those long-ago birth preparation classes. A wave of exultation sweeps over her, overcoming another brutal spasm that feels as if somebody has grabbed a handful of her entrails and twisted them. The hem of her dress is soaked: her water has broken.

Mor reaches for her phone to call an ambulance. A hand closes on hers.

"No need," says a familiar voice.

Deftly, Maggie rearranges the cushions on the couch to prop up her back. Dazed, Mor looks around. Familiar faces look back at her. Ruth smiles shyly; Victoria pulls clean sheets out of a large tote bag; Zoe plugs in the kettle in the kitchen. Liliana shoos out the men who crowd at the door. George waves at her; somebody else—Mikhail?—flashes a V sign.

Mor pushes Maggie aside and tries to stand up. But she can't: the pain is too strong.

"Why?" she cries. "What are you doing here?"

"We want to help you," says Ruth.

"We want to be here when the King is born," says Victoria.

She looks at them mutely, and they look back: War, Famine, Plague, Old Age, and Voodoo.

"Do you acknowledge my son, then?" asks Mor.

"He is our King," says Maggie. "We have been waiting for him since the beginning of time. And you are our Queen. You will intercede for us with your son."

The labor pains are almost continuous now; she can feel the baby impatiently pushing out of her womb. There are faint screams, booms of explosions, rattle of gunfire; it takes her a moment to realize they are coming from the TV.

"But aren't you afraid of him?" she cries. "Aren't you afraid, Death, that you shall die?"

She sees ambiguous smiles on their faces, but another twist of her guts makes her collapse on the couch, unable to push away Maggie's solicitous hand. Zoe removes her helmet and she sees the old brown bones of a skeleton rotting in some anonymous grave. The empty eyeholes are filled with light, and Mor still has the strength to wonder: Is it the longing for oblivion or the certainty of triumph?

White Curtain

Pesakh (Pavel) Amnuel

I recognized him immediately although we had not seen each other for eleven years, having last met under very different circumstances. There was a change in him: he looked older, yet, somehow, better.

"Hello, Oleg," I said.

"Hello, Dima," he answered, as if we had spent the day before as we used to, in years past, drinking and arguing about the cascading splice theory. "I knew you'd come. Sit. No, not on this chair, that's for visitors. Sit here, on the sofa."

I sat down, and the sofa squeaked in protest.

"Of course you knew," I said. "You are the prophet."

"I'm no prophet," he said sadly. "Who knows that better than you?" He spoke more slowly than ever before, enunciating each word to the last syllable.

"Yes," I said, not trying to hide the sarcasm. "Who better?"

"How did you find me?" Oleg asked.

"With difficulty," I admitted. "But I found you. You were . . ."

"No matter," he interrupted, "it does not matter at all, what I used to be. Why?"

"Why what?"

"Why did you come? I don't think you came just to make sure it's me. You want something from me. Everyone does. Success? Luck?"

If there was irony in his voice, I did not notice it. I did not need luck. Especially not from him.

"Irina died last year," I said, looking in his eyes. "We had been together for ten years, two months, and sixteen days."

He turned away from me to look at the curtained window. What did he see in that blank screen, that white expanse where all the colors of his life were mixed together? Himself, young, walking Irina to a discotheque? Or only Irina, on that long-ago day when yet another dazzling presentation he made at that morning's seminar inspired him to believe himself irresistible to women? The day I watched, from the auditorium door, as he proposed to her with this newfound confidence, as she kissed the corner of his mouth and said that he was a little late because she loved another, and cast an eloquent glance in my direction, and he followed it and understood. The day Irina and I left him behind, defeated and deflated, useless even to himself.

The day I saw him for the last time, until now. On the following morning Oleg Larionov, previously a promising theoretical physicist, submitted his letter of resignation. The dean, though loath to lose him, eventually would have allowed him to leave on good terms (he stamped the letter with "Approved at the end of semester"), but Oleg left without waiting for the response. He left without saying goodbye to anyone. He had been seen boarding the forty-three bus in the direction of the train station; except for that, no one had even an inkling of where he was going.

And that was all.

"Why did she die?" Oleg asked, his gaze still on the white, screenlike curtain. *Why did you not save her?* was what I heard.

I could not. I could do nothing. My strength was in theoretical work, I excelled at splice calculations, perhaps not all, but up to a very high complexity, up to twelve branches of reality, that's quite a lot, almost unheard-of for an analytical solution—but in reality there was nothing I could do. Irina fell ill unexpectedly and died soon after. How soon? She was diagnosed in March, and in July she was gone.

"Brain tumor," I said. "Could not have been predicted. There wasn't a nexus of branching ..."

"Theoretically," he interrupted, and I could not decide if his words mocked mine, or were a simple statement of fact.

"I've been looking for you for an entire year," I said. "And found you. As you can see. Do you remember Gennady Bortman?"

Oleg turned toward me at last. I had expected something in his gaze, a feeling, anything. But there was nothing. He looked at me as calmly as a doctor at a patient suffering from a cold.

"I do remember him," said Oleg. "It's a pity."

"He stayed on the branch," I said, "which you predicted for him. Was there anything he could have done?"

So much depended on Oleg's answer. I did not want to think about my life. But Ira's. . . .

"Dima," said Oleg and rubbed his hands together, an old familiar gesture with which he once rubbed chalk dust off his hands after a long presentation, adding it to the floor already littered with chalk crumbs. "Dima, he could have chosen any branch in his reality. The months he had until. . . . Of hundreds of decisions, you understand, each time a new branch grew, but always in the direction ..."

"In our reality," I interrupted, "only your prophesy could come true. Your branch was stronger, more resilient."

"Yes," Oleg nodded, "My branch had higher probability, a million times higher."

"In other words," I said, and it was important for me to be clear, so very important that I had searched for Oleg for a year, an excruciating year of living on memories, "in other words, for a million possibilities you choose, there may be one chance for someone else's choice?"

"Maybe not a million," he said, still rubbing his fingers, his gesture irritating me so much that I fought the urge to slap his hands. "Maybe ten million. Maybe a hundred billion. There is no way to measure, no statistics."

"You've had years to compile statistics," I said. "You set yourself up as a prophet to compile statistics, don't try to tell me you didn't! For God's sake, don't tell me you are disillusioned with pure science and became a practicing prophet only to help people!"

"I do help them ..."

"Some of them! Oleg, I've hung around here for a week; I listen to people waiting for their turn, some for six months, they come every day, they wait and walk away and come back, and once in a while one of your secretaries will come out and say, "He won't see you, sorry," and it's no use arguing back. And some, people you pick out from the crowd, you'll see them right away, only them, predict a happy, creative life with luck in business and personal fulfillment."

"Have I been wrong?"

"Never! You are one hundred percent reliable! This means you choose the necessary branch of the multiverse with an accuracy of at least ten sigmas!"

"Eight sigmas," he corrected. "I have compiled enough records for eight sigmas, I need another three years . . ."

"The hell with that," I said. "I looked for you so that . . ."

"It is impossible, Dima." Oleg stopped rubbing nonexistent chalk off his fingers, put his hands on his knees, and looked me in the eyes. "You know it's impossible. You were the one who proved the theorem, according to which . . ."

"Yes," I nodded. "I proved it. If in Branch N of the multiverse the world-line of object A is a segment of length L, this line cannot be extended within its branch by grafting it to other realities."

"You proved it. And what do you want from me now, Dima? Ira does not exist in this here-and-now. You could not keep her."

"I could not . . ."

"You could not hold on to her," Oleg repeated. "And what is it to us that our Irisha . . ."

He said "our." He still lived with the feeling that she had only temporarily left him for another and would come back.

". . . our Irisha is still alive in a billion other branches of the multiverse?"

"You could," I said. "You are a genius at splicing. You can tie branches together and graft them, like Michurin grafted an apple branch to a pear tree."

"And how did it end?" Oleg chuckled. "Michurin. Burbank. Lysenko."

"Won't you even try!" I yelled.

Oleg stood up and walked toward the window as if to put as much distance between us as possible, as if my presence made it hard for him to breathe, to think, to live.

"I tried. All the time, I tried," he said, his voice as hollow as if he spoke under water.

"You. . . ." I mumbled in confusion. He could not have known about Ira.

"I can do nothing for myself, you see? Think, Dima, you are one hell of a theoretician. If I am in Branch N, then all possible splices that can change my fate . . ."

"Are bound by the causality of that branch—yes, I proved that in my third year of study," I said. "But you said that you tried. . . ."

"I couldn't avoid trying. What if the theory were wrong?"

We sat in silence, each thinking about what had been said.

"How did you know about Ira?"

Oleg turned and looked at me with a silent accusation.

"Well, Dima, if you found me. . . . You didn't have to look for me, I checked the university web page every day, I knew about everything that went on. I could not stand not knowing."

"That never entered my mind," I muttered. "I would have figured out where you were long ago."

"I doubt it," he said. "I took measures. When Ira died, the alumni association ran an obituary the same day. I tried, right there and then. God, Dima, I leaped from branch to branch like a neurotic monkey, spliced more realities than I had ever allowed myself before—and, after that, never again.

"I didn't . . ."

"Of course you didn't feel a thing!"

"Sorry," I said. "I am not myself today. Stupid; I should have known, I could not feel a break, my reality was contiguous with my past."

"You had hundreds of realities, and in all of them Ira died, and I was always late, I made it to the funeral in one hundred seventy-six branches."

"You went to a hundred seventy-six funerals?" I said, horrified.

He didn't say anything, and I understood why he looked so old to me. I would have gone mad in his place.

"Then," I said, "there was nothing . . ."

"You are the one who proved that theorem," said Oleg roughly, "and I never found experimental evidence to the contrary."

"So that's how it is," I muttered. Something hit me all at once, a year's worth of fatigue, perhaps, and maybe now I made decisions one after another, each taking me to a different branch, each branch beginning with: "So that's how it is" parroted over and over.

"Well, that is all," said Oleg and stood up abruptly. He reached to shake my hand; his fingers were, for some strange reason, dusted with chalk. "Enough already with the histrionics. You lived by hope alone for a year, looking for me, and I lost hope a year ago and had the time I needed to come to terms with it. I can do nothing for you, Dima. Not—a—thing."

I stood up.

"Leaving?" Oleg asked, his voice flat, without giving me his hand. "You looked for me for such a long time. We could have coffee, dinner, you could tell me about the university. Did Kulikov defend his dissertation?"

"You've been on their web site." I shrugged.

"No, not since. . . ."

"You," I said, from the doorway, "you splice realities to make lives better."

"Of course," he nodded.

"And those you turn away?"

"So that's the question." He came closer and with a long-familiar gesture put both his hands on my shoulders. His palms were unpleasantly heavy, and I sagged like Atlas under the weight of the sky.

"You think I turn away those whose fate I cannot channel in a better direction," he said, looking straight into my eyes. He did not even blink, and I tried not to blink as well. "You are mistaken, Dima. I have rules. Well, not quite rules; I want nothing to do with unpleasant people, or with people whose happiness depends on the suffering of others. I choose, yes. Do you think I have no right?"

"Oh, come on," I muttered. "It's just that . . ."

"You thought of what I could have done for you?"

"No." I chuckled. "You would not do this, and it's not what I would want."

"You do want," he said roughly. "Don't lie, your eyes betray you. You want to be happy, everyone does. You want her specter to stop haunting you. You want to forget . . ."

"No!"

"Fine; to remember, just about enough to light a candle, that is sufficient. And live a happy life. You came to have your life spliced with a branch in which you are happy and prosperous . . ."

"No," I said, but blinked and lowered my eyes. I wanted that. So what? This he could do, I knew. I also knew he would not lift a finger to help me.

"Yes," he sighed and pressed even harder (or did I imagine it?) on my shoulders. "You know, Dima, when you came in and we recognized each other, the first thing I did was run through a list of splices, in my head, that I could have made. For you. Even if you had not asked me, I decided to do it. Because to live without Ira. . . . I know how it was for me, but I cannot do anything for myself because of your damned theorem. But I could help you, yes, or else what purpose do I have?"

He took his hands from my shoulders at last, and I stood straight, feeling suddenly light. Was it the lifting of that weight that made me feel relieved, or thinking, for a moment: *Oleg can, Oleg will?*

"There isn't a single line in all of the multiverse," he said, "where all is well for you. Not one. What can I do with that?"

"Nonsense!" I exclaimed and stepped back from him. "You know that's nonsense, why do you even. . . . We discussed this problem since . . ."

"Yes, we discussed," he interrupted.

"The multiverse is infinite!" I exclaimed. "There is an infinite number of branches of reality, and all without exception can be embodied as our reality, any version of any event, phenomenon, process, and that means . . ."

"That means," said Oleg regretfully, "that you were right, not I. You proved there's only a finite number of branches because the wave function for each event has a limited number of solutions."

"Yes, but since then . . ."

"But I," Oleg raised his voice, "I maintained that there is an infinity of branches, and in the multiverse's infinity there must exist all possibilities of human fate—happy and unhappy. I was sure! But now I know I was wrong. The branching of destinies is limited, Dima. Forgive me. I wanted. Very much. At least in Ira's memory. It's no use. There is a huge number of versions of your life, but none where you are happy."

"Well, then," I said, feeling an emptiness in my soul which I now knew could never be filled, "we've resolved an old scientific debate. For once you have admitted that I'm right."

"The branching is finite," he said. "Aren't you happy to be right?"

Did he intentionally torment me?

"Farewell," I said and closed the door quietly behind me. Three of the prophet's secretaries sat at their computers, not even lifting their eyes to me.

"The office hours are over for today," a ceiling speaker screeched, and dozens of people crowded into the waiting room sighed as one with disappointment.

It was windy outside, and a drizzle soaked my hair. The rented car was parked two blocks away, and by the time I sat behind the wheel my shirt was plastered to my body, and thoughts had deserted me entirely, all thoughts but one: Who needs a life like this?

I drove slowly in the right lane without knowing where I was, in what part of the city, until I saw a Dead End sign. I turned toward the curb and killed the engine.

We had debated once, with Oleg. Not just us; it was a popular question, fifteen years ago, in theoretic everettics: Is there a limited number of events in the world of continuous branchings? I said yes, it is limited, and my arguments. . . . God, I had no idea I could win the debate and lose my own life!

Rain. It will always be raining now.

The phone rang, its ringtone a Hungarian dance by Brahms. I fumbled in my bag and brought the phone to my ear.

"Dima!"

I did not recognize the voice at first: it was Mikhail Natanovich, the doctor who treated, but could not save, Irina. "Dima, I've been calling you all day!"

"My phone was off," I said.

"No matter! I wanted to tell you: today's test results are much better than before. Much better! This new drug, it's really.... Dima, I think it will all turn out for the best, now. Do you hear me, Dima?"

Will turn out for the best. New drug. Ira.

"How is she?" I asked, squeezing the phone as if I wanted to break it.

"Slept well all night."

"Ira?"

"Irina Yakovlevna had breakfast this morning, for the first time...."

"Yes," I said. "Thank you for calling. I will be at the hospital no later than nine this evening, as soon as I can get there."

I dropped the phone on the seat next to me.

Oleg succeeded? How? He said himself—not quite an hour ago—that there's a limited number of splices, that if she died, then....

Was he mistaken? Or did he accomplish that which he himself considered impossible? Or found an infinity of branches and among them, one in which everything, simply everything, works out?

I lifted the receiver and dialed his number. It was my duty to thank him, at least.

"I need to speak with Oleg Nikolaevich," I said when one of his secretaries answered.

"Unfortunately..."

"This is Mantsev, his old friend and colleague. I was just with him and want to..."

"Unfortunately," repeated a voice as gray as the rain beyond my window, "it's impossible. Oleg Nikolaevich passed away immediately after you left."

How could that happen? He had appeared healthy and acted perfectly well when....

"I do not understand," I muttered. "How is this..."

"The police are here now," the secretary said. "I think they might want to speak with you. You were his last visitor of the day. Ten minutes after you left..."

"Out with it!"

"Oleg Nikolaevich threw himself out the window. And we are..."

"On the sixth floor," I finished for him.

This is how it ends, I thought. He pushed the white curtain out of the way and stepped through.

Rain ended. I drove to the airport as fast as I could go. At nine I had to be at the hospital. With Irina. My Irina.

I was right after all: there is a limit to the number of splices. Oleg proved it, conclusively this time. He said he could do nothing with his fate. Of course. Except for one thing: he could interrupt it. Only then could my fate where Ira died be spliced with the branch where she survived.

You can extend one branch by cutting off another. The law of conservation. Oleg knew.

Why did he do this? He had every reason to hate me. What would I have done in his place, knowing there was only one possibility? What am I? A theoretician. Oleg worked in practical, experimental everettics. He did what I could only guess at. Or calculate.

I sped up, no longer watching the speedometer.

I knew that Irina and I—that all will be well.

How can I live, knowing that?

A Man's Dream

Yael Furman

"Rina! Rina!" Galia screamed at the top of her lungs, trying in vain to climb out of bed. The man at her side was fast asleep. She already knew there was no point in trying to wake him up. Only Rina ever managed to do that.

"Rina!"

She heard a toilet flush in the bathroom and then the familiar tapping of Rina's shoes.

"Yair!" Rina screamed. "Wake up, right now! Wake up!"

The man on the bed stirred, and Galia felt that the invisible barrier that had enveloped her had dissolved. She quickly jumped out of bed.

"I was driving!" she said with tears in her eyes. I was driving on Namir Avenue, and there were pedestrians."

"Oh, poor thing," said Rina softly and hugged Galia. "Let's get you into this robe and find out what happened to your car."

A few minutes later Galia sat at the kitchen table, dressed in a robe and holding a hot cup of tea. Rina sat next to her, talking with the police over the phone. Yair fell asleep again; the two of them preferred to let him sleep as long as Galia was there.

"I understand," said Rina into the receiver, "so except for the old man who was startled, no one was hurt."

Galia wrote on a note: *Ask him what happened to the stuff in the car.*

"I understand. Yes . . . yes, let her insurance company fight it out with ours— It's not her fault, poor thing. It's my husband's fault."

She looked at the note while listening to the voice on the other end. "Thank you . . . yes. She wants to know what happened to all her belongings in the car. . . . Aha . . . thank you."

She put down the receiver. "He said your bag is at the police station, and they don't think anything was stolen. And he said you should take the police report to the insurance company, showing that it was a Dreaming accident. The insurance has to compensate you for the damages. Worst case, they can talk to *our* insurance company."

"Even though you weren't involved in the accident?" asked Galia.

"But Yair caused it," said Rina.

"I don't know what to do," said Galia. She looked pale and confused. "I'm going crazy. Have you been to your psychiatrist?"

"Yes. And he gave us pills, but they gave Yair an asthma attack. The psychiatrist is consulting now with his colleagues about an alternative medicine."

"And what about the traditional treatment? Talks? Find out why he keeps dreaming about me in the first place?"

Rina sighed and held her head in her hands. "I asked him," she said. "He told me that many men dream about women they've seen for a moment. It's natural and usually harmless. Most men who dream about a woman dream about her for one night and usually don't even remember the dream the next morning. At most, they may create an alternative dream duplicate, and then it disappears when they wake up. Sometimes they don't even remember it. But Yair? He's so utterly uncreative. So when he first dreamt about you, instead of creating himself a dream duplicate of you he simply pulled you to him, which created a sort of self-perpetuating effect. Since you appear next to him and he knows you really exist, it makes him go on dreaming about you. It's an endless cycle."

"So maybe I should sleep with him once, let him get it out of his system."

Rina answered in a feeble voice, "I even asked him about it, as long as it would make him calm down. He said 'no way.' Bringing you here naked is the top of Yair's creativity. If you sleep with him it will only give him more stuff to dream about. And it will be even worse. If, when he dreams now, he can confine you to the bed, you don't want to imagine what will happen if he would actually dream that. . . ." She let her words trail off and sipped her coffee quietly.

Galia drank her tea.

Yair woke up and was relieved to find he was alone on the bed. He got up and went barefoot into the living room. Rina was sitting watching TV.

"Where's Galia"? Yair asked.

"I took her home an hour ago," Rina said. Her gaze was fixed on the screen. It was a program about nutrition. A man in a chef's uniform was discussing sprouting legumes.

"I'm sorry," said Yair. "I didn't mean to fall asleep. I was just lying down for a rest. I didn't sleep all night. . . ."

"There's coffee in the thermos," Rina said without taking her eyes off the screen.

"Thanks, honey," said Yair.

He went to wash his face in the bathroom. Staring back at him in the mirror was a balding man in his late forties. His face was already beginning to show wrinkles. Small bags hung under his hazel eyes. The mirror didn't show it, but he knew that his belly also showed. He wasn't the kind of man a good-looking woman like Galia would be attracted to. Even when he was younger and had abundant hair, they were not attracted to him. Rina was different. She saw in him something else, something that none of the Galias could see, but he wasn't sure anymore how much was left in him, of whatever it was that brought him Rina. He washed his face, shaved, and went back to the kitchen to pour himself some coffee. Rina still sat in front of the TV. The cook was inspecting the fresh lentil sprouts.

"Did Galia suffer any damages?" Yair asked. He sipped his coffee and slightly burned his tongue. He put the coffee down on the table to cool a little.

"Her car was left without a driver, and it hit a lamp post," said Rina.

"Did anyone get hurt?"

"No."

He took the coffee and went to sit beside Rina. He wanted to put his arm around her, but she got up and went to the bathroom. Yair sipped his coffee carefully to avoid burning his tongue again. The cook in the television finally cooked the lentils and went on to beans. Rina came back from the bathroom and went to the kitchen. He heard her pulling out some kitchenware from one of the cupboards.

"Maybe I'll try the pills again tonight," Yair said.

"It almost killed you last time," said Rina.

"Maybe it was something else. I have to try it again. I'm so afraid I'll dream about her again that I can't go to sleep."

The sound of rattling from the kitchen stopped abruptly. Rina came and stood between him and the television.

"It nearly killed you." She looked at him sternly.

"Maybe it was something else."

Rina went back to the kitchen. Yair went back to watching the show. The cook was now on to soaking beans in water. It was fascinating.

By one o'clock in the morning, with an inhalation mask strapped onto his mouth, Yair regretted taking the pill. His lungs relaxed after a long and terrifying struggle, and his breathing settled. The doctor Rina had called determined it was an acute allergic reaction to the pills, which could potentially be fatal.

"Thirty percent of the population is allergic to this pill," the doctor told Rina. "There have been quite a few reported deaths. Allergies can develop even after a certain amount of time. They give the pill only in cases in which the dreaming becomes a danger to the dreamer's life."

"And what if it puts someone else's life in jeopardy?" Rina asked.

"Next time the attack will kill him," the doctor said.

Yair removed the mask from his face and asked, "And what if I keep an inhaler or this inhalator, and use it right after I take the pill?"

He felt the pressure in his lungs again and quickly put the mask back to his nose.

The doctor looked at him as if he was mad. "It doesn't work that way," he said.

Yair managed to remain awake until six o'clock in the morning by reading a book. Rina slept next to him. He wondered what she was dreaming about. Was she dreaming about other men but not realizing them? He switched off the bedside lamp because the light coming in through the window was sufficient to prevent him from falling asleep, and he stared at his wife, trying to think only about her and not anyone else. For him there was nobody else. Just Rina. He looked at her dark, lifeless hair and at the slightly low angle of her eyes, her nose with the tiny protrusion and her thin, pursed lips.

"Yair, Wake up!" shouted Rina.

Yair woke up to find Galia sitting naked on the bed next to him, screaming. Judging by the light from outside, it was already late in the morning.

Rina was standing next to the bed.

"What are you doing sleeping in the morning, you moron?" Galia screamed. "I have a meeting with Ossem's CEO in an hour. I was just sitting with my boss to go over the final details. I don't know what I'll do if they fire me because of you."

She grabbed a pillow and started beating him with it in a rage. He flinched away from her and fell off the other side of the bed.

"Galia, I'll take you home quickly," said Rina, "and then to work. Come on, Hurry."

Galia got off the bed and opened the closet to take out a robe. Her face was distorted, on the verge of crying.

"I was wearing my best suit. It cost me more than a thousand shekels. I spent half an hour this morning doing my makeup; I was at the hair dresser. And now because of your stupid husband I'll look like some market girl at the meeting."

She covered herself with the robe and turned to Yair.

"If you fall asleep again, I swear I'll kill you! At least sleep at night, so that you don't completely screw up my job."

She left the room with Rina following her in silence. Yair got up from the floor, rubbing his aching back, and went to the bathroom.

Galia called her boss to explain what had happened. When she hung up she looked like she was going to put her fist through a windshield.

"He's furious," she said. "I was holding some very important document in my hands and they disappeared. Now they're making more copies, and he's trying to postpone the meeting, but it's Ossem's CEO. It's not simple. I hope I'll make it on time. You'll have to take me to work and then to Ossem, too."

"No problem, I'll take you."

"Oh my god, what am I going to wear? My other suit is at the cleaners. And the third one is for winter."

"I'll go upstairs with you and we'll find you something nice to wear."

"And then do me a favor and go home to keep an eye on him so he doesn't fall back to sleep. Just because he is unemployed doesn't mean he should sleep during the day. He should show some consideration."

"He does. He's afraid of sleeping at night because he doesn't want to dream about you."

Galia moaned. "It's better he dreams about me at night than during the day when I'm trying to live a little. Try and get that retarded monkey husband of yours to get it into his head!"

"I'll watch over him. Look, we're doing everything we can. Honest."

"I know you're doing everything, but I don't know how much more of this I can take. I really don't want anything bad to happen to Yair. I know he's not doing this on purpose and that you're good people, but this is ruining my life. One day I will have no choice but to file a complaint against him."

Rina drove through a red light and turned into Galia's street. She parked the car near her house.

"Yesterday he tried to take that pill that stops the dreams again. But he got a terrible asthma attack and I had to call a doctor. The doctor said that another pill might kill him."

Galia went out of the car and hurried up the stairs.

When Rina got back home she found Yair in front of the television watching the Fashion Channel.

"What are you doing?" she asked.

"Trying to stop dreaming about Galia."

"Galia at least lives here. What would we do if you brought some American model here? Not everybody is as patient as Galia."

Yair pressed the remote. "You're right" he said.

"So is Galia. It's not wise for you not to sleep at night. When you fall asleep during the day you're destroying her job, too."

Yair let out a moan and stretched on the sofa.

"No," Rina said. "Don't you dare. You will not fall asleep today and ruin the girl's career. No! Get dressed. We're going on a trip."

Yair got up from the couch with a moan. He looked at Rina and saw that her face was pale.

"What's wrong?"

"Galia said something about filing a complaint. She said she didn't want to do it, but soon she won't have a choice."

"What good will that do her? The psychiatrist knows about it, the police know about it, nobody cares."

"There are rumors about a new special unit that's supposed to deal with Dreamers. It scares me."

"Nonsense. I haven't committed any crime. I'm not doing this on purpose."

"If this doesn't stop, someone might do something. Let's go on a trip so you don't fall asleep on me."

They got into the car and drove up north. The sunlight was bright but not unpleasant, and a light breeze was blowing. They went up to Mount Carmel and took a walk in the reserve. The weather was excellent, and everything around was green. Yair held Rina's hand like he used to do when they were young and had only started dating. He looked at her and noticed for the first time that her black hair was not dyed like that of most women her age. And her face was gentle and almost without wrinkles. She also put on a beautiful red lipstick that made her lips look thicker. Rina smiled and said that maybe instead of continuing the futile search for a job they should open their own business. Yair thought it was a good idea. He had good hands. He could work doing carpentry or take a course in electricity.

In the afternoon they went further north to Acre and found a hummus place in the old city. They used to do it often during the first few years after their marriage. Yair watched Rina sipping her coffee. There was a light on her face, and for a moment she looked as beautiful as she did when they got married.

"I'm going to the bathroom," he told her.

He went out the back door of the restaurant, hurried to a flower shop down the market, and bought the most beautiful bouquet they had. When he came back, he crept up behind her, raised the bouquet and said, "Flowers for my flower."

She smiled, and her smile was like a rainbow after the rain.

"What's the occasion?"

"The occasion is that I love you."

On the way back he started singing along with the music from the radio. Rina joined him. They kept singing even when they got stuck in traffic. Only the sound of Rina's phone stopped the singing.

"Hello."

Rina listened, her face went pale.

"What's wrong, honey?"

"Who is it?" Yair asked. But Rina hushed him with her hand and turned off the radio.

The cars in front started moving again and Yair focused on the driving.

"I understand. . . . Yes, do you want me to talk to them?"

She listened again for a long time.

"Don't cry sweetie . . . there's no problem getting you a permit."

She stared at the glove compartment and didn't move her eyes from there.

"They have to. There are laws in this country. . . ."

"Is it Galia?" Yair asked.

Rina nodded.

"Do you want us to come there right now? Do you want me to come alone?"
She listened without moving so much as a muscle in her face.

"Look, we won't make it today. We're near Hadera now, and the traffic is jammed. But tomorrow we will straighten this out first thing in the morning. I promise. . . . It's going to be alright, sweetie. We'll see you tomorrow." She hung up.

"What happened?" Yair asked. "Did they fire her?"

"No. She got arrested."

"What? Why?" He lost his concentration and the car drifted to the right. He turned his eyes back on the road and went back to the lane.

"After the meeting this morning she discovered that her ID was gone, probably along with her clothes and her documents. She went to the Ministry of Interior at noon to get a new one. But because it was the fourth time in the past two months, they arrested her on suspicion that she's selling them to criminals."

"Are they nuts? It was a dreaming accident."

He glanced quickly at Rina. She was still sitting frozen in the same position, the phone resting in her lap.

"We won't be able to bail her out until tomorrow. So first thing in the morning we'll head to the psychiatrist and issue a new permit for your dreaming disorder, and then we'll go and get her out of there as soon as possible."

"But why can't we get her out today?"

"They want to make sure that she's not a Dreamer herself. That's the procedure."

"But I'm a known Dreamer. They should arrest me, why her?"

"Because it isn't your ID that keeps disappearing."

Yair punched the steering wheel. "Why? Why is this happening to me? When will they find a normal cure for this thing? All my life I've never smoked, never drunk. . . . Why me?"

They hardly exchanged a glance during dinner. Yair had planned a romantic evening, something to bring back the lost flame, but neither of them were in the mood. They went to bed early.

Rina woke up feeling cramped. The first rays of sun were already coming through the window, and she found herself pressed to the edge of the bed, next to a feminine body. Galia was fast asleep between her and Yair, who was also sleeping.

"Yair!" She screamed.

Yair woke up in second, and so did Galia. She sat up and looked at them in surprise with her mouth slightly ajar, just as she had looked the first time Yair dreamt about her in his bed.

"I don't believe this," she said. "You pulled me out of the detention center. Now they'll be sure I'm a Dreamer. That's it. I'll be fired. No one will believe I'm not guilty now, no matter how many permits you two give!"

Galia burst into tears. She fell on the pillow and started to sob. Rina got out of the bed and took out a robe. Yair also got up and went into the bathroom.

"Come on, get dressed," said Rina. "We'll get the permit and go to the police together. We'll bang on some tables. They'll understand."

Galia went on crying.

"Now my whole life will be ruined. I'm sick and tired of this!"

"Come on, get dressed. I'll make you a cup of tea."

"At least that moron could dream a normal dream; if he'd dream about me in a big house or something, at least then I'd have some compensation...."

"Galia, we will fix this."

"You can't fix this. Why do you think Yair can't get a job? You've seen what they do to Dreamers. Nobody wants to hire them. Everyone is afraid of them. Now I'll be branded too...."

There was a loud thud from the bathroom.

"Yair?" asked Rina.

Silence.

"Yair?"

She threw the robe at Galia and ran into the bathroom. Yair was lying on the floor letting out gurgling sounds. Next to him she saw the medicine bottle.

"Yair, what have you done?" she screamed.

"What happened?" Galia asked from the bedroom.

"Call an ambulance, quick!" Rina called. She opened the medicine cabinet and searched for the inhaler. It was supposed to be there, but she couldn't find it.

"Hurry, he's having an attack," she screamed.

"I'm dialing."

"Yair, what did you do with the inhaler?"

She started tossing out the entire contents of the medicine cabinet.

"Where is the inhaler?"

Galina walked into the bathroom dressed in the robe.

"The ambulance is on its way," she said. "Rina, he's not breathing!"

Rina looked down and saw that Yair's chest was not moving.

"Yair, breathe!" She kneeled beside him and put her fingers on his main artery.

"He's still got a pulse. Do you know CPR?" she asked.

Galia bit her lip.

"Please," Rina pleaded.

Galia knelt down and started performing CPR. Rina continued to fumble through the cupboard. This time she found the inhaler. "Got it," she said. She shook it and handed it to Galia, who pushed it into Yair's mouth and pressed twice.

They went with the ambulance to the hospital. The paramedics already managed to steady his breathing, but he did not wake up. The doctor in the emergency room was not optimistic. His experience taught him that people who developed such an acute allergic reaction to the medicine either died or went into a coma from which they never woke up. Rina was sobbing on the bench outside the emergency room. Galia sat next to her and put her arm around her shoulders.

"This is all my fault," she said.

Rina wanted to say that it was not true, that it wasn't her fault, but she cried so hard she could not talk.

"I pushed him into it," Galia went on in a shaking voice. "I knew he wasn't doing this to me on purpose. I shouldn't have talked like that."

Rina kept crying. Galia stood up. She went to the nurses' station and talked with them for a while. Then she brought a cup of water from the nearby water fountain.

"Drink," she told Rina. "You have to drink."

Rina took the cup from her hand and forced herself to sip a little. The water was cold and made her cough.

"It wasn't your fault," she said. "He was probably desperate because. . . ." Her sobs took over again, and she could not complete the sentence. She rubbed her eyes, which started to burn from the tears. Galia hugged her shoulders.

"I asked the nurses to let the police know that I'm here, to explain what happened," she said. "They'll probably be here any minute now to take me away, but the minute they let me go, I'll come right back to help you, okay?"

One of the nurses went up to them to let them know there was no news. Yair was unconscious and the doctors said that these were the familiar symptoms of the coma. They were getting ready to transfer him into a ward. She promised to let them know when the transfer would be done.

Two policewomen approached her.

"Galia Kena'an?" asked one of them.

"Yes, it's me," Galia sighed. "The doctors will issue a permit that states that this was a Dreaming accident and that I didn't break out of custody. The man who's responsible tried to commit suicide, and he's hospitalized now."

"We know," said the officer. "But we still need to get you back into custody. They'll let you out today."

"Can't we wait a little with this?" asked Galia. "This is his wife. I can't leave her like this."

One of the officers sat down next to them. The other went into the emergency room.

"Would you like some more water?" Galia asked Rina.

Rina nodded. Galia stood up and started to walk towards the water tank. Then she vanished.

The cop called out.

Rina fell silent. They heard the screams coming from the emergency room. They looked at each other and then stormed into the hall. On Yair's bed, Galia was sitting naked again and calling out for help. She tried to climb off the bed, but the invisible barrier blocked her. The medical staff started to gather around her.

Rina ran forward and started to shake Yair.

"Yair, Wake up!"

His head tossed from side to side, but his eyes did not open. Galia threw herself at the invisible barrier. She screamed with all her might. The doctors, the nurses, the cops and the patients, all stood and watched the spectacle.

"Yair, wake up!" Rina begged. "Please, wake up! Wake up! Wake up!"

Two Minutes Too Early

Gur Shomron

In retrospect, Tommy knew his suspicions should have been aroused from the very beginning. The deliveryman did not have the respectable appearance of an official representative of World Wide Puzzles and Riddles Organization. The hovercraft that conveyed him, despite the display of the well-known logo, was also rickety and dilapidated. But the most glaring of oddities was the fact that the package was delivered two minutes too early—something strictly forbidden by the rules of the competition. In their haste and enthusiasm they never gave this infraction a second thought and just blessed their good fortune in having those two extra, illegal minutes to try to complete the puzzle. And they opened the package, thereby instigating the sequence of events they could never have foreseen.

The very fact that the package had been delivered to the Lintons' home was no trivial event. It was one of the hundred packages sent to the finalists of the 2137 World Puzzle Championship, and indeed, just qualifying for it evoked high esteem in itself. The entire population of the little township of Cape Cass was proud that three local children had made it to the finals of the most prestigious competition in the world. A lengthy article, including a large picture of the three, appeared on the front page of the Cape Cass Gazette, and the media had at least one item on them every day for the past month.

It was the second occasion that Tommy, David, and Lily Linton had appeared in the press, the first being about a year earlier, when they surprised the world by finishing second in the Youth Open Tournament. This was quite a sensation, as it was the first time ever that the New York, San Francisco, or London teams, the so-called brain tanks, had failed to walk off with the top three prizes. Furthermore, the Lintons missed first prize by a mere thirty seconds. Everyone joined in the wave of adulation for the modern-day Cinderella story, wherein regular kids (albeit very talented) succeeded in outshining teams of certified geniuses of the highest order. The teams in the first three places were eligible for entering the world adult championship, thus placing the children among the elite group of one hundred competitors for the coveted title of World Puzzle Champion.

The contest pitted groups of geniuses, three members to a group, against each other, somewhat akin to the chess championships of a century ago (which lost much of their popularity due to the advent of simple computer programs that could easily beat any grand master). The challenges provided by Professor—the organization's computer—could be approached only by teams of exceptionally brilliant solvers equipped with advanced accessories and appliances. The sealed boxes, each containing exactly twenty thousand pieces, did not contain a picture or model of what should be constructed out of these fragments. The competitors were expected to derive the method of assembling the pieces and create a three-dimensional replica of an image or scene designed by Professor. This replica could rise to a man's height, and its base diameter could be twice as long. It could depict any random idea that Professor might have had at the moment of creation; a wild lunar landscape and a bustling city scene were two of the subjects used by Professor in previous contests.

All solvers had forty-eight hours to carry out the building of the representation they had received. However, in order to rank among the first three, thereby acquiring world acclaim and sizable amounts of cash, a team had to complete the task in less than half that time. The world record, established nine years earlier, was twenty hours, fifty-five minutes, and seven seconds.

Tommy assisted Alfred in wheeling the trolley with the package onto the Lintons' porch. Alfred Collins, the man who lived next door, was a rather timid, frail-looking gentleman in his sixties. He had moved to the neighboring cottage a couple of years earlier and had befriended the Linton children almost immediately. Their love for puzzle solving could be ascribed largely to Alfred's close companionship—something the youngsters unconsciously craved while their parents were busy with their career activities. Alfred coached and managed the Linton team, contributing enormously to their success in the previous year's competition.

"Hey, guys, it's here!" Tommy shouted, opening the front door. "Thanks, Alfred, for helping me roll it in. You really should be more careful with that leg of yours."

Alfred never stopped grinning. "You'd better get started."

There was a flurry of activity—not a second was to be lost. Tommy and Alfred lugged the large package into the puzzle room. Dave and Lily hurriedly removed the wrapping, and Alfred hastily made his way out so as not to be caught by the automatic tracker lens. This was an advanced telecamera operated to ensure that the solvers received no outside assistance and that only authorized computing equipment was used. It was triggered by the removal of the top panel of the box.

"Good luck!" yelled Alfred from behind the closed door.

No one bothered to answer him. The game was on!

"Operating the disperser," called Tommy. "All hands to the assembly deck."

The disperser was a huge contraption with bellows, trunk, and hose. It, together with the computer, was the only mobile machine permitted in the puzzle room, according to the competition rules. Its job was to suck in all the pieces from the box and arrange them individually on the large apron surrounding the assembly deck. It was a relatively old model, and it took over a minute to finish the job.

"All pieces taken out," announced Lily, extracting a small, star-shaped piece from the bottom of the box.

Apart from the disperser, the Lintons' puzzle room was quite highly developed. All the previous year's winnings, five thousand credits, were invested in innovations and improvements. The three-thousand-credit loan they had taken from Alfred was never returned (in fact, Alfred refused to take it back), and with it they bought an enormous ceiling mirror, allowing all of them to see all the pieces from anywhere. The room itself was very large, with a round deck in the middle that could snugly have accommodated a sumo ring. The deck was fitted on a hydraulic booster that could sink below floor level, and the surrounding apron was equipped with sliding metal plates that could carry a person toward the center of the deck. This machinery, standard to puzzle rooms everywhere, was absolutely vital for providing access to all points of the puzzle without endangering any of the unused pieces or partly erected sections.

The race against the clock had begun.

"First observation: ocean fragment with part of a coral reef. Also an unidentified brown object," announced Piper, in its typical piping voice.

Piper, the Lintons' compact computer, hovered lightly over the deck. Its spatial navigation was enabled by the repelling forces acting between the powerful electromagnets installed in its base and beneath the floor of the room. A tiny processor controlled the electromagnetic intensity, thereby allowing Piper motion anywhere within the room. This hovering capability was developed by Alfred and was approved by the Organization. It gave the computer a slight advantage over other puzzle computers, which traveled through a complex mesh of wires and cables.

"Restrict your scrutiny to the ocean and the ocean bed," instructed Tommy.

The three siblings regarded Piper as their smart younger brother. Eleven-year-old Lily named him, and the brothers constructed him with the necessary computer intelligence for participating in puzzle contests. Tommy and Dave, fifteen and thirteen years of age, respectively, found that endowing the computer with the appropriate competence, while at the same time remaining within contest regulations *and* installing it into very compact resources, was a challenging effort indeed. Without Alfred to guide and advise them, their task would have taken triple the time.

The construction was necessary; the Organization wished to prevent an unfair advantage to the resource-affluent competitors such as the brain tanks. Therefore, all competing computers had to be confined to a size no larger than a tennis ball and weighing no more than three kilograms. Within these restrictions, the computer needed to cope with vision, speech, hearing, motion, and display—not to mention the actual solution processing itself. Indeed, enhancing one of the functions usually deteriorated one or more of the others. The solution processor needed to be able to scan all twenty thousand pieces and group them in ways that made sense to the solvers. This capability was directly dependent on its size and the quality of its programming.

"Detecting a sandy segment with marine vegetation. Probably extending all the way to the reef. Assembling," called Lily.

"Okay," confirmed Piper.

One of the three small lenses on Piper's surface was focused on Lily. The computer could therefore confirm that the pieces she was handling did, in fact, match. What actually occurred was that any piece could be attached to any other piece by setting their surfaces together, and they would adhere to each other by magnetic force. However, nonfitting matches would fall apart about ten minutes later. It was the computer's job to verify that such mismatches did not occur.

"I see the base of a large coral," reported Dave. "I'd say about . . . umm . . . four hundred and fifty pieces."

Tommy eyed his younger brother with unconcealed admiration while deftly putting together a submerged boulder. Dave was rapidly becoming an indispensable factor within the team. The very same Dave, until last year the team's weakest link, was now revealing an uncanny photographic memory, enabling him to identify hundreds of matching parts at a glance. If he would only improve his coordination, mused Tommy, he could easily become one of the great masters.

The assembly work continued briskly. Portions of ocean bed and occasional corals began to appear on the deck. Dozens of crabs, sea urchins and starfish were strewn on the reef and within the vegetation covering it. The sea urchins were so lifelike that Lily actually pricked her finger while positioning one of them on a coral. The oysters were also very faithful to nature, and Tommy even fit a small pearl into one of them.

"Thirty minutes have elapsed," announced Piper. "Crab and coral size ratios indicate a scale of one to ten. Unidentified object probably an ancient sea-going vessel. Attempting design of initial overall view; results in approximately five minutes."

The picture that appeared on the 3-D screen exactly five minutes later was just a rough outline. It displayed a small coral reef surrounded by ocean. On the ocean bed, and adjacent to the reef, was the crude depiction of an antediluvian ship.

"Quite a coincidence," pondered Tommy. "Just a couple of months ago we assembled a puzzle of a sunken ship named the *Titanic*."

He sincerely hoped that the image on the screen closely resembled the solution. He realized that it was just a rough sketch, but Piper would henceforth update it continually with every piece assembled. Tommy knew that the closer the image was to reality, the easier their work would be.

They worked on without a break. An hour later, many more details surfaced; the ship was a sailing ship of some kind, damaged by the reef and half buried in the sand.

"Guessing—cannon on the bow indicates late-seventeenth-century British warship," chimed in Piper. It had accumulated considerable naval historic data while solving the *Titanic* puzzle.

"I'm handling the aft section of the craft now," said Lily. Dave and Tommy smiled at her choice of words. "It's full of crates and boxes and stuff strewn around. I suppose that the open boxes need to be filled with all kinds of merchandise. Request double monitoring."

"Okay," attested Piper, and swiveled a lens from Dave to her.

Tommy marveled at his sister's expertise. This thin, dark-haired girl had undertaken the hardest part of the puzzle—the ship's interior. Yet chances were she would make only slight, if any, errors. Her talent for spatial orientation, combined with her extraordinary color perception, made her an invaluable asset to the team.

The first problem arose after seven hours and twenty minutes, about ten minutes after their first meal break. The mainmast that Dave had just completed erecting suddenly broke loose and fell into the watery area below it. To the team's horror, the mast started sinking through the water pieces as if they really were liquid, and its base landed on the seabed. Tommy, who was assembling the nearby reef, reached out instinctively and grabbed the top of the mast before it, too, slid under.

"This isn't possible," yelled Tommy, flailing his free arm to keep himself from falling into the "water." "The pieces sank through solids!" He lowered himself to a prone position on the floor plate.

"I've heard about this," said Lily. "It's some special substance that they developed last year. Alfred told me about it and said we could expect it in the competition. If you hadn't caught the mast in time, we'd have to dismantle all the assembled water pieces."

"I can't understand why the mast broke away," muttered Dave. "It fitted exactly, and Piper confirmed it."

"That is correct," said Piper. "Cannot discern anywhere else to place it."

Lily shook her head, and after a couple of seconds said, "I think I know what went wrong."

"Yes?" Dave and Tommy chorused together.

"There are *two* places that could possibly be suitable for a mast. I believe we've just encountered the trap of the puzzle, and that we're very fortunate to have passed it with so little collateral damage. Let's have a look at it. . . . Yes, some pieces have shaken loose from the mast, but they shouldn't take more than a minute to restore."

Tommy's heart skipped a beat. In the heat of construction they had quite forgotten that every puzzle had a hidden trap. The temptation to rush ahead and complete the mast had nearly cost them dearly; they would have had to redo the puzzle from almost its starting point.

Piper piped: "Location found!" Tommy thought he detected a hint of embarrassment in Piper's tone but immediately realized that this was his own wishful thinking. "Tip of mast is on other side of reef, not yet assembled."

The image on the screen dissolved, and a new, updated image replaced it, the mast relocated now to its new position.

"Great!" exclaimed Tommy. "Now will someone please help me extricate this mast out of here, before my arm falls off?"

The team pulled gingerly on the mast and laid it aside. They had lost only three minutes, and work was renewed with full vigor.

"This looks like a trunk full of old books," called Lily. She had completed the stern of the boat and was handling the various goods and merchandise that were supposed to fit therein. "The script is so tiny that I can hardly make out the titles. Here's one called *Gulliver's Travels*, and here's another called *Huthering Weights*. Anyone heard of them?"

"*Wuthering Heights*," Tommy sounded a bit exasperated. "Have you tried to close the trunk lid?"

"Yes. I tried, but it won't fit. And now it won't open again"

"Correct," interjected Piper. "Please remember, we are permitted only one more error of this magnitude. Therefore, it would be a waste of time and effort to attempt to open the trunk."

"Guys, please—no more individual attempts. If anyone has any doubts or queries, bring them up at once for all of us to consider. We lose three minutes for every error—two more of these, as Piper has pointed out, and we'll be disqualified."

"Thirty nine and one-half percent of all pieces are assembled," intoned Piper, in his reedy voice. "Elapsed time is ten hours and twenty-seven minutes. At this rate you will break the world record."

It was as if they all had woken up from a refreshing nap. Usually the first third of the puzzle consumed about half the solution time. It began to look as if they could complete the puzzle in less than twenty hours, if no further unforeseen surprises occurred.

Indeed, the replica began to take shape on the assembly deck, and the image projected by Piper became sharper and clearer. At the sixteen-hour mark, the toughest part of the ship's assembly was nearly completed. The only major task that remained was the bow, jutting above the water's surface, with its lion-head bowsprit, according to Piper's projection. Piper had returned his lens to Dave, who appeared to be completely exhausted. Despite the fact that he was allocated the simplest tasks—the final touches to the body of water, with a few fish and eels swimming therein—he needed constant monitoring.

"You didn't get enough sleep last night," rebuked Tommy. "Just look how Lily is working like a demon."

Tommy was about to complete the reef, placing every coral in its proper location and interspersing fish and vegetation expertly in the nooks and crannies. His past experience became more and more evident as the hours progressed. The number of unattached pieces was diminishing rapidly, and many of them could be found strewn around Tommy, whose deft fingers were picking them up and joining them to the others as efficiently as a master bricklayer.

Nineteen hours, thirty minutes, and ten seconds from commencement, and the puzzle was completed. Tommy pressed the red button on the telecamera, and a loud bell rang as the camera took in the assembled puzzle, together with a time stamp, and broadcast the image to the control desk of the contest.

Lily sank to the floor, tuckered out. Dave, who had stretched out exhausted five minutes earlier, held up a limp hand with his fingers extended in a V sign.

It seemed like just a second after the bell that Alfred burst into the room, as if he had been waiting all the while for just that moment. He hugged and kissed the children, clapped his hands in glee, and called up the Organization's main office.

"Yes, yes, I am their manager. Thank you very much. Yes, we're all very pleased. Yes, we'll all make sure to be there tomorrow for the prize awarding ceremony. No, please, no press interviews before then. The children are very tired and very excited. They need to catch up on sleep hours."

He hung up and danced a little jig.

"It looks good, guys, it looks good. You're the first to submit the solution, meaning that you'll take first prize! Tomorrow we'll appear on SuperVision."

The three siblings smiled at him, bleary-eyed.

"He has every right to dance and be ecstatic," mused Tommy, as he leaned with half-closed eyes on a wall. "If it weren't for him we wouldn't have gotten anywhere. He financed the building of this room from his uncle's inheritance money, and it was he who bought the computer's components. He believed in us from the start, even though we were not certified geniuses—just smart kids. Well, we sure justified his faith in us."

The doorbell rang. Alfred shooed them into the bedroom, then went to answer the door. As the children slipped out of the assembly room, they heard him arguing loudly with a herd of news-hungry reporters clustering outside.

The ceremony took place in the main auditorium of the Organization's headquarters. The old building, considered an architectural masterpiece of the twenty-first century, was in the shape of a globe, and its highest point matched that of the ancient Eiffel Tower. Its surface was an exact map relief of the continents and oceans of the earth but had the appearance of being assembled from a puzzle. The main entrance was through a wide door in the south of the Pacific Ocean, and the Linton children remembered the sight from the many SuperVision broadcasts of similar ceremonies that they had witnessed over the years. Today *they* were the heroes of the show. Their parents, beaming proudly, chose to remain in the background and allow their offspring to bask in their moment of glory. Alfred, who was constantly repelling overeager reporters by waving his cane, made room for them to immortalize their historic entrance to the building on digifilm.

They were received with thunderous applause. They briskly followed the green-clad usher to their places of honor in the first row.

"I wonder if these people already know that we've broken the world record," commented Dave.

"I don't think so," replied Tommy. "The results are kept secret and are first announced on this very occasion. I believe they don't even know what place we took."

"Shh," hissed Alfred impatiently. "The ceremony is beginning."

The majestic ceremony was relatively short. The world head scientist gave a speech, and the chairman of the Competition Board delivered his congratulatory address to the winners.

The master of ceremonies called upon the Clarke team from Sunnyvale to ascend and receive third prize. Their excellent time was twenty-one hours, thirty minutes, and fifty seconds.

". . . With only one assembly error," announced the MC as the audience cheered and applauded.

Next was the team from the Einstein Institute in New York, who took second prize with the amazing time of twenty-one hours, eighteen minutes, and seven seconds.

"Without a single assembly error," roared the MC. "Only twenty-three minutes from the previous world record." The applause was long and loud, and in it were mixed whispers of anticipation and excitement. The allusion was quite clear—the audience was about to witness history in the making. The breaking of a world record!

"And first prize, by a very large margin, goes to a team that has continually surprised us this year," announced the MC, his excitement mounting. "I am honored to invite to the stage an independent team from Cape Cass: Lily, David, and Tommy Linton. And their manager, Alfred Collins."

The three children skipped onto the stage amidst deafening applause. Alfred limped after them more slowly.

"For the past nine years the world record was held by the Peterson team, and it was considered to be the ultimate in human puzzle-solving endeavor," continued the MC, his enthusiasm gaining. "And here we have a group of children, not even of the elite priority study program, who have broken this record. Ladies and gentlemen, it is with no little pride and elation that I tonight announce new limits to the human capacity to solve puzzles. In first place: the Linton team, with a new, fantastic world record of fifteen hours and forty-two minutes exactly!"

It was as if an earthquake had struck. The cheers, the clapping, the whistles, the yells—all made for a roar so deafening that Tommy, who had opened his mouth to correct the MC, closed it in consternation. He glanced at Dave and Lily and saw the confusion in their faces as well.

"And now, a few words from the head of the team—Tommy Linton!"

Tommy found the microphone shoved in front of his face. He swallowed hard and said:

"We are very happy to have won first place in the competition. It has been our dream for a long time. We'd like to thank our parents who gave us all the backing we needed. We'd also like to thank all the citizens of Cape Cass for their support and encouragement. And very special thanks goes to Alfred Collins, without whom we would not be standing here tonight."

The applause shook the auditorium, and Tommy waited for it to subside before continuing.

"However, there has been an error in the MC's announcement. Yes, we *did* break the world record, but our time was nineteen hours, thirty minutes, and ten seconds." He paused briefly and then went on. "And we need to add two minutes to this timing, because the package arrived two minutes early."

The huge auditorium became as still as a cemetery.

"Just what do you mean, young man?" boomed the Competition Board chairman. He waved a large sheet of paper and added: "I have here the photo-image of the puzzle you constructed, with its time stamp. The time is exactly fifteen hours and forty minutes!"

Tommy took the photo-image and his blood froze. The chairman was right about the timing. But the picture, instead of showing a coral reef and a shipwreck, displayed a savage volcanic scene—bubbling lava flowing down a mountainside studded with fabulous, overturned statues. Something was definitely very wrong. The paper sheet fluttered to the floor, and Tommy turned desperately to Alfred.

"Can anyone explain what is happening here?" thundered the head scientist. The audience started to mutter and exchange whispers.

"I can, Dr. Daniel Carter, if you'll permit me," said Alfred suddenly and picked up the microphone.

"Alfred Edelberg!" exclaimed the head scientist in astonishment.

"Not anymore," corrected Alfred. He turned to the audience and addressed them directly, his voice carrying confidence and authority. "Today my name is Alfred Collins. In the past my surname was Edelberg. You may remember the Edelberg vaccine against aging—in fact, I'm pretty sure many of you have actually used it. It is named after me, as it was I who discovered it. Others may remember me due to the scandal that resulted when I accused the World Science Committee of limiting the freedom of research. I consequently lost my job, and I was expelled in disgrace from USA-Tech."

His gaze scanned the audience. The whispers and murmurings intensified as several of those present recalled the episode that shook the scientific world some twenty years earlier.

"But I did not abandon hope," continued Alfred, and he turned to face the head scientist, who sat motionless in his chair, his face as pale as a sheet. "I changed my name and continued my research, which now was, unfortunately, illegal, and I may be immediately arrested for it. I developed a series of biological grain types, easily produced by common plants, that raised the intelligence of the organism that ate them."

He bent down to the floor, picked up the picture of the puzzle, and held it aloft for the audience to see.

"The puzzle in this picture was not assembled by Tommy, Dave, and Lily Linton. They assembled a different puzzle—a puzzle as difficult as this one, but a puzzle of my own design—and they completed it in nineteen hours, thirty minutes, and ten seconds. Two minutes must be added to this timing, because I delivered the puzzle to them two minutes too early. Thus, while they were busy with my puzzle, I intercepted the messenger with the real puzzle and took it to my house, next door to the Lintons'. There, in a simple and primitive assembly room, without the aid of a computer, the puzzle was assembled by the Zoko team in only fifteen hours and forty minutes."

He smiled reassuringly at the three children who were staring at him, their mouths agape, their complexions ashen.

"However, the title of Humanity's World Champion Puzzle Solvers still belongs to the team you see before you. There is no person, or team of persons, on this planet who could do the job better or faster than they."

Alfred unscrewed the top of his walking cane, and withdrew from it a large roll of paper. He flattened it out and showed the stunned audience the picture printed on it.

"This is the team that broke the world record," he cried. "They are only seven years old, but their individual IQs are higher than that of any other creature on this planet."

The three orangutans in the picture were grinning broadly. Each of them held a yellow banana in one hand and a red portable supercomputer in the other.

"We're so glad that you've managed to prove your theories, and that your banishment has been revoked," said Lily. "But it's such a shame that you're returning to the university. We'll miss you very much."

The three champions sat in the large assembly room, watching Alfred wrapping up his memory cubes and placing them carefully into a large container.

"I won't be so far away," said Alfred. "Just about three hours' drive from here. And you'll always be welcome at my new location."

"Lily will not be available until next year," said Tommy. "We won't travel to New York without her."

"But you could visit me on holidays, couldn't you?"

"Of course," replied Lily. "We've long forgiven you for what happened. We love you very much, and we're grateful to you for, well, adopting us, in a way. Even though your motive was to snatch our puzzle away from us. You know, Alfred, you were very lucky in choosing to coach us when you moved to Cape Cass as our neighbor. What would you have done had we *not* won second prize last year?"

Alfred did not respond. He hugged the little girl, and tears welled up in his eyes. There was no point in revealing to them what was contained in those spinach pies that they loved so much. They would never forgive him, and the world would exorcise him for illegally experimenting on humans. Even the fact that he himself was his own guinea pig for the past thirty years, and that all his discoveries stemmed from these experiments, would not have saved him.

My Crappy Autumn

Nitay Peretz

I knew something was going to happen. Everybody knew something big was coming. I can still remember people walking around with that feeling. But these things, even when you expect them, they still take you by surprise. For me it was a double whammy: first Osher's rotten stunt, and then Max's revelation. God really kicked my ass that autumn month, you could say.

Before it all happened we were having a pretty good time. The three of us sat down on the living room couch that evening with a bag of sunflower seeds to snack on. Max was on my left, Osher on my right, and the TV opposite me. Channel 1 was showing a soccer match, Maccabi Haifa v. Beitar Jerusalem, which had the potential to be a twofer: you get to see Haifa win *and* Beitar lose. Expectations in the living room were high. It was one of those evenings when anything could happen, or, as everybody's favorite sportscaster Zuhir put it: "Good evening Meir! Good evening viewers! Here in Kiryat Eliezer the tension is colossal! Sky-high!" Haifa was leading 1–0 by halftime—Beitar never saw it coming. Roso was on a roll. Every time they scored, we sang and cheered and waved our green scarves. Max had bet on Beitar, and he realized pretty quickly he was screwed. Haifa trounced them 3–0. We ordered a pizza to celebrate. The loser delivery guy got there super fast, so no free drink, which they give you if they're ten minutes late. Max paid him, cursed, and swore it was the last time he bet me on anything. And he didn't tip the pizza guy.

I live on pizza. I'm crazy about pizza. I've tried their whole new international menu. My favorite is the Tuna Crème Fraîche. I can easily finish half a large one and down a 50-ounce Coke with it. Life is good.

After the pizza, Max rolled us a joint. We went out to the balcony, passed it around, and talked about life. When we realized how late it was we went inside, emptied out the ashtrays of their cigarette butts and sunflower seed shells, washed the glasses and plates, threw the pizza box in the trash, and went to sleep.

Osher was already in bed. I hadn't noticed when she'd left the living room. I got into bed carefully, thinking she was asleep. The last thought that went through my head before I fell asleep was: Why is Osher tossing and turning?

I got up in the morning and brushed my teeth. I walked out of the bathroom with my toothbrush in my mouth. Osher was sitting in the living room. There was an empty coffee mug on the table and a lit cigarette in her mouth. Osher doesn't smoke. Her eyes were puffy and red, like she'd been crying or something. I realized she'd been sitting there for a long time, even though I didn't remember her getting out of bed.

"Hey, Ido," she said, and there was something different in her voice, like a quiet, blue sea after the storm passes. "Ido, I'm done," she said.

"Done with what, babe?" I asked. Then I noticed there was an ashtray full of cigarette butts next to her. When had she taken up smoking?

"I don't know, all I know is I'm done." She sniveled, as if something was about to stream out. "It's not you. Not at all. The opposite—you're so gentle and sweet and considerate and everything. It's not you. You need to understand that. It's me."

Osher burst out crying, with tears and everything, and couldn't stop. I sat down next to her, my toothbrush still in my mouth. I stroked her back, at the top, near her neck, where she likes it, just to calm her, but she shifted awkwardly and said, "No, Ido, it's over."

"Okay, honey," I said. "I don't have time now, we'll talk about it when I get home this evening."

"There's nothing to talk about. I'm done."

"Okay, babe, I have to run to work," I said. Even though that wasn't true and I had loads of time before my shift started. Osher knew I was lying but she didn't say anything.

I fixed my hair in the bathroom and rinsed out my mouth. I looked in the mirror, just to make sure this was really happening to me. I threw on a sweater and grabbed my bag. I tried to kiss Osher, but she turned away. "Bye, honey," I said. "We'll talk this evening." I left before she could answer and slammed the door behind me.

I took my usual route to Café Gross. The sky was grayish black and the air was still. It started raining, and everyone sped up, or ducked into a corner store until it stopped.

I didn't give a shit. I walked down the middle of the sidewalk and felt the drops run off my hair into my sweater and inside my sweater down my spine, all the way to my ass crack, then into my pants and my shoes, wetting Osher's Winnie-the-Pooh socks that she loved so much.

I stood outside Café Gross. It has big windows, and you can see everything going on inside. There was a couple sitting by the window, and not just any couple—they were tall and beautiful, tastefully dressed, as in a European TV commercial. They were drinking steaming hot cocoa in tall glasses, eating croissants, and laughing, snuggled up in their private paradise. Rina went over to ask if everything was all right, and the man must have told a joke or something, because they all started laughing.

The rain was getting harder. There was a pretty scary clap of thunder; lightning lit up the street and little pellets of hail started coming down. I couldn't feel my feet. Everything suddenly seemed so unfair. There was a lump of burning anger in my stomach, which climbed up and got stuck in my diaphragm. My eyes filled with tears, as at school when the older kids used to beat me up. I wanted to fight back, but there was no one to fight with.

I decided to go back home. Skip out on my shift. No one at the café had seen me anyway.

The apartment was empty. Osher had left. She'd emptied out the ashtray, rinsed it, and put it in the drying rack with all the coffee mugs she'd used at night. A closer examination of the apartment revealed that her toothbrush was also gone, and the clothes she left there for when she stayed the night. Her teddy bear was gone too, and her pillow, which she couldn't sleep without and even took with her when she went on a trip to the US.

There was no question about it: Osher had left, without any explanations or apologies. Just like that. What a crappy world. After four years together you'd think you deserve a warning—but nothing. I wanted to yell, I wanted to scream loud enough to shatter the windows. I wanted to kick and punch, break and smash—but that's childish and silly. I sat down on the couch and lit a cigarette. I felt all the anger that was bubbling and sizzling inside me begin to cool down and slowly congeal and harden into determination. I decided that this world, which had taken Osher away from me, did not deserve to have me in it. And not only that—I would not suffer alone. If this kind of shit could just hit me out of nowhere, without any warning, then it would have to hit someone else too. I was going down, baby—and I was taking a few assholes with me. Woo-hoo!

Max walked in, eyed me from head to toe, and said I looked wet. He had this talent, Max, for stating the obvious.

Max is my roommate. Sometimes people think we're brothers, because he too is one of those tall, skinny guys who look like they're about to topple over. I don't know how anyone could think that. We don't look anything alike. Max is a sound man, and he does customer phone support for a credit card company. And almost every Saturday he goes to a rave in some forest. I think he comes back high on molly, but we don't really talk about it.

I told him Osher left me. Max said that was too bad, we seemed like a great couple and he was sure we were going to get married. He asked me if I threw her out. I said she was the one who dumped me, and she didn't even tell me why, she just said she was done. Max's eyes glazed over. He stared into space and said he could really relate to that, that he's also done, and he feels like things can't go on this way, that something needs to change in a big way soon. It's not like Max to talk that way. I expected him to be on my side.

I blew off Max's bullshit. Usually he's awesome to talk with. He knows how to listen, which is an important quality that lots of people don't have. He gets things, and he has a good head on his shoulders. He's really a great roommate. He didn't deserve it, that whole tragedy that happened to him afterwards.

Right from the start I made up my mind that nothing was going to get in the way of my depression. I'm a serious guy. Everyone says that about me. So when I say nothing, I mean *nothing*. I settled on a daily routine, and for the next month, despite all the insanity going on in our place, I tried not to deviate from it.

It went like this: I'd get up at twelve-thirty on the dot every day and make myself some Turkish coffee, no milk. I'd make sure not to brush my teeth or even rinse out my mouth first. I'd sit down at the kitchen table and drink my coffee. I'd spread out a white sheet of paper and crumble all the weed I wanted to smoke that day. When I'd finish the coffee, I'd put my cup in the sink. I had a rule against washing cups. I was only allowed to do it when I was completely out of clean cups, and even then I'd only wash one, just so I'd have something to drink out of. When I couldn't be bothered, I wouldn't even do that. I'd just empty out the old coffee grounds and cigarette butts, flick out whatever was left with my finger, then pour fresh coffee into the same cup.

After the coffee I'd empty out five Winston Lights and make my spliffs, then smoke my first one with another coffee. Then I'd go down to the corner store and buy a new pack of cigarettes and a large bottle of Coke. I'd come home, go into my room, and lie down in the dark with my eyes open. I'd lie on my left side until two-thirty and think about what a whore Osher was for leaving me, and how much I hated her and felt like killing her. At two-thirty, give or take ten minutes, I'd turn over onto my right side and think about how much I loved her, and how, if she wanted to get back together, I'd take her back with open arms, and how much I missed her. At four I'd watch *The Bold and the Beautiful*. Then I'd channel surf. If there was anything interesting on, I'd watch it. If not, I'd turn on the light, open up my datebook at the end, where I wrote down phone numbers, and think about who I could diss today.

My voyage downwards to the depths of despair and depression had a few upsides. The main one was that I didn't give a fuck about anyone. I just didn't care. This evil world, which had taken Osher away from me just like that, without any warning, didn't deserve my caring. I felt that as long as I was wallowing in the dregs, no one else had any right to be happy—and if they were, then yours truly was going to put an end to it. And I'm talking especially about the assholes who'd insulted me or humiliated me. There seemed to be a lot of them, come to think about it.

I'd go through the list and try to pick someone. It was really hard: so many attractive options. My finger was on Dori's name when the phone rang, and it was Gross. I'd missed three shifts, and he thought maybe I was sick or something was wrong. He was worried about me, the angel. I told him nothing in particular was wrong, I just didn't feel great. Gross didn't get mad. He was really nice, in fact. He asked if I had a fever and if I'd been to see a doctor. I told him dryly that what I had, no doctor could cure. Gross snickered and said, "Oh, so it's that kind of disease. I get it. What's her name?" "Osher," I told him, "and it's incurable."

Then his voice got kind of formal and he said I could have let him know ahead of time, 'cause I really screwed up his shifts and he had to beg people to fill in the gaps. I told him he could get his fudge-packing friends to fill up his gaps, since all they did was sit there all day eating for free and trying to hit on me when I waited on their tables, and they never tipped, and his coffee sucked. I couldn't believe how easy it was to tick off Gross. I must have hit a sensitive spot, because he yelled that he hated my guts and he was sick of all these cocky assholes who'd moved to the city two minutes ago looking down their noses at him. He yelled so loud that I had to hold the phone away from my ear. Then he said that if I came anywhere near his café he'd throw a glass at my head and that he'd use his connections to make sure I never worked in this town again, ever. I hung up on him in midsentence. I took a red pen and put a thick check mark next to his name and number. I grinned to myself: my sweet revenge on the world, for what it had done to me, was moving along.

Max asked what all the yelling was about. I told him I just got fired from Café Gross and that I was newly unemployed. He shrugged his shoulders and went to make us some instant coffee. When the water boiled and he poured it into the cups, he realized we were out of milk, so he went down to the store.

And that's when Max had it.

Call it an accident, a prophetic revelation, an epiphany, a hit-and-run, or a cosmic event. Doesn't matter. What really happened at that moment, on Shenkin Street, corner of Ahad Ha'Am, no one has yet been able to truly explain.

What's certain is that there was a long, black Chevy Caprice Classic driven by a wealthy contractor, a short Mitsubishi Pajero SUV driven by a very tall young woman with short-cropped red hair who was so beautiful it hurt your eyes to look at her, and there was Ahmed the junkman with his cart. The first to recover from the accident was Tony, Ahmed's lame donkey, who sat up on his ass and started shouting: *"Alte zachen! Alte zachen!* Old stuff! Fridges, cabinets, washers. . . . *Alte zachen!"* Then the young woman and the contractor got out of their cars and started screaming at each other in a rabid fit of hatred, and their faces turned bright red and contorted with rage. The SUV and the Chevy were crumpled against each other, and there was shattered glass all over the place. Total loss. The furniture on Ahmed's cart had toppled out onto the road. Ahmed himself sat on a broken oven that had landed on the sidewalk, held his head, and sighed, *"Ya Allah! Ya Allah!* Oh Dear God, I've lost everything, I've lost everything. . . . *Ya Allah. . . ."*

And Max?

Max lay motionless on the road. He looked up at the sky and his pupils were enlarged like he was tripping on molly. All he could get out of his mouth was "Whoa . . ." like he was blazed or something. He just kept lying there saying

"Whoa . . ." very quietly, every twenty seconds, until the ambulance arrived. They put him on a stretcher, but as they were about to lift it into the ambulance, he sat up and said calmly, "No need. Thanks. I'm fine."

Max ran his hand over the doctor's body, and the ugly psoriasis all over the doctor's neck disappeared. Then he tapped his fingers on the paramedic's throat three times and cured the stutter he'd had since age six.

Max picked up his bag, which had been thrown to the sidewalk, and said in a loud, clear voice, "I'm going home, guys." And that's when things got crazy. Mor, the hot chick from the Pajero (she even had a hot chick's name) said, "I'm coming with you wherever you go." Azulay, the contractor (he even had a contractor's name), said, "Me too. Wherever you go." They both forgot how they'd tried to claw each other's eyes out only two minutes ago. Tony, the donkey said, "Anywhere with you. Through fire and waaaaater." His voice came out a little brayish because he wasn't used to talking yet. (Later, when he became the movement's spokesperson, Tony would sit on the balcony with me and say, "Believe me, Ido, everyone's an ass. But at least this ass knows what he's talking about.") Ahmed, who was a little confused, given Tony's condition, said, "I'm coming too. For sure!" Because he didn't want to be different from everyone, and also because without Tony he had nowhere to go to anyway.

And then they all started walking, single file, toward our place.

I was in the toilet with a lit joint between my lips when Max and his disciples walked in. It was my fourth for that day. Life looked sort of melted down, a bit rounded at the edges, and it made no sense to get mad about anything. I was high as a kite.

"Hi Maxi," I said to him, "want a hit?" I offered him the jay, burning side up to keep it from dropping. "No thanks," said Max—and that was the first time ever I've heard Max say no to dope. "I've changed, Ido," he said. "I'm not the same Max. I'm a saintly person now." And it was true, something about Max was different: he opened his eyes, and there was fire in his pupils. His eyes sparkled, as if he'd had two little lamps transplanted there.

Next morning I made a definitely final desperate attempt to get Osher back to me. I called her and heard in her voice that she was not at all happy to hear from me. She sounded tired on the phone. I insisted, until she agreed to meet with me at lunchtime in a café downtown. She actually suggested Gross's, but I explained I wasn't working there anymore.

Then I went to select a handgun for myself. They already know me at the Recoil shop in the mall. I've been there three times looking at guns, but never bought one, 'cause until that day I didn't really need a handgun.

The salesperson was called Ozz. Before I met Ozz, I'd thought it was a name fit for a Rottweiler, but it turns out there're all kinds of name-giving parents in this world. He opened the glass cabinet where all the handguns were locked and explained each one of them. I kept nodding my head, "yes, yes," and even asked a few questions, just to let him know I was really interested and also that I understand such things. Every once in a while I went so far as to hold a gun in my hand, to feel its heft and see if it was well-balanced. This was just for show. I knew exactly what I wanted. I waited for him to get to the chrome-plated Jericho Magnum, then I took it in my hand and caressed it lovingly. It had a good smell of gun oil and metal. When it comes to death, only Made in Israel will do. The big, heavy gun was a perfect match for my hand, precisely fitting all its curves and folds, sending silent vibrations up my arm all the way to the elbow, and then on to my chest and spinal column. Then I chose rounds—hollow point, of course. I looked at the silvery lead ball that I could see through the slits in the copper jacket in the bullet I was holding in my hand. When this round hits flesh, the copper around the lead opens up, becoming a little rosebud spinning at a terrific speed and leaving a wound you could throw a tennis ball through, never touching the edges.

If it's got to end, I was thinking, I want to make sure it really ends. I didn't want to miss accidentally and then lie for ten years in the Levinstein Rehabilitation Center staring at the ceiling and waiting for the nurse to come and feed me porridge with a teaspoon.

I ordered twenty rounds. They won't sell singles. I'd already asked. I gave Ozz a check for the down payment, and we agreed I'd give him the rest in twenty-six days, when I'd come to collect the gun, with all the paperwork done in the meantime.

I even had time to visit the Ministry of the Interior and fill in a request for purchase of a firearm. On my way to the coffee shop I lit a joint just to pull myself together. I got to The Other Café ten minutes ahead of time, lit a cigarette, and asked for a beer. I sat down to wait for Osher. Osher, as per usual, was late.

It's not so good, mixing alcohol with weed. When she arrived I got up to hug her, but I never saw this chair. Stumbled against it and fell right between Osher's sweet-smelling tits, which were projecting way out because of the tight black woolen blouse she was wearing. Usually, Osher hates it when I mix dope and alcohol and lose it. Last time it had happened, we were still an item. She'd cried and screamed at me for ruining myself and what a shame it was to see an intelligent guy like myself wasting himself like that. This time, Osher didn't get mad at all. She just helped me sit down again. Then she seated herself opposite me, looking at me as if she'd never cared. She took one of my cigarettes, lit it, and scrunched her face with the first drag. "Phooey," she said, looking at me, pouting her lips and blowing a thin jet of smoke in my direction. "I can't figure out how you people can smoke this shit."

"Give us E for effort," I said, smiling at her. Osher smiled back—and for a brief moment it was like old times, and my stomach got all warm inside. But just for a moment.

"I got a gun today, Osher," I told her. "Jericho Magnum with dum-dum bullets, like I've always wanted."

"You're mental," she said. "What do you need a gun for, anyway?"

"To blow my brain and get out of here," I said, and saw her cringing in her seat. Then, suddenly, there was a tired look in her eyes, like she was seventy years old. She told me I'd come looking for help at the wrong place, because she was all empty inside and no longer had anything for me. She took my hand in hers and looked me in the eyes: "Believe me, Ido, I'm not trying to lie to you or something. I can't help you. I'm really done." Tears came out, smearing this black stuff she puts around her eyes. "I don't know how to explain this to you," she said, "but something that'd always been there inside and I'd always known would be there the next day—it's gone suddenly, all at once. Now I must search for something else. Everyone's searching. I'm not the only one who's had it disappear."

I've never heard Osher talk like that. But she got back together real quick, saying, "Sorry, I don't know what I'm going through. You don't need my bullshit on top of everything else. I'm terribly sorry."

Then there was nothing left to say. We sat facing each other silently for maybe ten minutes. Osher smoked another one of my cigarettes, with obvious disgust, and finally got up, gave me a twisted smile, the sort that comes on by mistake, and left without saying goodbye. I walked home. Going slowly, in no hurry to get anywhere, dragging my feet, quiet and despondent. An exhausting sense of defeat spread inside me. I let my long legs carry me. They were up to the job, making long strides, rapidly swallowing those Tel Aviv streets. I gave myself up to the feeling of striding, forgetting myself.

The bus door closed. The green bus backed out of its bay. I realized I was sitting in an Egged Line 552 bus to Ra'anana, on my way home. I stared outside as if what I saw was the most interesting thing in the world, even though I knew each tree, each traffic light along the way. I'm going to Ra'anana, to see Mother.

I got off at my station near the Wars Memorial. My legs, still on autopilot, kept taking me along those side streets, imbued with suburban tranquility, to the four-story grey building on 58 Hahagana Street.

I took the stairs, reaching the door that bore a simple sign, "Menashe." I buzzed, and Mother opened the door. "Oy," she said. "Ido. I just called you. You weren't home, so I had a chat with your roommate, Max."

"What did you talk about?" I asked.

"Nothing in particular," said Mother. "Life."

The hall fixture spilled yellow light, sad and weak, deepening the shadows made by the creases in her face. The Menashe Family Map of Troubles, I secretly called Mother's facial creases. It was a one-to-one topographic map of all the shit this family has eaten over the last twenty years. Mountains, valleys, nothing missing. Just get on an air-conditioned tour bus and take the guided tour. *Ladies and gentlemen, if you'd look to your right, you can see a fold running from the side of the nose to the corner of the upper lip. It got much deeper the day the family business went bankrupt.* Mother said this was because *he* was a good-for-nothing jerk. Although they wouldn't admit it, this was what finally killed their marriage. *If you'd look to your left, you can see the central crease across the forehead. Yes, right there. Watch your step, Ma'am, it's very deep.* This one came from *him*: my idiot of a father. It came into being overnight, complete, when *he* took off to India with Rina. It started a lengthy geocosmetic process, which slowly but surely deepened this crease, during those long nights when Mother was left alone with her nightmares.

Look here, everybody: this is very interesting. Right here, in the middle of the forehead, between the eyes, rising vertically through the eyebrows, a crease I'm particularly sentimental about. My handiwork. Each little fold has something to say. Each tiny crease represents a stage in my growing up. *Bottom left, you can discern the time I went with Tomer Freistadt down to Sinai without telling anybody. A bit higher up, on the right-hand side, you can see my glorious motorcycle crash in the orange orchard, two weeks after I'd got the bike.* Flew twenty feet through the air into a tree. The tree came out alright, not a scratch. The bike was a total loss. Its carcass is still lying there in the backyard, rusting away in the rain. I got platinum nails in both my legs, and all the girls in my class came to the hospital to scribble on my cast, great fun. *Here to your right you will notice the classic crease known as Recruit's Mother Canyon, proudly borne by every Israeli mom.* It got a bit deeper each day during my three loony years in an infantry battalion.

"Come in, sit down," she said. "Eat something. If I'd known you were coming, I would have done some shopping and cooking. Just for myself, like this, I don't bother." She got some vegetables out of the fridge and started slicing them for a salad. "You want egg?" she asked, but didn't wait for an answer before putting a small frying pan on the gas fire, which shed a gloomy light on her narrow, darkish kitchen. When the pan got hot, she poured in some oil which started bubbling noisily.

"I'm not hungry, Mom, I've already eaten back home," I murmured my line, like an actor on his two-hundredth show. But a few minutes later I had in front of me a plateful of omelet and green salad; a couple of buns, hot from the microwave oven, lay beside my plate.

Mother made black coffee for herself, lit a Time cigarette. "Need money?" she asked. Hope lit up her face.

"No, Mom, the problem ain't money," I said. "I don't know what I need. What can you give me?"

"I can write you a check, if you want."

"Besides," I added, "I broke up with Osher."

"Why?" asked Mother, getting up to stand by the open window. Dying daylight lit her face when she blew cigarette smoke out into the open air. "Osher's always been such a nice girl."

"She dumped me, Mom. She'd said she was done, *puff*, just like that. Three years went out in smoke, because Madame Osher Yehoshua was done overnight. So she smokes two packets of my Winstons, uses up all the coffee and tissues in the place, and lets me know this is it. I'm done," I said. "Game's over. I'm taking a break from life—and terrible things are going to happen. Mostly to me, but also to you. To all of you. Shit's about to hit the fan—and no one's going to stay clean. I'm through waking up every morning to see who crapped in my plate, eat it like a good boy, then smile and say thank you kindly. You all will be sorry."

Mother remained standing by the window, her face still turned outside. She took another deep drag off her cigarette. Then she let it out with such an *ouch* sound, reminding me of Grandma's soul-rending sighs, the ones she used to make when she was still alive. "Okay, so what do you want? Like I was part of some conspiracy against you. I'm your mother, Ido. I'm just a mother, that's all." She crashed the cigarette in the ashtray. "What is it with the two of you? First *him*, now you too. I'm worried, is all, must I be punished for it?" She sighed again. "You do what you feel like doing. I'll write you a check if you want."

There was nothing left to say. So I took off.

It was only when I got back home that I discovered the horror.

The apartment's yellow, peeled up walls were covered with lengths of white, clean cloth. The rickety orange couch, the one I brought in from Grandma's old home, was gone. And something very strange happened to the floor: you could see the tiles' original color. This was quite bizarre. Something about the apartment's air was fundamentally different. The stench and general ickiness so typical of bachelors' shared rental places in central Tel Aviv were completely replaced by something else.

Max was in charge of Operation Cleanup, waving his arms in broad, slow gestures as he spoke and sounding quite serious. Seeing him like that, I could no longer be mad at him for the missing couch. I was just sorry for him, terribly. Poor Max. He just didn't have it coming to him. He used to be one of the good ones.

From the kitchen smells of home cooking wafted in, such as never before filled the air of this place. A pair of chubby twins, with long, blond, curly hair, were standing there, stirring two gigantic pots on the gas stove. They said hello, it was their pleasure to meet me, they've heard a lot of stories about me from Max. It was all I could do to avoid their attempts to hug me. They *did* try. Orit and Hagit, they introduced themselves with dimple-deepening smiles. Hagit offered me a chair, and Orit pushed a wooden plate in front of me loaded with rice and vegetables. She actually wanted me to eat it. When I saw those pieces of celery in the rice, I politely declined.

What the fuck, I thought. Lucky for them I don't have the energy right now to deal with this entire mess; otherwise I would have kicked the lot of them, just like that, out of my apartment. I turned aside to hide in my room. I got in—and immediately got out again, slamming the door. This can't be. Sheer horror.

I stepped back into the room. The first thing that hit me was the odor of orchids. The floor, believe it or not, was just like in the commercials, smelling of orchids. The windows were wide open, and fresh, pure air came in—who knows how long it's been since such a thing had happened. The floor was sparkling clean. All those pizza crusts, empty Coke bottles, and unidentified food leftovers that used to carpet it, all gone.

A week before, I'd stopped washing my clothes. When I got tired of any of them, I would throw the dirty ones on the floor and choose some other dirty clothes instead. The clothes that used to be on the floor were no longer there. I opened my closet and found them, washed and ironed, neatly folded up, lying in heaps, arranged by type and color. Even the condom I'd thrown under the bed, the last time I was with Osher, had disappeared. Motherfuckers. It had some sentimental value for me.

I didn't have to look far for the culprits responsible for my disaster: Azulay and Mor were on their knees, rubber gloves covering their hands, carefully and thoroughly cleaning the panels with toothbrushes that they dipped every once in a while in a bucket full of soapsuds.

Mor, still on her knees, straightened up. "Hi there," she said, taking off a glove and gracefully wiping sweat off her brow. "Sorry to have invaded your room like that, without permission," she went on, "but Max said it will be an excellent exercise for us in personal development and ego attenuation. And when Max says something, you know. . . ." She shrugged, smiling. Azulay, ignoring me completely, kept scrubbing energetically. His trousers were pulled down, revealing the crack of his red, sweaty arse.

"*Get—out!*" I said quietly, emphatically stretching out these words, because this had for some reason a calming effect on me. "*Get—out—now!*" I told them. Azulay quickly wiped off leftover water, and Mor removed the remainder with a damp rag. They got out in haste, and I realized my hands were trembling. I felt I had to leave this room, this apartment, at once, get some fresh air.

At first, nobody took their little cult seriously. After all, in Tel Aviv that autumn you could just throw a casual stone and hit two gurus and a prophet. Nobody took anybody seriously in Tel Aviv that autumn.

It turned out, however, that there was life outside Tel Aviv, too. I went out of the apartment, and my long legs took me north—deep in thought, barely noticing time. Reaching the entrance of Yarkon Park, I saw a lot of people there, a lot even for a Friday afternoon. Oh well, I said, it must be Town Hall having another one of their silly festivals: "Food in the City," "Jazz in the Park," or something else to offer an excuse for clean, happy, well-off young people to go out with their fashionable, high-bosomed girlfriends.

But it turned out to be something completely different. Neither "Food in the City" nor "Jazz in the Park." It was the landing of a UFO from outer space. I managed to see it after pushing through a multitude of people, knocking down a trembling old lady and landing, unintentionally, a terrible elbow blow on a patrol cop who blocked my view. It was a kind of silvery bubble standing on thin legs and spoiling City Hall's lawn.

The patrol cop's name was Nissim. He wasn't mad about the elbow blow. He just put a hand to his eye, where the flesh around it was swelling up quickly and getting an alarming blue color. "A historical event," he said to me. "A historical event, I'm telling you"—and I realized, by the very fact that he didn't drag me to his precinct to beat the shit out of me, that he must be right.

Around the UFO there were some SWAT types with their Kevlar vests and short-stocked rifles, the ones with the telescope sights; there's no knowing how they thought they could use those against a silver-colored bubble. Apart from them were parked three Merkava Mark III tanks and one Chabad Mitzvah tank, illegally parked, and blatantly so, beyond the police cordon. Only God knows how those crazy religious fanatics managed to work the system and get this close to the UFO.

Everybody around was really devastated by the fact that the bubble showed no sign of life. Especially the reporters. There were about one hundred TV crews over there who, having nothing better to do, kept interviewing each other and pushing everywhere with their minicams, their gigantic microphones, and their lights, knocking down trembling grandmas and unintentionally elbowing patrol cops.

"What is it? Why don't they say something? If they came from that far away, they must know real important stuff," said Nissim, rubbing his shoulder that got bruised by a cameraman wearing a Sky News badge who'd crashed into him with his camera while trying to move over from nowhere to nowhere and then added insult to injury with a thick Brit accent: "You bloody idiot, don't you have eyes?"

"Why is he talking to me like this, what did I ever do to him?" said Nissim to me, and I realized I chanced upon the geekiest cop in the Yarkon District and told him he should arrest that impudent cameraman. I kept trying to get Nissim mad at the Sky cameraman, in vain. He seemed far more interested in the aliens than in the cameraman, who stood near us, sunburned, shooting his reporter, who was chattering in English, accented so heavily I couldn't understand one word of it.

Everybody around us in the crowd started talking excitedly and pointing their fingers: a small hatch opened up in the silvery bubble, and the cameramen became ecstatic. Something that looked like an old gramophone loudspeaker came out very slowly. Everybody was completely silent until it was completely out, except for those ecstatic cameramen who were climbing on top of each other, trying to get a better angle. "Pheeew," said Nissim, "it's going to speak. Must have something important to say."

But the speaker remained silent.

Then it said, "Shalom."

The Chabad fanatics went crazy. They grabbed each other's shoulders, formed a circle, and started singing, "*Hevenu shalom aleichem.*" Very quickly they switched to sing "Messiah—Messiah—Messiah," until the crowd broke through the cordon and forcibly shut them up, because people wanted to hear what the UFO had to say.

And the UFO *did* have something to say: "Bring Maxim Kornfein of 28 Ahad HaAm Street. We have an important message for him."

Two white cars with blue lights on top went out, their sirens blaring. And I thought that with all those drugs screwing with my brain, I didn't hear very well what they were saying. What did they need Max for?

The squad cars were back in fifteen minutes; they must have been driving like crazy. The back car's window was open, and I could see the head of Tony, Ahmed the *alte zachen*'s donkey, looking out. He saw me in the crowd and winked at me.

Max came out of the car. He looked very impressive, so tall and wearing a white robe. He got on Tony's back, and then he looked even more tall and impressive. They moved together, trotting in a noble sort of way toward the silvery bubble. When they were real close, the bubble started vibrating and twisting, like the surface of a pool when you throw in a stone. Then the bubble puckered out a pair of lips and—*schluk*—swallowed up both Tony and Max. The Sky News cameraman swooned ecstatic.

And then nothing happened. For the longest time, maybe twenty minutes. The Chabad fanatics put on their phylacteries and started shaking and quaking. Nissim gave me a friendly elbow in the ribs and smirked: "Look, they're trying to listen in on the ship's communications network." I lit up a joint and offered Nissim a drag. Nissim looked fearfully left and right and then took it. He handed me back the joint and said, "just that you know, I'm not really a patrol cop. I'm with the patrol's computer unit, but I came here anyway, because this *is* a historical moment."

Finally, the ship's surface started twisting a little, made waves, and the lips puckered up again and spat out Max, still on Tony's back. The lips pulled back again. The waves grew stronger, the UFO bubble went *blip, blip, blip—zababababam!* and disappeared abruptly, leaving no trace except for a sharp smell of burning brakes, four little circles of yellow dead grass, and one of the Chabad fanatics, who disappeared leaving no trace.

The media waxed hysterical. The Sky News cameraman used the opportunity to crash again into Nissim, even though he wasn't in his way at all. I couldn't take it any longer and pushed him back. The cameraman fell down on the grass, but immediately got up and raised his minicam, taking no notice of me. That should teach him for interfering with a policeman in the fulfillment of his duty.

I took Nissim by the hand, and we ran forward with all those reporters and cameramen. When the police tried to stop me, I pointed at the heavily breathing Nissim and said, "I'm with him!" and they let me go through.

Max was sitting on Tony's back, absorbed in deep meditation. The reporters made a siege circle around them and kept asking a thousand questions: "How does the UFO look inside? Who were the creatures flying it?" and the question that was repeated the most, "What was the message?"

To the reporters' utter amazement, it was Tony the donkey who opened his mouth and answered all their question like a veteran spokesperson, in near perfect Hebrew and then almost fluent English. Sometimes it was a bit hard to understand him, because of the structure of his mouth, 'cause every word came out as kind of a braying *"brrr. . . ."*

Eventually the reporters realized that while a talking donkey was indeed a hell of an attraction and a hot news item, he wasn't going to betray (bray?) any real information about the UFO's cosmic message. So they returned to questioning Max, who wouldn't give them the time of day. When he got fed up with all this aggravation, he opened his eyes and stretched his neck. Silence fell among the ranked reporters.

Quoth Max, "It was a personal message for me. Can't tell you what they said." Before the stunned reporters could make a protest, he gave Tony a kind of giddyup with his knees. Tony made a sprint, jumped mightily above the alarmed reporters, who immediately ducked for cover, and started galloping west. He and Tony rode into the sunset, which indeed had amazing pink and orange hues to it. I thought, now they're going to take them a bit more seriously.

When I came back home, I lay on my bed staring at the ceiling, with the light on, for I don't know how long, until I got tired of it. Then I called Mr. Eliahu. Mr. Eliahu was my landlord, and a highly valuable archaeological relic he was, too. It's a wonder the Antiquities Authority hadn't laid their hands on him a long time ago. He dates back to the time they still thought they could set up a proper European nation here, where people will be nice and decent with each other. This is why he was called "Mr. Eliahu." His first name was Naphtali, but no one, not even his wife, I think, called him that. When I'd told him I was from Ra'anana he got terribly excited and said that that was where he'd met his wife, working at the Ra'anana orange groves in June of '47. They were building a homeland, but the entire experiment blew up in their faces once the Levantine Indians took over, he said. Now, I decided, Mr. Eliahu is going to get a living demonstration of Levantine Indiancy, courtesy of the Bezeq Phone Co.

Mr. Eliahu's Hebrew was old-fashioned. He was capable of saying things like "You shall pay me right on the dot for being exceeding kind to you, Mr. Menashe." I told him, "Naphtali sweetheart, I got fired from my job, my overdraft passed the five thousand shekels mark already last week, I don't have a penny in my pocket, and I'm rotting away at home all day not even looking for a new job. So you can forget about your money. I don't intend to pay you any. You won't see a penny coming from me to you. You've made enough money at the expense of losers like myself. What are you going to do with so much money? You're already rotten inside and half dead. Forget about it, Naphtali sweetheart. You won't see a penny from me."

Mr. Eliahu was not fazed one bit. Apparently I was not the first Indian to hit him. He said dryly, "I understand you, Master Menashe. I understand you much better than you realize. Just be advised that breach of contract is a serious matter—you are in way over your head in this."

"Naphtali sweetheart," I rudely interrupted him, "you can take your contract, roll it tight and good, and shove it deep inside your asshole!"

I hung up on him. Now it looked like I was on the right track, having greatly enhanced my prospects of becoming homeless. I've always wondered whether City Hall's wooden benches were good to sleep on.

Wandering footloose in the city did nothing to improve the way I felt. I couldn't stop looking at the benches, asking myself which one was going to be my home. Rows of benches kept passing in front of my eyes whenever I closed them—and this was getting too hard to bear. I felt I had to relax, clear my head somehow.

That's why I gladly accepted Ahmed the *alte zachen*'s invitation. He was sitting in the Yemenite's kiosk in Cordovero Street, near the Lehi Museum, looking bored.

"Backgammon?" he asked. "Come on, set it up," I said to him, "but only if you feel like losing." Ahmed smiled under his moustache, took out a packet of Time, offered me one, and lit another for himself. To Yossi he said, "Two black coffees, my man, and make it strong."

"You talk too much, you," said Ahmed, opening up the board and laying it on the brown Formica table. He arranged the pieces in a dizzying speed, rolled a die to see who goes first, and got a six. Ahmed stared at me with his one good eye, the other one roaming uselessly in space. "Play for money?" he asked.

"No thanks, I'm broke," I said and rolled my die. Got a one. "Never mind," said Ahmed, "coffee's on me." "You start," I said to Ahmed. We played silently, not talking at all, rapidly moving those worn-out pieces. The only sound was the rattle of rolling dice, until the end of the first game, which I lost to Ahmed by a gammon.

"You talk too much, you," said Ahmed again, never raising his eyes from the board. "All day long, your head's just running around thinking about girls, about life, you never notice what's going on 'round you. You're all like that. All day long, your head's into bilosophy and girls, not looking where you're going." Ahmed stressed the *b* in *bilosophy* to show his disdain. When he spoke Hebrew he hardly had any accent, usually, and he could pronounce his *p*s without any difficulty, unlike so many Arabs. I had a feeling that since the accident Ahmed was rather bitter with us Jews.

As well he should be. A week before, he got a new donkey, but they didn't quite get along. The donkey couldn't understand what Ahmed wanted it to do. Wouldn't move an inch, and when Ahmed told it what he thought about it, the donkey broke two of his ribs with a massive two-hoofed back swing. Ahmed returned the donkey to the person he bought it from, and since then he's been sitting all day at the Yemenite's, inviting passers-by to backgammon and coffee, trying not to breathe too deeply. It's not like he's out of pocket. Tony puts money in his bank account twice a week. But this is not what you'd call living. Ahmed is a man of principles and dignity. He shouldn't be living on handouts from his previous donkey, like a beggar.

Ahmed offered me another cigarette, took a long and noisy draft from his cup of coffee, and said to me, "Believe me, Ido. You have nothing to worry about, you. In the end, everything will be back the way it used to be. I've got eyes, I see people, and I've been around some. Last year it was Kabbalah, two years ago it was Hare Krishna, five years ago, Emin. Soon this too will get out of their system, the way all the others did."

"*Inshallah*," I closed our conversation. Wind started blowing, sweeping with it droplets of rain from the sea. We picked up the table, moved it inside the kiosk, and kept on playing, fast and silent. Eventually I beat Ahmed twelve to two, got up, and shook his hand. Ahmed ordered some more coffee. I went back to the apartment.

In the stairwell I found myself face-to-face with Mr. Eliahu, accompanied by an execution office cop. I was going up, he was going down. "You are extremely lucky, Master Menashe, because Mister Azulay is a real mensch, and thanks to him you may keep staying here rather than live on a bench in the street."

"He paid you?" I asked. All of a sudden, my face became red and hot.

"He most definitely has," said Mr. Eliahu. "Paid everything, with arrears interest and also for the next six months—adding a handsome compensation for all your smart-ass shenanigans. A right upstanding gentleman, Mr. Azulay is. I just cannot figure out what he sees in you."

Max and Co. were going out for a walking meditation. They passed me on the way down. When Azulay came down the stairs toward me, I looked him in the eyes. Shame on him. Did I ask him to pay for anything for me? I'm willing to live with the consequences of what I do. No, rather, I *want* to live with the consequences of what I do. Sink down, hit the bottom, with nobody to care about me. Now even this was taken away from me.

But Azulay didn't look away. On the contrary, he looked directly at me in a really annoying way. "You spoiled-rotten piece of shit," he said to me, aloud. "Say what?" I asked. Max kept going down with the whole troop behind him. "You spoiled-rotten piece of shit," Azulay said again, this time more loudly. Mor and Hagit turned their heads to look at us.

"You must be thinking you're something," said Azulay. Mor grabbed Hagit by that chubby hand of hers and they kept going down the stairs, in a hurry to catch up with the rest of the group. Azulay moved towards me. I suddenly realized he was quite a large man, about as tall as myself, but very broad and well-muscled, with a healthy beer gut dropping down from above his belt. "You think you're special, huh?" he asked, and his thick black eyebrows came closer as he stared at me. "Why don't you play alongside with Tony in *Florentine*, if you're so special?"

With Azulay standing in my way, I felt not so good, suddenly. He was one step above me, so close I could smell his sour sweat. I only wanted to sit down, maybe smoke a joint, clear my head. I had no time for him. "Don't you have to go with them?" I asked, smiling. Azulay raised his gigantic, heavy hand and brought it down on my cheek. The sound was not pleasant. My right ear started humming, and my eyes lost focus for a second. Azulay turned away from me and went down a couple of steps in a slow, dignified walk. Then, suddenly, he started running heavily to catch up with the group, which was now way ahead of him.

What's going on here? Has everybody gone completely bonkers?

When I came back to the apartment, my cheek was still smarting from the slap Azulay landed on me. I found Tony sitting on the floor watching *Ricki Lake*. "Come on, Ido," he winked at me. "I'll treat you to a beer from my private stock." He pulled out a six-pack of Tuborgs from under the box Max used to sit on when lecturing and took out a cigar from the pocket of the black jacket he was wearing. Tony snapped the cigar's end in one asinine bite, lit it, and gestured, in a twist of his cleft lip, to come with him to the balcony.

The balcony has always been our apartment's garbage dump. As part of Max's efforts to break down Mor's and Azulay's egos, all those dry leaves, empty beer bottles, broken furniture, and other junk that used to fill it were all gone. Now the floor sparkled (smelling of orchids, you guessed it). Pots with flowering geraniums (that also smelled like orchids for some reason) were hanging from the ledge, lit by hidden lamps at night. To complete the setup there were two chairs and a plastic table covered in a tablecloth of handmade lace, on which stood a vase full of fresh flowers, replaced each day.

Tony had told Max he's done enough walking meditation in his former profession and didn't need any more of it, thank you very much. So Max excused him. Tony used these breaks to have the time of his life.

He asked me to open a can of Tuborg for him. Because of his hooves, he couldn't do it for himself, despite persistent attempts. He then took it in in one swig. Finally, he let out a lengthy burp and took a drag from his cigar.

"Howzzit going, Ido?" he asked, laying a finely filed, nail-polished hoof on my shoulder.

"What can I tell you?" I said. "Life sucks."

"Behhh," said Tony. "C'mon, tell me about it. Four hours of meditation every day, two hours group singing and dancing—and pit-bottom, round-table talks. Getting under your skin, telling you you feel bad because you're alienated from the world. I'm just an ass, I'm not cut out for this shit. So I cut corners here and there, to make it barely bearable. That's how you have to take it, one day at a time."

Tony squashed the can and let it fly in a splendid volley shot to the neighbors' balcony. Then I opened another can for him, and he swallowed this one, too, in one swig. "So why are you staying on?" I asked.

"You may laugh at me until forever, Ido, but something about this makes me feel good. Can't describe this feeling—but for the first time in my stinking life, I'm being taken seriously; they listen to me. Maybe they're a little overenthusiastic, but they really care about me. For the first time I matter to someone, and not just as horsepower."

Tony spoke real plain, but everything he said went right into your heart. That's why they liked him on TV. More precisely, that's one of the reasons. The other reason, of course, was that he was a talking donkey. Since the accident, Tony's become a ratings buster—and Max realized this real quick and took advantage. TV stars and producers from Channel 2 would beat a path to our place begging Max to allow Tony to appear on their shows. However, Max didn't actually need this publicity. He's acquired a lot of following anyway. Therefore, even though he didn't need money either—he's rounded up some heavyweight contributors—he demanded incredible sums of them. As he explained to me, hitting their pockets was the best way to bust their egos. Those producers would come out of their meetings with Max with their cheeks wet, having gone through whole boxes of tissue, their souls pure as a baby's smile and their pocketbooks much lighter.

That memorable *Florentine* episode, with Tony as the spiritual donkey who makes Iggy see the light, was a hit, a bombshell. Busted all ratings records. The bank account of the Insights of Love LLC expanded accordingly.

I, too, liked Tony. There was something easygoing about him. He wasn't as fanatic as the rest of them. After a chat with Tony, a small joint, and a few beers, life seemed like something I could cope with.

The Coast Guard has arrived. That's how I called her privately, in my mind, in my long sessions with myself: *the Coast Guard*. It started on the beach: "Ido, put on your sun screen!" "Ido, don't take off your hat!" "Ido, don't go into deep water!"

"Ido, don't talk to strangers, because who knows what kind of maniacs you can see today at the seaside, now that the country is not what it used to be twenty years ago; then you could walk the streets without any worries. Just read the paper. Only yesterday they killed someone because of an argument over a deck chair."

"But Mom, you wouldn't let me go to the beach twenty years ago, either."

"Okay, what's the matter with you, sweetheart? You were little then."

"What are you doing here, anyway?"

"Resting, learning, healing myself."

"Over here?!"

"Yeah, over here. What's wrong with over here?"

"This is my place, Mom. I moved here to get away from you. You can't just barge in without invitation. This is a place where people live, it's not the Carmel Forest."

"*My place* . . . and who pays your rent? Never mind. It's not any business of mine. Besides, I do have an invitation. You never call home and you've received another notice from the army. You're bound to end up in the stockade. So I called here to tell you. Max answered, and we talked a great deal. A very nice boy, Max is. I was highly impressed by his views. He invited me to come visit. He said maybe he could help me become a whole person again. Shame on you for not letting me know what's going on in your place. I could have started working on myself a long time ago."

"Enough with it, Mom!"

"Enough with what, Ido?"

"Stop with it already."

"Stop with what, Ido?"

"Stop with this game. It's stupid and it doesn't fool me any longer. I know what you're trying to do."

"Of course you know. Wouldn't have thought you didn't. Big secret. . . . What do people come here for? Purification, meditation techniques. Making the world a better place. Becoming whole again. . . ."

"People, yes. You? No. You've come here for one reason only: to keep an eye on your little Ido'leh, lest he regrow the wings that you clipped. Keep me close and small underneath your apron. That's what you've always wanted."

"Listen, sweetheart, it's not at all like that. Things change. . . ."

"What things? What change? Nothing changes. Well, perhaps things change, but you don't. An equation with zero unknowns. The Soviet Empire may have collapsed, but you've remained the same: never let up, not for a moment. Help! Save me! The Polish Secret Service is after me!"

"Enough with the histrionics, Ido. You're making yourself a nuisance. People here are trying to concentrate on their meditation. You're a nuisance to me too. I'm in the middle of the Third Cycle, the crucial one. Why don't we have this conversation later on? You find me during suppertime, we'll sit down over a dish of rice and celery and talk about your anger and frustrations. Okay, sweetheart?"

"No supper, no nothing! Get out of my life, right now, this moment! You know how much I hate celery!"

"You haven't changed, Ido. You'll always be mother's little spoiled boy. *Ommmm Shaaaanti, Ommmm Shaaaanti, Ommmm Shaaaanti, haiiii!*"

Mother closed her eyes, took a deep breath, and began chanting mantras in ancient Indian. These were not my mother's words. Could it be the aliens messed with her head?

I was left alone with a deep sense of betrayal, a burning disappointment with life and one huge question mark: *Et tu, Mommy?*

Disco time. I pulled out the disc already in the player, threw it minus its box into the drawer that already was a disorderly mess of discs. None in its original box. Pulled out the Pixies disc from the Deep Forest box and put it in. Turned the volume all the way up to help them with their evening meditation.

Lay back on my bed, hitting the wall with my feet to the beat of the music. Happy as a clam. Really. Got everything I needed right here in this room. No reason to go anywhere else. In the top drawer I had a carton and a half Winston Lites, so I won't get stuck with nothing to smoke. In the middle drawer there were two boxes of Hogla tissue paper, should I wish to cry (Cry? Crying is for cunts!). In the bottom drawer I kept two dried bushes, courtesy of my friendly neighborhood dealer. Crumble half a leaf into your cigarette, it helps you go through the day. In the closet there was everything needed for munching: two giant bars of milk chocolate with raisins and nuts, Pringles, and three family-size bottles of Coke. On the bedside table there was a carved wooden box from India, which always had a few bills inside to pay for this partying. Where did the money come from? I didn't know, I never asked. But the footprints of Tony's polished hooves were quite obvious. Like everything else done in this cult, Tony always came and went, moved and shook, got everything organized.

And there was, of course, my phone: pretty, small, black, lying quietly in a corner.

I went through my address book and couldn't find anyone whose life I could telephonically ruin. But this gave me an idea. I went through the drawers until

I found my old phone book. Opened it on D and called Doron. Mali answered. She didn't recognize my voice; it's been a long time.

I didn't say who's talking. I asked for Doron and got him.

"Hey, you worm, what about the MAG? Ready for inspection?"

"Ido! You blob of organic fertilizer, why don't you ever call?" Doron enthused. "Howzzit with you, you piece of nothing?"

"All's well," I said. "I'm in Tel Aviv, doing nothing in particular."

"I've left a million messages with your mother, even sent you an invitation to our wedding. We'd said we'll remain friends for life."

"So we said, but. . . ."

"No buts. You're coming over for a visit with us right this week."

"Tell you the truth, Dori, I didn't want to come to yours and Mali's wedding. It would have been awkward."

"Awkward how? We never kept secrets from each other. What's the fuss, ha ha, did you screw my sister or something?"

"No. I mean, not your sister. Mali. In our end-of-service party. Remember how we both disappeared? Mali took me to some fortress by the sea. There was this nice sand on the floor, and she screamed and scratched my back when I fucked her. Lucky for me, she didn't have long fingernails. Then she wanted some more. We did it slow that time. She smiled and looked me in the eyes as I nailed her. She then said size does matter. I screwed your wife, Doron, and she told me you have a small pecker. Like I didn't know, after three years of taking showers together."

There was silence at the other end of the line.

"See you 'round, Dori. I just thought you should know."

I hung up. Just as it seemed things were going downhill all the way, it turns out I still have it in me. Besides, I only did my friend a favor. Dori deserves better than this Mali. Come on, I don't even know under what rock he'd found her. I left the room in high spirits. Everything's going my way today.

My happiness was temporary, quite temporary. As I opened the door, I saw Osher in the meditation hall. Suddenly an idea came to me. Holy rage filled me, a desire to take revenge burned in me. I improvised freely, not thinking at all.

"Hello! What's my girlfriend doing here?"

The small crowd in our living room shook off their meditation trance all at once. They all turned toward me, gawking. Osher opened her eyes and turned toward me too.

"I'm no longer your girlfriend, Ido. I may do whatever I want to. Get used to it."

"That you're no longer my girlfriend, I already know. What I'm wondering about is why?"

"Ido, get out. You're interfering with the community's search for light," said Max calmly, majestically.

"Search for light my ass. Search for my girlfriend, you had to say," I said to him. "I know this was what you wanted from the start." I turned to Osher. "How long has he been 'guiding' you?"

"Almost from the beginning, but I never came out to the living room. Didn't want you to see me. Didn't want to hurt your feelings."

"Of course you didn't want to hurt my feelings. You were fucking Max."

"Ido, stop this crazy nonsense. You know that is not true," said Max. His voice wasn't all that calm now.

"No fucking way I stop. I've just begun."

"Ido, not in front of everybody. It's disturbing to them. Let's go out, talk about it like two civilized people."

"Contrariwise, in front of everybody. Why the fuck not? It's only me you screwed with? You screw with them as well. They have a right to know."

"That's true, we have a right to know what you were doing with Osher when you sent Mor and me to clean up everyone's apartments in this bloc." Azulay got up. He demanded an answer, and he looked threatening.

Max tried to reply, but other voices joined with Azulay's. They demanded to know more stuff: what he did with all this donation money, who did he sleep with other than Osher. Other than Rabin's assassination, they accused him of everything. Max's protestations were drowned in a sea of accusations and charges.

The snowball started rolling, and it will be very difficult to stop it now.

I opened the bottom drawer to take out a joint I had ready in my emergency stock. Moving around there, my hand hit something else. It was the gun I'd bought the other day from Recoil, having received my Ministry of the Interior permits. Ozz had patted my shoulder, saying in his most serious and authoritative voice, "This is some serious piece, boy, don't you fool around with it, do you hear me?" I wanted to tell Ozz I wasn't going to fool around any, just stick the muzzle in my mouth and fire a shot into my brain, but you can't afford to joke with the likes of Ozz. They don't have even the slightest sense of humor. It'd be a waste of time. They won't get the joke, and you'd only come out the fool for it. Besides, they always know lots of people in the police, the border guard, the security service, and God knows where else; you could get into lots of trouble that way. It really never pays to joke with Ozz-like persons.

How glad I was that I wasn't tripping when I came to the store, 'cause I wouldn't have been able to stop myself trying to outsmart a fool like Ozz. I just smiled and said that I'd take real good care of my gun.

It was time to give up and admit I wasn't all that good in this. At any rate, I did achieve one objective: I'd burned my bridges behind me. The way I'd messed up the cult, it'd take them a lot of time to fix it. I could forget about working for Gross, which wasn't a great loss, let's face it. Dori was no longer my best friend for life, as we'd agreed, and I'd proved to Osher that I was a jerk. Now there was no chance in a million years that she'll come back to me.

The serene harmony and the singing that used to dominate the living room were replaced by shouting. I couldn't hear what they were saying, but any number of people were speaking out loud, interrupting each other. Through the music that still filled the room some words filtered out: "betrayal of trust," "charlatanism," "fraud," "end of the road," and other stuff like that.

That's it, this is final. As I'd planned in advance, I had ruined everything, and there was nothing important left to say. I picked up my faded jacket and wore it. I stuffed the Jericho into one pocket, and put two joints, a pack of cigarettes, and a lighter in the other. Closed the door behind me, moved quickly down the stairs. Got out to the street and started walking. After two blocks I realized I hadn't taken my notebook. I felt I needed a notebook and that it'd be a horrible mistake to shoot myself in the head without jotting down a few words first. I didn't have anything important to say to the world before leaving it for good, but I felt I mustn't blow it. Like Mother always says about weddings, "You do it once in a lifetime, so you'd better do it right."

I went back upstairs to get my notebook. When I came in, Max was sitting on his cube with everybody surrounding him. I've never seen the place so chock-full of people. They kept up the shouting, but when they noticed me in there, they all fell silent, looking at me. There were really a lot of people there.

I went into my room and got the violet copybook Osher had given me for my birthday a couple of years ago, together with a copy of *Zen and the Art of Motorcycle Maintenance*, which I could never read through. She wanted me to express myself, but the copybook remained blank, except for this little dedication at the top of the first page, in Osher's neat handwriting.

Ido dearest at twenty-four,

Write about yourself, write about the world. Write poems or just notes,
the important thing is that you write. Say what you have to say, but never
be quiet. Scream and shout, but never remain taciturn.

Love you, Osher

What a lovely word, *taciturn*. I've never heard Osher use it, perhaps because
it's a word you only write, not speak. Anyway, I was through being taciturn. I
added the copybook to my pocket, which was becoming heavy and bulging. A
moment before I got out I remembered one more thing and took a Pilot ballpoint
pen. Junk wipes you out. I've become forgetful recently.

Before leaving I lingered a bit in the living room. Something funny was going
on there. The atmosphere was heavy, unpleasant. The gun's grip was sticking out
of my pocket, and people turned to look at me. I felt like a black-hatted cowboy
entering the town's saloon in a second-rate western.

All the way to the beach my hand lay on the plastic grip of my lovely Jericho. Its
weight pulled down the right-hand side of my jacket.

The beach was quiet. Despite it being a pleasant evening, there was no one at
the seaside. Not that I wanted anyone to be there. Suicide, after all, is something
you do by yourself. I walked north. The Bugrachov Beach breakwater seemed
to me fit for my task.

Funny word, *suicide*. I said to myself, out loud, several times, just to get used
to it: "Ido committed suicide"; "Ido's dead, he committed suicide"; "Ido Menashe
committed suicide"; "Ido shot himself in the head"; "He committed suicide last
night." Then I said, "I committed suicide," and this brought up a terrible laughter,
to have such an expression in Hebrew. Must be the least-used phrase in the whole
language. So I kept laughing out loud, saying again and again, "I committed
suicide, I committed suicide, I committed suicide." An old man who passed by
me, wearing a baseball cap, trainers, and training suit, gave me a funny look and
started walking faster.

Enough with the laughs. Must find a logical place to do it.

I walked to the end of the breakwater. Couldn't be seen from the beach,
darkness surrounded me, swallowed me whole. Recoil's Ozz had explained to me
that the length of the barrel determines noise dispersal. The shorter the barrel,
he'd said, the sound of the shot disperses more, can't be heard from a distance.
A handgun's report—I hadn't realized until then that a *report* is also the sound

a gun makes—is carried just a few dozens of meters, and the waves will cover it anyway. Nobody on the beach was going to hear my shot.

I stepped carefully over those large rocks. The last thing I wanted was to fall over and break my neck. Got to the end of the breakwater, sat down on a rock. Took the gun out of my jacket pocket and the ammo box from my trousers pocket. Loaded ten rounds into the magazine, even though I needed only one. Sniffed the oil-and-metal aroma I liked so much. Looked at the magazine. The lead of the dum-dum core looked back at me through the closed copper rosebud, as if it were waiting only for me.

I cocked the gun. This was quite difficult, because it was a double-action mechanism: cocking and releasing the safety with just one pull of the hammer. Took aim at a rock and fired one shot. Lime dust rose up and rocky shrapnel flew all over the place. The noise was staggering. My ears started buzzing. Under the circumstances, it had seemed idiotic to put in earplugs. Good God, you should have seen what it's done to the rock. Blasted the shit out of it.

Okay, now I know the gun works properly, and I can move on to the next stage. I took out my pack of cigarettes and lit one, covering the lighter with one hand against the wind, the way I'd learned in the army. And so I sat there on the rock, smoking my cigarette in long, deep pulls. Wind hit my face, chilling it. I've never enjoyed a cigarette more than I did this final one.

I threw the stub of my final cigarette into the dark, roiling water. Didn't even hear it going *tsssss*. Put the Jericho's muzzle in my mouth and felt the barrel, still warm after the previous shot, pressing against the back of my mouth. It tasted of smoke and gunpowder.

I closed my eyes, because this is what you do when you commit suicide. It's instinctive, like closing your eyes when you kiss.

"I wouldn't do it if I werrrre you," said a voice behind me, emerging between cleft lips. Tony was sitting there on a rock, cross-legged, smiling an asinine smile. "Look at the macro, dude," he said. "Keep your head down till the wave passes over. This is just a rough patch. Good times will come; it would be a pity to end up like this." Tony got up, put a hoof against the gun and removed it gently from my mouth.

"Go away, Tony," I said. "You're just like them." I put the muzzle back in my mouth, closed my eyes and put my index finger on the trigger.

Tony reached out with a hoof and removed the gun again. "There are still those who care about you, Ido," he said. "You won't have it this easy; I'm not giving up on you."

With my right hand, I shoved the gun into my mouth. With my left hand I gave Tony the finger. I started increasing the finger's pressure against the trigger, gradually. "A gentle squeeze of the trigger," as I'd been taught in firearms lessons in boot camp.

Tony lifted again his hoof towards me, trying to remove the gun. He was quite serious about it, but I had no intention of allowing him to spoil it for me.

Suddenly we were both rolling on the ground, fighting for the gun. Tony was sitting on my chest, and he was not some skinny donkey. It was all I could do just to breathe. "You shall live, Ido; I will not let you ruin everything," he said, and I heard in his voice an insistent decisiveness I've never heard before. "I love you," he said, grabbing the barrel forcibly with his strong teeth and pulling. My finger was still caught in the trigger guard.

The gun fired, like it had a will of its own. Tony's head exploded, bursting like a ripe watermelon. Headless, Tony stumbled two more steps to the right, then fell rolling into the sea. My eyes were burning because of the gunpowder, and a thin buzz filled my aching ears. All over my clothes there was a spattering of blood, brains, and bone fragments. The ugly slush pooled up in various depressions on my body and flowed inside my shirt in warm, sticky rivulets. Some of it got in my mouth, and I have to tell you that donkey juice is the most disgusting thing I've ever tasted. And it had to be Tony juice, the only ass ever who really cared about me. I threw away the gun with all my strength. It hit the water far away, making a little splash, and sank deep. The headless corpse floated in the water, and black currents swept it rapidly into the sea.

Up in the sky a point of light appeared, growing larger. The UFO came in fast, stopped, and hovered above the body. A hatch opened in its belly, a yellow ray of light emerged, and Tony's corpse was pulled up slowly, majestically, into the flying bubble. The corpse was sucked inside, the hatch closed fast, and the bubble went *blip, blip, whoosh!*—and flew away. Quiet reigned. Only the crash of the waves could be heard. The wind carried towards me a smell of burned out brakes.

"Do you want to acquire merit, sir?"

I turned around quickly. The religious fanatic, the one who'd disappeared at Yarkon Park, was standing behind me holding a prayer shawl in one hand and a prayer book in the other. "Will you say Kaddish for him?"

"But he was just a donkey," I said.

"Let me tell you," said the fanatic, "that some Jews have the heart of a donkey, and some donkeys have a Jewish heart. He has no speaking relatives—so perhaps you, as his friend, could. . . . It's a great mitzvah, you know. . . ."

I couldn't take any more of this. I lied without hesitation: "I'm a Druze," I told him. "We can't say Kaddish."

I turned my back on him, stripped down to my underwear, threw the rest of my clothes into the sea, and jumped in myself. I scraped my body fiercely and felt the blood and brain fragments wash away in the cold water.

A thunder blasted, and lightning lit up the sea. Heavy rain started falling, and in a minute I could hardly see the figure standing on the breakwater, in black jacket and hat, shaking all over and chanting aloud, in an Ashkenazi accent, "*Isgodol veiskodosh shmei rabo. . . .*"

I swam away, leaving the breakwater behind me. For the first time in weeks I felt a twinge of sadness in my heart. He really cared about me. The jackass.

I came back home. Mor was standing on a chair in the hallway, removing a white sheet from the wall. Beside her there was a heap of folded up sheets, and the yellow-grey flaky walls of our beloved apartment were revealed in all their glory.

"Mor," I asked, "what are you doing?"

"I figured, if it's all over, and there's no more use for these sheets, I may as well take them back home."

"What do you mean, it's all over?"

"Why, haven't you heard? *Alllll* over," she said, pulling it out like she was giving birth to it. "He's a nobody, there's nothing to him, as everybody knows now."

I thought she sounded a bit angry, but surely I was wrong, because Mor is one of those people who never get angry.

Mother came out of the kitchen. "I'm leaving, Ido'leh," she said in a squeaky voice. "I left some good stuff in the fridge for you to eat. How could you get along without my schnitzels?" She gave me a sticky kiss, leaving a wet smudge of lipstick on my cheek, and went out.

Azulay came in from the balcony, carrying under each arm a pot of geraniums, which for some reason spread orchid smell all over the place. He made his way to the door, grunting in my direction, "See ya, Ido." He turned his back and kept going, heavy and awkward, never waiting for an answer.

The place looked empty as it had not been for a month now, since Max's accident. They put the TV set back in place, but without the couch it didn't look the same.

I went into his room. Max was lying on his bed in a torn training suit and a T-shirt, his arms and legs spread out, listening to trance music through earphones, but so loud that I could hear it as well as he did.

"Max," I said. He didn't react. "Max!" I shouted again. Max saw me. He got his earphones off at once and tried to escape. Stepping on the strings of his open shoes, stumbling and falling spread-eagle on the floor.

"Don't beat me up, Ido. I never fucked Osher. I swear on the Bible."

"I know you didn't. I knew all along. I thought maybe we could go back to the way things used to be before."

"Why are you wet, and where are all your clothes?"

"What's going on? Why did everybody leave?"

"Because of the mess you made," said Max. He sounded indifferent. "They asked some tough questions, and I no longer had any answers for them. So I told them it's all over and they may go away. There was some crying and some shouting. A few of them read me the riot act. But generally speaking, I think they'll get over it. Let it go, I've had enough bullshit for one day. I really have no energy to talk about it anymore. Say, is it at all possible that you've got some stuff for me to smoke?"

Max was right. It would be stupid to fight when you could smoke some good junk instead. I went into my room to get the stuff, because all I had in my pocket got lost when I tossed my clothes into the sea.

I was thinking about a small gob of quality Moroccan hash stuck underneath the bottom drawer of my cabinet for six months now, waiting for a special occasion.

In my room I found Osher sitting on my bed.

"Osher, you're here too?" I asked.

"I'm back, Ido," Osher said.

"But I thought you were done. You told me you're not my girlfriend anymore."

"That's true, I was done, but I've come back now."

"You're not mad because of the scene I made about you and Max?"

"Oy, Ido," Osher said in a voice I hadn't heard for a month now. "When are you going to get it? You've always been too heavy." Osher placed her hands on both sides of my head, covering my ears and temples. It was a very pleasant feeling. "Let this head of yours rest. You keep it running all the time. This is not healthy, Ido, and it does nobody any good. You and your thoughts, alone against the whole wide world. Somebody is bound to get hurt eventually."

"But Osher," I felt I had to protest, "I thought such things, when they happen in our lives, are supposed to make us grow, make us more ready for life or something. Has nothing happened to us during this last month? Haven't we grown, haven't we learned something, isn't there some lesson we're missing? Doesn't this story have any moral?"

"Don't you want to be back with me?" Osher asked, hurt. She leaned her head against my chest. She was five foot three, so she barely reached my lowest ribs, because we were both standing up. Her ribs were trembling with the beginning of a cry, and when I put my fingers over her eyes, they were salty. Then we just stood there hugging.

I still wanted to tell her lots of things. I didn't feel this was over and done with, but it was no use anymore. For myself, I really thought I've grown, I've been through something, this month has had some value. But there was no one I could tell it to. So I hugged Osher again, buried my head in the cavity between her shoulder and neck, smelled the nice scent of her deodorant, and thought that while I was right, there were more important things in life than being right.

"Sure I want to be back with you, Osher. I'm happy you've come back," I said. For a moment I became sad and wanted to cry.

We hugged each other like this, not speaking, for several minutes. My sadness passed away. I felt everything became as per usual, the way it used to be.

Osher put her hand on my hip. "What happened to your clothes? Where's your gun?" She asked.

"I threw them all into the sea. What do I need a gun for now?"

"Great," Osher said. "Just wear something, or you'll end up getting pneumonia."

Alte zachen! Alte zachen! Old stuff! Fridges, cabinets, washers. . . . *Alte zachen!*" Ahmed was shouting in the street below. He'd found a new donkey, a small brown one with a patient look in its eyes; a donkey that never spoke, just pulled the loaded cart wherever Ahmed told him to. They got along famously, and Ahmed was very happy. "At long last, a donkey with no bilosophy," he'd told me.

It's Azulay I'm going to miss the most. A real gentleman. It was quite nice of him to come with his truck and return my late grandmother's ugly orange wedding couch right to our living room. Despite all its cigarette holes and the stains of coffee and cum on its pillows, for me this couch meant home—and that's irreplaceable.

Good days are back, in a big way.

We were slumped, the three of us, on the couch in front of the TV. Max was wearing worn jeans that were a bit too short on him, felt slippers with a hole through which his big toe could be seen, and his favorite New York Knicks T-shirt.

"What's with the pizza?" he asked. I told him I'd ordered it twenty minutes ago, a gigantic tuna crème fraîche, which we all liked, with some extras. I'd also ordered a couple of large bottles of Coke, so we won't go thirsty. I told him that if the delivery guy won't make it within the next ten minutes we'd get the sodas for free, in line with Domino's hot pizza policy.

My mouth was actually watering, thinking of the delivery guy ringing our doorbell, of the moment I'd open the pizza's carton and a wonderful wave of smell, melted cheese commingled with the scents of tuna, onion, and pepperoni, would hit my nose. My stomach rumbled in anticipation of the pizza it was going to host soon. I had a feeling this was going to be a perfect night.

Channel Two had commercials and promos. In a few minutes the Haifa derby was going to start. The picture moved to Kiryat Eliezer. An excited Zuhir Ba'aloul said there already were ten thousand fans in the stands, chanting and shouting. Behind him there was a roiling sea of green scarves and shirts. Smoke grenades were thrown, enveloping the stadium in pinkish fog. Rolls of toilet paper and calculator paper flew onto the pitch. The mayhem was just beginning.

The doorbell rang. I got up to open the door. There was the delivery guy, handing me two family-size pizzas. In the nick of time. "Why two?" I asked him. He told me they now had a bargain to celebrate Domino Pizza's thirty years in Israel. Every third customer ordering a pizza gets another, identical one, for free.

The delivery guy was looking over my shoulder, into the apartment. He asked, "Don't you have an ashram or something here?" I told him there used to be one, but not any longer. The delivery guy asked if it wasn't by any chance the ashram of Tony, the donkey from *Florentine*. I said yes, but Tony won't be back. The delivery guy told me that with the sodas it comes up to fifty-seven shekels, sixty agoroth. I yelled out to Max that I've got no money for the pizzas, and he yelled back that I can take it from the Grace and Charity Box in the kitchen, he thought there was a lot of bread in there. I paid the delivery guy and added a generous tip.

I went back, sat on the orange couch, and moved closer to Osher. I lay my hand across her shoulders. Her feline body clung tight to me, and I felt her sweet ass pressing against mine. She stretched out, gently nibbled my earlobe, and whispered that she was glad we're back together and we'll never split up again.

"Pity about Hapo'el. Maccabi will tear them to pieces," said Max.

"Rubbish, Maxi," said I. "Giovanni Roso and Ben-Shimon are on a roll; they're going to teach the Maccabi defense some good lessons. Wanna bet?"

"Quiet, shuddup, it's starting," said Max, as the ref blew his whistle for the opening kick. I slid my hand under Osher's sweater, letting it cover her warm, firm breast. Moved my finger in circles around her nipple, feeling how it got hard and erect. Osher purred pleasantly and snuggled against me. A soft, long-fingered hand crept from below into my shirt, moving up slowly. "Just you wait for what I'm going to do with you after the match," she whispered in my ear before nibbling it again, not so gently this time.

They Had to Move

Shimon Adaf

They had to move. There was no other choice. She did try to keep it together. With all the washing, all the food she had to prepare, all the cleaning up. And she had to learn how to do all these by herself. With no help. With her slowly decaying mother who was looking at them, her and No'am, but saw other persons, times past. No'am was sinking too. When not moping around, he was fighting with kids in the neighborhood, and she had to hide him away and apologize for him. For one month she was able to hold on. Lucky for her it was summer vacation at school, but neighbors would come around occasionally to check up on her, asking questions, and finally Aunt Tehila, whom neither she nor No'am had seen for quite a few years, showed up. Their mother didn't recognize her at all. Just looked at her with those vacant eyes. No. They weren't vacant. Transparent, for all those tears, and all the light hitting them, which should have painted reflections and images, was deflected back the way it came, as though they were two little mirrors. And she was examining Tehila, who said, "Aviva, you've really grown up," and then offered her hand to No'am, who was staring at her too. And refused to approach her. "What a mess," she said, observing their home. Then she went to her sister, who lay folded on the living room's couch, and kissed her on both cheeks.

A strange one she was, Tehila. All dressed up, perfect makeup, looking ready to go to a party, her hair pulled back in a ponytail, and her makeup—rouge and blue eyeliner. Also what she wore, a simple dress, but nearly an evening gown. Yet, and this was the funny bit, her shoes didn't fit. That is, they were perfect colorwise, but they were old, cracked, blue lacquer shoes. What's with all this blue? Aviva asked herself, her hand moving to grasp the locket she wore on a chain around her throat, becoming a fist over that oblate silver egg. She wasn't quite sure what it was actually, except that her father had given it to her before he was gone.

She almost screamed, now it was just *almost* a scream. All through that month her pain folded in on itself, becoming a hard shell, so she didn't cry now when she remembered; it was only the pain banging on the shell from the inside, and she felt the thuds of these bangs, and she almost screamed. There were no stabbing pangs now, like there were when she'd heard from the soldiers who came to speak with her mother, to say things that her mother had already guessed, in the middle of the night, and she woke up and got them out of bed, screaming horribly, and No'am clung to her not understanding anything; fear made him cry, but she'd already realized, though she wasn't ready to admit it, until the soldiers came. And a couple of weeks later the war in Lebanon was over, but it made no difference to her; she felt the Katyushas that kept falling and the fire that kept burning, breaking pieces off her brain. Then she screamed too, because knives were cutting her inside, every one of her organs was being cut, and seeing her mother give up and start decaying, and No'am uncontrollable and full of rage and looking for pretexts to quarrel, she tried to choke down on her screaming, breathe it in, soften those knife thrusts, and she almost made it, she just *almost* screamed, and soon she'll lose her pain completely and will remain empty of her father, his memory, all those moments when he was her father and she was somebody's daughter, and she'll get on with her life. She knows this, it wasn't she who'd set the price, only her locket will remain, sort of an oblate sphere, and she couldn't figure out why somebody should have made it in the first place, and her father's words, "Aviva, so that you don't forget."

She started crying. Not really crying. She just allowed a few tears to get out. Tehila sensed, how fast she sensed those tears, and came beside her and held her tight. "Well," she said, "no way you're staying here. You're coming to live with me."

Live with her? In another city? Their mother hardly complained. She said, "The one I lived here for is gone," and Tehila just took her by the hand after Aviva had packed up for the three of them, but No'am ran out and kept running and running until he got to the royal poinciana tree—she knew its name because her father made her memorize the names of trees and flowers and birds—and No'am started climbing, holding on to its branches. And Tehila went out there, her lacquered shoes going *tak, tak, tak* on the pavement stones, and Aviva, standing at the window and watching, could hear her shoes even at this distance, but what Tehila whispered to No'am, which made him climb down off the tree and come with her, she couldn't hear. Even though she saw her lips move.

There was still a week left of the summer vacation, before they had to go to school. Both of them would go to the local high school, which included a junior high, since No'am was just going on to seventh grade and she to tenth, and No'am wasted no time getting on the wrong side of the neighborhood's kids. Kids in Yehud were tougher, and Tehila's home was at the end of town, in a neighborhood of old single-family houses, and it is well known that kids in single-family-house neighborhoods are the toughest. It's been a few days already that No'am would come home bruised and bleeding. Always, their mother lets her glance linger on him, and Tehila looks bemused, with this frown that doesn't fit in with her made-up face. And Aviva takes him by the hand and cleans his wounds with iodine or Polydine, or puts on a compress, and gives him a piece of her mind, but he doesn't listen, he just tightens up his lips and growls behind them.

"This can't go on," Aviva said to Tehila. Since their arrival they haven't talked much. Tehila showed them their rooms. She had a big house, with a den—she called it her study—in which she enclosed herself all day, working on her sculptures. She was unmarried and had no children, and when Aviva asked, she just smiled and said nothing. But her old lacquered shoes she wore every day, even when working in her study. Aviva saw some of the sculptures. They repelled her, deformed human figures that they were, with too many hands or too few, with two heads and sometimes more than one mouth where mouths aren't supposed to be, nor tongues, and still more parts sticking out or gaping, which Aviva recognized but was too embarrassed to tell herself what they were. And all of them, all these monsters, wore new shoes. Sometimes Nike or New Balance or Timberland, sometimes shiny with high heels, or square-toed leather shoes. Tehila also had a library. A huge one. In her living room. It had all of Jane Austen's novels. And Aviva, who had read only *Pride and Prejudice*, felt hope biting at her chest.

"No," said Tehila, "this can't go on."

"He needs something to keep him busy," said Aviva.

"I wish he would read, like you."

"But once, before, he used to read."

"Like what?"

"Books you don't have in your library. Adventures, and thrillers, and fantasy."

"But I do have fantasy," said Tehila, giving her a long stare. "And science fiction."

"My daddy . . ."

"I know. You think it would help No'am?"

"I never saw any of it in your library."

"It's not in the library." Tehila turned her back and made a few steps toward her den. "Come on," she turned back to Aviva, "follow me."

The far wall of her den had a small door Aviva hadn't noticed before. A low one. Tehila walked in with a straight back. Aviva, taller than Tehila by a head, had to bend to pass through.

A strange room. Even stranger than the den. On tall stands and in glass cabinets of all sizes there were assorted disassociated objects, including a jug and a watch and a book and a razor blade and a wallet and a handheld computer and a pair of eyeglasses and more. Each display cabinet was labeled by name: Alon. Dan. Yogev. Levi. Yaron. Yekutiel. Zvulun. And more. Aviva thought, *only guys' names. And the room looked like a museum.* Tehila went to a large glass cabinet holding a cardboard box. Aviva saw the label: Shim'on. Tehila lifted the box effortlessly, although Aviva suspected it must be quite heavy, and put it on a table in the middle of the room. "There you are," she said. Aviva opened the box and looked inside. A pile of glossy magazines, brand new. On the top one she saw *Fantasia 2000* printed in yellow letters, and the cover was purple and blue with an illustration of an alien traversing the sky in a teacup. *Interesting,* she thought, and started digging in. All those magazines inside had the same title, *Fantasia 2000.* Must be magazines from way back, she told herself. The year 2000 was a long time ago.

"There are stories here No'am will find interesting." Tehila answered the question she meant to ask.

"They're yours?"

"No," said Tehila. "They're Shim'on's."

"Who's he?"

"One of my ex-lovers," said Tehila, looking at her closely. Aviva turned pink. "He used to collect all these magazines. This one was important to him, helped him consolidate his identity as a reader. At least, that's what he claimed."

Aviva moved her eyes, looking around the room. All those guys' names. "All this stuff. . . ."

"Yes," said Tehila. "Keepsakes."

"There were many of them."

"Sure. Usually, the story lasts for just a few months."

"And then what? They leave?"

"No. I get tired."

"And you tell them to go away?"

"No. I kill them and capture their essences inside some object that belonged to them."

Alarmed, Aviva immediately turned her roving eyes to look at her. Tehila laughed. She went to a glass cabinet. Behind its doors there were small books bound in leather, neatly arranged. "Sometimes I need more than an object to remember them by." She took one of them out. Now Aviva saw that each of those books bore one of the names attached to the objects. The one Tehila handed to her was marked "Shim'on." Aviva opened it—a photo album, not a book. Shim'on and Tehila on the beach, Shim'on and Tehila with a tower in the background, Shim'on and Tehila somewhere at night. In all those photos Tehila looked just the same, the way she looked ever since Aviva had seen her first, in those bluish cracked lacquer shoes. But Shim'on was changing. Growing older. She followed the sequence of photos, and her heart stopped. Froze. In this photo, yes, in *this* photo, under the big tree—a walnut tree, she knew—Shim'on and Tehila, and behind them, on a bench in the corner, someone. Not someone. Her father. She said, "that's Daddy," in a broken voice, and raised her eyes to Tehila, and Tehila bent to see for herself, and said, "That's right, I never realized Netan'el was here. How strange. He really was friends with Shim'on."

Aviva grasped her locket, closed her hand around it, squeezed. She felt the room closing in on her; she had to get out. She picked up one of the *Fantasia 2000*s and started for the door, actually ran, and her forehead hit the frame head, but she didn't feel it. She went out of the house. Her mother was sitting on the couch staring at the TV set, which was turned off, and she ran out to the porch, and there she stopped. From a distance she saw No'am approaching. He was limping. *He mustn't see me cry.* She tightened her lips. "Who did you fight with this time?" she asked, making every effort to smile.

"None of yer business."

"Sit here a moment, I'll get you something to drink."

She went inside, came back with a glass of Coke and saw that No'am was sitting, bristling with anger, and that he was crying. He, too, was crying. "Look, No'am," she said. "Look." She pointed at the magazine. He wouldn't comply. She felt his frustration radiating out of him, shining like a little sun. She extended her hand to caress his hair, which was exactly like their father's, dark and smooth. He pushed her hand away, rudely, and she grasped her locket the way she always did when she didn't know what to do with her hands. With her left hand. With her right hand she opened the magazine, issue number 41, she saw, and leafed through it fast. "Look, No'am, aliens and spaceships, like in the books Daddy used to like." No'am looked at her. His eyes were bright, bright because of his tears. She cringed and squeezed her locket tighter. With her other hand she pointed at a random page. "Shadow, Shadow on the Wall," it was titled. "An interesting one, seems to me," she said desperately, looking closely at No'am, but his eyes were glued to the page. He was swallowing the words. "No'am," said Aviva, but No'am didn't reply. He picked up the magazine and, walking and reading, went into the house.

Aviva wasn't quite sure what it was all about. She sat all morning in the backyard, in the shade of the trees, reading Jane Austen's *Northanger Abbey*. About some stupid girl who begins to suspect that the mansion in which she's a guest conceals dark secrets. Obviously, there aren't any; she only fell in love with the son of the host family, and she's making up all this just for kicks. Nevertheless, Aviva never noticed how fast time was passing. It was already noontime and hot, and sun rays were filtering through the treetops—sacred fig and Indian banyan and sycamore—in bright, shiny patches, but what brought her out of her book was the sound from the front of the house; there was a woman on the porch, and she was shouting. She bolted for the front of the house. Tehila, too, emerged from her den. But not her mother, who remained on the couch. On the porch stood a heavyset woman, her black hair splayed over her shoulders. She was holding a tall, skinny boy by the hand. Would have been handsome if he weren't so full of sharp bones, she thought. Bigger than No'am, who was leaning against the wall by the door, on the other side of the table. No'am looked very calm. He even grinned. He crossed his arms and looked back at her.

"I'm gonna break both that boy's legs," said the woman. "You just let me lay me hands on 'im and you'll see."

"What happened?" Aviva asked. She was looking at Tehila, who didn't answer her.

"Yer brother, that little bastard, see what he done to m'boy."

Aviva saw. The boy's arms, his throat, and every other bit of exposed skin were covered with blue bruises. She turned to look at No'am. "You did this?"

"Not just to 'im," the woman added, "a couple more kids, m'boy's friends. I'm gonna tear 'im to pieces. And you," she said to Tehila, "you got nuttin' to say? You got no control over the kids yuh brung into the neighbor'ood?"

Tehila said, "Take a good look at No'am, see how small he is. Half the size of your son. You really believe he can beat up your son and his friends?"

"You tell 'er," said the woman to her son. "C'mon, ya little jerk, tell 'er."

"He got help," said the boy, sucking in the snot threatening to drip out of his nose. "He brung another kid to the woods." He pointed in the general direction of the woods at the edge of the neighborhood, a place Aviva had passed once. "That's where we was playin'."

"Two boys?" said Aviva. "Against a hulk like yourself?"

"I wanna go," said the boy, pulling at his mother's hand. *Tak, tak, tak,* Tehila's shoes sounded as she went down to the gate and opened it for them. The woman gave her an angry look but stepped down from the porch. Then she turned around and said to No'am, "I'm warnin' you. You come near m'boy, it's the end of you."

The grin Aviva thought she had seen on No'am's lips grew wider. He waved them both good-bye.

"What was that all about?" asked Aviva.

"No clue," said No'am. And Tehila looked at him again, her frown returning to spoil her carefully painted face.

No'am came to her room at night, asking whether he could get more *Fantasia 2000* magazines. He liked these stories, he said, and Aviva sent him to Tehila, and he returned with the whole bunch of them. "Help me pick a story," he said. "The one you chose earlier was a good one."

"I'm too tired," Aviva said. "Choose for yourself."

He went through the magazines and finally selected one by its cover illustration.

The next evening he came back. All roughed up and disheveled, like scuzzy hair in the morning, she thought; the neighborhood kids must have caught up with him. "What happened?" she asked. "You got beaten?"

"Help me pick a story," he said. "I can't find any I like."

"Come on," said Aviva. "Don't be such a lazy dog. Next thing you'll ask me to read to you." They were sitting in the living room. Their mother was sitting there too, chewing on a piece of bread Aviva pushed into her hand. The food on her plate was getting cold. "Can't you see I'm busy?" And to their mother, "Come on, Mommy, you've got to eat." And their mother said, "I've already told you. Me, I have nothing to eat for."

"Daddy always used to read to me when I asked him to," said No'am.

I'm impervious. I'm as impervious as a wooden door, Aviva said to herself, moving her left hand to her locket. She squeezed, she could almost feel her hand bones cracking around the locket. *I'm giving up crying, and pain, so that something will be left.* "Get the pile," she said, making every effort for her voice to come out steady. And clear.

No'am obeyed immediately. Again she picked one, almost at random. This time she chose the magazine she'd already seen, the one with the alien in a teacup. And opened it. The first story began with a couple of lines about a teacher and a school. Very good. She pointed at the title—"Ararat"—and said, "There, this one looks interesting." No'am became absorbed almost at once, breathing quietly while she urged their mother to eat.

This time she saw No'am running. She felt uneasy, perhaps because of that business with the boy who'd complained about him and his strange behavior. She should keep her eyes open, she thought. And indeed, when she raised them from *Sense and Sensibility,* she realized he was making towards the woods, followed by a bunch of kids, with the tall boy leading. She leaped to her feet and ran there too.

First No'am disappeared into the woods, then the kids who were shouting bad names after him. Two boys who looked the same, pudgy and menacing, caught up with their tall leader, shouting, "We'll get 'im."

Three white egrets were sitting on the branches of the outlying trees like ornate hairpins. When she got into the woods she saw no one. The silence was deep. In this heat the eucalypts were standing tall, green and sweating, the bright light making their trunks shiny, their pungent smell stinging her nose. Then she caught sight of a swift movement and headed for it. Through the trees she saw the kids bunching up, and then, coming closer, there was No'am facing them, grinning, his arms crossed. What she saw then she couldn't believe. Everything that happened next was blurry, as in a dream. The kids had sticks and stones in their hands. And No'am said, "Come out now." And the eucalypts' tops started moving, and out of them came more kids. They were flying. In the air. *Flying kids,* Aviva thought. And they had with them an older woman, but still young. Pretty. She looked American. And lonely. Aviva knew this expression. She could see it in the mirror every day. The flying kids were holding ropes as they came closer to the other ones, those from the neighborhood. One of the flying kids was waving his hands, and it looked like the neighborhood kids were unable to move—they were paralyzed. And the flying kids separated the neighborhood kids from each other and prodded them into the thicket and tied them up. Then they alighted. And the young woman raised her hands high in the air and started moving them like she was pulling strings, but they were invisible. And a small cloud appeared above the underwood where the neighborhood kids were tied up, screaming and trying to free themselves, and hail started falling on them. Heavy, pounding hail. And No'am was laughing. Aviva hasn't heard him laugh since their father. . . . *This is not possible*, she told herself, *I'm dreaming*. She started to back away, then turned around and ran.

In the afternoon, when No'am returned from his wanderings to eat, she interrogated him. But he looked at her as if she had a few screws loose. *Maybe he's right*, she thought. *All the same, there is something weird about those woods. I must look into it*. And in the evening, while she was insistently entreating their mother to eat, with Tehila looking at her in silence and No'am restlessly leafing through *Fantasia 2000*, she asked No'am again if anything unusual had happened in the woods. And No'am said, "What's all this about the woods? First that broomstick Aviel accusing me of roughing him up; now you too? I never go anywhere near those woods."

Tehila asked, "Why are you asking about the woods?"

"No reason," said Aviva.

"Okay, then help me pick a story," No'am said. "I can't find any by myself."

"No'am," she said, "you must learn to find stories you like on your own."

"But you find them so easily. You've already picked two, and I couldn't find any."

She looked at Tehila, who seemed to be grinning to herself. Her cracked lacquer shoes were clicking on the floor. Their mother started coughing. "What's the matter, Mommy?" Aviva asked. "Are you ill?" She laid a hand on her forehead. And their mother said, as if she was speaking with someone far away, "What could happen to me anyway? What could happen? The one who took care of me is gone. There's no one to take care of me anymore."

The locket was waiting for her hand. She grasped it. She mustn't cry.

"Come on," said No'am. He picked up one of the magazines and shoved it into her hands.

"Enough, No'am," she said angrily. "I picked those stories without even thinking. It was sheer luck." And to prove her point she opened the magazine and pointed at a page. "There, this one looks good to me." Truth to tell, it didn't look good at all. It had a surprising title, "5,271,009."

No'am snatched the magazine away from her and started reading. And she turned her attention back to their mother.

Going to her room, exhausted after this evening, she thought she must do something about No'am. Early next week they'll both have to go to school, and she'll have to look after him. *Something is happening to him*, she thought. *And it has to do with this* Fantasia 2000 *magazine and with Tehila. She's involved, too, with those cracked-up shoes of hers. And who was this Shim'on who knew their father, anyway?* She went into No'am's room. He was lying in his bed. The light was on and his head was pushed into the pillow. He was snoring a little. The *Fantasia 2000*—issue number 5, she saw now—fell onto the carpet. On his desk there was a sheet of paper. No'am had written one line on it: "Dear Mr. Solon Aquila."

She picked up the magazine and went into her room.

The story, "5,271,009," was fascinating. It was written by an author named Alfred Bester. She seemed to recall that her father had read one of his books, something about a man with a tiger's face or suchlike, and her hand tightened around the locket. This one was a story about an artist gone mad and a character called Solon Aquila, who was some kind of witch doctor or angel or Satan and had a power to make people live their dreams, or their nightmares. *Dear Mr. Solon Aquila*, she thought. Her eyes were already heavy, but before shutting them she could hear Tehila's footsteps coming closer to her room: *tak, tak, tak.*

When No'am left the house in the morning, she followed him. He seemed deep in thought, holding a letter in his hand, unaware that she was not far behind him. He made for the woods, and she followed. For a moment he disappeared among the trees, but then she saw his back on her right-hand side, beyond a trunk. Like he was giving a wide berth to the place where she dreamt of the flying kids. She hurried to close the gap and didn't notice how near she was before she realized she could hear No'am murmuring to himself, "Now I'll show 'em. . . ."

She stopped for a moment, to let him get farther, then kept following him. No'am took a path that only he could see; otherwise she couldn't explain how they went around in circles part of the time or went straight ahead into the woods at other times.

No'am stopped. He stopped beside a mailbox, bright red, shining as if it was just recently painted. He glanced down at the letter he was holding, then dropped it into the box.

"No'am," Aviva said, coming towards him among the trees. No'am stared at her. "A . . . Aviva," he stammered, "What are you doing here?"

"What did you do with that letter?" she asked.

"Oh, it's nothin', just a game."

"A game? What kind of game?"

"Nothin'."

"No'am, you told me you never go anywhere near these woods. Aren't you afraid they'll ambush you here? Aviel and his pals?"

"No, not really."

"I'm surprised. What are you hiding?"

"Nothin', I told you. Don't be such a bore."

"So what's the game?"

"I don't want to tell you."

"Okay. Can I guess who you sent the letter to?"

His eyes narrowed. He looked at her suspiciously. "I have to go," he said. He took a few steps, and suddenly disappeared.

"No'am," she called.

He returned. "We have a problem," he said. "If I leave you here you won't find your way back."

"What's going on, No'am? Does it have anything to do with Tehila?"

"Tehila? Why should it? Tell you the truth, I don't know."

"You sent this letter to Solon Aquila, didn't you?"

No'am started. "How did you guess?"

"Why would you send a letter to a character out of a story?"

"'Cause sometimes they come."

"They?"

"Those I send letters to through this mailbox."

"That boy that Aviel claimed you brought in for help?"

"His name's Bobby. He can. . . . Well, in the story his stepmom is abusing him and he can make silhouettes with his hands, live ones, and then he calls a creature out of the shadows to come take her. I wrote to him to come out and help me. After I'd read the story I went for a walk in the woods, and suddenly I got here, to this mailbox, and I thought, why don't I send this Bobby a letter to come help me. And that's what I did, and he did come. But . . . but he was more wicked than in the story. He brought creatures out of the shadows, scary creatures, and they attacked Aviel and his pals."

Aviva looked at him, shocked. *He's pulling a fast one on me*, she thought. *His inventions are getting more sophisticated. Like Father's.*

"Then I wrote to those kids from this story, 'Ararat,' the ones who came from another planet and were afraid to show their powers, and their teacher, too. They looked nice. Only they weren't so nice. They made fun of me and spat at me."

"The . . . flying kids? They were for real? And their teacher? The one who makes hail?"

No'am nodded. His face seemed sad. "They didn't go away as fast as Bobby. They shouted that next time I call 'em, they'd have enough power to get me as well."

"I knew it, I knew it all has to do with those magazines Tehila gave you. What is she up to, Tehila?" said Aviva.

"At least some of the magazines," said No'am. "I don't know why, but it doesn't always work."

"You tried some more?"

"Yeah. I sent a couple of letters to people from other stories, but nothing happened. And somehow I knew nothing would happen. Those stories, they weren't. . . ." he fell silent.

"They weren't what, No'am?"

He looked at her in horror. He was terrified. "They weren't alive, like the ones that you picked."

"That *I* picked?"

Now Aviva felt as alarmed as he was. Her hand went to the locket. The woods started closing in on her. She tightened her fist around the silver egg. No'am kept looking at her, waiting for an explanation.

"Do you know what Solon Aquila does?" she asked.

"Yes," said No'am. "I asked him to come over here and make Aviel's worst nightmares come true."

"You didn't get the point, No'am," she said. "Solon empties people of their childhood, after letting them live their fantasies. He takes away their inner world, all their dreams. He leaves them with nothing."

"Here he comes," said No'am. His voice was trembling.

In the air, beside a eucalypt standing not far from them, a block of air lit up like a flame. The woods shook. Aviva squeezed her left hand around the locket. She whispered, "The locket, Daddy's locket. . . ." With her right hand she held on to No'am.

She shuddered, thinking of flying kids.

Afterword

Aharon Hauptman

It was in 1996, during the first annual convention of our newly founded Israeli Society for Science Fiction and Fantasy. I proudly strolled, with Emanuel Lottem and other friends, through the corridors of the Tel Aviv Cinematheque, crowded with enthusiastic young fans. One of them stared at me, and I could hear him whispering in a friend's ear: "I think this is Aharon Hauptman, he was the editor of *Fantasia 2000*." And his astonished friend replied: "What? Is he still alive?!"

Well, here I am, twenty years later, alive and kicking (or at least trying to), and what is more important, the Israeli SF scene is alive, kicking more than ever. Yes, there are no regular printed magazines anymore (the time of printed magazines is over anyway). But the online activity is flourishing: three or four sites, rich in contents. Conventions attract thousands of visitors each year (amazingly, sometimes two parallel events competing with each other), an annual collection of original stories is regularly published, several local publishers specialize in SF, Hebrew SF is being translated, Israeli writers win awards, films are produced, academic theses are being written. Who would have dreamed about this back in 1978, when we conceived the late *Fantasia 2000*, the first Israeli SF magazine that besides translations encouraged submission of original Hebrew stories? (Funny, once upon a time the year 2000 sounded futuristic).

Well, we dreamt. Science fiction is the stuff of dreams, isn't it? SF dreams (and nightmares) are products of imagination, but they are inspired by reality, and they shape reality by inspiring and enriching human knowledge and actions. I write these words just after attending an academic meeting about artificial intelligence. The chairman reminded the audience that the origins of AI and robotics are rooted deep in SF. They will soon be an integral part of our lives. The same with space travel, of course, as well as with human-machine interface, cyberspace, cyborgs, nanotechnology, you name it. And, as every SF fan knows (or should know), the point is not the technology (real or fictional), not even speculative science, but their interaction with humans, with us. Good SF can help us to better understand how we are (or will be) shaped by science and

293

technology and how science and technology are (or will be) shaped by us. For me, an SF story at its best is a thought experiment about alternative realities, with plausible technoscience ingredients, in a way that makes you think differently and perhaps better understand our world, other worlds.

If humans fail to understand our potential futures, our alternative realities, it is mostly due to the failure of imagination, something that the SF community is not short of. Arthur C. Clarke wrote (in *Profiles of the Future*) that although only a very small fraction of SF readers would count as "reliable prophets," "almost a hundred percent of reliable prophets will be SF readers—or writers." Today, we should better replace the word "prophets" with "futurists" or "foresight practitioners," as foresight and futures studies are finally (but yet not sufficiently) taking their place in research and policy making.

What's more, in these fields (which don't deal with prophecy but with analyzing alternative futures) there is growing interest in the contribution of SF and SF thinking. We constantly face unforeseen surprises in economy, politics, climate, and technology that challenge conventional thinking and methods. In order to enrich the outcomes of foresight studies and to strengthen their effectiveness, it is important to encourage nonconsensual views about potential wild cards: future events with (currently perceived) low likelihood but high impact. And there is no better source of wild ideas for wild cards (including their possible implications) than science fiction. Yes, you may think about teleportation.

Indeed, in recent research activities, such as some projects in the research program of the European Union (in which yours truly was privileged to participate), imagining wild cards played an important role, and the projects' work plans explicitly encouraged the researchers to explore the SF literature for inspiration. And that's what they did. In one of those projects many imaginative wild cards were analyzed in order to point at possible new (currently overlooked) research directions for technology-society interaction. Some of them had distinctive "SF flavor"—for example, the one about a society in which people are becoming addicted to dream manipulation enabled by brain-computer interfaces. Another project dealt with wild-card scenarios about potential abuse of new technologies. One of them described future everyday gadgets (enabled by nanotechnology or 4D printing combined with the Internet of Things) that are capable of (remotely activated) self-healing, upgrade, or recycling, thus being vulnerable to a malicious signal that triggers their self-destruction (and thereby making flea markets the most attractive places to buy reliable products). The project even sketched the outlines of so-called narrative scenarios—we may call them SF stories—with the help of an SF writer (my good friend Karlheinz Steinmüller) who also happens to be, not coincidentally, a professional futurist.

With the accelerating pace of advances in science and technology, and of social changes in general, it is becoming a cliché to say that "we witness SF coming true" or that "we live in the future" (although some current societal phenomena should make one wonder if we are not going backwards to live in the past, which in turn has also to do with SF: the alternative history branch of the so rich SF tree). But as the only constant thing is change, and the future will always surprise us, the role of SF is not over. SF is the future; the future is SF, long live SF!

ACKNOWLEDGMENTS

The Tribes of Israel wandered in the Sinai Desert for forty years before they could enter the Promised Land. This book took nearly the same amount of time to gestate. Many people helped us navigate the often treacherous wadis, passes, dry holes, false turns, and dead ends we traversed during this otherwise interminable slog. These included Robert Silverberg, who introduced us to our agent, Eddie Schneider, of the JABberwocky Literary Agency, who ran with this effort long after any other front-ranking agent would have shown it—and us—the door.

Sheldon Teitelbaum would like to offer thanks to our legal Godzilla Guy Mizrachi; Aharon Hauptman, who volunteered for the odious task of translating his words into Hebrew during the heyday of *Fantasia 2000*; Hanan Sher, who ran his book reviews (he used to refer to them as "Yids in Spaaace!") in the *Jerusalem Post*, the first Israeli daily ever to publish a monthly column on SF/F; and Ian Watson, John Clute, and the good folks at *Foundation*, who at various times offered up much-needed erudition, insight, and other assistance

Emanuel Lottem wishes pay respect to the late Amos Geffen and Aharon Sheer, as well as Dorit Landes and Adi Zemach, the trailblazers, and to add thanks also to Liat Shahar-Kashtan and other members of the Israeli Society for Science Fiction and Fantasy who offered help and advice, in particular Nadav Almog and Ehud Maimon; to Danny Manor and Gabi Peleg, who got me involved with *Fantasia 2000*; to the many readers who gave me feedback on my SF/F translations (good ones or bad, they were always helpful); to Larry Niven, Brian Stableford, and Ian Watson for their encouragement; and finally, to my good friend Aharon Hauptman.

We both thank Avi Katz, our illustrious illustrator and good friend; Alex Epstein, Elana Gomel, Danielle Gurevitch, Gail Hareven, Eli Herstein, and Noah Mannheim, who helped comprise our editorial board; Adam Rovner and Jessica Cohen-Rovner, who provided early and timely counsel regarding research and translation-related issues; Bill Gough, who went over the manuscript and made some cogent remarks; Adam Teitelbaum, Lance Cody, Adam Roth, and Eric Menyuk, the intrepid gang behind our Kickstarter promo, and Lionel Brown, who supported it wholeheartedly; John Robert Colombo, who first showed us how it was done; and Robert Mandel, who made it his business to ensure that Israel, despite the trepidations of every other publisher we encountered, got a fair shake. Other staff at Mandel-Vilar Press, as well as Noel Parsons and Barbara Werden, were ever helpful. Without their stalwart contributions, and those of so many others, *Zion's Fiction* would likely never have emerged from the desert. To them, and everyone else who helped light our way, we remain profoundly grateful.

And of course, we owe a debt of gratitude to all the authors featured in this collection and an apology to the many left out for lack of space. We fervently hope to rectify this in future volumes.

ABOUT THE CONTRIBUTORS

The Editors

Emanuel Lottem, born in Tel Aviv in 1944, has been a central figure in the Israeli SF/F scene since the mid-1970s: translator of some of the best SF/F books published in Hebrew and editor of others; advisor to beginning writers; a moving force in the creation of the Israeli Society for Science Fiction and Fantasy (ISSF&F) and its first chairman; and founder of its annual ICon convention and other activities.

Lottem's first SF translation was Frank Herbert's *Dune*, which has become a classic. According to Israeli literary historian Eli Eshed, "This translation is considered a masterpiece of SF translations." More SF/F translations followed, and Lottem's name became familiar to and respected by Hebrew-reading fans.

After a few career changes, Lottem became a freelance translator and editor. In addition to SF/F, he also specializes in popular science and military history. In 1983 Lottem became chairman of the editorial board of the Israeli SF/F magazine *Fantasia 2000*. A few years later, in 1996, he presided over the inaugural meeting of the ISSF&F, which he founded with a small group of devoted fans. Visiting author Brian Aldiss officially announced the ISSF&F open for business, and Lottem was unanimously elected its first chairman.

To date, Lottem's SF/F translations include works by Douglas Adams, Poul Anderson, Isaac Asimov, Alfred Bester, Edgar Rice Burroughs, Lois M. Bujold, Jack Chalker, C. J. Cherryh, Arthur C. Clarke, Hal Clement, Michael Crichton, Philip K. Dick, Robert L. Forward, William Gibson, Robert A. Heinlein, Frank Herbert, Ursula Le Guin, Ann Leckie, Anne McCaffrey, Larry Niven, Mervyn Peake, Frederick Pohl, Christopher Priest, Robert Shea and Robert A. Wilson, Robert Silverberg, E. E. "Doc" Smith, James Tiptree Jr., J. R. R. Tolkien, Jack Vance, and Connie Willis, among many others. In 1994 Lottem won one of Israel's highest translation awards, the Tchernichovsky Prize, for rendering into Hebrew Richard Dawkins's *The Selfish Gene*. The ISSF&F gave him in 2016 a Life Achievement award on its twentieth anniversary.

Sheldon (Sheli) Teitelbaum was born in Montreal in 1955. He attended Concordia University, where he earned an honors degree in history. Upon graduation in 1977 he left Canada for Israel, where he joined the infantry, completed IDF officer training, and served as a staff officer for the Paratroops Brigade. During his compulsory military service in Israel he moonlighted as a member of the editorial board of the seminal Israeli magazine *Fantasia 2000* and as in-house SF reviewer for the *Jerusalem Post*. Upon concluding a five-year military stint, Teitelbaum began a journalism career, working for the *Jerusalem Post*, which put him to use as a night desk subeditor and, on weekends, as a feature writer. During the days he worked as a writer for the Weizmann Institute of Science.

Teitelbaum moved with his family to Los Angeles in 1986, where he took up new duties as West Coast bureau chief for the acclaimed film magazine *Cinefantastique*, as founding reporter for the *Los Angeles Jewish Journal*, and as a senior writer for the *Jerusalem Report*. Additionally, he held down a day job for three years at the University of Southern California as a science writer and, later, three more as a subcontractor to the US Department of Energy.

Teitelbaum has commented on SF/F-related themes in the *Los Angeles Times*, the *New York Times*, *Forward*, *Time*-Digital, *Wired*, *SF Eye*, *Midnight Graffiti*, *Foundation: The Review of Science Fiction*, the *Encyclopedia of Science Fiction*, and the *Encyclopedia Judaica*. He is the recipient of Canada's first Northern Lights Award and three Brandeis University–based Jewish Press Association awards.

The Artist

Avi Katz, a veteran American-born Israeli illustrator, cartoonist, and painter, evinced interest in SF/F illustration early: while still a teenager in Philadelphia he sent a pack of his *Lord of the Rings* art to J. R. R. Tolkien and received an enthusiastic response from the author, who told him he was the first illustrator to portray the dwarves as he had intended.

At age twenty, while studying art at Berkeley, after being interviewed by John W. Campbell he decided to avoid the draft and Vietnam and complete his studies at the Bezalel Academy of Art in Jerusalem; he has made his home in Israel since then. He has been the staff illustrator of *Jerusalem Report* magazine since its first issue in 1990, and is active in the international organization Cartooning for Peace as well as the Association of Caricaturists in Israel. He has illustrated some 170 books in Israel and the United States, which have won the National Jewish Book

Award, Hans Christian Andersen honors, the Ze'ev Prize, and others; he was a nominee for the lifetime achievement Astrid Lindgren Award.

A founding member of the Israeli Society for Science Fiction and Fantasy, Katz created many original book covers for SF/F published in Israel; his illustrations graced the covers of society posters and all the issues of *The Tenth Dimension* fanzine over the decade of its publication. He has exhibited at various SF/F conventions, including WorldCon 2003, and was guest of honor at ICon 2002. He is featured in the book *Masters of Science Fiction and Fantasy Art* (Rockport Press). In 2000, Katz created for the Israeli Postal Service a three-stamp series on science fiction in Israel.

The Authors

Shimon Adaf, a well-known poet, prose writer, musician, TV writer, and university educator, was born in 1972 of Moroccan parentage in the town of Sderot, near the Gaza Strip. He attended a religious school as a child and later segued to an ultra-Orthodox Sephardic junior high school, which he left after six months. Adaf completed his studies at secular schools.

Adaf began to publish poetry during his military service. Moving to Tel Aviv in 1994, he published his first short-story collection, *The Icarus Monologue*, which won a Ministry of Education award. This and other poetry achieved widespread translation, earning Adaf a reputation as a literary wunderkind. From 2000 to 2004 he worked at the Keter Publishing House as the youngest editor of their original Israeli prose line, discovering such genre stalwarts as Ophir Touché Gafla and Nir Bar'am. In 2004 he wrote a murder mystery, *One Kilometer and Two Days before Sunset*, and a young adult fantasy, *The Buried Heart*, the latter steeped in Jewish mythology. In 2008 he published the fantasy novel *Sunburnt Faces*, Adaf's biggest hit until his most recent one, *Aviva-Lo*, about the unexpected death of his sister. In 2006 he launched his *Rose of Judah* sequence, including the Delanyesque epic *Kfor* (*Frost*) in 2010. Adaf followed this in 2011 with *Mox Nox* (Latin for *Soon the Light*), an alternate-history *Turn of the Screw*–inspired tale, winning the prestigious Sapir Prize. This was followed by *Earthly Cities*, or *Netherworld*, in 2012.

Adaf's literature and literary persona pose several problems to modern Hebrew literary gatekeepers. He is a polymath, and there is no gainsaying his place as one of the most erudite Israeli writers today. But his preoccupation with Talmudism, the powerful mythologies he derived from his Sephardic background, his shifting from Israel's geographical periphery to its center and back again, from the biographical to the universalist, from the distant past to the present to the far future, as well as his sometimes hard to parse yet rich Hebrew, render his output challenging in the view of some non-genre-savvy critics.

Pesach (Pavel) Amnuel was born in 1944 in Baku, Azerbaijan (then part of the USSR), and is known as a brainstorming astrophysicist and SF writer. Amnuel, with O. Guseynov, predicted in 1968 the existence of X-ray pulsars, which were later confirmed by the American Uhuru satellite. Amnuel and Guseynov's catalog of X-ray sources was considered for a time the world's most complete.

Amnuel first began publishing SF/F in Russian in 1959, his first story appearing in *Technology for Youth*. His first collection of stories saw publication in Moscow in 1984. Since 1990 he has lived in Israel, where he has taught at Tel Aviv University and edited several Russian-language newspapers and magazines, including *Time, Aleph,* and *Vremya*. Since emigrating to Israel, he has published the novels *Men of the Code* (1997), *Three-Universe* (2000)—the latter involving social satire and kabbalistic mystery, with events transpiring in a mid-twenty-first-century Moscow run by the Russian Mafia and Israeli rabbis—and *Revenge in Dominoes* (2007), as well as sundry SF/F collections, short stories, and detective novels.

His work appears regularly in Russia, where he continues to claim a large fan base. He has won multiple awards, including The Great Ring, for achieving the greatest popularity among contemporary Russian writers, the 2009 Bronze Icarus Award of Russian Science Fiction, and the Aelita (the Russian equivalent of the Hugo) in 2012. "White Curtain" is one of several stories and novellas in his Multiverse cycle. These include the yet-to-be translated novellas "Branches," "Facets," "What Is Behind This Door?" and "Seeing Eye." Appearing in *The Magazine of Fantasy & Science Fiction* in 2014, "White Curtain" figured in Gardner Dozois's *32nd Best SF of the Year* anthology in 2015. It was Amnuel's first publication in English translation.

Rotem Baruchin grew up in Tel Aviv, Ramat Gan, Petach Tikva, and Giv'at Shmuel, all in Israel, as well as in Swiss suburbia. She began reading science fiction and fantasy at the tender age of eight and started writing it at about the same age. For years she has combined fanzine writing with original fiction, published in both printed and online magazines, and then went on to study screenwriting at Tel Aviv University's School of Film and TV.

For the past ten years she has been writing plays for Israeli LGTB groups, such as the Gay Ensemble, produced on commercial stages. She was a dialogue writer and consultant for a children's show, *The Dreamers*, broadcast by an Israeli TV channel, and has directed several plays and musicals for a number of theaters, festivals, and conventions, including an interactive production involving audience choices. Her Internet series, *The Grey Matter*, filmed in the United States, can be seen online. For the Israeli youth magazine *Rosh 1* she wrote two story series, published over a couple of years.

Rotem won three Geffen prizes for her short stories and is currently working on her first full-scale novel in a planned series, The Cities' Guardians, which is based on the premise that every community has a "spirit of place" that manifests itself as a living entity—supernatural, eternal, and almost omnipotent. Some of her stories have been translated into English. Rotem has opened an account with the international website Patreon, which allows content creators to receive communal support for their work; she now has some one hundred regular supporters.

Rotem Baruchin is a regular participant in Israeli SF/F conventions and is also a member of a volunteer group dedicated to the prevention of sexual harassment at conventions. She lives in Ramat Gan with her two cats. Her favorite genre is urban fantasy, and she loves looking for magic in cafés and bars, in dazzling streetlights, in broken pavement stones, and in anyone alive in the city's boulevards after three a.m. who is still drinking coffee.

Yael Furman, born in Ramat Gan, Israel, on October 7, 1973 (a day after the outbreak of the Yom Kippur War), began publishing work of genre interest with "Hatzva'im haNechonim" (The right colors) in the online magazine *Bli Panika* in 2001. For the next few years she published several well-regarded short stories in Israeli genre publications such as *Halomot beAspamia* and the annual anthology series Once Upon a Future, for which she was nominated for the Geffen Prize a remarkable eight times.

Her novel *Children of the Glass House* (2011) is notable as a genuine example of Israeli young adult science fiction. Set in a future Israel, the novel concerns humans genetically modified to live in water, existing in conditions somewhat reminiscent of James Blish's underwater inhabitants in "Surface Tension" (1952) or Cordwainer Smith's *Underpeople* (1968). A human child befriends a water child against the background of a civil rights battle, partly carried out by members of the "Human League," who want the captive water people released. Although the theme of the book is not unusual in SF, the Israeli setting *is* uncommon, and, in a nice use of location, at the end of the novel the water people are transferred to the Sea of Galilee, where they are now free—or at least freer. The novel was illustrated by artist Yinon Zinger and was based on Furman's earlier short story, "Empty Walls," winner of a first prize in a 2009 Olamot Convention short story contest. Another novel, *The Portal Diamond*, was published just before this volume went to press.

Elana Gomel, born in Kiev, Ukraine, emigrated to Israel with her mother, noted writer and essayist Maya Kaganskaya, in 1978. She obtained her PhD in English literature from Tel Aviv University and went on to postdoctoral study at Princeton University as a Fulbright Scholar. She subsequently taught and researched at many world-class universities, including Stanford, the University of Hong Kong, and Venice International University. She served as chair of the Department of English and American Studies at Tel Aviv University, where she is currently an associate professor.

Gomel is the author of four academic books: *Bloodscripts: Writing the Violent Subject* (Ohio State University Press, 2003), *Postmodern Science Fiction and Temporal Imagination* (Continuum, 2010), *Narrative Space and Time: Representing Impossible Topologies in Literature* (Routledge, 2014), and *Science Fiction, Alien Encounters, and the Ethics of Posthumanism: Beyond the Golden Rule* (Palgrave/Macmillan, 2014). In 2006 she published a book in Hebrew, *Us and Them*, about the experience of Russian emigrants in Israel—one of the first comprehensive treatments of the subject. It was subsequently published in the United States as *The Pilgrim Soul: Being Russian in Israel* (Cambria Press, 2009). She is also the author of numerous scholarly articles.

Active in the science-fiction community in Israel since its inception, Gomel participated in the development of the annual science-fiction conventions ICon, Utopia, and Worlds. With her graduate students she has organized an international science-fiction symposium at Tel Aviv University, and she has striven to bring Israeli science fiction and fantasy onto the world stage by writing and lecturing about it and by coediting the groundbreaking collection of essays *With Both Feet On the Clouds: Fantasy in Israeli Literature* (Academic Studies Press, 2013).

Gomel has published more than twenty fantasy and science fiction stories in *New Horizons, Aoife's Kiss, Bewildering Stories, Timeless Tales, The Singularity, Dark Fire*, and many other magazines and in several anthologies, including *People of the Book* and *Apex Book of World Science Fiction*. Her fantasy novel, *A Tale of Three Cities*, was published by Dark Quest Books in 2013.

Gail Hareven was born in 1959 in Tel Aviv to celebrated author Shulamith Hareven and to Israeli intelligence and senior Mossad officer and, later, Foreign Ministry official Alouph Hareven. Dr. Yitzhak Epstein, her great-grandfather, who immigrated to Palestine in the 1880s, was one of the founders of the Academy of the Hebrew Language, to which Hareven's mother and then Gail herself were subsequently inducted.

Hareven grew up in Jerusalem, where she now resides. After receiving a BA in behavioral sciences from Ben Gurion University in Beersheva, she spent five years at the Shalom Hartman Institute in Jerusalem, reading Judaic studies and Talmud.

Hareven made her mark in Israeli SF/F in 1999, when she published an unabashedly genre-infused short-story collection called *The road to Heaven*. "The Slows," published here, was placed in *The New Yorker* through the efforts of translator and researcher David Stromberg, an editor at the cultural journal *Zeek*. The collection's title is telling, as the loss of paradise recurs as a theme in much of her work. Her access to the *fantastique*, in contrast, is joyful, profuse, and infused with a sense of wonder.

A journalist and book reviewer, she has written for most of the major Israeli media outlets as well as for *Tikkun*, *Lilith*, and other progressive American publications. In 2006 she was a guest lecturer at the University of Illinois, teaching writing and feminist theory, and in 2012, a guest lecturer at Amherst College.

So far, Hareven has written seventeen books: short story collections, children's stories, novels, a thriller, and some nonfiction. Major Israeli theater companies have staged five of her plays. *The Confessions of Noah Weber: A Novel* (2009) garnered the Sapir Prize in Israel as well as rave reviews in the United States and elsewhere. In 2015 she published *Lies, First Person*, earning similar accolades. Her work has been translated into English, Russian, Italian, Spanish, Serbian, Czech, and Chinese. She is also a recipient of the Prime Minister's Prize.

Guy Hasson, born in 1971, is an author, playwright, and filmmaker who crafts plays in Hebrew and prose in English. His books were published in Israel (*Hatchling, Life: The Video Game, Secret Thoughts*, and *Tickling Butterflies*), the United Kingdom (*The Emoticon Generation*), and the United States (*Hope for Utopia* and *Secret Thoughts*). He has won the Israeli Geffen Award for Best Short Story of 2003 ("All-of-Me™") and 2006 ("The Perfect Girl"). Since 2006 he has been focusing on the production of original films, including the feature-length *A Stone-Cold Heart* and the web series The Indestructibles.

Eschewing Hebrew in his SF/F has served him well in accessing a wider readership but has also caused a modicum of confusion at home, especially when some of his work found itself translated back into his native Hebrew. In either language, however, Hasson is a force to be reckoned with, and his work has been translated into seven languages. His stories can be found in the various Apex

World SF anthologies and in Apex's *Horrorology*.In 2013, Hasson created an independent comic book company, New Worlds Comics, and its flagship title *Wynter*, written by him, was hailed as one of the best SF comic book series in recent time. In 2015 Hasson created an online comic book store for the blind and the visually impaired called Comics Empower.

SF/F writer Lavie Tidhar says of Hasson: "In his refusal to compromise on commercial principles, and in his ongoing experimentation with various forms of media, it has become clear that he is following an intensely personal vision; one to which his commitment is whole."

Hasson's latest book, *Tickling Butterflies*, was released in Israel in 2017; currently he is writing and directing a feature-length horror film, *Statuesque*.

Keren Landsman, MD, is a mother, an epidemiology and public health specialist, and an award-winning SF author. In 2014 she volunteered to go to South Sudan to instruct local health care workers in epidemiology and public health. She is one of the founders of Mida'at, a voluntary organization dedicated to the promotion of public health in Israel. She currently works at a free STD clinic and at the mobile clinic for sex workers.

Landsman first started reading SF in school, in spite (or because) of the librarian's claim that "it's not for girls," and has been reading it ever since. Her interests come through in her works, where one may encounter children fighting medically accurate space epidemics. From motherhood to friendship and coping with loss, all these and more find their way into stories that balance emotion, plot, and vision. Landsman published her first story in 2006, winning three Geffen awards, Israel's top prize for science fiction, twice for best original short story and once for best original book: *Broken Skies*, a collection of her short stories.

"Burn Alexandria," she says, is the literary fulfillment of her wistful yearning to have saved, together with her editor, close friend and Israeli SF maven Ehud Maimon, the Great Library of Alexandria.

Savyon Liebrecht was born in Munich in 1948 as Sabine Sosnovsky to Polish Holocaust survivors (her father had emerged from Buchenwald, his first wife and baby had not). She was two years old when she arrived in Israel, where her family finally settled in Bat Yam. She started her military service in a kibbutz and was later transferred to the Tank Corps as a communications specialist. During that time she started working on her first novel, about a girl who leaves a kibbutz for the big city. After her service Liebrecht departed for London, where she took up journalism studies. A year and a half later she returned to Israel, changed her first name to Savyon, and began to study English literature and philosophy at Tel Aviv University. After graduation, she taught English to adults, studied sculpture, and began writing for the women's monthly *At* (You). She attended a writers' workshop run by noted Israeli author Amalia Kahana-Carmon and submitted the resultant story, "Apples from the Desert," to the editors of *Iton 77*, who published it in 1984. It was reworked for theater two years later and subsequently (2015) became a feature film.

Liebrecht writes novellas, novels, and plays, but her forte is in short stories. Much of her fiction falls under the category of psychological realism, as testified by titles such as "Horses on the Highway" (1988), "It's All Greek to Me, He Said to Her" (1992), "On Love Stories and Other Endings" (1995), and "Mail-Order Women" (2000). These provided adequate cover for her rare forays into the *fantastique*, of which "A Good Place for the Night" (2002) serves as the most accomplished example. She is known as a meticulous craftsperson, building her narratives out of objects she finds in her personal life and experiences. Liebrecht also translated the Jewish-American writer Grace Paley into Hebrew. She wrote a number of teleplays as well, which eventually found their home on Israeli television. These won her the Alterman Prize in 1977.

Nitay Peretz, born in 1974 in Kibbutz Revivim, where he lives now with his family, studied scriptwriting at the Camera Obscura school of art and became a researcher, scriptwriter, and documentary director. He is also a social activist, involved in various projects, and a blogger. Since 2004 he has been directing, shooting, and editing the life stories of many Israelis. His writing career so far includes one children's book, *Eyaly's Heart*, and the novella *My Crappy Autumn*.

Mordechai Sasson (1953–2012) was a chemist, an artist, and a writer. Born in Jerusalem to a family that has lived there for many generations, Sasson became a self-taught painter, specializing in oils. Since early childhood he avidly collected science fiction books and magazines, comics, and films. His worldview was ahead of its time in Israel, especially in matters of literature and poetry, art and music.

During his military service he participated in the Yom Kippur War, and he subsequently started painting. While studying chemistry at the Hebrew University in Jerusalem, he began to write science fiction. One day he left his notebook in class, and the assistant professor who found it decided to send one of the stories to *Fantasia 2000*, which published it forthwith. Having won some success with further stories, including the one that follows herein, he began publishing stories in more venues, mainly children's magazines. These stories were accompanied by his own illustrations. He published one children's book, *The Toads' Party* (1993), also illustrated by him. Sasson dedicated his stories to his good friend Eli Altaretz and to his own two daughters, to whom he always emphasized that knowledge is the greatest power.

Sasson was involved in helping the poor and was severely critical of Israeli society for generally ignoring them. His stories featured the city of Jerusalem and its folksy citizens with gentle humor, kindness, and deep love.

Nava Semel was born in Jaffa in 1954 to Romanian Holocaust survivors Mimi (Margalit) and Yitzhak Artzi, née Hertzig. Her father was a member of the Romanian Zionist Youth Movement, which became involved in a first-of-its kind rescue attempt in Transnistria. The family emigrated to Israel in 1947 but was stopped en route by the British, who sent them to a detention camp in Cyprus. Upon their arrival in Israel, Yitzhak Artzi served as deputy mayor of Tel Aviv, a post he would hold for twenty years, after which he was elected to the Knesset as a representative of the Independent Liberal party. Semel's brother, Shlomo Artzi, is regarded as one of Israel's most iconic balladeers.

Semel attended Tel Aviv's Gymnasia Herzliya, then served in the army as a reporter for the IDF radio station. She worked for Israeli television and the fledgling Beit Hatfutzot while completing a degree in art history at Tel Aviv University. In 1976 she married Noam Semel, a theatrical producer who went on to become theatrical director of Tel Aviv's iconic Cameri Theatre. Through 1988 she worked as a book reviewer, film critic, and journalist. That year she left to the United States with her husband, who had been appointed cultural consul to the Israeli Consulate-General in New York.

Semel's scrapes at the scar tissue of the Holocaust, searching for the effable behind the determined silences in Israeli survivor families. Her SF/F, most particularly the novel *And the Rat Laughed* (2001), deals with the ostensible inability to confront the unmentionable. This novel was staged by the Cameri Theatre and is slated to become a major international film. *Isra-Isle*, published in 2008, is an alternate history novel that posits the creation of a Jewish homeland in upper New York State. It was published well before Michael Chabon embarked upon his similarly themed *The Yiddish Policeman's Union*. Semel is an SF aficionado and is unapologetic about what others may see as rummaging behind the cowsheds.

Nava Semel was the recipient of several awards, including the American Jewish Book Prize, the Prime Minister's Prize, Austria's Best Radio Broadcast Prize, and Israeli Woman Writer of the Year. She succumbed to cancer in 2017.

Gur Shomron is a writer, poet, and technology entrepreneur and inventor. He co-started his first technology company, Quality Computers, at the age of twenty-two and took it public in Israel. He continued his career as an entrepreneur and investor and spent thirteen years in the United States building high-technology companies. At the same time he started writing science fiction. In his first (as yet unpublished) book, *A Message from Nowhere*, Shomron envisioned a network similar to the Internet more than thirty years ago. His second book, *NETfold*, was selected by *Kirkus Reviews* in 2014 as one of the best in its category (Indie). It describes a virtual world where people have twenty-four times more time and can lead alternate lives. *NETfold* was published in Israel by the Modan Publishing House.

Currently, Shomron divides his time among writing, charity, and serving as chairman of various Israeli technology companies. He is the chairman of WalkMe, a world-leading company in the Internet guidance and engagement field, and of Coldfront, which develops medical devices for the treatment of brain stroke. Gur Shomron lives in Raanana, Israel. He is married and has four children.

Eyal Teler was born 1968 in Jerusalem to a literature teacher and an astronomy buff. Teler took to SF/F in high school, advancing from Hebrew translations of genre standards to English, largely, he says, thanks to a seeming inexhaustible supply of Perry Rhodan novels. He attended the Hebrew University in Jerusalem, graduating with a master's degree in computer science, and has been a software developer ever since, creating, among other products, games, an AI chip, and a 3D 360-degree camera. Teler credits the online Critters writing workshop with his first and only sale so far, "Possibilities," to *The Magazine of Fantasy and Science Fiction* in 2003. The story was a response to Bradbury's story, "Quid Pro Quo," published in 2000. Teler later sold the story through the online service Fictionwise, earning a majestic $2.20, the proceeds of which he never banked, as check-cashing charges in Israel exceeded the value of the check. Henceforth, writing took the far back seat to family and work responsibilities—Teler is married and has two children—and although he has considered writing a novel centered on the female protagonist of his story, time, he says, has eluded them both.

Lavie Tidhar is winner of the World Fantasy Award for *Osama* (2011) and *The Violent Century* (2013) and of the Jerwood Fiction Uncovered Prize for *A Man Lies Dreaming* (2014) and is author of many other works. He writes across genres, combining detective and thriller modes with poetry, science fiction, and historical and autobiographical material. Tidhar's work has been compared to that of Philip K. Dick by the *Guardian* and the *Financial Times* and to that of Kurt Vonnegut by *Locus*.

Tidhar was born in 1976 on a kibbutz in northern Israel, where he discovered SF/F in a cache of the Israeli SF magazine *Fantasia 2000* gathering dust in the collective's library. Upon moving with his family to South Africa in his teens, Tidhar adopted English as his primary creative language. His first publication, however, a collection of verse translated as *Remnants of God*, appeared in his native Hebrew in 1998. He launched his career as an English-language SF/F writer in the online magazine *Chizene* in 2005.

The *Encyclopedia of Science Fiction* (www.sfe.com) describes the writer, who now resides in the United Kingdom, as a postmodern pioneer of equipoisal fantastika. "Tidhar's literary strategy," it intones, "repeatedly relies on the recycling of stereotypes and clichés drawn from classical pulp SF and detective fiction, traditional mythologies and contemporary popular culture."

This penchant can be identified in his first English-language collection of linked short stories, *Hebrewpunk*, published in 2007. It reaches full steam(punk) in his *Bookman* sequence (2010–12), three linked novels transpiring in an alternate Victorian England under the claws of a reptilian alien race. But it is in his World Fantasy Award–winning novel *Osama* (2011), which channels noir, alternate history à la Philip K. Dick's *The Man in the High Castle* and *Timeslip*, that Tidhar breaks free into new psychological and genre-shifting territory. "The Smell of Orange Groves" is featured in *Central Station* (2016), winner of the John W. Campbell Award and a Locus and Arthur C. Clarke Award nominee. It is a mosaic novel set around a spaceport erected several hundred years hence on the ruins of the eponymous Tel Aviv bus station.

Nir Yaniv, a Tel Avivian, is a musician, writer, editor, and occasional director. He describes himself as a hi-tech wizard with a background in computer programming and an instrumental vocalist, a devoted a cappella performer, bassist, composer, and arranger. Yaniv performed at the Red Sea Jazz Festival in 1999 and 2002 and at numerous other festivals. He records his own music at his own studio, The Nir Space Station. Yaniv performed live music with a dance company for ten years and created music for films and TV. Indeed, he starred in a short, award-winning Israeli horror film as the monster. Yaniv has participated in numerous musical groups and bands and says he still hasn't had enough. His short-story collections include *One Hell of a Writer* (Odyssey Press, 2006) and *The Love Machine & Other Contraptions* (Infinity Plus, 2012).

Short films include *Conspiracy* (2011), *MicroTime* (2013), and *LiftOff* (animation, 2013). Yaniv draws weird caricatures, sometimes to be found on T-shirts and coffee mugs. He founded Israel's first online SF/F magazine and served as its chief editor, then moved on to edit the printed SF magazine *Halomot beAspamia* and to found the website of the Israeli Society for Science Fiction and Fantasy. He writes columns, articles, and reviews for various publications.

Yaniv's short stories appeared in magazines in Israel and abroad (notably *Weird Tales*, *ChiZine*, *Apex*, and other publications, electronic and printed). He wrote two novels with fellow author Lavie Tidhar: *Fictional Murder* (Odyssey Press, 2009) and *The Tel Aviv Dossier* (ChiZine Publications, 2009).